Sylvia was a pretty little
attracted. Suddenly, the
fore his eyes and he did.
mancin'. More to get rid of her than anything else,
out and caressed her.

She stiffened. "Am I to take that as a compliment or a challenge, Mr. Long?"

He didn't answer. He couldn't answer. The room was spinning. He was going to be sick . . .

And then he was in this funny big room with red velvet drapes and a mess of undraped women were coming at him from all directions. They had painted faces and high-heeled shoes and they were grinning from ear to ear. But they were grinning evil and they had guns in their hands . . .

. . . from Novel 8: . . . the Nesters

"Would you do me a great favor?" she asked.

"Sure if I can," replied Longarm.

"Be my messenger to my countrymen. Tell them of my interest in their well-being, convince them that I will help them."

"That's a pretty big order. What makes you think they'll listen to me?"

"They trust you. And so do I." Ilioana stood up and came to his side. "It would make me very happy if you would do this for me. And I always respond to men who make me happy. I try to make them happy, too." She bent over Longarm and lifted his chin with a soft, warm hand. "Men say I have a great talent for pleasing them. You are a man I would enjoy pleasing, Longarm."

Before Longarm could move, her lips were on his . . .

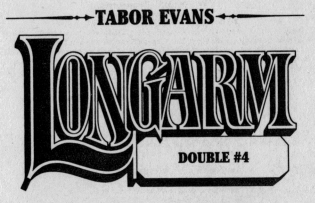

TABOR EVANS

LONGARM

DOUBLE #4

LEGEND WITH A SIX-GUN

JOVE BOOKS, NEW YORK

THE BERKLEY PUBLISHING GROUP
Published by the Penguin Group
Penguin Group (USA) Inc.
375 Hudson Street, New York, New York 10014, USA

Penguin Group (Canada), 90 Eglinton Avenue East, Suite 700, Toronto, Ontario M4P 2Y3, Canada
(a division of Pearson Penguin Canada Inc.) • Penguin Books Ltd., 80 Strand, London WC2R 0RL,
England • Penguin Group Ireland, 25 St. Stephen's Green, Dublin 2, Ireland (a division of Penguin
Books Ltd.) • Penguin Group (Australia), 250 Camberwell Road, Camberwell, Victoria 3124, Australia
(a division of Pearson Australia Group Pty. Ltd.) • Penguin Books India Pvt. Ltd., 11 Community
Centre, Panchsheel Park, New Delhi—110 017, India • Penguin Group (NZ), 67 Apollo Drive,
Rosedale, Auckland 0632, New Zealand (a division of Pearson New Zealand Ltd.) • Penguin Books
(South Africa) (Pty.) Ltd., 24 Sturdee Avenue, Rosebank, Johannesburg 2196, South Africa

Penguin Books Ltd., Registered Offices: 80 Strand, London WC2R 0RL, England

This is a work of fiction. Names, characters, places, and incidents either are the product of the author's
imagination or are used fictitiously, and any resemblance to actual persons, living or dead, business
establishments, events, or locales is entirely coincidental.

LONGARM DOUBLE #4: LEGEND WITH A SIX-GUN

A Jove Book / published by arrangement with the author

PUBLISHING HISTORY
Jove edition / December 2012

ISBN: 978-0-515-15351-4

JOVE®
Jove Books are published by The Berkley Publishing Group,
a division of Penguin Group (USA) Inc.,
375 Hudson Street, New York, New York 10014.
JOVE® is a registered trademark of Penguin Group (USA) Inc.
The "J" design is a trademark of Penguin Group (USA) Inc.

PRINTED IN THE UNITED STATES OF AMERICA

10 9 8 7 6 5 4 3 2 1

ALWAYS LEARNING   **PEARSON**

NOVEL 7

Longarm
and the
High-Graders

Chapter 1

Longarm entered the Manzanita Saloon to the lilting strains of "Garryowen," being played very fast on what sounded like tin pans. Had he come through the front entrance, he'd have been able to see who or what was making all that racket an hour before noon. But when a shifty-eyed stranger tells a lawman that someone is waiting for him in a saloon, then darts away before he can be questioned further, common sense dictates a prudent avenue of approach. So Longarm came in the back door.

There was a pantry to his right. The kitchen to his left was deserted. Longarm nodded. Drawing the .44-caliber Colt Model T he carried for just such mysteries as this, he eased toward the barroom on the balls of his feet. He moved quietly for a man of his size, but the music out front was so loud that he probably could have ridden a horse along the corridor without being noticed. It was a noisy place, considering that it seemed to be empty.

That was something to ponder. August was hotter than the hinges of hell in the Sierra foothills, and the dusty streets of Manzanita were devoid of life as the siesta hour approached. He'd only been in town about a half hour, and hadn't climbed up on a soapbox to announce his arrival. Yet the rat-faced little cowhand had been waiting in the empty street as Longarm had come out of the livery after leaving his army issue gelding in a cool stall. The hand had just said something about Longarm's being wanted over at the saloon, and then had slithered away like a sidewinder seeking shade under a flat rock.

Who in thunder could know he was in Manzanita? They were expecting him up at the mine, and he'd intended to pay a courtesy call on the local law before beginning his investigation, but he'd deliberately arrived two days early. It was surprising what a lawman could stumble over that way. Yet he'd been spotted the moment he had ridden in. Someone probably had a reason for watching the trail from Angel's Camp.

There was a bead curtain across the doorway into the barroom. The tall deputy stood in the shadows behind it as he studied the barnlike space on the other side of the beads. There was no bartender behind the long oak bar to his right. The rinkytink music was coming from a coin-operated harmonium against the wall to his left. In the middle of the room, seated at a table with his back to Longarm, was a dark figure in a brocaded charro outfit. A black sombrero hung on his back between his shoulders. The exposed hair was dishwater-blond. Some Anglo had apparently taken to the Old California style, which made no never-mind to Longarm, but he did think the double-barreled shotgun the stranger held trained on the swinging doors to the sunlit street was a proper thing for any lawman to take an interest in.

Training his .44 on the man at the table, Longarm said, "You just freeze in place and listen, friend. I've got the drop on you. A sudden sneeze could get you killed. You got that much of my message, old son?"

Without moving a muscle, the man in the charro costume asked, "Is that you, Longarm?"

"Deputy U.S. Marshal Custis Long, at your service. In a minute, we'll palaver about who *you* might be, and why you have a scatter gun trained on the doorway you invited me through. Right now I want you to slide your chair back away from that gun on the table. Then I reckon you'd best put both hands on top of your golden locks and stand up slow and easy. I'll tell you when I want you to turn around."

The man at the table didn't do as he was told. He crabbed sideways off his chair, shotgun and all, and pivoted on one knee to fire.

He didn't make it. The twin barrels were three-quarters of the way around when the Colt kicked in Longarm's palm and the lawman's first slug slammed into the man's chest. The shotgun went off, blowing a hole in the baseboard of a corner as Longarm fired again. Between the recoil of the twelve-gauge and the .44 slug that caught him just under one eye, the would-be ambusher was thrown flat on his back to the sawdust-covered planks. A booted heel drummed mindlessly a few times, as if dancing to the music box, and then the corpse lay very still, staring up into the drifting blue gunsmoke with a bemused smile.

Longarm parted the beads and strode over to stare down at the man he'd just shot. He was a total stranger. Longarm reached into the side pocket of his Prince Albert coat for two fresh rounds as he studied the odd situation. The harmonium tinkled merrily on as he thumbed the spent brass from his cooling weapon, wondering how to go about shutting the infernal contraption off. He muttered to the dead stranger, "You likely thought you were as smart as an old he-coon in a henhouse when you put a penny in and cranked her up, huh? What was I supposed to think it was, a piano being played in a crowded saloon?"

Holding the Colt in his right hand, Longarm dropped to one knee, being careful not to get the spreading blood on his tobacco-brown tweed as he went through the dead man's pockets with his free hand. The man he'd shot was about thirty, with one of those uninteresting faces you see every day. He'd backed his shotgun with a brace of Smith & Wesson .45s in a silver-mounted gunbelt. Longarm noticed that one of the ivory grips had been notched four times. He sighed and muttered, "Jesus, you've been reading Buntline for sure. No calluses worth mention on your gun hand, so despite the vaquero outfit, you ain't a dally roper. You're tanned enough to have been out in the sun a few years, so you ain't some loco Easterner playing big bad cowboy, either. But those notches don't make you look like anyone with a lick of sense. Who were you trying to scare?"

At that moment a shadow appeared in the front doorway and a voice called out, "What's going on in here? You are talking to the law!"

Longarm looked up at the worried-looking newcomer in the doorway and replied, "I'm law, too. Just shot it out with this cuss for some fool reason. I'm still trying to find out why." He reached into his inside coat pocket. Producing his wallet, he flipped it open. His badge glittered dully in the dim light filtering in from the street. "Custis Long," he said. "Deputy U.S. marshal out of Denver. Now who the hell are you?"

The Manzanita lawman came in to join him, introducing himself as one Constable Lovejoy. As he got his first good look at the body, he said, "Oh, Jesus H. Christ! You've shot the Calico Kid!"

"Is that who he was? The name doesn't mean much to me, Constable. I pride myself on a tolerable memory, but if any wanted fliers on a so-called Calico Kid have ever come my way. I disremember seeing them."

Lovejoy said, "God, this is awful! We have a nice quiet little town here, and I don't have deputy-one who'd go up against the Calico Kid and all."

Longarm got to his feet, dusting off his trousers and holstering his six-gun as he studied the concerned-looking smaller man. Lovejoy was gray around the edges and had a slight pot. He had the kind of politician's face that seemed to be made for smiling a lot. But right now he looked as if he were getting ready to burst out crying. Longarm said, "He did seem to think he was one mean fellow, but I doubt that he'll give anyone any more trouble. You reckon he really shot four men like he bragged?"

"Hell, it's more like a dozen. I'm going to have to do something about this mess, Longarm."

Longarm managed not to raise an eyebrow. He had no memory of having told the constable his nickname. Counting the dead man at his feet, that made at least three people in Manzanita who had been expecting him to ride in early.

Playing dumb, the tall deputy said, "Well, it was open-and-shut self-defense, even if I wasn't packing a federal badge. I'll make a statement for the county before I mosey on."

Lovejoy said flatly, "Longarm, you ain't going nowhere in *this* county! You just shot the Calico Kid!"

Longarm pushed his Stetson back from his forehead. "You keep saying that like it's important. Who was he, the bully of the town?"

"Damn it, he was a killer. Meanest son of a bitch we've had in these parts since Joaquin Murietta rode through in '53!"

"Well, don't get your balls in an uproar. His killing days are over."

"Hell, I'm talking about his friends, Longarm!"

Longarm looked down at the glassy-eyed corpse and shrugged as he mused, "He had friends? Well, anything's possible, I reckon. The way it seems to read right now is that he recognized me as I rode in and decided to build his rep some more with an easy murder. If his plan had worked, you'd likely be telling him right now what a serious thing he'd just done. I've got friends, too. They call themselves the U.S. Justice Department."

The constable was sweating profusely now. "Yeah, but *your* friends ain't likely to ride in shooting in the next hour or so. The Calico Kid's friends *are!* You take my meaning?"

"I'm not sure. Since I don't have the calling for raising folks from the dead, what is it you've got in mind?"

"I want you to *git*, damn it! If you've a lick of sense, you'll fork that pony you have over at the livery and ride out sudden and far!"

Longarm shook his head and said, "Can't. My outfit sent me here to do a job and I don't aim to ride anywhere till it's done. I'll help you put what happened here on paper, then I've got to head up to the Lost Chinaman diggings. I was aiming to poke around here in town for a spell before I rode up for a look-see at the mine itself. But since everyone seems to know Uncle Sam has a man in the field already, I don't reckon it's worth my time to jaw with the local barber and such."

Lovejoy hesitated. Then he nodded and said, "I figured you were on that case. We'd best go over to my office. If you won't leave peaceable, we may as well take down your statement and at least get you out on the trail. Calico rode with a mean bunch and at least one of them knows you just killed him."

Longarm thought, *Strike two!* but didn't say anything aloud as he followed the constable out the door. Other men were standing in the street now, and Lovejoy called to one of them, "Hawkins, go fetch Doc Forbes and tell him we got a fellow who needs planting. Me and this deputy U.S. marshal will be at the jailhouse if you need us."

The little crowd parted as they crossed the street to the shady overhang of the opposing frame buildings. Longarm was now aware that the local law knew how he'd been set up. Yet he didn't remember having told Lovejoy about the rat-faced hand by the livery. That could be taken several ways. Lovejoy might have heard it from the stablehands. It seemed a bit soon to conclude that he was in cahoots with the gang against a fellow lawman.

The Manzanita jail was a thick-walled adobe structure with a redwood-shingled roof. Lovejoy ushered him in and Longarm saw that it was a one-room building partitioned by iron bars.

A morose-looking Indian sat crosslegged on the floor of the lockup. He didn't look at them as they entered.

The office was furnished with a rolltop desk and some bent-wood chairs. There was a typewriter on the green blotter of the desk. Beside it stood a funny-looking contraption of a kind that Longarm had never seen before. He asked, "Is that one of Professor Bell's newfangled talking telegraphs?"

"It sure is," Lovejoy said proudly. "We're up to date in California. Got us a line running all the way to Sacramento, now."

Longarm was impressed. "You must have some budget. My boss, Marshal Vail, has been trying to get him one of those back in Denver. Washington keeps telling him it's a passing fad."

Lovejoy put a sheet of paper in the typewriter and began to hunt and peck, standing. Longarm snorted and said, "Hell, let me type it up for you. I ain't got all day."

"You know how to play a typewriter?" Lovejoy said incredulously.

"Some. I've been fooling with the one in the office in Denver."

He sat down at the desk and began to hunt and peck a bit faster than the constable had, but not much. For the life of him, he couldn't see why everyone was in such an all-fired hurry to change things. He'd been writing his reports in longhand for six or eight years and nobody had ever said they couldn't read his Palmer penmanship.

He had typed out, *REPORT BY CUSTIS LONG, DEPUTY U.S. MARSHAL, DISTRICT COURT OF DENVER*, before Constable Lovejoy got up the nerve to place the muzzle of his revolver against the nape of Longarm's neck.

Longarm stopped typing. He asked, "Do you have a reason for whatever you're trying to pull, Lovejoy?"

The constable licked his lips and said, "You just keep them hands up there. I don't want no trouble, Longarm."

Longarm said, "Hell, old son, you've already *got* trouble." But he did as he was told. As Lovejoy held the muzzle of the revolver against the base of Longarm's skull with one hand, he frisked and disarmed him with the other. As Lovejoy took the derringer from Longarm's right-hand vest pocket, the lawman nodded and sighed, "Yeah, they gave you a pretty good rundown on me, didn't they? Not many folks know about the derringer on my watch chain. Who are you working for, those jaspers who've been stealing high-grade from the Lost Chinaman?"

"State of California," Lovejoy said, adding, "You could have rode out like I asked, but they said in Sacramento that you was a stubborn cuss. You get up, now, and move slow for the lockup. I don't want to shoot you, but . . ."

Longarm rose slowly to his feet, the gun pressing against his back, but he protested, "Lovejoy, you are starting to piss me off a mite. You can't lock me up."

Lovejoy cut him off. "You ain't the law in California. You're out of your jurisdiction, and Justice Field, down in Sacramento, says you have no call to mess in local matters."

As the constable opened the jail door and shoved him inside, Longarm snorted, "Hell, if you mean Justice Stephen Field, *he's* in trouble too! I wasn't ordered out here by the Denver office. I'm on a special assignment from Washington! It seems they've been wondering why the federal marshals out here can't seem to get a handle on those missing gold shipments." As the door slammed shut, he added, "We're talking about gold being sent to the U.S. Mint in San Francisco, Lovejoy. We're talking about Uncle Sam's money. Savvy?"

"Look, I just do my job as best I know how. Sacramento says your badge don't mean shit on this side of the Sierras and, damn it, it was your own idea to go and shoot the Calico Kid!"

"Come on, the silly son of a bitch was trying to murder me!"

"Maybe. We'll see about it at your trial."

"My *what?* What the hell charges are you holding me on, God damn it?"

The constable holstered his six-gun. "Don't know. Maybe murder. Maybe manslaughter. That'll be up to the district attorney, won't it?"

Longarm laughed, still more puzzled than alarmed, and said, "Lovejoy, this ain't going to work. I know you old boys up here in the Mother Lode play rough, but we're not talking about jumping some greenhorn's claim or robbing a Mexican. We're talking about over a dozen gold shipments sidetracked between here and the mint. You don't seem to grasp that it's federal gold we're talking about!"

Lovejoy shrugged and turned away. One of the townies came

to the door and yelled in something about the undertaker. Love-joy said, "I'll talk to him. Keep an eye on the jail, will you?"

As Lovejoy left, Longarm called out, "They'll send someone else, you damned fool! Even if you kill me, you're going to be combing U.S. deputies out of your hair until Justice finds out where all that ore's been shipped!"

And then the constable was gone. The man he'd deputized to take his place went over to the desk and sat down with his back to the lockup. He put his feet up on the desk and lit a smoke. Longarm asked, "You mind telling me something, friend?"

The man didn't answer. Longarm swore softly and turned away from the bars. The Indian on the floor said, "I am not a bad person. Don't hurt me."

Longarm went over to the fold-down bunk and sat down, saying, "I'm not a bad person, either. What are you in for?"

"My name is Bitter Water. I am a Miwok. What you Saltu call a Digger Indian."

Longarm had recently come to know and respect these groups of foraging Indians contemptuously called Diggers. They were peaceable, graceful, and intelligent peoples who were often ruth-lessly exterminated or driven from their lands by avaricious whites. He had recently had occasion to help a group of Paiutes in eastern Nevada whose stores of their staple food—pinyon nuts—were being destroyed by uncontrolled, illegal logging. Longarm extended a large, callused hand toward Bitter Water, and the small Indian shook it firmly. "Well, I'm Custis Long," he said, "and I'll call you a Miwok. You didn't say why they ar-rested you."

"Yes I did. I told you I was an Indian."

"Is that against the law?"

"In this county? Yes. Some. Saltu came to the valley where my people have always gathered acorns. They said it was *their* valley now. They said they had a paper from Wa Sentan telling them they could keep cows there. When I asked to see the paper, they hit me. So I ran away."

"I'm sorry, Bitter Water. I hope you don't think all of my people are like that. But how'd you wind up in this jail if you got away?"

"You have a good heart, but you do not listen. I said I ran away. I did not say I *got* away. While I was running from the men with cows, I crossed some other Saltus' mining claim. They caught me with a rope and brought me here. They say I have been stealing gold. Someone has been stealing gold around here, and, as I said, I am an Indian." Bitter Water shrugged as he added, "I think they will hang both of us as soon as it gets dark."

Longarm shot a glance out front. Lovejoy had taken his watch along with his badge, gun, and last three smokes, but he could see it was still early afternoon. Turning back to the Indian, he said, "Lovejoy said something about a trial. How often does the circuit judge come over from the county seat?"

"I don't know. It does not matter. They will not hear of us over in San Andreas. The men in Manzanita who hang people call themselves vigilantes. It is said nobody knows who they are, but I think this is a lie."

Longarm frowned thoughtfully. Then he got up and went over to the bars again, calling out, "Hey, this fellow says you have a vigilance committee in this town. I thought that sort of thing went out with the forty-niners."

The deputy, if that was what he was, didn't answer. Longarm insisted, "Look, I don't know if Lovejoy told you boys the facts of life, but I am a federal officer. You just try lynching a federal man and you won't have to worry about the Justice Department. You'll have the U.S. army up here asking all sorts of questions."

Again, there was no reply. Apparently the man at the desk knew how hard it is not to give anything away, once you start talking. The people behind this had their henchmen well-trained.

All right, he decided, *let's take as gloomy a look at this mess as possible and see where that leaves everyone.* His investigation had been nipped in the bud, either by some very clever plotting indeed or just a bit of quick thinking on the part of a skunk wearing a badge. It didn't matter whether the late Calico Kid had been in on it or not. By shooting the inept gunman, he'd delivered himself into their hands. The Indian's idea made sense, too, damn it. Longarm knew there was no way they'd ever hang a murder charge on him in open court. On the other hand, if he and Bitter Water were killed, by vigilantes, friends of the Calico Kid, Or simply "trying to escape" . . .

"It still won't work," he called out, adding, "My office knows I'm here in Calaveras County. The Lost Chinaman is fixing to ship another carload of high-grade ore down to the stamping mills, and if I don't ride in with the gold, they'll send in another team."

No answer.

Longarm insisted, "Sure, you and your pals might steal at least one more shipment, but then what? You're spreading yourselves a mite thin already, you know. I figure even if we're talking about the highest grade of ore, it still can't run more than a few thousand dollars a trainload, before it's refined. I can see you've bought your own law all the way down to the state capital, but, like I said, there's only so much gold and there are a lot of palms to grease."

Hoping the silent man was at least listening, he insisted, "Look, you can bribe almost anyone to look the other way about a trainload of ore. But the rates go up as soon as you start killing folks, and a deputy U.S. marshal comes high as hell. I know you won't answer, but I want you to study on my words. Up to now, I don't have a thing on anyone. But once the government starts getting serious about you boys, it's all over. You have too many people in on it. One of you, only one, just has to get worried about his own hide, or maybe pissed off because he thinks he should have had a bigger share and—"

The man at the desk swung his boots to the floor and turned around to snap, "You just *hush*, mister! You don't know what you're talking about!"

Longarm was a bit relieved to see that the man wasn't deaf. "The hell I don't. I'm talking about a U.S. deputy being hindered, or worse. You're not going to like it in Leavenworth, boy."

"God damn it, you got no call to say I'm a thief. I've never stole a penny in my born days. Me and every other honest man in the county is as riled as you are about them jaspers robbing the ore trains, and I'll not be tarred with the same brush as them!"

Longarm saw that the man was young and rather simple-looking. He smiled and asked, "Why are you holding me, then? Can't you see you're helping the high-graders, even if you're not in on it?"

The guard shook his head and said, "Don't fun with me, mister. You know you shot the Calico Kid."

"Then you must be one of *his* friends, right?" Longarm prodded him.

"Hell, I just said I was an honest man. I got no truck with them wild gunslicks Calico used to ride with."

Longarm shook his head wearily and marveled, "Loco. The whole bunch has busted out to nibble locoweed, unless I missed a turn a ways back. If you and Lovejoy ain't with the high-graders, and you ain't with the Calico Kid's bunch, what in thunder am I doing behind these bars?"

"You're in jail 'cause it's where you belong, damn it. You had no call to come here and stir up trouble."

"I'd say the trouble sort of came my way. I was only trying to do my job."

"No, you wasn't. You don't belong in these parts, mister. We got a town constable and a county sheriff. We got our own federal marshals down to Sacramento. You're just a durned old carpetbagger! Nobody around here ever asked you to stick your nose into our business, did they?"

"I hate to call such an honest man a liar, but you are purely full of shit. I *was* asked to investigate those gold robberies. Uncle Sam asked me, real polite. Are you saying Calaveras County's not part of these United States?"

The youth hesitated. Then he said, "You're trying to mix me up," and turned away again. This time he meant it. Longarm tried reason. He tried argument. He tried saying mean things about the man's mother. Nothing worked. After a while he got tired of talking to the back of an obviously thick skull and went back to the bunk. As he sat down again, the Indian muttered, "We have nothing to worry about as long as they are guarding us."

Longarm started to ask what Bitter Water meant. Then he nodded in sick understanding. He'd investigated enough lynchings to know the form.

If that was indeed the plan, Constable Lovejoy would go through the motions for the rest of the day. A rural community like Manzanita went to bed early. Or at least, the honest elements did. Later, in the dark of the moon, Lovejoy would probably be called away from the jail on some obscure mission. That was when the night riders would arrive.

Later, some luckier lawman might put it all together and they'd know at last whether the late Custis Long had been lynched by men in the pay of the gold thieves, by pals of the Calico Kid, or by someone he hadn't figured out yet. Yeah, they'd get to the bottom of it, in time. You don't steal federal gold and murder federal marshals and hope to get away with it forever. But he didn't have forever. He had maybe eight or ten hours if he intended to crack the case himself. It wasn't a bit comforting to think some other lawmen might track down the answers, after he was dead.

The Indian's voice was soft as he asked, "Would you get mad at me if I made a suggestion?"

Longarm smiled and said, "No. I think it's a good idea."

Bitter Water looked puzzled as he asked, "Do you read my words before they are spoken?"

"Hell, if you're thinking about anything *but* busting out of here you must be loco, too. What's your plan?"

Bitter Water suddenly looked even more dejected. "I was hoping *you* had one. All I know is that we can't stay here overnight. Right after dark would be the best time, don't you think?"

Longarm shook his head and said, "That's when they'll be expecting us to try and bust out. One of the oldest tricks around is to leave a prisoner unguarded and sort of let him think he's escaping."

Morosely, Bitter Water studied the floor between his knees for a time before he sighed, "Heya! Waiting outside with rifles. Forgive me for being stupid. I have spent little time in Saltu jails. When do *you* think we should get away?"

"Right about now would suit me just fine. It's mid-afternoon and hot as hell out there. Half the town'll be taking a siesta, and the restless souls are likely holding a funeral for the cuss I just shot."

"I agree. But I don't see how we can get out of this place. If I had a knife I could dig through the adobe wall, but—"

"It'd take too long," Longarm interrupted. "I think we'd better try an old trick and hope that jasper out front is as dumb as he looks. The old prison fight would never work on anyone who's worked as a guard for six weeks, but he might not have heard of it."

"He does look stupid," Bitter Water agreed. "But what is this trick you speak of?"

"Oh, you're going to start beating me up. I don't think he'd care if *I* started slapping *you* around, but—"

The suggestion caused a flicker of enthusiasm to brighten the

Indian's features. "Yes. No Saltu is going to stand by and allow a brother to be bested by a dirty Indian. But what are we supposed to be fighting about?"

"Hmmm, we'll have to make it look a mite serious, won't we? Let's see now. What's a good old boy likely to have strong feelings about? I'll tell you what, Bitter Water. Take off your pants."

The Indian looked thunderstruck and muttered, "You are making a joke. What do you take me for?"

"That ain't important. It's what we want *him* to take you for. I want you to act like a wild, crazy Indian with a hard-on. Come on, old son, I know you ain't a jail-wolf."

Bitter Water shrugged and stood up, turning out to be taller than the lawman had expected. The Indian dropped his ragged britches and stepped out of them, naked from the waist down. Longarm shouted, "You ain't gonna do no such thing, you crazy red bastard!" and then he grabbed the startled Indian by the shirt and pulled him against his own frame, crying out, "Help! This crazy Digger's after my white ass!"

The guard swung around to stare openmouthed as the two men rolled over and over on the floor. Then he sprang to his feet and shouted, "Hey, what the hell kind of jail do you think we're running here? We don't allow that sort of thing in Manzanita, boys!"

Longarm whimpered, "Get him off me, then! He's as strong as a goddamned elephant and I reckon he'd fuck one, given the chance!"

The guard fished a key from his ring and fumbled with the lock, saying, "Hit back, damn it! You're a white man!"

"He's killing me! He must have been chewing that crazy Indian medicine they use to get riled up!"

The door was open and the guard stepped in, muttering, "Oh, for God's sake," as he drew his gun. Longarm saw what was coming and tried to shove Bitter Water out of the way, but the gun barrel slammed down against the side of the Miwok's head and Longarm felt him go limp. He rolled the Indian off, hooked a toe behind the guard's ankle, and kicked him hard in the kneecap with the other booted heel.

The guard went down, gasping in pain, but still holding on to the gun as Longarm rolled to his hands and knees and dove headfirst over his victim's thrashing legs. He landed with all his considerable weight on the man's chest and grabbed for the wrist of his gun hand as he kneed the guard viciously. The man gasped in pain. Longarm grabbed his hair and pounded his head on the floor until he lay limp and silent. Then Longarm hit him once for luck and got up with the other man's gun in his own hand.

He stood for a moment, listening. The sounds of the struggle didn't seem to be drawing any attention from the blazing furnace of the town outside. Both Bitter Water and the guard were breathing, but were obviously out of it for some time to come.

The Indian looked sort of silly lying there with no pants on, but his appearance was the least of Longarm's worries. He stuck the gun in his waistband and picked up the Indian's discarded pants. As he knelt to fumble them on over Bitter Water's big feet, the Indian opened his eyes and asked, "What are you doing?"

"Trying to get you dressed and out of here."

Bitter Water sat up and said, "I can do that. Why didn't you run away as soon as you had the chance? Didn't you think he knocked me out?"

"You mean he didn't?" Longarm asked, astonished.

"No. I was only dazed. It came to me as I lay there that I would be wise to let you run away and then leave myself. You are a good person, but you are Saltu."

"You mean you figured you could lose yourself in the timber easier without a white man tagging along?"

"Of course," Bitter Water replied with assurance. "No white man can track me in my native hills. But you did not run away. You stayed to help me. This is a new thing I must consider."

Longarm shrugged and said, "You light out on your own if you've a mind to. I've got to see if I can find my gun and badge."

But as he went out front to rummage through the constable's desk, the Indian, now dressed, took his arm and said, "Come, Saltu brother. The siesta will be ending and we must have at least an hour's start on them through the trees."

Longarm looked at Bitter Water with some surprise. "I thought you aimed to make it on your own, Bitter Water. Just let me find my stuff, and—"

"You are a good person, but a fool. You *had* your badge and they arrested you! When they find their friend unconscious, the whole town will be after us!"

"*Us?* All for one and one for all?"

The Miwok nodded. "You have me in your debt. Come with me and no Saltu will ever cut your trail."

"Well, maybe if I can get a few miles off and study my next move a spell . . ." Longarm speculated.

"Come. I will show you things no Saltu knows about these hills. Later, you can go back to Wa Sentan. Agreed?"

Longarm nodded, but then he said, "Not hardly. This case is just getting interesting."

"You mean to come back to this place? Without your badge? Without your gun? Without a friend in the county?"

"Hell, old son, I've got a gun. The other odds just promise to make the game a mite more interesting."

In a white man's town, wearing a white man's cast-off rags, Bitter Water had seemed a rather shabby specimen. But crouched on a granite outcropping beside the lawman, the Miwok was a wild creature in its own element. The Mother Lode country lay in the oak-covered foothills of the Sierras, rather than in the evergreen slopes he'd half expected, so they were no higher than the Colorado prairie he was used to, yet Longarm was out of breath. His Indian companion had set a killing pace since they'd skulked out of Manzanita. Bitter Water had led them downslope for a time, which made sense, since anyone trying to cut their trail would figure they'd made a beeline for the high country. But then he'd led them in a series of hairpin turns through canyons thick with undergrowth and over hogback ridges too steep for a billy goat to consider, and, except for knowing that they were somewhere to the south of, and slightly higher than Manzanita, Longarm was completely lost.

He could only hope that anyone following them was as bushed and mixed-up as he was. As he rested his cramped calves by sprawling on the granite on one elbow, Longarm began to recover his bearings as well as his breath. The lookout Bitter Water had selected was a cunning choice. Longarm knew most men moved to the highest ground they could find when they wanted to see out across the world. The Miwok had led them to one of many boulders running in a horizontal band two-thirds of the way up this particular ridge. Anyone sweeping the high country with field glasses from the valley below would have no particular reason to study the rocks they were on, and their outlines were well below the skyline.

At the same time, they had a spectacular view to the west, north, and south. The sun was low and blazing red as it headed for China. The tawny, rolling foothills lay below them like some huge, wrinkled carpet, stitched together by the Great Spirit from odds and ends of animal skins—mostly cougar. The ridges ran north and south, under a cover of cheat grass and wild mustard, in rounded muscular curves that reminded one of the feminine strength of a great cat. It was easy to see, from up here, why California was earthquake country. The lower slopes of the Sierra looked as if they were about to spring at the North Pole. The folds between the smooth rolls of the slopes were dark with canyon oak and manzanita. To his left and right, the land grew rougher as the slopes became steeper, with a darker pelt of ponderosa pines and other evergreens disputing the claim of the lowland vegetation. He couldn't see the snow-covered crests of the High Sierra behind them, for the range climbed to the timberline in graduated waves, steeper toward the east and gentler toward the sunset. The western slope of the Sierra would hardly have been noticeable, in fact, had not time and the patient running waters of a million brooks carved the main slopes into thousands of smaller ridges and canyons.

Bitter Water was watching one of the brush-choked canyons. They had come through it on the way here, and he was worried about his attempts to hide their sign. He'd called the place Spider Valley, Longarm remembered it as a winding stretch of dusty hell where he'd crawled on his hands and knees under waist-high twisted branches that smelled like medicine. He didn't remember seeing any spiders in Spider Valley, but the place had been crawling with sassy little lizards who stuck their tongues out before they darted away along the branches.

He couldn't locate it now. Spider Valley could have been any of those wrinkles down there, sinking into twilight well ahead of the still brightly illuminated ridges. He squinted his eyes against the red sun and managed to make out the distant flatness of the Great Valley between where they stood and the lower coastal ranges. The lowlands shimmered under a flat haze of dull orange and woodsmoke gray as the late afternoon breeze moved in from the invisible Pacific, beyond the horizon. He knew Sacramento was down there, somewhere. That son-of-a-bitch federal judge who'd disputed his jurisdiction was probably watching a nice sunset and planning a night on the town. In a state notorious for political corruption, Justice Stephen Field had gained a reputation for innovative crookedness.

The trouble with federal judges, Longarm mused, was that they were appointed for life and were often given the job as a reward for getting out the vote instead of for juridical literacy. Justice Field was one of those old-timers who'd come West to do good, and he had done a lot of it—for himself. They said he'd killed a few men in his day, and he was widely known for his draconian views on the rights of Greasers, Chinks, Niggers, or Injuns, as he called them. He was reputed to be thick with the railroad barons and bankers. He'd elevated the art of land-grabbing and claim-jumping to a fine science. This very year, at a place called Mussel Slough, U.S. marshals from the judge's district had done battle with a group of small ranchers and farmers who had failed to see the justice in their homesteads being seized by Justice Field for his richer cronies. Longarm was glad he hadn't been assigned to that case. The Battle of Mussel Slough had been a bloodbath California was going to remember. Five settlers had been gunned down by federal deputies, but they had taken two members of the attacking forces with them before losing their lands. It was easy to see why someone in Washington had asked for a deputy from another district. The California marshals had said they had no idea who had been stealing that gold bound for the San Francisco Mint. Longarm wondered if they were all in on it, or if he only had a few key men in high places to worry about. He felt a certain sense of loyalty to his fellow deputies, but in truth, he knew his own good reputation was mostly the result of his having a certain amount of common sense in an outfit tending to hire cheap help. He knew a lot of federal deputies who didn't have sense enough to pour piss out of their boots. They'd go where they were told and see what they were told to see. The cover-up that Washington suspected was pretty obvious. Yet, wasn't it a mite *too* obvious?

Longarm chewed thoughtfully on the edge of his full, dark brown mustache. Aloud, he muttered, "I don't understand it. We just ain't talking about all that much money!"

Beside him, Bitter Water asked, "What money are you talking about?"

Longarm said, "I've been thinking about those gold shipments. A federal judge is expensive and I've been adding it up. Those high-graders haven't been running off with gold bullion; they've been stealing whole trainloads of ore. You know what ore is, don't you?" Bitter Water looked at Longarm a bit reproachfully.

"Of course. My people roamed the Mother Lode before the Saltu found out there was gold in that band of yellow-brown quartz that runs north and south through these hills." He chuckled softly and added, "We used to make arrowheads out of it. If the Saltu were less unfriendly, we could show them places where the flecks of gold in the rock are visible to the naked eye. We never had any use for it. Gold is softer than lead; it makes very poor tools. In the old days our children used to find the beads of gold washed out of the rocks by running water and, being children, they'd bring them to their mothers. Once, when I was a boy, I found a nugget as big as my thumb. My mother said not to be foolish. It was the time of the year to be gathering acorns."

Longarm nodded and said, "I sometimes wonder myself why so many men have gone crazy over the stuff. Though I don't hold with eating acorns. Pinyon nuts ain't bad, but acorns are bitter as hell."

The Miwok laughed and pointed a finger at Longarm. "You are a Saltu. You don't know how to wash the bitterness from our food. Your people have no patience; you only eat what's easy. Over to our west, there is a valley where a whole party of your people starved to death many years ago. They were very crazy. They starved surrounded by food, had they but seen fit to gather it. Yet they cried like women and started to eat one another. My people have often joked about those crazy Saltu."

Longarm frowned and asked, "Are you talking about the Donner party, back in the gold rush?"

"I think that was what they were called. They got lost in the High Sierra and were snowed in for the winter. There were roots and nuts all around them, but they ate each other. The ways of your people are very strange."

Longarm had had this same conversation with other Indians, so he didn't want to get into it. Unlike some whites he knew, Longarm liked most Indians. But he didn't buy the "noble savage" myth. As a man who'd lived with, slept with, and fought with Indians, he knew them better than either the bigots who hated them or the poetic writers who, never having swapped shots with Apache, tended to picture them as misunderstood supermen. The tragedy of the American Indian was simply that, save for a few tribes he could think of, they saw the world they shared with the white man as something *different*—something no white man could fully understand. Bitter Water seemed neighborly enough, and they were in this mess together. But Longarm knew that, no matter how it all turned out, they'd never really understand each other, so he didn't waste time trying.

He said, "The sun's going down. You aim to spend the night up here on this rock like some big-assed bird?"

The Miwok shrugged and said, "One part of this country is as good as any other. I don't see dust against the sunset. If they are trailing us, they are on foot."

Longarm stood up, shook the kinks out of his leg muscles, and stretched in the red glow of the setting sun.

"I could have told you that. We went through places no pony could have gone. Come to think of it, I wouldn't have laid odds on a mountain goat."

"If I had run off alone," Bitter Water continued, "I would not think anyone was taking the trouble to search for me. They consider us pests rather than game worthy of a great hunt. But you seemed important to them. From what you have told me this day, important people want you out of the way. There may be a reward offered for your capture. Saltu will do anything for money."

The tall deputy nodded grimly. "That's for damned sure. But you purely puzzle me, Bitter Water. You *know* what money is."

"Of course. Did you think I was a stupid person? You know I speak your tongue. 'Fuck' and 'money' are the first words anyone learns around you people."

Longarm chuckled. "Well, maybe 'son of a bitch' comes almost as early. Where'd you pick up English, at some mission school?"

"No, my band avoided the padres when Mexico owned California. They were nearly as cruel as your people. When I was young, I was captured by some gold miners. They made me work for them one summer. Your tongue is less complicated than my own. You Saltu speak a sort of baby talk with very few words. It was easy to learn your speech, although your ways will always be a mystery to me."

"White folks keep surprising me a mite, too," Longarm admitted. "But what do you mean about us talking like babies? I know your old ones like to make long speeches. Most Indians I've met could talk the horns off a billy goat. But where'd you get such a big vocabulary with no books or telegraph lines?"

The Miwok shrugged and said, "We talk about things your people do not seem to find important. When Saltu speak, they only skim the surface. For instance, you only have one word for a horse."

"Wait a minute. We have lots of words for the critters. We call them horses, ponies, studs, mares, pintos, roans, all sorts of things."

Bitter Water waved this away with an imperious gesture. "Bah. Those words only deal with the surface. You say the same word for the poor animal no matter what it's *doing!*"

The lawman looked puzzled. "I don't follow you."

"Of course you don't. Suppose I said I saw a horse. What would this mean to you?"

Longarm stared down into the low country and asked, "*Do* you see a horse down there?"

"No. I am hoping that when it gets dark, anyone following us may build a fire and give his position away. To a Miwok, the word 'horse' would have little meaning. He would want to know how old the horse was and which way it was going. He would want to know if the horse had a rider. He would want to know if it was running, walking, or standing still. He would have no word that simply meant 'horse.'"

"You mean in your lingo you use a different *word* for a horse running and a horse standing?"

Bitter Water nodded. "Also for every other thing a horse can do. We have no word that means 'woman.' To a Miwok, it is important whether a woman is young or old, ugly or pretty, awake or asleep, and so forth. No Miwok would ever ever say he had a woman. He would say he had a pretty woman who'd had children and made good acorn mush, or—"

Comprehension flickered in Longarm's steely dark eyes. "I'm getting your drift. That's why when I ask what you folks call a man, I get all sorts of answers, right? I mean, as far as I can grasp your lingo, a 'ho,' a 'wa,' a 'pai,' or a 'ute' are the same critter!"

"They are all men, doing different things," Bitter Water concurred. "Your wise men are very funny. They keep writing down names of things they call tribes. They don't understand that when they asked the so-called Paiute, Ute, Hopi, and so forth what they were, they were given the same answer. We all call ourselves 'people.' What the wise men wrote down was simply what the people they met were doing, or felt like, that day."

"Well, I thank you for the language lesson, but I never came out here to study Indians. I'm looking for some jaspers given to stealing federal gold. For some reason, you have as much trouble grasping the idea of money as I do understanding Miwok."

"I understand money. I just see no use for it," the Indian said.

"That's what I mean. Hell, can't you see that a couple of dollars would buy you a decent set of jeans instead of those rags you're wearing?"

Bitter Water shrugged and said, "I wear cotton this time of the year because it is cool on the skin in the heat. Later, when it's cold, I will wear skins. In the green of spring I will go naked. It seems very sensible to me."

"Sure," Longarm persisted, "but if you had money you could buy all sorts of outfits and have them ready as the seasons changed."

"You speak foolishly. Why should any man carry everything he might need for all the months he can't possibly need them?"

Longarm started to argue. Then he reconsidered and nodded. Since the Diggers wandered constantly, following the game and harvests of wild vegetables, it *did* make sense to travel light. But he saw a hole in that argument and, even though he knew better, he asked, "Haven't you folks ever considered sort of staying put? I mean, you ain't dumb and you must see the advantages of a permanent home, with maybe a garden and some livestock. Farm folks don't have to wander all over creation just to rustle up a meal."

The Miwok grimaced and asked, "Would you have us live like some sort of Mexicans? Even if we were content to spend all our days looking at the same hills and trees, drinking water that always tasted the same, smelling flowers that always smelled the same, eating food that always tasted the same, would we be left to enjoy our new bland lives?"

"Well, the Indian agency would protect you, on a proper reservation."

Anger darkened the Indian's features. "As a caged bear is protected by its keepers? No, thank you. There were villages of my people in the Great Valley when the gold seekers came. They had learned farming from the Mexicans. They ate well, as you say. Then a general called Fremont came over the Sierra to fight the Mexicans. The Mexicans had guns and knew how to fight back. So your Fremont had his war with the mission Indians. He killed many. Today their farms are owned by Saltu. They boast that they won their homesteads from wild Indians."

Longarm said, "You win. It's nigh dark enough for anyone on our trail to be thinking of setting up camp for the night. You think we can find your village in the dark?"

"My people have no villages. They wander. They sleep wherever they are when it's time to sleep."

"Then how do you expect to find your band?" Longarm asked.

Bitter Water shrugged and said, "We shall meet when we meet. There are only so many valleys where a person can find food. At this time of the year my people will be gathering manzanita. I know where it grows thickly. If I don't find them in the manzanita groves, they will be harvesting acorns soon."

Longarm started to say he'd tasted one of the little crabapple things off a manzanita bush once, and never intended to try again. Instead, he pointed with his chin and said, "Smoke. Over there to our right, behind that saddleback ridge." The distant plume of smoke was tinted violet by the setting sun.

"I see it. It is a Saltu fire. You people put too much wood on when you make camp. It is very foolish. A Miwok builds a small fire and sits over it, keeping warm. Saltu build big fires and have to sit back, roasting their fronts and freezing their backs. From the smoke, I would say there are a lot of men in the party. The fools are mounted. We have nothing to worry about."

Longarm was getting tired of being treated like a greenhorn, so he tried to figure some things out for himself. He wasn't a bad woodsman, if he said so himself, but he'd have missed the part about horses, had not the Miwok made him study on it for a spell.

He said, "You're right. They must be mounted. I can see how the land rolls gentle on the other side of that saddleback. They've been following the natural lay of the land, hoping to cut our trail as they rode. If they don't give up come morning, they'll likely ride up that draw to the north. I'd say they're about four miles away right now, as the crow flies. But they're riding ponies instead of crows, so the grain of these hills will carry them directly away from this rock."

Bitter Water said, "I know. Why did you think I led you this way?"

Longarm laughed and said, "I thought you were aiming to kill me. I can see now how you folks can stay so wild right on the edges of settled country. It's a good thing for our side that you old boys are less warlike than Apache. I'd hate to try and lead an army patrol after you poor primitive bastards."

Bitter Water smiled grimly and said, "The idea has been discussed around our campfires. We are not a warlike people, but many of your people are evil. Just a few years ago some men of our kind, led by a breed called Captain Jack, tried fighting you, to the north of here."

"I heard about the Modoc War. Your Captain Jack and his braves made the army look sort of silly."

Bitter Water shrugged and sighed. "It didn't matter. In the end, they were all killed. It is better just to avoid your kind."

Longarm suddenly understood something he'd started to wonder about. He had a gun, though, so it was as good a time as any to have it out. He said, "You have no intention of leading me any closer to your own kith and kin, right?"

Bitter Water kept his face blank as he answered. "I am in your debt. My people are not. You are a good person, I think, but they would want to kill you if we met them far from any settlement."

"I've heard that white men have a habit of sort of vanishing in the high country from time to time. But what are we supposed to do, walk hand in hand through these bushes forever?"

"When I am sure we have lost those who wish you dead, I will take you to a place called Murphy. There you can steal a horse and be on your way. Will you be going back to Wa Sentan?"

"Not hardly. Nobody seems to savvy that I came out here to do a job."

"You keep saying that. If you go back to Manzanita, they will kill you and all of my efforts will have been wasted."

Longarm shook his head and explained, "I ain't as dumb as I look. I've been studying on my next best move. Can you put me on a trail that leads to San Francisco?"

"Of course. You can go down to Sacramento, then catch a steamboat to the big bay."

"No. I don't think they like me in the capital. I've got to get to Frisco without anyone in Sacramento knowing about it. Can you do it?"

The Miwok thought for a moment before he nodded and said, "Yes. We will move along the ridges until we are well south of Sacramento. Then I will lead you to a Mexican village in the valley. They are good people and may give you a horse. From there you simply ride due west toward Mount Diablo, on the coast. San Francisco is on the other side. Are you going there to get help?"

Longarm shook his head and said, "Not exactly. I'm going over Judge Field's head. You see, he's only the *second* biggest crook in California. If I can make a deal with the *biggest* crook, I might uphold some law around here yet!"

Chapter 2

They called him "The Blind Boss," but this appellation was only partly accurate. Christopher Buckley was getting on in years and had cataracts, but he could see well enough with his ghastly gray eyes, and didn't miss one hell of a lot. Boss Buckley was the undisputed owner, lock, stock, and barrel, of the California Democrat Party, and who was in the White House made no difference to him and his henchmen, a band of boisterous bullies known as Buckley's Lambs. Finding out where Boss Buckley was, the night Longarm arrived in San Francisco, was no problem. Getting to see him was a bit more difficult.

Longarm caught up with Buckley at a whorehouse near the waterfront. It was late evening. The cobbled streets at the foot of Telegraph Hill were dark, and a peasoup fog was rolling in through the Golden Gate. Longarm was on foot and tired of chasing false leads by the time he got to the frame house and knocked, as instructed, on an alley entrance. The door opened a slit and a wary-looking Chinese asked who'd sent him.

Longarm said, "Marty, the bellhop at the Palace Hotel. I have to talk to Boss Buckley."

The doorkeeper said, "No savvy," and tried to close the door. Longarm stiff-armed it open, Chinese and all, and stepped inside, saying, "Sure you do. Where is he, upstairs or in the parlor?"

The Chinese yelled something in his own language and a trio of his countrymen boiled out of the woodwork, yelling.

Longarm sighed, punched the doorkeeper flat, and waded into the others, swinging. Since nobody seemed to be waving a gun at anyone, he decided to settle for a friendly fight.

The confrontation was short, savage, and noisy. Longarm emerged with a split lip, leaving four Orientals stretched out on the red carpet in various states of disrepair. As he sucked a knuckle and got his breath back, a tall, statuesque blonde wearing little more than red garters and a wisp of black lace appeared in the nearest doorway to observe, "Hell, honey, if you want to get laid that badly, you should have made an appointment."

Longarm smiled at the tall whore and said, "I didn't come for that, this time. I have to see Boss Buckley."

"Oh, now I see why Wang attacked you. You'd better get lost, handsome. We only do business in this place. We don't introduce customers to one another."

"Where is he? It'd save time and furniture if folks would be more neighborly hereabouts."

The whore insisted, "Honey, if I were you, I'd fold my tent and steal silently away. Since I don't want you to beat me up, I'll tell you all you really need to know. The boss is holding a meeting in a side room, and he has a couple of his lambs with him. So what are you waiting for? *Run*, you damned fool!"

Longarm started toward her. She noted the look in his eyes and got out of the way, but yelled out, "Hey, Curly! There's trouble headed your way, and he's a *big* son of a bitch!"

Longarm found himself in a high-ceilinged stairwell, appointed richly with brocaded wallpaper and, for some reason, a suit of armor. A door across the way opened, and a man only slightly smaller than a steam locomotive appeared. He had curly red hair, so Longarm didn't wait to be introduced. He swung as hard as he could and connected firmly with the bodyguard's lantern jaw.

Nothing happened.

Curly not only looked like a locomotive; he seemed to be made of the same materials. He shook his head as if dimly aware of the blow and then, as the deputy hit him again, he simply reached out and hugged Longarm like a big bear, crooning, "Now, Jasus, me bucko, is it trouble you've come for? Faith, and it's trouble you've found, for it's in the bay I'll be after putting you, dead or alive."

Longarm tried to knee the monstrous redhead as he felt the breath being squeezed out of his creaking ribs. But Curly had his knees together against such a move and sighed, "Now, is that a decent way for a wee thing like you t'act?"

Longarm butted his forehead into Curly's mouth, as hard as he could. Curly roared like an annoyed grizzly and warned,

"You're beginning to *annoy* me, bucko! You jist come quiet, and I may be after depositin' you in the water alive. Another trick like that and it's a dead man you'll be!"

Longarm felt his feet leave the carpet as the giant started waltzing him toward the front door. He reached down with the only hand he could move, got a firm grip on Curly's family jewels, and started to twist them off.

The bigger man howled and literally threw Longarm across the hall into the suit of armor, shouting, "Jasus! Now I really am starting to dislike you!" as the lawman sprawled in a welter of disjointed steel plates. He crabbed sideways, clattering and scattering bits of armor as Curly charged. The big man crashed into the wall as Longarm got to his feet, holding the battle mace he'd found on the carpet amid the debris. As Curly moved in on him, growling low in his throat, Longarm could only hope the studded steel club might stop him.

He never found out. A new voice whipcracked, "What in hell is going on out here?" and Longarm recognized the white-eyed older man standing in the doorway. He said, "Buckley, I'm a deputy U.S. marshal. If you don't call that gorilla off, I'm going to have to pull a gun on him!"

Boss Buckley said, "Back off, Curly." But Curly said, "He went after me privates. I'm going to tear off his arms and legs. I'm going to twist off his head. And then . . . I'm going to kill him!"

Buckley laughed and said, "Later. After I hear what he has on his mind. What's this all about, Deputy?"

"I've come to ask a favor," Longarm gasped as he tried to regain his breath.

"You and everyone else. Let's go inside and sit down. Would you mind telling me how you found me here?"

"Like to. Can't. The man who told me where to find you made me promise not to tell on him. I can see why."

Buckley led the way to another room. It was expensively furnished and smelled musty. Buckley had a cigar in one hand, but there was no smell of tobacco smoke in the small room, so Longarm knew he'd been taken to one the boss hadn't been in that evening. The political meeting he'd been holding in some other part of the house must have been private indeed. But it was none of his business, so he didn't comment.

The boss waved Longarm to a chair and took a seat across from him, near a marble fireplace that smelled of damp ashes. He leaned back and fixed the lawman with a shrewd look from his oyster-colored, half-blind eyes, saying, "All right, this had better be good."

Longarm told his story, beginning with his assignment to the case and ending with a brief sketch of his escape. When he'd finished, the boss said, "I think you're barking up the wrong tree if you think Steve Field is in on it, son. I happen to know he's about to be made a justice of the Supreme Court."

Longarm exhaled heavily and shook his head. "God help the country!"

"Now cool down, son," the old boss admonished him. "I know old Steve. He's twice as tough and almost as mean as they say he is, but he wouldn't take a bribe from penny-ante thieves."

"What about *big* thieves, Mr. Buckley? Are you saying Field hasn't his price?"

Boss Buckley chuckled and said, "Of course he has his price. As does everyone, which makes my career so interesting. But a man slated for the Supreme Court's bench has expensive tastes—too expensive for what you have in mind. I know the Mother Lode like the back of my hand. The Bonanza reefs are played out. In fact, the Lost Chinaman bottomed out a good ten years or more ago. There can't be enough gold in that whole mountain to buy Steve Field—or even me."

Longarm chuckled and said, "I wouldn't know what your price is, sir, but you're dead wrong about the mine being played out; I read the reports from the assay office. It's true the original owners hit bottom back in the fifties. At least, they thought they'd hit bottom, but we live in changing times. The old-timers just skimmed the cream when they found the Mother Lode. They took the stuff you can wash out with running water. The new owners up there use chemicals the forty-niners never heard of and they found the veins weren't all that pinched out after all."

Buckley nodded. "I know about the cyanide process. I've shoveled, hydraulicked, and cradled gold in my time! These new-fangled methods explain why they've been shipping the ore down the mountain instead of stamping it out on the site, eh?"

"Yes sir. The old-fashioned stamping mills up in the gold fields can't extract enough gold from the country rock to make it a paying deal. So the Lost Chinaman's been sending it by narrow-gauge down to Sacramento where it's supposed to be leached out, melted down to bullion, and transferred here to the mint. But like I said, it ain't been getting here."

"So I heard," the boss said. "Where are the trains being held up?"

Longarm wondered if he dared ask the man for a smoke, but decided against it, and said, "That's the spooky part they sent me to find out about, Mr. Buckley. You see, the trains ain't being held up. They leave Manzanita with a shipment, chug down through the hills right peaceably, then turn up in Sacramento with worthless rock. Our government assay boys say the high-graders are substituting the same salmon-colored quartz the gold is found inside, only it's worthless. It looks like gold ore, but it ain't."

Boss Buckley puffed his cigar thoughtfully and said, "I give up. How the hell do you suppose they manage such a slick trick?"

"I don't know. You're right about its being slick. If the jaspers just stopped the train and rode off with the stuff, we'd have some notion where to cut their trail. But by switching worthless rock for gold-bearing ore somewhere along the way, they leave us with some sixty-odd miles of trackside to study." He paused for a moment before adding, "If I could get some cooperation around here for a few days, I might be able to answer better."

Buckley ignored the hint. "Do you suppose they have a railroad siding up there somewhere? You can't unload and then reload an ore car while it's moving. The only way I can see it is that they have a set of duplicate cars, loaded with dross rock and waiting along the right-of-way. Somehow, they must be uncoupling the ore cars, switching them for the others, and—Yeah, you'd only need to start with one string of empties. Each time you switched cars you'd wind up with more empty ones for the next time. You'd best start looking for a siding near a tunnel or switchback. Maybe someplace where they stop the train to jerk boiler water."

Longarm took the bull by the horns and said, "I'd like to. But I need your help, Mr. Buckley."

The older man snorted. "*My* help? Before we go a step deeper, I'd like you to tell me why. You're working for those shit-for-brains Republicans the voters were dumb enough to put in, last election. I wouldn't want this to get around, but I run the Democrats in this state!"

"I know. That's why I came to you. Most of the folks up near the diggings are Republicans. If any government people are mixed up in this high-grading, I should think you'd want me to expose them before it's time to vote again."

Boss Buckley chuckled and said, "I admire your gall. You must have been told by now that I'm supposed to be a scoundrel and a thief."

"Yes sir, and if this was my assignment, and if I could prove half of what I've heard, I'd arrest you. But I catch my crooks one at a time, and right now I'm after those high-graders. If you could get the county government up there off my back, I'd likely get them, too."

"How do you know I'm not one of them?" Buckley asked pointedly.

Longarm shrugged. "Don't seem likely. The sheriff up there is a Republican. Another Republican named Lovejoy robbed me of my guns, my badge, my watch, a horse and saddle, and too much else to mention. He's welcome to all but my guns, watch, and badge, as long as he promises not to arrest me any more."

Buckley smoked a while, immersed in thought, and Longarm knew he'd aroused the older man's chess-playing instincts. Finally the boss asked, "What could I do if I was willing to? I run San Francisco, not Calaveras County, or even Sacramento."

"They'd listen to you, though. Every nail and barrel of flour they need up there in the Mother Lode comes through your port. I doubt whether a handful of deputies up near the mines would want to tangle with your lambs, either. I know I wouldn't!"

Buckley laughed expansively, and said, "Hell, old Curly is one of my *gentle* lambs. But I'm not about to loan you a posse of waterfront Irishmen."

Longarm leaned forward and asked intently, "What *are* you going to do, Mr. Buckley?"

The boss studied his cigar ash, and replied, "I'm not sure. With Steve Field on his way to the Supreme Court, and a mention in your case report saying I've been helpful to the U.S. government, I might feel more comfortable about those Eastern senators who keep questioning the way we do things out here on the coast. You did say something about mentioning me in your report, didn't you?"

"I sure did, Mr. Buckley." Longarm smiled. "Now that you mention it, I don't see how I could have solved this case without your help. I disremember just what you did for me, though."

"You let me worry about the wheels of government," Buckley said. "Take your time getting back to the gold fields while I pass the word to a few people."

"Like Justice Field and the marshal in Sacramento?" Longarm prompted.

"I told you Steve Field's not a thief. I doubt if he knows you're alive."

"Somebody in his office does," the deputy pointed out. "They came down hard on a jurisdictional dispute and signaled the county to get rid of me."

"All right," Buckley relented, "let's say there's a crook or two in the marshal's office. Let's say that once the marshal's personal attention is drawn to the matter, a smart crook would crawfish off, grinning as innocent as a shit-eating dog. You give me a day or two and I'll be surprised as hell if anyone wearing a badge tries to give you a hard time."

"I'll be in your debt if you can, sir. That still leaves me with the high-graders, whoever they may be, and they say the late Calico Kid had lots of friends in the county."

The older man growled, "Don't press me, son. Despite what they say about me, I don't have much truck with outlaws and roughnecks I don't have on my payroll. I'll tell the sheriff's department up there that it might not be advisable to gun you down like a dog. You'll be on your own as far as anyone else up there is concerned!"

The Sacramento boat left San Francisco after dark to arrive upstream at the capital in the morning. It was comfortable, but a slow way to travel, even that far west.

On the other hand, he'd promised Boss Buckley that he'd take his time getting back to Manzanita, so what the hell.

He'd wired Denver for expense money and bought himself some fresh duds before engaging a stateroom on the paddle-wheel steamer. As the night boat puffed its way through the San

Pablo narrows and headed for the tule marshes of the big inland delta, Longarm took a seat near a window in the dining salon and gave his order to an immaculate colored waiter who acted as important as Queen Victoria's head butler.

He was waiting for his steak and potatoes when a female voice at his side asked, "Forgive me, sir. Is anyone sitting at this table?"

Longarm smiled up at the expensive-looking brunette who'd spoken, and replied, "I'm sitting at it. You're welcome to that other chair across the table."

The girl smiled back at him and sat down, explaining, "A woman traveling alone has to be careful. The purser tells me you're a U.S. marshal."

"Only a deputy," he corrected her. "My handle is Custis Long."

"I'm Sylvia Baxter. Of the Boston Baxters, that is."

Longarm studied her, wondering what a Boston Baxter was. She had a veil over her eyes, hanging from a perky little blue velvet hat, but he could see she was pretty, in a snooty sort of way. The hat had been chosen to match her wide-set eyes. A hat like that cost money, no matter what color it was. He said, "I was in Boston, once. Had to transport a prisoner back from there. I didn't get to see much of it, but the harbor was right pretty."

"I'm afraid we lived on the Back Bay. You do know what the Back Bay is, don't you?"

Longarm found her approach a trifle offensive, so he nodded and said, "I can read, too. If we ever get served, you might be surprised to learn that I don't eat with my fingers." He saw the uncertain look in her eyes and added, "Might use my bowie knife if the steak is tough, but I promise I won't shoot the waiter."

She smiled uncertainly, and said, "Dear me, we are getting off to a bad start, aren't we?"

Longarm was beginning to enjoy needling her. "Don't know. Where are we supposed to be headed?" he asked with a blank expression.

She replied huffily, "I simply introduced myself in what I felt was a proper manner, sir."

"Maybe. Folks out our way don't fret much about which side of the tracks a person comes from. I'll say right out I was born and brought up on a hard-scrabble West Virginia farm, and I'll take on any man who says that makes me less than he is."

The woman blinked, apparently taken aback by the marshal's directness. "My word! I certainly never intended to start a fight with you! Are you always so sensitive about your background?"

Longarm's mouth smiled, but his eyes remained expressionless. "Honey, I never had any background. We were too poor. As to what coming from Back Bay Boston makes you, all I really want to know is whether you aim to pay for your own dinner or whether you're expecting me to."

Sylvia Baxter flushed under her veil and snapped, "That's a churlish thing to say! Of course I had every intention of buying my own meal!"

He looked elaborately relieved and said, "In that case, let's just eat and say no more about it."

He saw the snooty waiter passing, apparently with no intention of taking her order, so he snapped his fingers.

The waiter didn't look their way, but the girl said, "Please, it's not polite to snap one's fingers at the help."

Longarm shrugged, drew his revolver, and aimed it at the ceiling. The girl gasped, "Oh, my God!" in a loud voice, and that did the trick. The waiter swung his head to see what was wrong and, noting the gun in Longarm's hand, hurried over with a nervous smile, saying, "May I be of service, sir?"

He'd obviously been working here long enough to understand the frontier breed better than he'd been letting on. Longarm put the gun away, saying, "This lady wants to eat. So do I. Where in thunder is the steak I ordered?"

"It's coming right up, sir. Would madame care to order, now?"

Sylvia looked undecided and stammered, "Dear me, I haven't read the menu."

Longarm said, "Give her steak and potatoes, and tell them we ain't got all night."

As the waiter scurried away to do as he was told, the girl asked Longarm, "How did you know I wanted steak and potatoes, sir?"

"Everybody wants steak and potatoes. I read the menu. By the time you found anything worth ordering, we'd have likely starved to death."

The girl picked up the menu firmly and began to read it, try-

ing to ignore Longarm. He tried in turn not to drum his fingers
on the table. He was wondering what was wrong with him tonight. He was usually a friendly enough sort, and the girl was
pretty, but he felt edgy, impatient, and out of sorts. Was he coming down with some ague? He didn't feel sick, just sort of raw-
nerved about something. But what could it be? It wasn't the
snooty little Boston gal. Any other time he'd simply have laughed
her uppity notions off. They said ponies and other critters got
like this when an earthquake was fixing to happen. Could he be
sensing some disaster he couldn't see or smell?

The waiter returned with their orders, a nervous smile, and a
bottle. He said, "We'd like you to accept a complimentary bottle
of our California wine, Marshal. May I draw the cork for you?"

Longarm nodded and said, "Sure, you can draw it *and* quarter it." Then he shook his head to clear it, wondering, *What in
thunder is wrong with you, old son? You're acting like a school-
boy sniggering at a dirty joke!*

He knew he wasn't given to rawhiding colored folks or playing big bad Westerner to schoolmarmish little snoots. But he
was fighting a terrific urge to draw the gun again and shoot up
the overhead coal-oil lamps. The infernal lamps were too bright.
They hurt his eyes. It seemed pretty silly when he thought about
it. A high-plains rider who'd squinted against a searing sun for
many a summer shouldn't be blinded by a little coal-oil flame in
a smoke-glass globe.

The waiter poured a small amount of red wine into a long-
stemmed glass and handed it to Longarm. The deputy remembered the form and took a sip before nodding. The nod was a
lie, for the wine, if that was what it was, tasted like red ink
mixed with vinegar. The waiter filled both their glasses, put
the bottle on the table between them, and left with a relieved
expression.

Sylvia Baxter tasted her wine and said, "My, it is good, isn't
it? I mean, it would hardly pass for Bordeaux '53, but it has an
amusing bouquet."

Longarm stared at the bottle as if it had played a dirty trick
on him. The fancy label said it had been made in Riverside by
some colony, but it didn't say what river the colony was beside.
He remembered his manners and waited for her to start eating.
But she kept dawdling with the godawful wine until he muttered,

"Let's dig in," and started cutting his steak. She probably had him figured for a savage anyway and, what the hell, he'd never see her again. He intended to catch the stage in Sacramento in the morning, and take his own sweet time getting back to Manzanita. He only hoped Boss Buckley's word would arrive there ahead of him. If the word didn't help, he'd cross that bridge when it shot at him.

The steak tasted as though it had been fried in iodine, and he was about to say so when the girl smiled and said, "My, this *is* good, isn't it? I've been making do with shipboard fare since leaving Boston. Fresh meat is such a relief to my poor, tortured taste buds."

He didn't want to call the lady a liar, so he said, "Oh, you came around the Horn?"

She shook her head and explained, "No, I took the Vanderbilt line to Nicaragua, crossed to the Pacific by the Commodore's road, and arrived yesterday on the Matson clipper."

"You didn't get to see much of Frisco, then?"

"Forgive me for correcting you, but they tell me it's simply not called Frisco by gentlefolk."

He said, "Yeah," and took another bite. It was no use. The food was as bad as the wine and he was feeling . . . seasick?

That was impossible. They were steaming through a big flat swamp he could see outside in the moonlight. The night was dead calm and the water all around was as flat as a millpond. He could feel the vibration of the big stern-mounted paddle and hear the hiss of the engine if he listened carefully, but they were moving as smoothly as silk up the winding, shallow Sacramento.

The girl was saying, "I am in a hurry to reach Manzanita, but I did a bit of sightseeing in San Francisco. I rode all the way to the top of Nob Hill on one of those new cable cars. I must say they're up-to-date out here. I'm afraid I expected California to be much more primitive."

"Some of it still is. You say you're headed for Manzanita, up in Calaveras County?"

"Yes. That's the place Mark Twain wrote about in that amusing piece about the jumping frogs, wasn't it?"

"Yep. I read it, too. The last time I was up there, though, they weren't betting on frogs worth mention. Uh, do you have kin or something up in Calaveras County?"

"I'm joining my brother," she told him. "He's a mining engineer interested in some properties near Manzanita."

"Oh? Did he come out ahead of you, then?"

She looked down, avoiding his eyes as she murmured, "I hadn't planned to come at all. But Ralph is the only family I have now. You see, our parents are gone and . . . well, if you must know, I just divorced a man I never should have married. Ralph told me he was no good, but would I listen?"

Longarm nodded, understanding her snooty act better now. Divorces were legal enough, but still shocked a lot of people, despite the changes that had rocked the world since Victoria had been in the catbird seat of proper society. Sylvia Baxter was acting as if her armpits smelled of violets because she'd probably had a few snide remarks spit at her. To comfort her, he said, "I'd say divorcing a skunk is more civilized than shooting him or putting flypaper in his coffee."

She looked startled and said, "Flypaper? In coffee?"

"Coffee, tea, or whatever. That sticky stuff on flypaper is a mix of honey and arsenic. You'd be surprised how many mean husbands have died young since flypaper was invented."

She laughed, for once not stiffly, and said, "I should have met you sooner. The papers I paid for cost much more than those I could have bought in any general store."

He laughed with her and said, "We live and learn. Maybe next time."

She said, "I'm not sure there'll be a next time. I've had all of marriage I care for, thank you very much."

"Don't thank me; I wasn't proposing. You'll be taking the Wells Fargo stage up to the Mother Lode, won't you?"

"I don't think so. My brother wrote that there's a narrow-gauge railway winding up from Valley Springs. I think I have to transfer from the main line at a place called Lodi, and—"

"It's the long way around, but likely more comfortable than the stage," he cut in. He was disappointed in one way, but relieved in another. Ordinarily he had an eye out for a well-turned ankle, but there was something about this woman that made him as broody as an old hen on a cold glass egg. Besides, he hadn't come all the way out here to spark divorcees. He'd been on the case nearly a week and, up to now, hadn't even managed to get within hailing distance of the goddamned mine he'd been sent to investigate.

He took another sip of wine, gagged, and suddenly knew he was going to throw up!

Without a word, he got up from the table, moved off at a trot, and just made it out to the promenade deck in time. He leaned out over the rail and gave everything he'd eaten in the past couple of years to the croaking frogs protesting in the tule reeds they were passing through.

He heaved at least five times before a couple of dry retches told him he'd hit bottom. A male voice to his left said, "If you taste hair, swallow fast, or you'll be throwing up your asshole!"

Longarm turned to the amused deckhand and asked mildly, "Can you swim, sailor?"

"Don't take it personal, cowboy. I've been seasick myself. Though, come to think of it, it was out at sea. Ain't the waves in this delta a caution?"

Longarm wiped his sweating brow with the back of his hand and said, "I ain't seasick. I suspicion I've been poisoned. You have a sawbones on this tub?"

The deckhand shook his head and said, "Not in the crew. If you're really sick, I can ask the purser if there's a doctor on board."

Longarm shook his head and said, "I'll just go to my stateroom and flatten out. If I ain't dead by the time we make Sacramento, I likely threw up whatever it was."

He brushed past the amused deckhand and staggered to his stateroom, where he stripped without lighting the lamp, tore open the bottom bunk, and flopped face down on it, feeling as though he'd been run over by a Conestoga wagon. He ached all over, and though the California nights were cooler than he'd expected, he was sweating like a pig shoveling coal.

How in thunder had they done it? He hadn't had a thing to eat or drink at the whorehouse. The Boston gal hadn't been wearing any rings big enough to play a Borgia trick on him. It hardly seemed likely that the steamboat company had poisoned him. Could it have been those oysters he'd eaten for breakfast at the hotel?

He started feeling a little better. He'd most likely thrown up whatever it was, and it was time to reconsider living long enough to collect his pension.

Longarm got up, lurched over to the gunbelt he'd hung on a rusty nail, and drew the Colt he'd bought in San Francisco to replace the one the Manzanita constable had stolen from him. He hadn't had time to shorten the barrel or file off the front sight, but he thought he could manage a fast enough draw from under his pillow. The door to the deck outside was a flimsy-looking thing with jalousie slats for ventilation, but anyone busting through it would have to make some noise. Gun in hand, he walked naked to the door to slide the bolt in place.

The door opened before he could reach it.

Longarm whipped the muzzle of the gun up, trained it on the slim figure outlined in the moonlight, and snapped, "Freeze, you son of a bitch!"

Then he saw that it was Sylvia Baxter. She looked startled, which sort of made sense, even if nothing else did. Suddenly aware of his nakedness, he placed his free hand in front of his crotch and asked, "Don't folks knock in Boston, sis?"

"I did knock! What on earth is *wrong* with you, sir?"

"I've been shot at, thrown in jail, beat up, and poisoned. Now let's hear what's wrong with you. Are you in the habit of leaping at a person wearing nothing but his birthday suit?"

"Would you please stop pointing that gun at me? I only came to your cabin because you played a dirty trick on me back there in the dining salon. I had to pay for both of our dinners!"

He lowered the Colt, still covering his privates as he stepped back and said, "Come on in. My pants are hanging over there. You'll have to fish out my wallet and help yourself, because I've only got two hands."

She laughed nervously and said, "I know, but it's a little late now." Then she added, "Don't worry about it. I studied medicine for two years before they forced me out of it. I've seen naked men before."

He backed to the bunk and sat down, pulling the edge of the blanket over his thighs as she turned her back on him to go through his pockets. He was grateful that it was almost dark in the room, for he knew he must be beet-red. He said, "It's too bad you didn't graduate. I could use a doctor right now—even a female one."

She turned around and handed him his wallet, saying, "You owe me seventy-five cents plus the extra dime I tipped the waiter. I might have known you'd be like all the other men. Damn it, I would have been a *good* doctor! You men just don't seem to understand that a woman has a brain, too."

He put the gun under the pillow and took out a bill, saying, "I'll give you a whole dollar and we'll call it square. As to your brain, I ain't actually seen it, so I can't say whether you've got one or not."

She snatched the bill from him angrily and stuffed it into her purse as she sniffed, "I don't understand why a grown man should be afraid of a woman doctor. There are a lot of quacks and butchers who are men—name one who is a woman."

"Don't reckon I can," he concurred, not a little non-plussed by her belligerence. "Now look here," he continued. "First of all, I said I'd be right glad to see *any* doctor just about now—"

"Even a female one," she interrupted him acidly.

"Even a Paiute medicine man," he continued. "I'm purely sorry about the eighty-five cents, but I was a mite confused and in just a smidgin of a hurry. You wouldn't have cared for it much if I'd stayed."

To his surprise and further confusion, she sat down on the foot of the bed and said, "You know damned well it isn't the eighty-five cents; it's your whole attitude."

This conversation was starting to make his head spin even more. He said, "Up to a minute ago, I didn't have any attitude worth mention, but I'll admit I'm getting one pretty fast. Just to set the record straight, as a U.S. deputy sworn to uphold the Constitution, I can tell you I'd arrest anyone trying to deprive any citizen—yourself Included—of his constitutional rights."

"There, you see?" she exploded. "'*His* constitutional rights'—it's even in the language."

"Afraid I can't take responsibility for that," he said. "I only talk it—I didn't make it up."

"What about the right to vote?" she pressed on, leaning closer to him and jabbing a finger into the thatch of hair on his solid chest.

Longarm was beginning to wonder seriously what her game was, and he decided to feed her some more rope. "I'll allow that most *men* don't have the sense to pour piss out of their boots—

excuse me, ma'am—much less vote. I doubt that women would
do much worse, and maybe someday, when the country simmers
down and gets less hectic around the polls—"

He noticed that her face was growing flushed and little beads
of perspiration had appeared on her upper lip as she asked,
"Does the Constitution say only you men have the right to sow
wild oats? There's a parlor house in every town across the country, and you know very well that no man sniggering with the
others at the pool hall would ever admit that he was a virgin."

"Would you admit it?" he asked pointedly.

There was an unmistakable sparkle in her eyes as she replied,
"It's hardly a problem. I told you I've been married."

"And since I don't visit parlor houses," he said, "I guess that
more or less cancels out the entire issue."

Longarm felt now as if he were floating in the air a little
distance above the bed. He knew he needed to lie down, with her
or without her. As usual, his amorous parts were behaving as
though they had a life of their own, and he could feel himself
swelling beneath the blanket across his lap. Longarm decided,
with fireflies glittering before his eyes, that it was time to call
her play. He placed a hand on her knee. She glanced down at his
hand without moving away, then shifted her gaze to the promi-
nent bulge at his crotch. Her eyes rose to meet his, and she
asked, "Am I to take that as a challenge or a compliment, Mr.
Long?"

He didn't answer. He couldn't answer. Suddenly the room
was spinning around and he felt as if he were about to puke all
over them both. So he decided to lie down and die instead.

He was in this funny big room with red velvet drapes. A bunch
of naked women were coming at him from all directions. They
had painted faces and high-heeled shoes and they were all grinning from ear to ear. But their grins were evil and they had guns
in their hands.

He reached for his own gun, but he wasn't wearing his cross-
draw rig. He wasn't wearing anything at all. He was naked and
had a monstrous erection, and the painted women were laughing
at it. A big blonde with a mouthful of gold teeth and a Mexican
gunbelt riding low on her naked hips grabbed at him as if she
intended to milk him like a cow. He stepped back and discov-

ered that another naked woman had knelt behind him on her hands and knees. He fell backward to the thick red carpet and the big blonde jumped over the girl who'd tripped him, placed her French heels to either side of his chest, and squatted. Her aim was perfect and he felt his shaft going deeply into her as she shouted, "Powder River and let 'er buck!!"

It felt too good to be real. He decided he was having a wet dream. He wondered if he'd get to come this time, before he awoke all the way. The trouble with wet dreams was that he always seemed to wake up just as they were getting interesting. He started pumping back, but he couldn't quite make it and he knew he'd open his eyes in the little furnished room by Cherry Creek and discover that he had to take a leak. It was purely frustrating to wake up with a hard-on and nobody there to share it with.

He opened his eyes. For a long moment he wondered where he was. Then he remembered that he was on a steamboat. The stateroom lamp was lit. Sylvia Baxter was beside him, sitting up in bed and doing something funny to his eyelids. She was stark naked. Built better than he'd expected, too. Those starched lace dickies that women wore down the front of their dresses sort of flattened things out. Her pink nipples were turned up like her nose.

He said, "What happened? The last time we met, you had all your duds on. Then I must have passed out. I had the damnedest dream."

"It was a dream for *me*, too!" she said. "I didn't know you were unconscious until a moment ago."

"You mean we—?"

She smiled languidly. "Yes, darling, and I must say, you're better by reflex action than my silly husband ever was wide awake. I think you've got a concussion. Has anyone hit you on the head recently?"

He grinned wanly, and said, "Now that you mention it, doc, I did have a tussle with a big Irish wharf rat last night. He hit me with the wall of a whorehouse."

She nodded and said, "That explains a lot. I didn't think you could be as crazy as you've been acting. Have you had sudden mood changes? Any nausea?"

"I threw up a while back. What do you reckon I should take for this concussion, doc?"

"There's nothing you can take. What you really need is a few nights of bed rest. If I'd known you were ill, I'd have . . . well, what's done is done."

He grinned and said, "The hell you say! If I really did what I dreamed I did, I've got some catching up to do in the real world."

As he put an arm around her, Sylvia drew back and insisted, "Not in your condition. Maybe later."

He said, "My condition right now is hard as a poker and, what the hell, it ain't like we're strangers!"

She was still insisting that he was too weak as he rolled her to the mattress and started to mount her. Then, as he got his hips between her smooth ivory thighs, she went limp and breathed, "Do be careful, dear heart. I don't know what I'd do if you killed yourself with this foolishness!"

He got a hand between them and guided his shaft into her moist warmth, saying, "Yeah, it'd be a tough thrill to follow, wouldn't it? A gal who'd once come with a dead man in her would never be able to top it for an interesting experience!"

As he slid all the way into her, she gasped in mingled pleasure and annoyance. "I think I liked you better unconscious! Must you be so vulgar about it?"

He laughed and started moving. "Hell, lady, if you didn't want it he-man style, you never should have started it."

"I didn't start it. Oh, stop talking like a fool and *do* it!"

The fireflies were back again and the room was spinning like a merry-go-round, but he knew he wasn't going to black out. He gritted his teeth and muttered to himself, *Listen, God. I'm likely to take it personal if you don't let me do it right this time.*

This time, God listened.

Sylvia couldn't ride to Manzanita in the stage with him because her brother was meeting her at trackside in the mountains. So they kissed goodbye as the boat docked in Sacramento the next morning, and Longarm promised to look her up when he arrived in Manzanita.

He went to the Wells Fargo office and bought a ride to Manzanita. The agent told him he had a couple of hours to kill before the stage hauled out for the High Sierra. He had most of the

background material he needed, but Marshal Vail and the treasury boys might have missed a thing or two, so he moseyed over
to the land office to refresh his memory.

Longarm introduced himself to an elderly clerk as a deputy
U.S. marshal, without mentioning what district court he worked
for. The clerk was a friendly sort who didn't even ask to see his
badge, which was just as well, since some son of a bitch had it
up in the hills somewhere.

As he started pawing through the files, the clerk said, "I can
tell you just about anything you'll find in there, Deputy. I came
out here in '49."

"I'm interested in the Lost Chinaman claim, up in Calaveras
County."

"Hell, son, I was washing color in the headwaters of the
Stanislaus when Mark Twain wrote that fool story about the
frog."

"You ever meet the frog?"

"Nope, but I met Mark Twain and Bret Harte when they was
just starting to tell all them lies about us. You see, the gold rush
started down here in the low country, when they found color
washed down off the Sierra in the creek beds."

"I know about the gold rush, old son," Longarm told the man.

"No, you don't," the old clerk contradicted him. "Not if you
been reading Harte and Twain. Like I said, we started washing
color in the low country. By the fifties, we'd followed the gold
up the streams and found the Mother Lode—a big, wide belt of
gold quartz running a couple hundred miles up there. The color
we'd found in the creeks was just what had washed out of the
real lode. It was the hard-rock miners who had the capital to
move mountains to get at the good stuff."

"How many mines are still in Bonanza up in Calaveras County,
pop?" Longarm asked.

"Bonanza? Not a one. Most of the veins petered out some
time ago. A man named Hearst has a working claim in Calaveras, a mine called Sheep Ranch. But he's hauling low-grade out
these days. Hearst is a big shot who got in on the big Virginia
City strike, on the other side of the Sierra. He's got the capital
to crush his own ore. Angel Camp's about dead. Murphy has a
low-grade mine nobody's interested in these days. They had a
copper strike up there a while back, but it never amounted to

much. Copper's too cheap to haul over all them ridges and they just couldn't compete with Arizona Territory."

"So let's talk about the Lost Chinaman. I understand the owner is a man named MacLeod?"

"That's right. Nice young jasper, for an Easterner. Him and his pretty little wife bought the mine for next to nothing. It seemed to bottom out a good six or eight years back, but Mac-Leod's some sort of geologist and he hit a vein the others overlooked. They say he's been shipping tolerable ore."

"He may be shipping it," the deputy agreed. "It's not getting anywhere, though. You got a railroad map of the county?"

The clerk nodded and slid open a wide, flat drawer, saying, "I know what you have in mind. Other marshals have been studying the same crazy situation. You won't find the siding everyone's looking for. Half of the old narrow-gauge tracks up there have been pulled up for scrap."

Longarm spread the map on a nearby table and ran his finger along a red line between Manzanita and the Big Valley. He mused aloud, "If there's unused track laying around up there to be claimed by any junkman, it wouldn't be impossible for somebody to build his own siding in some wooded stretch of canyon."

The clerk shook his head. "The other lawmen have been all up and down the line. Besides, the train crews say they've never stopped or been stopped between the mine tipple and the mills down here."

"What about this other fellow, Hearst?"

"George Hearst? He lives in Frisco. Ain't heard about him missing any gold. Like I said, they crush their own ore up at Sheep Ranch and ship it almost pure. They send it down in freight wagons, under guard. The way I hear tell, nobody wants to tangle with old Hearst. He's in politics in the city and thick with the Big Five. This young MacLeod likely don't have as many friends who'd back his play against high-graders."

Longarm smiled thinly. "He has the U.S. government in his corner. He contracted with the treasury to deliver his gold to the mint. Where does this Hearst jasper send his gold?"

The clerk shrugged. "Same place, of course. Nobody else buys gold in quantity on this coast." He saw Longarm's puzzled frown and asked, "Did I say something important, Deputy?"

"Maybe. These robberies have added up to a mess of gold,

no matter what the quality of the stolen ore might have been. But you're right. You can't sell a real pile of gold to anyone but Uncle Sam—not without attracting a lot of attention."

"Mexico?" the clerk suggested.

The marshal tugged at a corner of his mustache. "Doubt it. For sure, they couldn't haul it that far as ore. They have to have a refinery we don't know about. If MacLeod's extracting with the cyanide process, it can't be just some backwoods stamping mill, either, You say the Hearst mine has its own mill?"

The old man shook his head. "Wrong tree, Deputy. The mill in Sheep Ranch is just a simple crusher that runs the slurry over mercury beds. They boil the mercury out of the results and wind up with rich dust. If the Lost Chinaman's ore needs cyanide to leach it from the rock, the Hearst mill couldn't extract it worth mention."

"How about those other ghost towns up there, like Angel's Camp?"

"They ain't quite dead, for one thing, so you'd have witnesses. There ain't no cyanide mills, either, so you'd get no gold."

"Try it this way. What if MacLeod's wrong? The ore might be rich enough to run through an old-fashioned mill and settle for half, letting whatever gold the cyanide might get out stay where it is?"

The man scratched his wispy-haired pate vigorously. "Well, high-graders is called high-graders 'cause they skim the cream. You could get some gold out of nigh *any* rock with a pan and running water. They're going to a lot of effort if that's their play, though. MacLeod's ore is marginal. Wouldn't be worth digging if they hadn't come up with new methods in the past few years. Hell, if *I* was up there high-grading, I'd rob George Hearst's mine. It's a third richer in color."

Longarm thanked the clerk and left. He went next to the offices of the *Sacramento Bee*, where he found another friendly cuss who was more than willing to jaw about the newspaper's back files.

He knew he was wasting time asking about the high-grading. If the case could have been solved by reading old reports on paper, the treasury never would have come bleating to Justice for a helping hand.

He asked about the Calico Kid and was told, "He got the name and the rep down near Los Angeles. Mining camp called Calico. Nobody knows who he was or where he came from before he started shooting folks as a hobby."

Longarm pursed his lips and said, "Hung out in mining country, did he? Now that's right interesting. You got anything in the morgue about him robbing gold shipments?"

The reporter shook his head and said, "Nope. The way they tell it, he was just a wild saddle tramp. Rode with some other young owlhoots of the same stripe. They've shot up a few towns for the hell of it, and been run out of twice as many. But the kid never had any robbery pinned on him."

"What *did* he do for a living, then? Folks can't just ride around like something in a Ned Buntline novel with no visible means of support. Bullets cost a nickel apiece and drinks are three cents a shot!"

The reporter shrugged and said, "He probably let folks grub-stake him some. Lots of people sort of like to stay on friendly terms with a mean-eyed jasper with a rep."

The deputy pondered this for a moment, then said, "I don't see him as a man who begged for handouts. If he didn't work, he must have been stealing for a living."

"Could be," the newspaperman agreed. "If he ever robbed anyone, they never saw fit to press charges, which isn't hard to understand. They say he had about five sidekicks riding with him, all of them just as mean as he was."

Longarm saw that he wasn't getting anywhere, and left. He found a café and had some chili and a beer. They both stayed down, so he figured he was getting over the set-to with Curly.

By the time he got to the Wells Fargo office again, the stage was loading up for its run up the slope. The jehu holding the reins was a fierce-looking old man of about seventy. The shotgun rider at his side was a consumptive-looking hunchback with a bullet hole in the brim of his dusty Stetson. Longarm saw that two passengers were already aboard, so he climbed in.

His fellow passengers were a tall man wearing a business suit and a blond mustache, seated across from a girl of about twenty-five. She wore black Spanish lace and her face was a dusky shade of rose. If she wasn't at least half Indian, he'd never met one. Her dark eyes smoldered angrily in a way that led Longarm to believe that anger was a natural condition with her, so he just smiled and sat beside her, introducing himself to the man in the opposite seat.

The man held out a hand and said, "I'm glad to know you, Deputy. I'm Kevin MacLeod."

Longarm blinked and asked, "The same Kevin MacLeod who owns the Lost Chinaman? I was beginning to think I'd never find you. This must be your pretty little wife I've heard so much about, right?"

The girl gasped in dismay and MacLeod said, "Not hardly. Allow me to present Señorita Felicidad Vallejo. One of the Vallejos of Old California."

The girl looked away, trying to ignore them both. MacLeod shrugged and said, "She doesn't like gringos very much."

Longarm refused to be snubbed, and he said, "It's an honor, ma'am. I read about your kinsman, General Vallejo. He sort of chased our army through a few canyons before they called the war off, didn't he?"

She didn't answer. So he shrugged and turned back to MacLeod as the jehu atop the stage cracked his whip and shouted, "*Move*, you oat-wastin' sons of bitches!"

The stage lurched into motion and took off in a cloud of dust, swaying on the rawhide thoroughbraces as if it were a small craft plunging through choppy water. MacLeod grinned and said, "It gets worse when we reach the high country. I think old Logan, up there, has been trying to die young. You can see he never made it, but it's not for lack of trying."

Longarm turned toward Señorita Vallejo, touched the brim of his Stetson, and asked, "Mind if I smoke, ma'am?" She kept her face averted, gazing out the window, and made no answer. The deputy shrugged and, taking her silence for consent, produced a cheroot from an inside coat pocket and planted it between his front teeth. He turned back to MacLeod and said, "Let's talk about rocks. Just how many shipments have we lost track of, so far?"

MacLeod's smile faded as he said, "Thirteen. I don't know what I'm going to do if you can't find out who's been doing it, Deputy. We've been digging damned decent stuff out of that mountain, but my men have to be paid and my wife and I are down to bread and beans. If they keep robbing us, we're just going to have to cash in our chips. Our original grubstake's about used up."

Longarm struck a match on the coach's window frame, and touched the flame to his cigar. "Haven't you made *any* money on the mine?"

"Not a red cent! I figure, allowing for a rough assay, we've shipped at least a quarter of a million in extractable ore since we reopened the mine. Not a speck of it's ever reached the mint."

Longarm blew out a large cloud of smoke that dissipated rapidly in the breeze from the window. He was tired of going over the same ground, so he didn't ask about the shipments. Instead he asked, "Do you know a mining engineer named Baxter?"

"Ralph Baxter? Sure. He's staying at the hotel in Manzanita. As a matter of fact, he's made me an offer for the Lost Chinaman."

The deputy's eyebrows rose slightly. "You don't say. Now that's sort of interesting."

"Not really," MacLeod said. "I have no intention of selling— not if I can help it. Baxter is fronting for an Eastern syndicate, and frankly he's been talking penny-ante. He knows what we have up there. I took him through the mine myself. You know what he offered us? A measly million dollars!"

Longarm whistled and asked, "You call that measly? For a man living on bread and beans, you think big, MacLeod!"

"Hell, I'd *be* big if they'd let me! The vein I opened promises to assay out a hundred times that amount. That reef of quartz shows no sign of having a bottom to it. Given the time and a little more backing, I can dig for gold all the way to China!"

"Maybe, but in the meantime we have to see about getting it to the mint. Have any others made you an offer for your mine? I've got reasons for asking."

MacLeod nodded and said, "I follow your drift. Ralph Baxter might be a crook, but I sort of doubt it. I checked out the people he works for. I'm not supposed to know who they are, but a man who's knocked around the mining business knows who to compare notes with. Baxter's outfit is made up of Boston bankers with solid reputations. I'd say his offer was legitimate, but it's way the hell too low to consider."

"How about the Hearst interests, over in Sheep Ranch? Do they seem interested?"

"They sent a man over to congratulate us when we hit pay dirt. He didn't make an offer. I showed him through the mine. He said the rock formation we're into isn't the same one Hearst is working. He said that was all he was really interested in. You see, some folks think the gold quartz runs all the way under the Sierra, clean over to the diggings in Nevada. But we agreed we'll have to dig some even to get near one another underground. Sheep Ranch is a good ten miles from Manzanita and the Lost Chinaman."

"Maybe. I'll ride over there and have a talk with them, though. From everything I've heard about George Hearst, your mine's just the sort of thing he's been buying up on both sides of the range. Didn't it strike you as odd that they weren't interested in buying you out?"

MacLeod frowned and said, "Not at the time. Now that you mention it, though, Hearst has the capital and muscle to make the Lost Chinaman a paying proposition. You see, you usually lose money on opening a mine and organizing things. A lot of small operators go broke holding rich enough claims. It takes money to make money, once you're into hard-rock deep mining. But they have money, and they know we've opened a new vein. Do you think—?"

Longarm held up a cautioning hand. "Let's leave off thinking till we know some more. You eat the apple a bite at a time, in my business. I'd best start with the suspects closer to home."

They rode on in comparative silence for a time. The stage was jarring hell out of them all as it started hitting rougher road. The Mexican girl was pouting fit to bust, and Longarm was heartily sick of running over the details of the mysterious high-graders. It seemed that no matter who he met up with, they all had the same impossible tale to tell. He knew they'd all missed something. Something simple. Nobody could simply lift a running freight car filled with gold ore off the tracks in broad daylight without the train crew noticing it. Someone had missed something—something important. He'd just have to bull on through till he spotted something in the pattern that nobody had seen up until now.

*   *   *

They were a couple of hours out of Sacramento and had just topped a rise when Longarm felt the stage slow down and heard the jehu cry out, "Son of a bitch!"

His oath was followed by the crack of a rifle shot and the sound of something or someone thudding to the dust outside. Then the stage was moving faster and a bullet slammed into the doorjamb near Longarm's head!

MacLeod gasped, "Road agents?" as he drew his own Smith & Wesson. Longarm didn't answer. He was leaning out the door he'd opened, gun in hand and looking back.

There were four of them, riding hard after the runaway stage and shooting from the saddle. Longarm spotted the body of the jehu on the trail as one of the road agents jumped his pony over it and kept coming. Longarm took aim and fired. He missed with his first shot. His second slug hit the pony he'd been aiming for and spilled the outlaw ass-over-teakettle into the dust.

He fired again, dropping another mount with its cursing rider, and then the survivors were reining in. One of them was shaking his fist.

Longarm climbed out on the side of the careening coach and looked up at the boot. There was nobody sitting up there, with or without the reins. He swore and climbed all the way to the top, holstering his gun as he crawled to the vacant seat. The shotgun rider was down in the boot, alive but bleeding like a stuck pig. Longarm saw that he'd managed to hang onto the traces, albeit with no control over the frightened mules. He said, "Good man!" and pried the blood-slicked reins from the shotgun's hand.

The hunchback made a gargling sound and tried to say something. Longarm said, "Just hold on, old son. You ain't hit bad. I'll have a look-see as soon as I get these infernal mules under control!"

He lied, of course. The poor bastard was done for, but he didn't think it would cheer the shotgun to hear it from him right now.

Longarm hauled back hard and kicked the brake rod, locking the wheels. The team dragged the coach a few yards, then came to a nervous, dancing stop. Longarm reached down with his free hand and groped for the shotgun wedged between the bulkhead and the dying guard. Then he looked quickly around in a full circle. They were alone on a stretch of rolling mustard meadow. Kevin MacLeod, gun in hand, stuck his head out and called up, "You seem to have driven them off, Deputy. What happened to the crew?"

Longarm said, "Both hit. The jehu didn't stop when they threw down on him. He was a good old man. Can you handle a scattergun?"

"Of course. Toss her down."

"Nope. You come up here and watch my ass while I turn the team around."

The mine owner joined him, gasping at the sight of the dying hunchback down in the boot. Longarm handed him the shotgun and said, "They may have given up. They may be back. They'll hit us from the rear if they hit us at all."

As Longarm hauled on the reins, MacLeod asked, "Where are we going, back to Sacramento?"

"Nope. Back to pick up the old man. Wouldn't be neighborly to leave him for the buzzards. There might be some sign to read back there, too."

MacLeod braced his heels on the boot above the moaning hunchback, and said, "I'm sure he's dead. I saw him hit the ground. But you're right. We can't just leave him."

Longarm swung the team back the way they'd just come and clucked them into motion, holding a tight rein to keep them from stampeding again. As the lead mules sniffed the body on the trail ahead, they started fighting the bits, but even without a whip the deputy managed to drive close enough. Then he set the brake and handed the reins to MacLeod, saying, "Don't let them have an inch of slack or you'll be on your way to wheresoever."

He climbed down and walked over to the body of the jehu. He didn't have to roll the old man over to see that he was dead. There was a gaping hole between the driver's shoulder blades. Longarm sighed, "Poor old bastard. You should have stopped, but I'm glad you didn't."

The door opened and the girl jumped down, asking, "Is there anything I can do?"

Longarm said, "Not for this one, ma'am. There's a man hit bad up in the boot who could use a woman's hand on his brow, if you have the belly for it."

Felicidad stared down at the dead man in the road and sighed,

"Ay, pobrecito!" Then she turned and walked to the front of the coach. MacLeod reached a hand down to help her, but she ignored it and climbed up beside him without comment. Longarm noticed that she climbed proficiently for a woman in skirts. She placed a foot on a spoke of the near wheel and went up like a hand climbing the side of a corral one jump ahead of a rogue steer. He surmised that she sat a pony well, too.

Leaving the dead driver for the moment, Longarm walked a big circle in the dust, searching for sign. The bodies of the two ponies he had shot carried no brands and had been stripped of their gear. He spotted a hoof print and muttered, "Son of a bitch. I thought so!"

Then he bent over, reholstered his gun, and dragged the body by its heels to the coach. The dead jehu was as limp as a dishrag, but a good deal heavier. It was a task getting him inside, but Longarm managed. He slammed the door and climbed up beside MacLeod and the girl, saying, "This other fellow might be more comfortable down there, too."

Felicidad shook her head and said, "He is dead. What do we do now?"

Longarm said, "For openers, one of us has to drive while another rides shotgun. You want to give her the shotgun, Mac-Leod?"

The young mine owner looked surprised, so Longarm explained, "I can see by the way you're holding that thing that you ain't a skeet shooter. Miss Felicidad, here, knows her country and moves like a lady who's used to traveling around it safe and quick. How about it, Miss Vallejo?"

The girl lowered her eyes and said, "I have hunted since I was six. If they intend to hit us again, it will be up past the next few bends, where the trail passes between high outcrops."

Longarm laughed and said, "There you go, MacLeod. Give the lady the scattergun. If you're any good with that .38, move back along the deck and keep an eye on the brush on either side. They'll hit us low if they don't hit us high."

MacLeod did as he was told, and once everyone was in place, Longarm swung the team around once more and yelled, "Heeeyah!!"

As they lurched forward, Felicidad asked, "Are we pressing on? I thought you'd head back to Sacramento for another driver."

Longarm said, "We've got a driver. Me. I've been trying for a week to get to the damned old mine, and it's getting tedious as hell."

MacLeod called forward, "I'm for that. My wife will worry if we're late. Did you find anything back there, Deputy?"

Longarm said, "Yeah. A hoof print. U.S. army issue. I thought one of the rascals was riding my gelding and shooting my old Winchester at us. Lucky he didn't know its windage is a hair off to the right."

"Jesus! You mean those rascals had the horse you say Constable Lovejoy took from you?"

"I do. It'll be interesting as hell to see what Lovejoy has to say about it. He'd best have one good story, and his stay on this earth depends on whether I believe it or not."

Chapter 3

A stagecoach got its name, of course, because it got where it was going by stages. Calaveras County lay a good forty miles from Sacramento, mostly uphill, and a good team can sustain a ten- or twelve-mile-an-hour trot for little more than two hours. So the coach had to stop for a fresh team every twenty miles. Like other lines, Wells Fargo maintained a cross-country network of road-side corrals with comfort stations and, occasionally, kitchens for the passengers. So Longarm hauled in eighteen miles out of Sacramento for a change of teams—and to get rid of the bodies before they started bloating.

They told the Wells Fargo crew what had happened and the telegrapher put it on the wire. So all stage crews, of any company in the area, would be watching for road agents. The man in charge of the station seemed to think Longarm should let him have his company's stagecoach back. He said that they'd send for another crew and that the three survivors should wait awhile. Longarm said he was commandeering the coach for U.S. government business. When the Wells Fargo agent said he'd have to check with his headquarters, Longarm told him to do anything he liked as long as Longarm, MacLeod, and the girl didn't have to hang around.

They were still arguing—or rather, the agent was arguing at Longarm—when the deputy whipped the fresh team into motion and left the bewildered man standing in the road, calling out, "Hey! Come back here with my coach, God damn it!"

Kevin MacLeod was roaring with laughter and, for the first time since he'd met her, the girl at Longarm's side reluctantly chuckled. She shifted the shotgun in her lap to cover an approaching grove of five oak and observed, "It's nice to see an

Anglo screaming helplessly for a change. I didn't know you people were as highhanded with one another as you are with us."

Longarm grinned and said, "There was nothing personal meant by it when we stole California from you, Señorita. We'd just as likely have taken it had it belonged to anyone else."

She no longer looked amused as she nodded and said, "I believe you. You people are natural bullies. You seem to have understood the survival of the strong long before Darwin published his outrageous book."

Longarm shrugged and said, "You'd best take that up with God, ma'am; He made the rules. Besides, we could have been even meaner, if you study on it. I'll allow that some of the forty-niners were a mite uncouth, and some of your people got the short end of the stick, but a lot of your Spanish grants were recognized by the U.S. government."

Her dark features took on an ironic cast. "I see. You think, because you only stole *half* of our land, that that makes it just."

"Not as just as it might have been, but a better deal than you folks offered the Indians who owned all this land in the first place," Longarm said evenly. He saw that he'd scored a point and added, "How much land did Cortez let Montezuma keep?"

She flushed and said, "That's not the same!"

"Sure it is," he insisted. "You Spanish found a land filled with gold and Indians, so, being tougher than the original owners, you just up and took it. The forty-niners found a land full of gold and comfortable Spaniards and they were just as tough on the Spaniards as the Spaniards had been on the Indians. Like I said, it was nothing personal."

"We were not living under the tyranny of Castile," the girl objected. "California belonged to Mexico, a friendly democracy!"

"Mexico was friendly as hell at the Alamo," Longarm countered, "and if you want to call Santa Ana's dictatorship a democracy—Well, what the hell, we've elected some funny folks ourselves, so you're likely right. I'd give California back if it was up to me, but it ain't, so let's talk about something else."

She smiled wryly, and replied, "It *is* a waste of time now, isn't it? Do you think those banditos are liable to come back?"

He shook his head and said, "Doubt it. I left two dismounted and we showed them we weren't schoolmarms. We're carrying some mail in the strongbox under the seat, but the agent says there's no gold aboard."

"Then why did they try to rob us in the first place?"

"Because *we* were aboard. There's usually a gold watch or a pretty gal aboard any stage. If that bunch is who I suspicion, they don't run to much common sense. You might say they rob folks on impulse."

"You know who they were?" the woman asked with a puzzled frown.

"Not for sure, "but I think they're what's left of the Calico Kid's gang. The one who was riding my gelding looked like a rat-faced saddle tramp I met in Manzanita near the livery stable. Either Constable Lovejoy gave it to them or they stole it."

Felicidad's lip curled contemptuously. "I know this Lovejoy. My people call him *el stupido*."

He chuckled and replied, "Fair is fair. When you folks are right, you're right. Do you live in Manzanita, Señorita?"

"No. Our rancho is just outside of town. We will pass it on the way in and I will get off there. How soon do you think we will be there?"

"A couple of hours, the Lord willing and the creeks don't rise. You say your people know Lovejoy well enough to call him names. Can you tell me if they have any notions about those high-graders stealing from Mr. MacLeod back there?"

The girl shook her head and said, "We have heard of the robberies. We would like to think it was one of our people, but that is too much to hope for. Some of our vaqueros are sure it is the work of Joaquin Murietta, but that is just wishful thinking."

He frowned and said, "It'd have to be. Joaquin Murietta was shot and beheaded nearly thirty years ago!"

"I know. But some of our people still see him, late at night on a moonlit trail."

They dropped Felicidad off on a wooded path a mile outside of Manzanita. Then Longarm drove the stage to the Wells Fargo office, where MacLeod's wife was waiting with a buckboard and a worried look. Lottie MacLeod was a pretty Utile dishwater blonde in a sun bonnet two sizes too large for her little head. Longarm could see that her face had been freckled by the mountain sun in spite of the bonnet. He told the MacLeods he'd be up to visit them as soon as he found something to ride. As the Mac-Leods drove off, Longarm explained to the suspicious-eyed Wells Fargo men whose hands were resting casually on their sidearms that he hadn't really stolen the coach. They'd gotten some of the story by telephone, they said. Everybody but the U.S. government seemed to believe in the newfangled things. The station boss said the company had posted a reward on the rascals who'd shot their employees. Longarm said, "I ain't allowed to accept rewards, but it'll be my pleasure, anyway. One of the bastards was riding my horse."

Leaving the Wells Fargo men to figure out how they were going to move the stage a mile farther east, Longarm headed for the constable's office down the street. He walked in the shadows of the overhanging wooden awnings with his new gun in his hand. The few townies he passed looked at him suspiciously, but he paid them no mind. Until he knew how much pull Boss Buckley really had up here in the hills, he was going to make sure they didn't get the drop on him a second time.

Constable Lovejoy must have spotted him through the window and been spooked by the sight, for he waved a white handkerchief out the door and called out, "Put that fool gun away, Longarm! It was all a mistake!"

Longarm stopped within strategic range of a watering trough he could duck behind in two jumps and called in reply, "That's one thing we're agreed on, Lovejoy. Come on out and let's talk on it."

"You must think I'm loco! You're pointing a goddamned gun at me!"

"You bring out my own gun, my badge, and the other things you stole, and I'll put this one away. You'd best make your next move careful and slow. I've taken just about enough shit off you and my job gives me a certain amount of leeway about dealing with coyotes and other varmints."

Lovejoy stepped timidly outside, holding the white kerchief in one hand and a big paper bag in the other. Longarm saw that he'd thought to leave his gunbelt where it couldn't get him in trouble, so he put his own gun away, but stayed near cover just the same. He was well within rifle range of the jailhouse window.

Lovejoy crossed over to him, saying, "I got all your stuff

right here, Mister Long. Like I said, I've seen the error of my ways."

Longarm took the sack from him, saying, "I know you have a telephone line to the capital. I'll take your word for what's in this bag, for now, but it seems a mite light. You don't have my horse, Winchester, and saddlebags in here, I'll bet."

"Listen, Longarm. I got a nice pinto stud with a new Visalia stock saddle for you. Got a spanking new Remington rifle I'd be pleased to offer, too."

"I don't want your horse and gear. I want *mine*. What happened to them?"

Lovejoy licked his lips and said, "Honest, I just don't know. After you run off, I went to the livery to see if you'd left any clues in your possibles. That's when we noticed someone had sort of, well, *stole* them."

Longarm nodded and said, "A little rat-faced tramp in a hickory shirt and gunbarrel chaps. He just chased me on my own mount, shooting at me with my own rifle. You sure run this town sloppy, old son."

"We heard about them smoking up the stage. Some of the boys're out looking for the rascals right now. I can see I had you wrong, Longarm. I'll just bet the Calico Kid's gang has been behind this high-grading all the time."

He waited for Longarm to answer, got nervous waiting and tried to grin, saying, "But, hell, we're on the same side now, right?"

Longarm said, "Maybe. You were about to tell me who passed the word that I was to be kept away from the Lost Chinaman and such."

Lovejoy hesitated, then shrugged and said, "Hell, no sense in me trying to cover for folks who can't make up their own durned minds. It was the U.S. marshal in Sacramento. The same hombre just called to say we were to leave you the hell alone!"

Longarm nodded, but said, "I want a name to go with your tale. Was it the marshal himself or somebody farther down his totem pole?"

Lovejoy said, "It was a deputy named Harper. Sam Harper, I think his name was. He said you had no jurisdiction the first time he called. Now he says the case is all yours and he hopes you choke on it."

Longarm nodded again and said, "You can start breathing again, Constable. I don't aim to shoot you after all. Did that deputy of yours get over the little set-to we had over at the jail?"

Lovejoy smiled shakily and wiped his heavily perspiring brow with the white handkerchief. "Old Pete? He's all right. I got him out looking for them road agents with the others. He said he still can't figure out how you slickered him. Pete says you and that Injun started a row and the next he remembers is me standing over him with a pail of water. How did you do it, Longarm?"

"I've got magic powers. But tell me something else. When Bitter Water and I ran off, did you trail us as far as a saddleback ridge about eight or twelve miles to the southeast?"

"You must be funning! We knew you had a gun and the Injun who knew the country with you! Do I look like the sort of fool who'd ride into a bushwhacking with night coming on?"

Longarm was too polite to say what sort of a fool he thought Lovejoy looked like. Instead, he said, "I'll take you up on the loan of that pinto."

"Sure, Longarm. Where you headed, up to the miner?"

"Not right now. I've got to get my own horse and rifle back."

"But you said them road agents had them!"

"They do. I think I spotted the smoke from their hideout a few nights back, too."

"Jesus!" Lovejoy gasped. "I'll deputize some of the boys and we'll ride with you!"

But Longarm shook his head and said, "No thanks. I got enough on my plate facing the four of them. I don't like folks behind me holding guns unless I know them real well."

"Aw, hell, you still don't trust me, Longarm?"

"Not as far as I can spit, Constable."

It was almost dark in the canyon when one of the four men hunkered around the firepit looked up and said, "Listen! Did you hear that?"

One of the other road agents poked at the fire and replied, "Hear what, Slim? You been listening for ghosts again?"

The first man who'd spoken said, "I could swear I heard a pony nicker, just now."

His companion glanced over at the two tethered to a live oak and said, "Of course you did, you durned fool. The two we got left are lonesome."

Another owlhoot nodded morosely and observed, "Thanks to your fool idea about that stage, we're riding double these days."

"Hell, how was I to know they had some sort of durned old sharpshooter aboard?" Slim protested. "I picked off that shotgun rider neat as anything, just like I said I would."

"Sure you did. Then some other son of a bitch blew two ponies out from under us and left us in the dust feeling foolish. Did any of you boys get a look at the jasper? We owe him, if we ever meet up again."

Slim said, "All I seen was some hombre in a brown suit. He was one shooting son of a bitch, whoever he was."

A smaller, rat-faced youth in gunbarrel chaps frowned thoughtfully and said, "The cuss who shot Calico was dressed in brown tweed. You reckon it could have been that lawman, Longarm?"

Slim said, "Shit, they threw that one in jail for shooting old Calico. Must have been somebody else."

A new voice in the canyon said soberly, "You're wrong, Slim. It *was* me."

The four owlhoots stiffened as Longarm stepped out of the underbrush, his gun in his hand and trained on them. Slim dropped a hand to the gun at his side and the .44 in the lawman's hand spoke once. Slim went over backward, wetting his jeans as he died with a soft sigh.

Longarm asked mildly, "Any other takers?"

Rat Face gasped, "Please, mister! You got the drop on us!"

Longarm said, "I know. I want the three of you on your feet and grabbing sky, but be sure you get up like the little gents your mothers always said you were. I still owe one of you to the ghosts of that stage crew, and I ain't particular who I shoot next."

The trio rose from the fire slowly, their hands raised. Longarm nodded to the one in the checkered shirt and said, "You first. Bring your hands down slow and unbuckle that gunbelt."

The owlhoot dropped his hands to his middle. Longarm fired and the outlaw jackknifed with a scream as the bullet tore his guts apart. As he went down, Longarm fired again and blew away the side of his head. The body lay limp in a spreading pool of dusty blood as Longarm said, "Damn it, when I say slow, I mean *slow*."

One of the two survivors gasped, "Are you crazy, mister?" and made the mistake of moving a step. So Longarm put a bullet in his chest. The man's hands flew reflexively to cover the gaping bullet hole. Blood spurted from between his fingers as his eyes rolled backward and he crumpled heavily to the dust.

The lone survivor in the gunbarrel chaps screamed like the frightened animal he was and fell to his knees, babbling, "Please, mister! You can't just shoot me like a dog!"

Longarm grimaced and said, "I can do anything I want to, you sniveling little pissant! What did you think this was, a game for schoolboys? You gave up any rights you had to life when you first strapped on those guns and started scaring folks."

"Oh, Jesus, I don't want to die!"

"Not many folks do," Longarm agreed. "Those men you shot today likely didn't enjoy it much, either."

He saw the trickle running down the inside of the terrified owlhoot's thigh and said, "Unbuckle that gunbelt or *draw*, you shithead!"

The rat-faced youth fumbled hysterically with his buckle, got it open, and let the gunbelt fall from his hips as he knelt in the dust, pissing in his pants. Longarm said, "That's better." Now we can talk. Your continued existence depends on how *well* you talk. What's your name, shithead?"

"Carson, sir. They call me Buck."

"No they don't. They call you shithead. We know you tried to rob the Wells Fargo, so let's not waste time on that. What do you know about that ore that's been disappearing off the narrow-gauge between here and Sacramento, shithead?"

"Ore, mister? We heard something about some high-grading, but that wasn't us, honest to God."

"How long have you boys been skulking about out here in the brush?"

"You mean here in Calaveras County, mister? About a month. We rode up from the Santa Monica Mountains with the Calico Kid about a month ago."

"You get one point for something that agrees with what I

knew already. I'm cheered a mite more by seeing that you've
taken good care of my gelding over there. You keep singing the
right tune and I just might take you in alive."

"Anything, mister! I'll tell you anything you want to know!"
Carson said with great enthusiasm.

"All right. If you boys have been roaming around out here,
looking for a chance to steal, you must know the territory pretty
well after a month. I'm interested in railroad properties. You
know the tracks to the low country?"

"Sure, we've rode over 'em plenty of times."

"You ever notice a siding? Maybe a spur line running off into
the trees or some old mine tunnel?"

Carson shook his head and said, "No sir. Not that I remember, and I'm thinking hard as anything."

Longarm nodded and said, "Let's try another one. You boys
have likely been keeping your eyes open for strangers on the
horizon line. Have you seen any others playing your same
game?"

"You mean another gang, mister? I don't think so. We've
spied greasers working cows a few times, and once we spotted
an Injun squaw picking nuts, but she got away."

"Lucky for her, I reckon. But I'd say if you stumbled over
Diggers you were moving pretty slick. You'd likely have noticed
white riders if they were about. So the high-grading has to be an
inside job. I want you to study on my next question before you
lie to me, boy. I noticed you and the Calico Kid had the freedom
to roam the streets of Manzanita. Can you enlighten me on how
the law felt about that?"

"Hell, mister, there ain't no wanted posters out on us."

"There are now; Wells Fargo just posted them. What I'm
aiming at is how the Kid happened to be on such friendly terms
with Constable Lovejoy and the sheriff's department."

Carson shrugged and said, "He was just scared of Calico, I
reckon. He was a pretty hard case and Lovejoy has a wife and
kids."

"What about the county sheriff?"

"Never met up with him. Calico said not to steal nothing near
the county seat."

Longarm thought this over. Then he nodded and said, "I can't think of anything else you might have to say, so we'd best get on with it."

Then he put his revolver in its holster and said, "I figure I've got one bullet left. Your gun is within easy reach when you've a mind to go for it."

Carson gasped, "Oh, no, I ain't about to try! You got to give me a break!"

Longarm stood with his hands out to his sides as he said, "I *am* giving you a break. It's against my nature even to step on a bug without giving it a chance."

"I can't fight *you!* You said you'd carry me in alive!"

"I said *maybe*. Your trial would be a needless expense to the taxpayers, since we both know you shot that old man and the hunchback."

"Slim shot the guard! Brown, there, killed the old man! I've never shot it out with nobody!"

"It might be a good time to start trying; I ain't got all night. I can see you've started to reconsider the error of your ways, and if you and I were the only folks I had to worry about, I'd be tempted to let you go, for I don't have time to trifle in a case I ain't assigned to. But you see, sonny, there're other folks out there that you might run into, and I'd hate to have a six-year-old kid on my conscience when and if you start feeling tough again."

The owlhoot started to cry.

Longarm said, "Come on, you've got at least five rounds in your gun and I cross-draw, so you have an edge on me."

"Oh, please, please, I'm so damn scared!"

"It doesn't feel so good to be on the receiving end, does it? Didn't you think anyone was ever going to call your play when you decided to be a big bad cuss?"

"Mister, I just want to go home to my poor old momma! I swear, if you let me live, I'll never wear a gun again!"

Longarm shook his head and said, "I'm counting to three, and then I'm going to draw. You do whatever you want to about it."

"Oh, no! You got to let me live!"

"One!"

"I'll be good! I swear I'll never do it again!"

"Two!"

"No, no, I don't want it this way!"

And then Longarm said, "Three!" and reached across his waist for the .44. The owlhoot screamed and dove for his gun as the deputy fired. The bullet hit Carson just under his nose, drilled through his skull, and blew his brains out the back of his head. His body didn't even twitch as it went limp and keeled over on its side.

Longarm stood silently, looking down at the four bodies as he reloaded. Then he swallowed the funny taste in his mouth and muttered, "I must have eaten something that didn't agree with me. Likely the chili I had in Sacramento."

He knew he'd done the only sensible thing; it wasn't as if they'd have treated him differently. So it surprised him a bit, as he walked over to reclaim his horse, that he suddenly gagged and had to lean against a tree trunk to throw up.

Chapter 4

By the time Longarm got back to Manzanita, leading the two other ponies and riding the army remount gelding he'd reclaimed, the posse looking for the road agents in other parts had ridden in too, bone-weary and out of ideas.

Longarm told Lovejoy he'd had a shoot-out with the rascals and added that the constable was welcome to the reward if he and his boys would ride up to the canyon and pack the bodies out, so Lovejoy didn't press him for details.

It was getting dark by then. Lovejoy asked if Longarm had a place to stay the night in town and he answered, "Nope. It's taken me a while, but I'm riding up to the damned mine."

He left them celebrating their good fortune and headed up the slope along the wagon trace that they said led to the Lost Chinaman. The mine was said to be only a couple of miles away. He'd gone maybe a quarter of the distance when he heard hoofbeats behind him, approaching fast, so he reined in just off the road and sat his mount quietly in the inky shade of a canyon oak.

It was Sylvia Baxter and a man he didn't know. They saw his outline at about the same time and reined in. The man called out, "Who's there? I see you, my good fellow."

Longarm saw that things were getting tense and called back, "It's all right, folks. I'm the law. 'Evening, Miss Sylvia."

"Is that you, Custis?" she asked, squinting into the darkness.

"Yes, ma'am. You had me spooked, too. It was dumb of me only to hide halfway till I took your measure."

Sylvia laughed and said, "Ralph, dear, this is the man I was telling you about—Marshal Long."

Her brother sniffed and said, "I daresay," and Longarm wondered just how much she'd told him.

Ralph Baxter was twice as snooty as his sister, but not as

pretty. He had muttonchop sideburns and a pouty mouth. He was wearing a little sissy hat and English jodhpur boots under too-tight whipcord breeches. Longarm wondered how he posted, trotting in that rented stock saddle. The only thing anyone could take seriously about the dude was the Webley revolver riding butt forward on his left hip. Longarm knew that most men who didn't know too much about riding armed favored fancier border rigs that looked mean enough until you had to draw quickly from the saddle. He couldn't see well enough in this light to be sure, but the black hard-rubber grips of the big pistol had a no-nonsense look to them that said Ralph had paid a good gunsmith to fit them to his palm. He wondered why a man who looked like a sissy was armed like a hired gunslick.

He asked where they were headed, and Sylvia said the Lost Chinaman. Longarm smiled and said, "We'll ride together, then. I met MacLeod and his woman earlier. I hope they don't keep early hours."

Ralph Baxter said, "My sister and I were *invited* to join them this evening. Do you make a habit of these rather informal social visits?"

Longarm clucked his mount out from under the tree and got them all started again before he said, "I don't pay too many what you'd call social visits, Mr. Baxter. I'll just let you folks sip tea with the MacLeods while I have a look around the diggings."

Before Ralph could think of a suitable snotty retort, Sylvia cut between them. "We heard about the attack on the stage, and I was so worried about your poor hurt head."

Ralph added, "Sylvia told me how she nursed you back from the grave. My sister has always had this sensitivity for those born less fortunate than she."

Longarm growled, "Let's back off a mite, Baxter. You can say what you like about me, but you're carrying this close enough to my kinfolks to rate my saving a dance for you, and I ain't talking about the waltz."

Ralph laughed and said, "You're really not good at veiled threats, Deputy."

"Hell, old son, there's nothing veiled about it. You keep sniping at me and we're headed straight to Fist City! What's wrong with you, anyway? We've never laid eyes on one another, and you're acting like I ran off with your silverware."

"My silverware isn't what I'm concerned about at the moment."

Longarm didn't answer. If he knew, he knew, and there was nothing he could say right now that wouldn't get them to rolling on the ground, if not shooting at one another. What was wrong with women, anyway? To hear them let on, you'd think they'd slash their wrists in front of stampeding buffalo to hide what they called their shame. Yet it seemed that half the times he'd had a little fun with a gal, she managed to let the whole blamed world know about it!

As if she knew what he was thinking, Sylvia tried to smooth things over. "Don't mind my brother, Custis. He's miffed because he's been stuck out here for months trying to close a deal, and the boys in town have been teasing him."

That seemed reasonable enough. Longarm said, "I don't tease folks much. MacLeod told me you'd been sent out here to buy his mine, Ralph."

"Would you mind calling me Mr. Baxter?"

"I'll call you the Prince of Wales if you'll tell me a mite about the Lost Chinaman."

Baxter said, "You'll see it soon enough. It's only a hole in the ground. The idiot seems to think he's found El Dorado."

"And you don't agree?"

"Oh, it's not a bad little strike, given a bit more science and some capital to put it on a paying basis. He's trying to run it with a crew of shiftless, unskilled Mexicans, digging the hard way, with hand tools."

"It doesn't take all that much digging, if it's high-grade ore, does it?"

Warming to the subject, Baxter said, "It's not high-grade. I'd say it assays at less than a thousand dollars a ton."

"Then you've been down the shaft and seen the gold?"

"Of course not. You don't *see* gold in medium-grade ore. The grains are microscopic."

"Then how do you know there's any gold at all?"

Baxter snorted and asked, "What do you take me for, an idiot? The man has an assay office report, and besides that, I've tested it for color myself."

"Do tell? How do you test for gold you can't see?"

"With aqua regia, of course. The acid dissolves any gold in

the rock and leaves a deposit in your test tube." Baxter frowned. "What are you suggesting, a salted mine?"

"The thought's crossed my mind," Longarm admitted. "I can't think of any way on earth they could be switching so much ore in bulk on the fly. But if they were loading barren rock on the train in the first place, there'd be no mystery at all."

To his credit, Ralph Baxter thought for a moment before he shook his head and said, "That wouldn't make sense. MacLeod is losing money every time he loses a shipment, and he's been supervising the whole operation. How in blue blazes could it profit the man to rob himself? It's his gold in the first place!"

"Maybe. I'll take your word that he's got a real gold mine, for now. But I'd be obliged if you showed me how you test for gold, before they send another load down."

Sylvia said, "Of course he will. But just what are you planning to look for, Custis?"

Longarm said, "Gold, of course. I'm making it my business to ride down the mountain aboard the next trainload of ore. Before I do, I aim to make sure that what they put aboard is real ore. Then I'm going to be interested as all get-out to see if anyone tries to switch it with me sitting smack-dab on the pile!"

They could see lights through the trees ahead, now. Ralph Baxter's tone was almost friendly as he asked, "Just what did you mean about a salted mine, Deputy? I'll confess you've made me thoughtful. My company just authorized me to offer more than we've been bidding up till now."

Longarm said, "I figured they might. I don't know about microscopic grains, but many a mining claim has been sold to unsuspecting folks by a smart jasper firing gold birdshot into a rock face with a shotgun. I'll go along with you that MacLeod seems like a tolerable cuss, but we live and learn. If I was you, I'd hold off till we test the next shipment and see if it gets through."

They were within sight of the mining property now, so Longarm dropped the conversation. He could see the MacLeods' cabin, off to one side of the diggings. The operation itself was a lunar landscape of torn-up earth. A high loading tipple built of logs hung over a narrow-gauge railroad siding. The whole area was illuminated by torches, and Longarm saw cotton-clad workmen loading a couple of small, tubby ore cars. A dog started to bark and Kevin MacLeod appeared at the cabin door as they rode in. He waved amicably, even though he hadn't expected Longarm.

As the three of them dismounted, Longarm said to MacLeod, "You folks just visit away. I came up here for a look-see. You got anybody who could show me through the diggings?"

MacLeod called out, "Vallejo?" and one of the Mexicans came over to join them. Before he reached earshot, Longarm asked quietly, "Is this fellow related to that gal on the stage, MacLeod?"

The mine owner laughed and said, "You know, I never made the connection? Half the Mexicans in this county seem to be named Vallejo. The rest are named Garcia or Castro."

The foreman was too close to discuss it further, so MacLeod introduced them and told Vallejo to show Longarm anything he wanted to see.

The foreman was a man of about thirty, with a friendly, open smile. He was either innocent of guile or a damned good poker player. As Longarm walked away from the cabin with him, he asked, "Are you any kin to Felicidad Vallejo?"

The Mexican answered, "We are distant cousins, unfortunately. She is *muy linda*, no?"

"I'll go along with that. I'm unfortunate, too. She doesn't like gringos much."

Vallejo laughed and said, "That side of the family was very rich before you people came. I come from a less fortunate branch of the family, so I've made out all right. Señor MacLeod is *muy simpatico*."

"Have you been working for him long?"

"Since he and his wife bought the mine. The last owners refused to hire greasers. What was it you wished to see?"

"Well, I was thinking of going down the shaft, but I hear it's a waste of time for a man without a degree in chemistry. When do you aim to ship those cars you're loading?"

"The engine is coming for them in the morning. That is why we are working overtime. If you don't wish to go down in the shaft, what can I show you?"

Longarm walked over to the siding. Grabbing a hand iron, he pulled himself up to the lip of an ore car, saying, "I ain't stealing. I'll put it all back in a while."

Then he reached in at random and selected three lumps of the salmon-colored quartz they'd been loading. He got down, went to the rear car, and did the same. Then he put the ore samples in his coat pocket and asked Vallejo, "Do you have a guard posted over this siding at night?"

The Mexican nodded and said, "Of course. We are not at all pleased by what has been happening."

Longarm thanked him and walked quickly back to the cabin. He went in without knocking, found Sylvia and her brother seated in front of a fireplace sipping tea with the MacLeods, and said, "Baxter, I'd like you to aqua-whatever these rocks."

Baxter said, "Oh, for God's sake," But MacLeod smiled a bit thinly, and said, "We've been talking about your suspicions, Longarm. It's all right with me, Ralph."

Baxter shrugged and said, "Well, I do have my kit in my saddlebags, but I assure you, all this is none of my doing!"

MacLeod said, "I insist. I think I see what he's getting at, and frankly, I haven't been assaying the ore, once it's out of the mine!"

Muttering to himself, Baxter got up and went out to his tethered horse as Longarm followed. Sylvia followed too, and as she and Longarm waited on the porch she nudged him and asked, "Where are you staying tonight, darling?"

He answered, "Right here. If that's really gold ore in those cars, I ain't letting it out of my sight this side of Sacramento!"

"Damn it, Custis, I want you so badly I can taste it!"

Longarm nodded. "I know the feeling, but I wish you wouldn't call me Custis. Now hush or he'll hear us, and he's suspicious already."

Baxter came up the steps with an oilcloth bag. He said, "I have to have some light."

From the doorway, MacLeod called out, "You can use our kitchen table, Ralph."

Longarm wondered if MacLeod had heard Sylvia's somewhat forward statement, but he didn't know how to find out.

They all went inside. MacLeod led them back to a lean-to kitchen, and Baxter set up his testing gear on the redwood table as Longarm watched. Baxter asked for a sample and Longarm handed him a hunk of ore. Baxter said, "It's supposed to be crushed first, you moron," but he took out a pocketknife and, using the back of the blade, scraped a few grains off the surface. Longarm strolled over to a nearby window and folded his arms. He could see both the table and the men working outside from this vantage point.

Ralph Baxter put the sandy dust in a test tube and poured something from a little brown bottle into it, saying, "Aqua regia is a mixture of sulfuric acid and nitric acid. It's the only acid that dissolves noble metals."

He waited a few minutes and poured a few drops of something else in the tube, holding it up to the light. The test tube started smoking like a lit cigar, and Longarm asked why. Baxter said, "I'm neutralizing the acid to precipitate any metal it's dissolved. Don't you know anything about basic chemistry?"

"Not much," Longarm said, "but, I'm willing to learn. What does it look like?"

Ralph held the test tube out to him and said, "See for yourself. But be careful. Even with bicarb in the tube, it's been known to burn skin away. This is hardly a chemical lab and my field methods are a bit roughshod."

Longarm took the test tube and held it up to the light, squinting at the muddy contents. He nodded and said, "Yeah, I can see the specks of gold in it. Are you sure it ain't fool's gold?"

"Iron pyrite? Don't be inane. Fool's gold settles a rusty red in the tube. I hope you're satisfied?"

Longarm took out another lump and said, "I will be, once you test them all. I gathered hunks from all over."

Baxter sighed and went back to work. It took him a half hour to satisfy Longarm, but in the end the deputy nodded at MacLeod and said, "I owe you an apology, sir. I'll allow that what you've just loaded must be the real thing."

MacLeod grinned boyishly and answered, "Oh, I don't know. I could have put a few chunks of pay dirt in with the dross to fool you."

Longarm said, "I know. That's why I sampled from both cars. To salt the load that rich, you'd have had to put enough aboard to make it worth shipping. So let's see if we can get those cars through to the mill."

MacLeod said, "We're shipping it in the morning. I suppose you want to come back early to ride herd on it?"

Longarm shook his head and said, "Nope. I'm staying put.

I'm going out right now to climb aboard with my Winchester. Then I ain't getting down until the train reaches the Big Valley."

"Longarm, you'll freeze out there and it's not yet ten o'clock," MacLeod said.

"I never said I hankered to be comfortable. I just said I aim to watch it from this moment on. We just made sure the gold's aboard, and this time, by thunder, it's *staying* aboard unless somebody shoots me right off the top of it."

Kevin MacLeod had been right, but Longarm had already learned the hard way how cold the Sierra nights could be. The Mexican crew knocked off before midnight and, at Longarm's suggestion, took the torches with them. He didn't want to sit up on the piled ore like a big-assed bird outlined in torchlight to anyone in the surrounding brush. Vallejo had explained that most of the miners went home to their local farms downslope. The foreman and a couple of men who usually took turns as night watchmen stayed in a shack near the mine entrance on the other side of the tipple. Longarm had told them to stay well clear of his stakeout. He was sitting on the uncomfortable, jagged lumps of ore with his feet braced against the bulkhead of the rear car and the Winchester across his thighs. It would be a hell of a mistake for anyone to wander into range unless they had something serious in mind.

He had a round in the chamber, so he could fire without levering the action. He was dying for a smoke, and knew he'd want it even more before the sun rose, but you could see the lit end of a cheroot for almost a country mile on a moonless night in air as clear as this. The unwinking stars hung above him almost close enough to brush his hat, it seemed, as the planet slowly turned under him. The high country was the place to spend a night if one admired stars. The Milky Way arched overhead from horizon to horizon, and every few minutes there would be another sparkle of movement in the silent sky as another meteor burned itself to nothing.

The crickets serenaded him for the first hour or so, then it got too cold for them and they faded away to wherever crickets go between songs. It became so quiet he could hear his own pulse in his ears, and once he heard a hoot owl that he judged to be about a quarter of a mile away. Longarm shifted his weight, and the crunch of the glassy rock he sat on was almost loud enough to make him jump. Anyone trying to lift so much as a single lump from either car would be heard.

He'd climb up in the loading tipple before the crew left, to make certain it was empty. He'd noticed that the ladder rungs squeaked under his weight at the time, so he figured he could ignore the black mass he could just make out against the stars. There were no trees or bushes close to the track, and the open, dusty ground all around was light enough to outline anyone moving sneakily across it. He couldn't see how anyone could sneak anywhere near him, and since nobody did, his watch became as tedious as hell.

Longarm was an active man, and the dull routine that makes up so large a part of a lawman's life was hard to take. But like a good soldier, a good lawman knows that the secret is in lasting as long as most people can, then lasting just a minute more. The average criminal, like the average human being, lives by an average clock. Few crooks he'd met up with had been men of infinite patience. Men who are used to dull routine seldom take to a life of crime. The whole idea of being a crook is *easy* money.

Longarm knew most night prowlers made their moves between three and four in the morning, when most of the world would be sound asleep. But three o'clock came and went and a million years later it was four, and nothing happened.

Longarm thought about that. The high-graders had to be watching for another shipment. Anyone on a distant ridge could tell just by looking when the ore cars were loaded. But he'd climbed up here with the lights out. If they knew he was staked out, someone had told them.

Sylvia and her brother had left hours ago, of course. The MacLeods hadn't stirred from their cabin at all, and there were no wires running from the mine to anywhere else. Only the foreman and the few workers sleeping on the site knew he'd planned to guard the shipment. He'd asked Vallejo not to gossip about it much. On the other hand, every man who had been there that night knew he was law and might have figured out what he was up to. There were just too many suspects to work with right now. He could see that he was going to have to start whittling them down one at a time, and that meant more dull routine that could take weeks. He estimated that there were at least a dozen men in the Mexican crew. His job would be a lot easier if the high-graders just came out of the woods for a good old-fashioned fight.

Another million years dragged slowly by. The ice age came and went, and mankind had invented fire and built the pyramids by the time the sky grew lighter in the east. By the time Columbus discovered America, the birds were sassing him from the treeline and he started making out colors as well as the forms of daybreak. Off in the distance he heard a train whistle, and a few minutes later Vallejo came down from the bunkhouse with a pot of coffee and a tin cup. He handed them up to Longarm and asked if anything had happened. Longarm poured himself some coffee and said, "Nope. I didn't even see the ghost of Joaquin Murietta."

Vallejo laughed and said, "You have heard of him, eh? I was only a child when he held up the stage over near Angel's Camp. At least, they say he held up that stage. Joaquin was very mysterious, even when he was alive. There are a dozen versions of who he was and what he did. Our people's stories have him all over the state at the same moment. There are even those who say he never existed."

Longarm sipped some coffee and said, "Well, they shot somebody they said was him, down in Kern County. Was that whistle I just heard what I hope it was?"

Vallejo nodded and said, "Yes. It will be here any minute."

Kevin MacLeod came down from the cabin with a Henry rifle cradled in an elbow and wearing a worried smile. As he joined them, Longarm said, "No, they didn't shoot me and steal this ore I'm sitting on."

MacLeod looked relieved and said, "Thank God, I'm riding down the line with you this morning. If this shipment doesn't get through, I'm going to be in a real fix."

He climbed up beside Longarm and explained, "I've barely got enough money left to meet my next payroll. I don't want to sell out to that damned Baxter, but he's got me by the short hairs and he knows it."

Longarm nodded, and asked, "Is he the only one who's made an offer?"

"For the mine? Yes. I've had a few ridiculous offers for the property, of course. I've filed on a full section of land, and apparently some of the local rancheros feel I'm sitting on enough grass to matter."

Longarm swept a thoughtful eye over the surrounding country. The mining claim was in rolling parkland. Most of the bigger trees had been cut long ago for pit props and lumber. The grazing looked like tolerable grass, but nothing to get excited about. He asked, "Do you pump your water, or is there a running spring on the spread?"

MacLeod said, "I thought of the water rights. I doubt if anyone's that serious about the brook cutting across one corner of the place, over beyond our cabin. These hills are well watered all around. Besides, the only serious offer was from Baxter's syndicate."

Before they could go into it at length, the narrow-gauge locomotive backed into view, the fireman waving to them from the cab. Longarm watched with interest as the little engine eased into the ore cars with a bump and they coupled up. The engineer called back, "Are you boys riding shotgun?" When Longarm nodded, he said, "Let's get cracking, then. I got a timetable to think about." He tooted his whistle and they started up with a jerk as Vallejo and another Mexican who'd just come down from the quarters waved goodbye.

Longarm saw MacLeod's wife waving at them from the cabin door and put a finger to his hat brim as her husband waved back. And then the ore train was in the trees around the bend and picking up speed.

The trip down the line was uneventful. The narrow-gauge tracks wound down the slopes in a series of hairpin curves. The train ducked through a few cuts and over a dozen bridges. Longarm and MacLeod sat back to back, rifles at the ready. But nothing seemed interested in them this morning. Longarm watched for an unmapped rail siding. He couldn't spot any. They crossed wagon traces where a Conestoga could move off with maybe a ton or so of ore, but there was no traffic on the dusty roads at this hour. They passed farms where kids ran over to the fence line to wave at them, and they chuffed through a couple of sleepy mountain towns where nobody paid any attention at all. Had he been asked to drive the train, Longarm would not have held the throttle as wide as the engineer did. But while the speed around a few drop-off curves was a bit hair-raising, it eliminated some possibilities from his mind. If they didn't get through this time, he was going to have to consider Joaquin Murietta's ghost as a suspect.

They got through. The train reached the flats of the Big Valley and tore out across it at thirty miles an hour. In what seemed no time at all they pulled into the yards behind a string of big wooden buildings. Even before the wheels stopped clicking under him, Longarm could feel the pulsing of the earth being pounded by the machinery of the stamping mills. They'd stopped near a tall chimney belching black smoke into the blue sky, and the sounds made by tortured rock set his teeth on edge.

A man came out on the platform with a sheaf of papers and waved up at them, shouting, "You from Lost Chinaman?"

When MacLeod nodded, the mill supervisor yelled, "Got to assay you before you unload. The boss is sore as hell about the worthless stuff you've been gumming up our machinery with!"

As he and Longarm climbed down, MacLeod explained that they'd come through with real ore this time. But the mill operator took random samples anyway and they followed him inside.

The noise wasn't quite as bad in there, but they still had to shout at one another to be heard, and Longarm wondered how the workers here could stand it day after day. Another man took the ore samples to a workbench and fed them into what looked like a big coffee grinder, operated by a leather belt feeding through the wall. The little crusher started chewing gritty quartz with a noise that made the boards tingle under their feet. The lab worker didn't seem to mind. He slid a tray filled with fine powder out from under the assay mill and put some in a glass jar. He poured aqua regia in as Longarm and the others watched. He seemed to follow the same routine Baxter had, but on a bigger scale.

After a time he shook his head and shouted above the general din, "Nothing! Not a sign of color! What the hell are you digging up there, MacLeod, a well?"

Kevin MacLeod paled and gasped, "Oh, shit! Not again!" He whirled on Longarm and added, "God damn you! You were supposed to be watching!"

At the assayer's words, Longarm had nearly bitten through the cheroot he was smoking. "I *was* watching!" he told MacLeod. "The stuff never left my sight!"

"But God damn it, it was gold ore when we loaded it!"

Longarm said, "I know. I saw the color myself." He scratched the back of his neck vigorously, then headed for the door. MacLeod followed him outside, bleating, "Where are you going? We have to figure this out!"

Longarm crossed the platform, picked out a few random samples of ore, and put them in his pocket, saying, "I've got to get on into town. I figure it's a half hour's walk if I don't shilly-shally."

"Can I come with you? Where are you going?"

"U.S. assay office. It's near the state house about two miles from here. You can come if you've a mind to."

"What about my ore?"

"Yeah, what about it?" Longarm asked rhetorically. "If I were you I'd sit tight right here and make sure it's all there when I come back."

"But they just told us it's worthless rock!" MacLeod protested.

"I know. I heard them. I'm aiming to get an opinion from somebody else."

MacLeod opened his mouth to ask something, then blinked and lowered his voice to say, "Jesus! I never thought of that! I've delivered these people fourteen loads and never gotten paid for one of them!"

Longarm nodded grimly and said, "That's as good a reason as I can think of for asking Uncle Sam, personal, who's been lying. Because someone has been lying like a rug!"

It proved to be a long, dusty walk to a dead end. The men at the government assay office tested the samples Longarm brought them and came up with the same results. The federal assayer held his test tube up to the light and said, "It's the Mother Lode formation all right, but there's not enough gold in it to matter."

Longarm asked, "Is there any gold at all?" and the lab worker explained, "There's *some* gold in seawater. Probably in you and me. But you don't get rich processing anything but ore. It's simple economics. You have to spend less getting gold out of something than the gold is worth. Every few weeks some idiot comes running in here with a rock he's found somewhere and I have to go over it all again. There's still plenty of gold in the Mother Lode, but it's spread out between hell and breakfast. A

pebble with a speck of color in it doesn't mean you have a strike.
The metal has to be in one place before you can spend it. If you
spend a thousand dollars refining a hundred dollars worth of
gold, you're going to wind up busted. Folks keep finding that out
the hard way, all over the West. Go down to skid row and you'll
find a hundred old prospectors mumbling in their beards about
a claim they have out in some neck of the woods, if only someone would grubstake them. The samples they'll show you have
real color, too. A dollar's worth of color in a fist-sized rock
makes a pretty paperweight."

Longarm nodded and asked, "Couldn't you show a profit by
busting up the rock and panning it?"

"Sure," the assayer said, "but men don't crush their dreams. A
few hand-picked samples from an otherwise worthless outcropping can make any man dream big. Over in the desert on the other
side of the Sierra there are places where a man can pick up a
burroload of fairly decent gold quartz in a couple of days. By the
time they haul it out of the dry country, figuring a dollar a day for
their time, they might break even. You have to have water, supplies, and plenty of money to make a profit even on a real strike."

Longarm said, "I understand that part. Let's stick to this shit
I brought in here today. You say it's worthless and I'll take your
word for it. But just last night I saw it tested the same damned
way, and there was maybe ten dollars' worth of color in the test
tube."

The assayer shrugged. "Then someone switched samples
on you."

"No. They couldn't have. I picked them myself, at random.
If someone had salted two freight cars with enough real ore to
fool me, there'd be enough aboard to be worth milling. Is there
any way to fake that test?"

The government man thought and shook his head. He said,
"Nothing but aqua regia, mercury, or cyanide will dissolve pure
gold. What did the other chemist use?"

"He said aqua regia."

"I'd say he had no reason to lie. Cyanide's dangerous to carry
around and you'd have known mercury on sight. If he got a real
precipitate, the samples you had him test must have been rich."

Longarm frowned and asked, "Is there anything else in that
rock he could have separated out? Maybe fool's gold or mica?"

The assayer said, "No. You don't find pyrite in quartz. It's a sulfide of iron you find in shale or slate."

"Maybe brass or tin or something like that?"

The man was growing impatient. "Damn it, Deputy, I just told you there's not enough metal of any kind in this stuff to matter. Don't you think I know my own business?"

Longarm sighed and said, "You likely do, but I can see I don't know *mine* as well as I ought to!"

He went outside and caught a hackney cab back to the mill. He told the driver to wait and went back to the loading platform, where he called to MacLeod and explained, "I got us a ride to the stage line. We may as well get on back to Manzanita."

"You mean they did it again? God damn it! I owe the railroad for hauling it and the mill supervisor just told me there'd be a charge for unloading it on their tailings dump!"

"You have a hard row to hoe and that's the truth, MacLeod. But we surely won't catch any rascals hereabouts. The U.S. government backs what they said. There ain't enough color aboard those cars to pay for our ride and breakfast, but that's all right. I'm on an expense account and I'm feeding you as a material witness."

As they left the mill in the hackney, MacLeod said, "I'm too sick at heart even to think of breakfast. I'd like to go straight home."

But Longarm insisted, "We can't help matters by neglecting our innards. Besides, we've got plenty of time."

"Well, just a quick bite. What's our first move, once we get home?"

Longarm had been afraid MacLeod was going to ask that.

He had no answer.

Chapter 5

Longarm rode up to the ranch house and tethered his gelding to the hitching post. As he climbed the steps, a suspicious-looking Mexican with a shotgun opened the door and snapped, "*Que pasa, señor?*"

Longarm said, "I'm looking for Señorita Felicidad, amigo. Is she at home?"

"For why do you wish to see La Doña Felicidad? She has no business with your kind, Americano!"

Longarm didn't think it would please the lady to have her employee shot on her doorstep, so he tried to figure out some politer way to get past him.

Then Felicidad herself appeared in the doorway behind the man with the gun and murmured something softly in Spanish. The man shrugged and went off.

The girl led him into a baronial living room and indicated a chair by the fireplace. Longarm sat down. He saw she had no intention of offering him any of the coffee she'd been drinking from a cup that sat on a little table beside her chair, so he took out a cheroot and asked permission to smoke. She nodded a bit sullenly, and he lit up, placing his hat beside him on another table.

She asked what he wanted and he said, "I understand you offered Kevin MacLeod a thousand dollars for his mining claim, ma'am."

The girl shrugged and said, "It was Vallejo land in the first place, but I see no other way to get it back."

"Ain't that a sort of miserly offer for a gold mine?"

Her smile was bitter as she answered, "Who cares about the gold? It is the land, Vallejo land, I want." Then she added, "I would offer more, if I had it. My late husband did not leave me enough to be imprudent."

"I didn't know you were a widow, ma'am. I'm purely sorry to hear it. Is Vallejo your married name?"

"Both my married name and my maiden name. We of the old aristocracy tend to marry cousins."

"Well, I never came to jaw about religion. MacLeod has another cousin of yours working for him. Do you know Tico Vallejo, ma'am?"

"I do not speak to him. He has become an Americano."

"Forgive me, ma'am, but since you're both American citizens and have been for a good long time, it doesn't strike me as such a foolish notion on his part." He smiled and added, "You couldn't have been born yet when California changed hands back in '48."

"Just the same," she said, "I shall never be an Americana. But we are wasting time discussing such matters. You still have not told me what you want."

Longarm smiled self-effacingly. "Well, you might say I'm sort of fishing. I know us lawmen can be a bother asking all sorts of fool questions, but it's the only way we can work things out. You heard the MacLeods got robbed again?"

She smiled the sort of smile he had seen on the faces of Apaches. It chilled him slightly. She said, "Yes. My vaqueros were laughing about it just before you came."

"I believe you. How many hands have you got working for you, ma'am?"

"Eight vaqueros, the house servant you just met, and a stable boy. I take it you don't suspect the chicas I have for cooking and cleaning?"

"I didn't see a man or a woman of any kind anywhere near that last shipment of ore they somehow got away with from under my . . . whatever. Let's get back to your real estate notions. A thousand is way low for a gold mine, but a mite high for a section of rough grazing. Half the spread is all torn up from the mining. What's left under the sod ain't worth a thousand dollars."

She shrugged again and said, "Once I have reclaimed what is rightfully mine I intend to have the men fill in the pits with the spoil and plant alfalfa. In time, the scars will heal."

He took a long drag on the cheroot, examined the lit end thoughtfully, then said, "I can see you're more interested in just owning it again than in any profit you might ever show."

"We may seem quixotic to you pragmatic Anglos. But what of it? I made an honest offer. Does this make me a suspect? How do you think I stole the gold?"

"I don't know. I was hoping you'd tell me."

She laughed a trifle wildly, and said, "We have the ghost of Murietta riding for us, didn't you know? I have the gold hidden under the house. Would you like to have me show you through the wine cellar?"

Longarm nodded and said, "Sure."

"You are joking, of course?"

"Maybe. Don't you have a wine cellar?"

"Certainly I have a wine cellar, but what do you think I have hidden down there?"

"You're the one who mentioned it. If you don't want to show it to me, well, I don't have a search warrant."

She rose to her feet and snapped, "Come. I insist you see it, now."

"Hell, honey, I was just running you. You're acting like you've got red ants in your never-mind. I just rode over to ask some routine questions."

"You suspect me of being a thief and I won't have it!" she said angrily. "I insist that you search the whole house!"

He got up and said, "All right, I'll take you up on it. I can play stiff-necked stubborn, too."

She led him through an arched passage and into a hallway. There she opened a thick door under a staircase and said, "Be careful. The steps are steep."

She struck a match as he followed her down into the musty, cobwebbed darkness. Felicidad lit a candle stub on an empty barrel and waved expansively, saying, "Behold the vaults of Monte Cristo! You can see they are a maze of treasure-filled caverns!"

He looked around the tiny hole and observed, "Looks more like a root cellar to me. Do you make your own wine, or are those barrels empty?"

"They are empty. We've made no wine since my grandfather passed away." She chuckled theatrically before adding, "It is just as well for you, señor. We sinister Spaniards are well known as poisoners."

He mulled that over as he followed her back upstairs. She was touchy as hell about being a Mexican, he thought.

She conducted him through the kitchen, insisting that he look in the beehive oven for the missing gold ore. He had a sudden thought as she led him through another room. He asked, "Your people make these 'dobe bricks by mixing clay and straw with sand, gravel, rocks, and such, right?"

"Of course." She turned to him, one eyebrow cocked. "Are you suggesting the missing high-grade ore has been built into the walls of my house?"

"Not hardly. Not this house. But I mean to sniff around the county for new construction. No trace of the missing ore's turned up, but ore is bulky stuff to hide. Building a wall or a barn with it and just leaving it there until the search wore off might not be a bad notion."

"My God," she said with amazement, "you have a lively imagination. Do you want to know what I think? I think there is no gold at all. My people owned the land the mine stands on for generations. If there had been gold they would have known it."

"You're wrong, ma'am. You folks had California for generations, like you said, but you never knew the gold was up here in these hills. It was a gringo who found the first nugget at Sutter's Mill. Your folks were cowboys, not prospectors, so they likely never *looked* for color. I'm a jump ahead of you on the Lost Chinaman. I checked the records down in Sacramento. It's a real mine. They shipped over a million dollars' worth of color to the mint in one year alone, back in the seventies."

"Perhaps, but it has been closed for years. MacLeod and his wife are fools. They should have accepted my offer."

They were in a bedroom now. Longarm said, "MacLeod's turned down bigger offers than yours, ma'am. Besides that, I saw the stuff he's digging tested and it was real. You see—"

Then he noticed the way she was standing there, looking up at him with her eyes limpid and confused. It seemed the most natural thing in the world to just reach out, haul her in, and kiss her full on her trembling lips.

For a moment she responded, running a hot tongue between his firmer lips. Then she stiffened and tried to pull away, mur-

muring, "What is happening? I don't want you to touch me! I hate you and everything you stand for!"

He said, "Sure you do," and kissed her again before drawing her closer to the bed and running his hand down her back. She wore no corset under the black lace and her buttocks were quivering like a nervous colt's. He pressed her closer to him. Her feeble struggles threw them off balance, so he rode with gravity and let it deposit them across the mattress of the old fourposter. They wound up with her half under him. He had a hand between her thighs, now. She churned her knees and one of her slippers flew across the rug to a corner as she gasped against his lips, "We have to stop! You're acting like a monster!"

But he noticed she had her arms around his neck, so he didn't answer. He unbuckled his gunbelt before he started inching her skirt up a fold at a time. She was kissing him with a fervor to match his own, but every time they came up for air she told him how much she hated him, so he decided it might not work if he took time to get undressed. He got her skirt up around her waist and she tried to cross her naked thighs as he slid his hand between them. But he was too strong, or she wasn't trying as hard to stop him as she was pretending. She was wearing no knickers under the skirt. Her sex was as moist as a ripe, sliced-open fig. He fingered her and kissed her until she started moving to meet his thrusting hand. Then he braced a boot on the rug, lifted himself up and over her, and unbuttoned his trousers. The respite gave her time to twist her head away, wild-eyed, and moan, "Please don't. I am not that kind of woman!" But she opened her thighs wide to him as he plunged into her.

He pinned her to the mattress with his pelvis and stayed like that long enough to rid himself of his frock coat. And then, as he started moving, she sighed, "Oh, you *are* a monster!" and dropping the maidenly notions, started pumping back.

She wrapped her legs around him and groaned, "Oh, *querido*, it's been so long since I felt this way!"

He said, "Can't we get out of these duds? This tweed must itch you some."

"Don't stop. I like it. You feel like a big, woolly bear and I'll never forgive you, but, *Madre de Dios*, don't stop! It's happening!"

For a woman who hated him, Felicidad nonetheless seemed

to be taking great pleasure from this encounter as she heaved, plunged, and bucked beneath him. When their movements quieted for a moment after their first climax, Longarm was surprised to notice that they had managed to get fully undressed. Her hips began to gyrate under him once again before his erection had had a chance to wilt very much. He felt himself growing hard again. He felt purely sorry for her poor husband, dying young with so much to live for, but one man's misfortune was another man's bliss. As he stopped to get his breath back after a second climax she said, "You are a terrible man and I hate you. But as long as you've defiled me—" Then she started kissing her way down his moist chest and belly on her way to further glory. They made love for a good two hours before she lay quietly in his arms, her lips against his chest, and murmured, "If you tell anyone about this, I will kill you before I kill myself."

He patted her bare back and said, "I ain't given to talking about such things. Your secret is safe with me."

"You must think I am a terrible slut. I suppose you'd laugh if I told you there has been no one in me like that since my husband died?"

"Hell, I believe you. I could tell you'd been saving yourself for me."

She laughed in spite of herself, and asked, "How could you tell? I didn't know how much I needed that, myself."

"I know. That's likely what had you acting so ornery. Maybe some day gals will be allowed to admit that they get just as randy as us men."

She giggled and snuggled closer, saying, "I thought I hated you that first day on the stage. But you were so brave about those bandits. You moved like such a beautiful big cat and you were so much braver than any man I'd ever known. I started feeling butterflies inside me, in a most indecent place for butterflies to be, and I told myself I was overexcited because of the shooting. You knew, even then, didn't you?"

"To tell you the truth," he said, "I was thinking more about not getting shot. You likely think I came out here with this in mind, but I really wasn't expecting to make love to you."

She smiled. "I am glad. It would shame me to think I'd been so transparent. But why did you seduce me, if you never planned it?"

"Honey, if I knew the reasons for half the things I do, I likely wouldn't do them. I did what I did because you're pretty as a picture and, well, because I could read the smoke signals in your big brown eyes."

"What are we to tell everyone?"

He frowned and said, "I just heard you ask me not to tell anyone at all."

"I wasn't thinking. If you are going to stay with me, the servants must be told something."

He'd been afraid she'd say something like that. He knew what she'd say if he explained that he wasn't the marrying kind, too. So he just said, "We have to keep it a secret for your own protection, Felicidad. I wouldn't want the men I'm after thinking they could get back at me through my woman."

She gasped with pleasure and said, "Oh, *mi caballero!* You are so gallant, but I am not afraid to share your dangers."

"You may not be scared, but I sure am. We're up against somebody who's as slick as goose grease. I'd fight hell and high water for you if I knew who or what was likely to come at us. But I can't do my job and guard your pretty little body at the same time. So we'll have to playact that we're only friends until I catch the rascals."

"I understand. And after you catch them, *querido*, I shall never let you out of my sight again!"

The county seat of San Andreas was a lot closer than Sacramento, but still a long ride from Manzanita. There was a library near the San Andreas courthouse, and it was stocked with more books on mining than Longarm cared to read. The librarian was a little sparrowlike woman, but she had a sweet smile and he noticed her well-turned ankle when she climbed up a ladder to reach him down some books.

He took them to a table and started reading. Every time he looked up, the librarian was staring at him. Immediately, she'd duck her head and pretend she hadn't been looking. *The womenfolk in Calaveras County sure are friendly*, Longarm thought.

He skimmed through local history without finding out much except that there had never been a frog-jumping contest in the county before Mark Twain made that story up. Some of Bret

Harte's tales of the forty-niners, however, turned out to be true. Calaveras had really been a humdinger in the gold rush days. Now it was withering on the vine as the mines played out. People here were raising cows and cutting timber for a living, for the most part, and it was hard-scrabble living at that. The country was pretty enough, but you can't feed scenery to cows and what timber was left was mostly second growth or tough old twisted oaks that had been passed over in the first place. Canyon oak burned well, but it didn't mill worth a damn.

He looked for someone opening a new mine more recently than the Lost Chinaman. He couldn't find one, so there went one good idea. He'd thought some tricky cuss might have thought to sell the stolen high-grade as his own, using a dummy mine as a front. But it didn't pan out. The nearby mine being operated by George Hearst shipped ore of the wrong composition. He intended to stop off at Sheep Ranch on the way back to Manzanita, but it was likely to prove a waste of time.

He cracked open a high school chemistry book and boned up on aqua regia. The book, like everyone else, said it was nasty stuff to spill on your pants and that it dissolved gold. He already knew alkali neutralized acid, so it was easy to see how the test worked. The acid picked up the invisible molecules of gold and they floated around in it until you poured in alkali, which turned the acid to some sort of brine that wouldn't hold the gold in solution any more. So it formed heavy crystals of pure gold and sank to the bottom along with other sludge it wouldn't mix with. Being heavier than lead, the gold settled faster than any other crystals. That accounted for the color he'd seen— the color that hadn't been there when the ore reached Sacramento. The damned book didn't make any mention of the part where the gold disappears without a trace. Once again, the possibilities flitted through his mind. Could he have dozed off? Could he have been knocked out somehow for a spell without his knowing?

It's impossible, he thought. *But so is stealing a carload of ore out from under a man with a Winchester, damn it!*

He walked back over to the desk and asked the librarian if she had any books on magic tricks.

She had a couple, and this time when she climbed the ladder

he got to see even more of her legs. He wondered if she was doing that on purpose, and decided not to find out.

He sat down and started reading about false bottoms, mirrors, black silk strings, and such. He found out how to make a rabbit come out of his hat, but not a clue to the shell game the high-graders had played with at least four ore cars, with him watching.

He was about to give up when he stopped to go back over a paragraph he'd skimmed: "Misdirection is the basis of most good stage magic. It is hard to perform before children because they allow their eyes to wander. Adults can be counted on to keep their eyes fixed where the skilled magician directs them. If one is certain everyone is watching one part of the stage, many things can be done with impunity in full view of the audience. Those watching know they are being tricked, therefore they are so intent on watching the magician's more *obvious* moves that they are oblivious to less subtle happenings, often in plain view."

Longarm nodded and muttered, "That's for damn sure."

The librarian smiled over at him and called, "Did you want something else, sir?"

He shook his head and thanked her. She looked disappointed. As he carried the books up to her counter, she asked, "Are you coming to the dance tonight, Marshal?"

He said, "I'd have asked you to save a dance for me if I was, ma'am. But I've got other chores."

She blushed from her hairline to her lace collar, but grinned like the Cheshire cat. He hoped he had made her day a bit brighter. He thanked her and went out into the bright sunlight.

As he walked out to his gelding, a hard-eyed, thoughtful-looking fellow leaned away from the awning post he'd been holding up with his shoulder and asked, "Are you Longarm?"

"I've been called worse. What's your pleasure, pilgrim?"

"The sheriff wants to see you. Over by the courthouse."

Longarm nodded and said, "I've been meaning to see him, too. Just lead the way."

The stranger pointed down the street with his chin, his thumbs hooked in his gunbelt, and said, "His office is just past that church steeple yonder. You can't miss it."

Longarm decided to walk, since it was less than a city block and there was no sense fooling with the gelding's reins twice more than he had to. He nodded and started toward the steeple. Then he remembered he'd ridden in from the other direction, and remembered what he'd seen down the other way. He crabbed sideways, going for his gun as a bullet buzzed through the air he'd just been walking through!

Longarm reversed his direction with a firmly dug-in heel and whirled about, gun in hand, as the man who had tried to set him up fired a second time. The misdirected slug went through the space the gunman had thought Longarm was headed for. Then the deputy fired.

The stranger was apparently not experienced enough to take on an old hand like Longarm. He stood in one place as he pumped lead. Longarm's first round took him just under the belt buckle and folded him up neatly as it knocked him down. Longarm saw that he'd dropped his weapon, so he held his fire and walked slowly back, covering the man he'd shot and keeping wary on all sides. The librarian came out, saw the man lying almost at her feet, and screamed. Other people boiled out of other doorways, ran halfway over, then stopped uncertainly as Longarm stood over the groaning gunslick.

Longarm kicked the man in the ribs to gain his undivided attention and asked, "All right, old son. Who are you working for?"

The gutshot gunman groaned and said, "Fuck you."

A man wearing a tin star and a worried look came down the center of the dirt street with a shotgun. He saw that Longarm was keeping his six-gun trained in a neighborly fashion at the dirt, so he called out, "What's going on?"

Longarm said, "Don't know. I'm a deputy U.S. marshal and this jasper just tried to shoot me in the back."

The man came closer, staring down at the wounded gunslick, and said, "He's a stranger to me, too. I'm Sheriff Marvin. My office is just up the street."

"I know. He told me you wanted to see me, but he pointed the wrong way. I don't know if it was ignorance or a better field of fire for him. Lucky for me I passed your sign riding in and remembered in time to ponder his words."

The sheriff frowned and said, "I never sent for anybody. Hell, I don't even know you!"

"I figured as much. I'm Custis Long."

"The one who shot the Calico Kid and his gang? Jesus, I want to buy you a drink, son!"

"I'll buy you one too, as soon as we figure out why this son of a bitch was gunning for me."

He kicked the downed man again as the sheriff walked over and picked up the revolver the man had dropped in the dust. He said, "Sonny, if you ain't aiming to die, you'd best tell me the facts of life and I'll see about a doctor."

The gunslick groaned and said, "Stuff it up your ass, lawman."

Longarm said, "Suit yourself, but it's going to smart like hell when the first shock wears off."

A man wearing a white apron had been watching and listening from the crowd. He came forward and said, "I served him in my saloon one night. He said he was with the Calico Kid."

Sheriff Marvin grinned and said, "There you go, Marshal. He was one of the gang you missed before, but now it looks like you've made a clean sweep of the rascals!"

Longarm swore softly and said, "Damn! I was hoping he was somebody important. I ain't got time to trifle with saddle tramps."

The sheriff said, "Just the same, you did the county a favor and the drinks are on me." Marvin pointed to a pair of town loafers and called out, "Luke, you and old Bill drag this skunk over to the jailhouse and send for Doc Cunningham. Mind you don't put him on a bunk. I don't want blood on my furniture."

Then the sheriff slapped Longarm on the back and, together with the bartender, they crossed over to the saloon, where half the town seemed bent on getting Longarm drunk.

As they bellied up to the bar, Longarm told the sheriff of his misadventures. Marvin knew about the high-grading over in Manzanita, but had no suggestions. The only thing Longarm learned was that he might owe other local lawmen an apology or two. Both the sheriff's department and the California marshals had gone over much the same ground before abandoning the case as embarrassing as well as impossible to crack. His notion of guarding the train from loading to delivery had been tried before, with the same results.

Longarm said, "We've missed something. I was just reading

about the way magicians trick folks. The high-graders are doing something we just ain't thought of."

Marvin said, "Hell, tell me something I don't know! You know what they did to me? It was purely spooky. I had a man watching every likely suspect—and I had a long list, too. I put two deputies aboard the cars; I staked out every Mex who works at the mine; I threw a cordon around the whole durned spread, then sat on MacLeod's porch with my own gun handy till the train pulled out with a load of ore. None of us saw even a pack rat near that ore. But it got stole just the same. Ain't that a bitch?"

Longarm nodded, his lips twisted in a wry smile. "Yep. I know the feeling. How come you gave up, though?"

"Hell, Marshal, it's an election year, and it gets tedious looking like an idiot. Besides, I only have so many men and it's a big county. While we were wasting time watching the Lost Chinaman, some rascals ran off thirty head of cattle up by Murphy. When they told me the government was sending in a man, I just thanked the Lord and handed it back to you folks."

Longarm regarded the sheriff for a moment, then downed his shot of Maryland rye in one throw. "I see," he said. "Well, I've only got one man. Me. Old Lovejoy over in Manzanita is a crook, and—"

Marvin cut in, "He's not a crook. Just dumb. I heard about the set-to you had with him. The way I hear tell, the marshals in Sacramento were a mite peeved at the government for not trusting them."

As the bartender poured him another shot, Longarm asked, "What can you tell me about George Hearst, over at Sheep Ranch?"

Marvin frowned. "Nothing. Hearst just owns that mine and a lot of others. He's a big hoorah down in Frisco and over in Virginia City circles. He don't dig his gold personally."

"What about the folks working for him, then?"

Marvin sipped his beer and said, "Eye-talians. A whole colony of Eye-talians who come over the mountains together from some town in Italy. They talk funny, but they never give us no trouble. I know what you might suspicion, but it won't wash. There's only one mule track between Sheep Ranch and Manzanita, and we been over it again and again looking for sign. No freight wagons could make it, even empty. Besides, the Sheep Ranch ore is another kind of rock."

Longarm shrugged and said, "I'll have a look-see anyway. Was that mining engineer, Ralph Baxter, one of the folks you had staked out when it was your turn to look foolish?"

Marvin shook his head and said, "He hadn't come up here yet. He wasn't in the county, as far as I know, when the robberies first started."

Longarm grunted, "He's here now, and he's offered a million for Lost Chinaman."

The sheriff's mouth fell open. "Jesus, I'd take it if I was Mac-Leod. He ain't making anything on the mine now, the way they've been robbing him. It's a wonder anybody wants to buy it at any price. There's no way to show a profit till we find out who's high-grading it, and make the rascals stop!"

Longarm nodded and said, "Yeah. Makes you wonder if Baxter thinks he can stop it any time he wants to, doesn't it?"

"Hot damn! You reckon that prissy dude is behind all this?"

"It's sure starting to look that way. On the other hand, some slick son of a bitch might just be wanting it to look that way. I'll know better when I catch him." Longarm tossed back his drink, thanked the sheriff for his hospitality, and strode out through the batwings into the brightness of the street.

Chapter 6

Longarm never found out why they'd named the little town Sheep Ranch. Nobody there knew. There was a billy goat grazing atop the town dump as he rode in, but not a sign of a sheep. Of course, he hadn't seen any disoriented Orientals over at the Lost Chinaman and he doubted that Angel's Camp had been built by celestial beings.

Sheep Ranch had a big frame hotel with a built-in taproom. The miners lived in less imposing accommodations—shacks that lined the single street, which was only a wider stretch of county road. The mine works were surrounded by a barbed wire fence. The fence was posted against trespassers with the additional warning that survivors would be prosecuted. So he went to the hotel bar and told the bartender he wanted to meet up with someone who could answer questions about mining.

The bartender said, "That'd be Herc Romero. He'll be here in a little while. They're about to change shifts."

Longarm said, "Romero, huh?" and the bartender snapped, "Do you know who the last man who saw Custer alive was?"

"Some Indian scout, wasn't it?" the deputy guessed.

"No. Custer sent his bugler, Trooper Martin, with a message for Terry, just before the Sioux wiped out the Seventh Cav."

Longarm was puzzled. "That's interesting as hell, but what's the point of your yarn?" he asked.

"Trooper Martin's real name was Martini. He came from Palermo, damn it!"

Longarm blinked, surprised at the intensity of the bartender's response.

"Well, don't get your balls in an uproar. Everybody has to come from some damn place."

"Palermo is in Sicily. Martini was an Italian. Herc Romero is an Italian. And I, God damn it, am Italian!"

"I don't aim to dispute your words, old son. I just don't savvy what you're getting at," Longarm said, pushing his hat back from his forehead.

Slightly mollified, the bartender said, "My folks came across the prairies and deserts in a covered wagon. Everybody seems to think that's funny as hell. You Irishmen weren't the only people who won the West, you know."

"That's for damn sure," Longarm agreed, "but I ain't Irish. Ain't an Indian, either, and they were here before damn near anybody else."

The bartender nodded and said, "Just wanted to set the record straight. They buried a Yankee over in Dorado for calling somebody a dago last year. Folks in this part of the county are just as Western and mean as anybody else."

Two men came through the swinging doors and the bartender called out, "Hey, Herc. Lawman here wants to talk with you. He sounds like he's all right."

Herc Romero was a bearish man of about forty with a red bandanna around his neck and rock flour in his hair. He came over to Longarm and offered his hand. He said, "I'll drink with you, but I'm wore out answering questions about the Lost Chinaman. I've never seen the damned mine."

The deputy smiled amicably. "I'll take your word for it. But Kevin MacLeod over there said someone working for the same boss as you rode over for a look-see a while back. MacLeod said he took the Hearst man through his diggings. Do you have any idea who it might have been?"

Romero shook his head and said, "Nobody working under me. The way I hear it, our ore is higher grade, and even that's not anything to get excited about. The Mother Lode is playing out. We'll be shutting down here in just a few more years."

Longarm frowned, wondering who in thunder *had* visited MacLeod. But he knew Romero couldn't—or wouldn't—tell him. So he asked, "If I was to ask you, would you ride over there with me right now?"

The foreman considered this briefly, then said, "Maybe. If you can give me two good reasons."

"One reason is that you ain't on duty," the lawman offered.

"My wife's expecting me for supper."

"The second is that you'll be helping the U.S. government. I want a man I can trust to have a look at a few things over there for me."

Romero smiled and asked, "How do you know you can trust me? You never met me before."

Longarm chuckled. "Sure I have. You've been married up with the same gal for nigh twenty years, you were cited for bravery in the Battle of Cold Harbor, and you've never been sued or arrested since you stole those watermelons when you were twelve."

Romero and his friend looked startled, and the mine foreman asked, "How in hell did you find out so much in the short time you've been here?"

Longarm said, "I didn't find it out here. I've been over to the county seat. I've read your whole record."

"Damn it, I don't have no record!" Romero protested.

"Sure you do," Longarm said. "Everybody does. Every time a man gets hitched, serves his country, or gets dragged before a judge for any reason whatsoever, there's a record kept. Since you've lived in this county most of your life, except for five years in the War, I know all I need to about you. I need an honest man to back my next play, too. Will you do it?"

The bartender said, "I'll be damned, you never told us you got a medal in the War, Herc."

The foreman shrugged and said, "It wasn't much. What do you want me to do over at the Lost Chinaman, Deputy?"

"Answer questions as I think them up. I'm going through the diggings from top to bottom and I need a hard-rock mining man I can trust as a guide."

Romero nodded and said, "You got one. Just let me tell my woman. Do you suppose I'm going to need a gun?"

Longarm said, "Don't know. If you've got one, you'd best bring it along. The folks we're after are pretty slick, and they might start playing rough if we get near pay dirt."

Kevin MacLeod's wife said her husband had gone down to Sacramento to see about another bank loan. But Tico Vallejo said he'd show Longarm and Romero through the mine.

As they moved down the gentle slope inside the entrance,

walking between the tracks with Vallejo holding a lantern, Long-arm held back and let the two other men talk. He knew Romero was likely to ask more sensible questions about the operation than he was. So he just listened.

Vallejo seemed friendly and at ease with the burly Italian. Romero was friendly too, but he'd been filled in during the ride over, and was asking more questions than the usual guided tour might call for.

Romero rapped a pit prop with a knuckle and asked, "How come you have live oak instead of cedar, Tico? Didn't you know oak gives all at once, without warning?"

"I think some of these tunnels were dug before my time. The hills hereabouts are thick with oak. Isn't oak stronger than cedar?"

"Sure it is, but cedar groans like a sick cat for at least a few minutes before it gives. If this mountain ever decides to sit down on you boys over here, it'll happen with no warning."

Vallejo looked morosely up at the hanging wall and said, "Well, we're solid rock, and it's lasted this long."

Romero grunted, "It always lasts *this* long. By the time you can say it lasted *that* long, it's too late. You folks are operating on a shoestring over here!"

Vallejo nodded and said, "There's no argument about that, Herc. Señor MacLeod says if the bank turns down his application for another loan he's going to have to close or sell out."

A workman was leading a burro hitched to a little ore car up the slope toward them, and the three men squeezed back against the wall to let it pass. Longarm reached out and snagged a lump of rock from the cart, but Vallejo laughed and said, "Save your-self the trouble. It's overburden."

Romero started to explain, "You have to dig ten tons of noth-ing much to get at a ton of high-grade ore," but Longarm cut him short, saying, "I've been in a few mines before."

Vallejo led them farther down the slope to a point where the main shaft ended in a lopsided T. As they turned to the left, Romero ran a finger along the standing wall and said, "Meta-morphic quartz, sure enough. I can see where they followed the vein as she pinched out."

Vallejo said, "It opens up again a bit farther, on. We're almost there."

He held his lantern high as they approached a wet dead end of glittering rock. Though hardly a geologist, Longarm could see how the pinkish, glassy quartz ran in wavy bands through darker, duller rock. He asked, "What are the middlings—quartzite?"

Vallejo sighed, "Yes, it's tough as a bitch to shatter. Takes twice as much dynamite to shave the face as it ought to."

Longarm could see the shallow craters from the last blast running in neat rows across the mine face like the stars in the American flag. Romero bent to pick up a loose lump of quartz and put it in his pocket.

Longarm followed suit with another sample, holding it up to the flickering light of Vallejo's lantern before putting it in his pocket. If there was gold in it, it couldn't be seen with the naked eye. Romero asked Vallejo for the lantern and held it close to the wet rock face. He ran his free hand over the rock and tasted his fingertips. He grimaced and said, "Metallic, all right. Sulfur, too. Are there any hot springs in the neighborhood, Vallejo?"

The Mexican shook his head and replied, "Not that I know of. Why?"

Romero said, "If the temperature starts rising down here, run like hell. You might be digging your way into a hot spring."

Vallejo muttered, "*Madre!*" but before they could get into a geology lesson, Longarm asked Romero, "What do you think, Herc?"

Romero said, "Looks like a gold mine. Tastes like a gold mine. I'll know better in a minute."

He squatted on an empty dynamite box and took a pocket-size kit from his loose wool trousers. He uncorked a small bottle, placed a shallow glass dish on one knee, held his ore sample over it with one hand, and dribbled some acid over the sample from a thin glass tube he had dipped in the bottle. As he corked the little vial of acid and opened another small bottle, Longarm observed, "That's a right cunning little outfit. Do you carry it all the time?"

"Sure," Romero replied, "when I'm working. It gets tedious digging worthless rock, and all this durned quartz looks the same."

"They say you have another kind of quartz over at Sheep Ranch," Longarm said.

Romero shook his head. "A deeper shade, is all. Ours has more iron in it. Gold is gold no matter what the rest looks like."

Romero dripped alkali into the little basin, put the glass tube away, and swished the dish around like a tiny prospector's pan. He asked Vallejo to hold the light closer. Then he held the dish up, peered at the muddy contents, and nodded. "Medium-high grade. Our stuff at Sheep Ranch is richer, but this rock's well worth digging."

Vallejo said, "I don't understand what you're trying to prove, Señor Longarm. We have told you from the first we were digging gold ore here."

Longarm nodded and said, "Just wanted to be sure."

The Mexican insisted, "Sure of what? Why on earth would we be working so hard if there was nothing down here worth our efforts?"

Longarm held up a cautioning hand. "I never said I doubted anyone's word, Vallejo, but somebody is tricking the shit out of us and I'm eliminating as many angles as I can think of."

"Damn it," Vallejo said, "we are digging real gold and loading real gold and shipping real gold. You were the one who was supposed to be guarding it. None of my crew were near you when you let the high-graders steal it!"

Longarm said placatingly, "Now don't get your balls in an uproar. If you weren't so sensitive you'd see we just gave you and your men an alibi."

Vallejo simmered down and said sheepishly, "Oh."

Longarm explained. "That's how I aim to find our culprit— by figuring out who *didn't* do it, till I whittle down to the only ones who *could* have." He ticked off possibilities on the fingers of his large, calloused hand. "So far, I know *I* never stole the gold. I don't think Herc stole it, and it looks like you and your men are home free."

Vallejo sighed deeply and nodded, "I understand. Forgive my outburst. One becomes a bit sensitive after being called a greaser a few times. Who else have you eliminated from your list of suspects?"

"Nobody. And there's a lot of folks in Calaveras County, too. Let's go topside. Maybe I can start crossing off a few more names."

Vallejo led the way with the lantern and they followed him

back to the main shaft. Romero asked where the other miners were. The Mexican explained that the three of them had come down at the end of the shift. He added, "We are only working one shift a day now. Señor MacLeod is having difficulty raising more working capital."

Romero said, "I can see you're running a shoestring mine with semiskilled labor, no offense intended. If I was MacLeod, I'd sell out. He sounds like a stubborn cuss."

Vallejo said, "He is. This mine means much to him. He says he put a lot of time and effort into finding his first decent strike and has no intention of letting others get rich from it."

They started up the slope. Vallejo was in the lead, with Romero in the middle and Longarm bringing up the rear. Longarm neither heard nor felt anything unusual until Romero suddenly whirled around and pushed him, yelling, "Run! Run like hell, and cut around the corner!"

Wondering why, but willing to learn, Longarm tore after Romero as the burly Italian raced down the pitch-blackness of the shaft. He could hear it now. Something was chasing them!

He reached the end of the entrance shaft in the darkness and ran full-tilt into the hard, wet standing wall. A hand reached out and hauled him into the side tunnel as an ore car, with an explosive, earth-shaking crash, slammed into the space he'd just been occupying. Longarm was hit in the back with a chunk of flying rock. A wooden plank slapped him across the behind like an initiation paddle wielded by a school bully who'd eaten gunpowder for breakfast. Longarm and Romero sprawled together on the sloping, muddy floor as things tinkled and shuddered into dead silence. Then Longarm got off Romero and helped him up, saying, "Thanks. You have damn good ears!"

Romero lit a match, saying, "I felt the air pressure building. A hard-rock man gets to where he can feel things before they happen, under a mountain."

He raised the little light over their heads and took a gingerly few steps back the way they'd come, muttering, "Jesus!"

The ore car that had chased them down the track was a pile of shattered debris against the standing wall at the bottom of the slope. The rock it had been filled with lay in a spread-out pile. A lantern lay on its side among the lumps of ore, its chimney shattered and its flame snuffed out. Romero's match went out, but he lit another, picked up the lantern, and lit the wick, saying, "This thing's warm. I think it was Vallejo's."

As he held the lantern up, Longarm pointed with his chin at a trickle of blood running out from under the piled rock and wreckage and said, "He came down the tracks with the car! He's under all that shit!"

Romero put the lantern down as he dropped to his knees and started lifting rocks, saying, "*Help* me, damn it!"

But Longarm was running up the slope, his drawn Colt in his hand, as he called back, "There's no way he's *alive* under there, but the son of a bitch who killed him can't be far!"

He boiled up out of the ground, dodged to one side as he left the overhang of the mine entrance, and took cover behind another ore wagon sitting quietly on a siding as he scanned the sunlit surroundings.

He seemed to have the mine head to himself. He'd come up out of the darkness so suddenly that the sun hurt his eyes. But he could see to the treeline all around, and it was just dusty and dead-looking in the late-afternoon light. There wasn't even a wisp of hanging dust to hint at anyone's presence.

The back door of MacLeod's cabin opened and the owner's freckled little wife stepped out. Longarm shouted, "Get back inside!" and then, as he saw she was just standing there like a big dumb bird, he swore and ran over to her, grabbing her as he whipped them both inside, slammed the kitchen door, and peered out the dusty kitchen window.

Lottie MacLeod gasped, "What's wrong? What happened?"

Longarm said, "They just killed Vallejo and damn near killed me and that other fellow. Have you been working in this kitchen, ma'am?"

"Of course. Kevin will be home any minute and it's getting on to supper time."

Longarm nodded at the pot of beans simmering on the kitchen stove and asked, "Did you see anybody moving about out there, just now?"

The girl shook her head and said, "Not since the men knocked off a few minutes ago."

"Did they all leave directly, or did some of them sort of hang back?"

"Heavens, I wasn't paying that much attention." She thought

for a moment, then shook her head again and said, "I just don't know. I'm so used to seeing men come and go up there by the diggings, I never notice who comes or goes."

He saw Romero in the mine entrance now. He went to the door again and called the husky Italian over, covering Romero's back as the big man dog-trotted to the cabin. As Romero joined them, he told Longarm, "You were right. They're going to have to carry him out in a sack." Romero saw the horror in Lottie's eyes and quickly added, "Sorry, ma'am. But facts is facts."

She gasped, "What happened down there—a cave-in?"

Longarm said, "Runaway ore car, ma'am. Romero, is there any chance at all it was an accident?"

The Italian shook his head and said, "The shift was over. I noticed the other cars were on a siding sloping *away* from the entrance. They've led the burros off, too. Somebody pushed that car in on us the hard way. From the speed it came down, I'd say they followed it a ways, still pushing."

"Could one man do it, or would it take more?"

Romero shrugged and said, "One man could have moved her if he really put his back into it. Once he had her headed downhill, of course, he was just pushing to be ornery."

Longarm nodded, looked out the window again, and said, "Whoever it was seems to be long gone. We'd best get you headed back home while it's still light, and I thank you for your help." He turned to Mrs. MacLeod. "When's your man due back, ma'am?"

She said, "His stage is due before sundown. He left his pony at the livery in Manzanita. Why?"

"I ain't sure it's safe to leave you up here alone. By the way, didn't a dog yap at us when we rode in?"

Lottie looked around at the floor and replied, "Rex? He was here just a minute ago."

"He ain't here now," Longarm observed. "He should have been sounding off about all the excitement we've just had."

Lottie said, "That's funny. He usually does bark at strangers."

She went to the back door and called out, "Rex? Here, boy!" a couple of times. No dog appeared.

Longarm glanced at Romero and said, "Stay with her a minute, will you?"

The miner nodded and put a casual hand on the grips of his six-gun.

Longarm stepped outside and walked over to the untrodden earth at the edge of the dust surrounding the cabin and mine works. He worked the grassy edge for tracks, but there was too much sign to read a pattern. He found rabbit tracks and deer scat along with plenty of prints that he assumed had been left by Rex. The dog had probably patrolled the grounds thoroughly and pissed on nearly every tree and bush.

There were human tracks too. Too many human tracks. The workmen lived in every direction and had walked home every damned way. So Longarm started looking for hoof prints.

He circled the whole site, crossing the road and the rail siding without spotting anything worth following up. He cut back toward the cabin, holding his gun loosely at his side as he walked. As he passed the mine entrance again, he wondered who he was going to send to break the news to the dead man's kin. They were probably waiting supper on him right this minute. He passed an ore car parked near the tipple. A flash of chestnut caught his eye between the wheels and he stopped. He walked over to the car, bent over, and muttered, "Oh, damn!"

The dog, Rex, lay under the car on his side. A bluebottle fly was crawling over his open eye and others were sipping at the bloody edges of his bared fangs. Someone had smashed the dog's head in with a club or a rock. The poor brute had died defending the property as best he knew how.

Longarm walked slowly back to the cabin. That woman was going to cry some when he told her. They were going to have to take her with them when they left. It wasn't safe to leave her up here alone.

Longarm had a sudden thought and stopped in his tracks, muttering, "Wait a minute!" Then he turned and moved back the way he'd come. The dead Vallejo had mentioned night watchmen. Sure. Nobody was waiting supper on Vallejo—he lived with two other workmen in that little shack just up the rise beyond the tipple!

Longarm cautiously approached the bunkhouse. The plank door was ajar a slit, but when he called out there was no answer.

He moved in carefully, kicked open the door, and stepped inside. There were two Mexicans in the bunkhouse. One lay on the floor and the other was sprawled across his bunk, staring up at the ceiling. The bunkhouse was filled with the smell of bitter almonds and both dead men had cherry-red faces, as if they'd blushed themselves to death.

Longarm had seen Death wearing this expression before. He knew cyanide was used in gold mining, so there was no mystery as to how they had died.

He stepped over to the body on the bunk and felt its cheek. The corpse was lukewarm. They'd died at about the same time as the dog, while he and the others had been down in the mine.

A bottle lay on the floor near the other corpse. Longarm picked it up and sniffed. The bottle was one-quarter full of red wine with just a hint of bitter almond to its bouquet. The dead men hadn't been fussy drinkers, but they'd probably known the man who had given them the free wine. That didn't tell him a damned thing. He already knew it was someone in Calaveras County.

Lottie MacLeod had been right about the stage. It arrived just before sundown and she was with Longarm when her husband got down from it. She threw herself against him and started to weep loudly as Longarm filled him in on what had happened up at his mine. He added that the bodies had been hauled into town and handed over to their kin for burial. MacLeod said, "Damn it, just as I get another bank loan, they start killing us!"

Longarm said, "Yeah, I'll be at the Manzanita Inn later, if you have any ideas. Constable Lovejoy's posted some deputies up at your diggings with orders not to drink any wine. So it's likely safe for you two to go home when you've a mind to. I've got work to do."

He'd noticed the stage crew ducking into the saloon across the street while the team was being changed for the next trot up to Angel's Camp. So he left the MacLeods to sort things out and moseyed over after them. He introduced himself to the jehu leaning on the bar and asked, "What time did you boys pull out of Sacramento this afternoon? I've got good reasons for asking."

The driver shrugged and said, "I never looked at my watch, but we've been on the road a good five or six hours. Why?"

"I'll pay for your drinks. You just saved me a ride in to Sacramento to talk with some bankers."

He placed a coin on the bar and went outside. He'd eliminated MacLeod as well as himself and Romero. That wasn't much, but every little bit helped.

He saw that the MacLeods had left. Constable Lovejoy had been in his office when Longarm and Romero had carried Lottie MacLeod and the news to town, but that meant nothing. The Baxters were staying in Longarm's hotel, but when he'd knocked on their door he had gotten no answer. Their horses were in the livery and nobody in town knew where they might have gone on foot.

He went to the Manzanita Inn and asked the desk clerk if they'd come back. The desk clerk said no, so he went upstairs. His own room was just down the hall from the suite Sylvia and her brother had rented. He knocked softly on Ralph Baxter's door, got no answer, and hit it a few hard licks. Then he took out his penknife and quietly opened the latch.

The room was empty, as he'd hoped. Knowing the room clerk was right under him, Longarm moved quietly on the balls of his feet as he gave the room a casual search, not sure what he was looking for.

Baxter's clothes were hanging in a closet. Longarm found a carpetbag under the bed, opened it, and found it filled with nothing incriminating or even interesting. The engineer's chemistry kit was in a dresser drawer. He uncorked every bottle and sniffed for bitter almonds. Some of the stuff smelled godawful, but he found no cyanide. He remembered that Baxter had said he was afraid of the stuff.

There was a sheaf of envelopes and papers in the same drawer. They seemed to be assay reports and a telegram. Longarm read:

ONE AND A HALF MILLION IS FINAL OFFER **STOP** WHATS
HOLDING UP THE PARADE **STOP** MORRISON

He folded the telegram and put it back the way he'd found it.

Wondering where in thunder the two of them could have gone, Longarm eased over to the connecting door between their rooms and tried the knob. The door wasn't locked. He opened it. Then he froze in the doorway.

They were in Sylvia's bed—asleep or dead, he couldn't tell which. They'd tossed the sheets aside to cool off. He imagined they'd been having a lively time. They were both naked. Baxter lay spread-eagled on his back with Sylvia cuddled against him. She was still wearing her black stockings and frilly garters, but nothing else. They didn't look as if they'd been poisoned.

As Longarm studied them for signs of life, Sylvia opened her eyes. Longarm stepped back and softly closed the door. He was halfway to his own room when Sylvia caught up with him and clutched at his sleeve. She'd slipped on a robe. She said, "You have to let me explain, darling."

Longarm opened the door to his own room and she followed him inside as he said wryly, "There's no need, ma'am. Incest ain't a federal offense, lucky for lots of folks."

"Damn it," she said, "he's not my brother. He's my husband."

"Adultery ain't a federal crime either, Mrs. Baxter. I wasn't prying into your personal habits. The high-graders have started killing folks and I was worried about you. I can see you're alive and healthy, so what the hell."

"Listen, Ralph understands my needs, darling. He knows I hold advanced views about sex."

"I figured that was why he's been so testy with me. But what's your play, Sylvia? How come you two are posing as brother and sister if you ain't?"

"We're a team," she explained, "We're fronting for a financial syndicate and, well, sometimes it gives us an edge if I'm free to have a romance or two along the way."

"The two of you are out to fuck folks either way, huh?"

"Don't be brutal. What happened on the steamboat was not in the line of duty. I let you make love to me simply because I wanted you."

"Maybe. Have you had Kevin MacLeod in your pants, too?"

"Of course not," she said righteously. "He's happily married."

Longarm noticed she had shut the door behind them and was already out of her robe. He asked, "If Ralph didn't sic you on me and you're not out to seduce MacLeod, why are you up here in the Mother Lode?"

"Why? He's my husband, of course. Don't you think poor Ralph has needs and feelings too?"

"He's got them under better control than most gents, I imagine. You'd best get back to him before he starts getting desperate again, Sylvia."

She smiled lewdly and said, "Ralph's done for the day. But I'm a warm-natured woman."

As she dropped to her knees and started to unbutton him, he shook his head and said, "I noticed that on the steamboat. But I'll pass, this time around."

She fumbled for him. As he backed away she followed him on her knees, protesting, "Pooh, you know you want me."

He bent over and pulled her to her feet, saying, "Put on your damn robe and git, girl. Aside from my delicate feelings, I've got work to do."

"You can't discard me like some used toy, damn it! The two of us are lovers."

"You mean we were," he corrected her. "I ain't any toy, either. If Ralph can't keep you satisfied, the saloon is filled with horny cowhands almost every night. So, like I said, I'm out of the game."

She shrugged and bent to pick up her robe, saying, "You'll be sorry, the next time you wake up with a hard-on. Ralph's left me more than once. But he always comes crawling back for more."

"Some men are like that. I ain't."

"Pooh, you men are all such hypocrites. There's not one of you who doesn't fool around on his woman, but when one of us acts the same, you act like you're shocked silly."

"You're probably right, ma'am. I reckon we ought to be horsewhipped for being like that, but that's the way we come."

"I'll bet you have somebody else lined up, right?"

He grinned and said, "Maybe."

She laughed and said, "I knew it." She put her hand on the doorknob and added, "Well, if it doesn't work out, don't go to strangers. Meanwhile, good hunting, darling."

She left. Longarm sat on the bed and lit a cheroot, wondering how Ralph was going to take her odd views on free love this time. He puffed furiously on the cheroot as he ran the day's events through his head. At least he supposed he could scratch the Baxters off his list of suspects. He wouldn't take Sylvia's word for it that the sky was blue, but the room clerk had told him he hadn't seen the couple for hours, and for now, Longarm was willing to go with the assumption that they had been exactly where he had found them. He was stuck for ideas. It was too dark to look for sign and he reckoned the murderers hadn't left any anyway.

For some reason he found himself thinking about the pretty little librarian over at the county seat. He shook his head to clear it. That was crazy. He had enough of that kind of trouble on his plate. There was a jealous husband just down the hall and a Mexican gal waiting for him who'd likely pull a knife on him if he looked at another woman. He frowned, blew a smoke ring, and thought, *Misdirection. That's what the book said. I ain't been looking at the right places. While I'm checking out a mine everybody says is all right, the rascals kill three men and a dog and damned nearly me, too.*

MacLeod would have his ore cars filled again in a day or so, since he had plenty of ore in the tipple at the mine head. Should he sniff around up there some more? No. That was what he would be expected to do. Check out the bank to see if MacLeod had told the truth about making another loan? That was also an obvious move. The stage crew had said MacLeod had really come up from Sacramento. What about wiring headquarters for a rundown on the Baxters? The girl's story jibed with what Mac-Leod had told him about their fronting for people who wanted to buy the mine. The telegram wasn't likely to be a plant. He doubted that they'd expected him to find them in bed like that. On the other hand, it was a neat alibi for folks to appear to have no shame. Ralph could have slipped out the back way. But what was his game? To crush MacLeod financially so he would sell the mine cheap? It was possible. But the snooty Bostonian couldn't move tons of ore all by himself, even with Sylvia helping. You'd need a whole crew to shovel all that ore and hide it. A man masterminding others didn't have to stage a bedroom farce; he'd just sic some sidekicks on you.

Had that gunslick over at the county seat really been just a pal of the Calico Kid's, or was that a set-up too? Wheels within wheels.

Misdirection, he told himself. *Nothing really matters but the way they've been stealing that ore. Find out how they work that one slick trick and you'll have the rest of it on a platter!*

He snuffed out the cheroot and checked his sidearm's ammunition. Guarding the shipments by sitting on top of the ore was useless; it hadn't worked for any lawman who'd tried it. There had to be something else he should be watching instead.

But what in thunder was it? They weren't switching the ore before it was loaded. They weren't switching it at the stamping mill. And he'd been sitting on it everywhere between. What they were doing appeared to be plain impossible. But they'd done it, over and over.

"Secret trapdoors?" He asked the .44 in his hand. Then he shook his head. If they'd been sneaking the ore out the bottom of the cars as they rolled, he'd have noticed because he'd have gone down through the trapdoor with it. If they'd somehow switched moving cars in a tunnel, say, he'd have been switched as well. But another shipment would be leaving and he knew if he didn't figure it out, the ore would never arrive at the stamping mill. MacLeod would go bankrupt and have to sell to that snooty Baxter. . . . *Back off. I've been down that trail and it doesn't lead anywhere I ain't thought of.*

He put the gun in its holster and rose to his feet. He knew where he'd be spending the night, and that part was just fine. He had a while to figure how to guard the next shipment. Meanwhile, Felicidad was waiting.

Longarm lay in the fourposter, smoking in the dark with Felicidad's head on his naked shoulder. She murmured, "That was lovely, *querido*. But I can sense you are troubled. Is it about poor Tico and those other muchachos?"

He said, "They tried to kill Romero and me, too. Romero has a wife and kids. I've been thinking of magic tricks. I'm usually tolerably good at spotting a cardsharp dealing funny. I've never been taken by the shell game. So, if nobody can shift a card or a pea without my noticing, how do they move two loaded freight cars out from under my big behind?"

"I like your behind," she purred. "It is solid as a rock and you are so good at moving it. When you finish that smoke, can we make love again?"

He nodded and stroked her naked shoulder fondly though a bit distractedly as he ran every move of the past few days through his mind. Damn, that little librarian had a nice pair of legs. The gunslick who had thrown down on him had probably recognized his gelding tied up out in front of the library. He hadn't told the librarian his name, so she hadn't been in on it. She was just a lonesome little thing who liked tall men. She didn't look like a gal who went all the way. He thought it was likely she'd want to take him home to meet her folks.

Felicidad broke into his reverie, asking, "When will you be riding with the next shipment?"

He said, "Don't aim to," wondering why she'd asked. Then he decided it was a natural enough question. He was in a line of work that made men suspicious by nature. Felicidad had bid on the mine property, but her offer wasn't even under consideration. If she was fronting for some local Mexican outfit who wanted the land back, they were certainly being clumsy. MacLeod wouldn't be their main worry now. The Baxters were offering over a million for the Lost Chinaman. Anyone else who was after it should have taken a shot at Ralph by now. Once his syndicate got control, there would be plenty of working capital to hire a whole squad of Pinkertons.

He reached out to snuff the cheroot and Felicidad said, "Let me get on top this time."

She rolled over on him and started fondling him, asking, "Is something wrong? You are not responding, *mi querido*."

He started running his hands over her body to help focus his attention and she leaned forward to pass her nipples over his lips. That helped a lot.

She murmured, "Oh, you have such a lovely body, and there is so much of it," as she slid her thighs up on either side of his chest. She raised her knees and braced a foot in each of his armpits, still jackknifed forward. It opened her so wide he could have gotten in soft, but he wasn't soft anymore. He closed his eyes and pictured the little library gal in the same position. Why was it a man always wanted what he couldn't have? He knew that if he was wrestling with the librarian somewhere, he'd be wondering what that Mexican girl back in Manzanita was like.

He started moving up to meet her as she rode him like a trotting horse, but his mind was up at the mine. Lottie MacLeod was pretty, too. But that wasn't the answer. Everyone expected him to be riding shotgun on the next shipment. What could he do that they wouldn't be expecting?

Felicidad said, *"Ay, que chihuahua!"* as he absently nibbled her breast. He saw she was about ready. So he rolled her over, braced both of his feet on the rug, and started plunging deeply into her with her ankles locked around his neck. She screamed aloud in pleasure and raked his back with her nails as she sobbed, "Yes, yes, all of it, all the way!"

He gave her what she was pleading for. That was easy. But the thinking part of him kept chewing like a bone on the next shipment.

Going through the same motions over and over wasn't as tedious in bed as it was in his job. But he and those other lawmen had just been jerking off at the high-graders. Billy Vail had sent him all the way from Denver to screw them *right!*

His anger at his own frustrated investigations added what the girl took for passion to his thrusts and she gasped, "Oh, my God, I love you! No man has ever made me feel like this before!"

She was making him feel like a shit, but he didn't say so. She was pretty and had her own land, and many men would have jumped at the chance to keep her permanently. How was he to make her understand that he wasn't one of them?

He'd met more than one woman in his time with whom he could have stayed. His badge, his gun, and the enemies he'd made kept Longarm moving on. Many a gunslick without the sand in his craw to come at him face to face would jump at the chance to hurt a lawman's wife or kids. He couldn't be married to a woman and do his job at the same time. He'd comforted too many lawmen's widows in his day even to think of it.

But he still felt guilty as the girl cried out and climaxed under him. He pumped her down from heaven and rolled off as she sighed, "Oh, I can't get enough of you, *querido.*"

He murmured, "Me neither. My back gives out ahead of the parts that count. That ornery little rascal would rut us both to death if I let him."

She laughed and said, "I'd hardly call him little. Do either of you love me, just a bit?"

"More like a lot," he lied. "But let's just be still while I slow my pump down and catch my breath."

If he told everyone he was giving up and let them send the ore down with some of Lovejoy's men guarding it, that would leave him free to skulk about a bit himself.

It hardly mattered whether or not Lovejoy could be trusted. He knew nobody on the train was going to see anything. But he wondered what *he* might see, watching from the sidelines.

Felicidad said, "I shall miss you so when you leave me, *querido*."

He blinked and asked, "Did I say I was going somewhere?"

She said, "You didn't have to. I have come to know the sort of man you are."

"Listen, Felicidad, it ain't like I'm not fond of you. You're the prettiest little thing I've ever met, and—"

"Hush, *querido*. No lies between friends. I shall never forget you. I shall probably always be at least a little in love with you. But I am not a stupid woman."

"I never said I thought you were. Does this mean you don't want me to come back any more?"

"You will always be welcome in my bed as well as my heart, my darling. I have tortured myself trying to think of some way to make you stay with me. I even thought of saying I was in trouble, but you must have heard that many times before, eh?"

He had, but he didn't say so.

His thoughts returned to the Lost Chinaman with an almost audible snap. He couldn't follow the next gold shipment on horseback. It wasn't possible to stake out every mile of the track. And if he *could* watch from the side, what was he likely to see? There wasn't a better view than right aboard the damned tram in any case; anyone could see that. He frowned and muttered, "Yeah, and that's what everyone's been doing! We've all been watching the magician's waving hand!"

Felicidad asked what he was talking about. He pulled her closer, cocking his right leg over her thigh. She laughed and asked, "Do you want to do it *again?*" and Longarm answered, "Yes ma'am, this time it'll be my pleasure."

"You mean you didn't enjoy it the last time?"

"Hell, you know I did," he lied, adding, "but I just thought myself out of a box and I'm feeling bright-eyed and bushy-tailed as hell!"

Chapter 7

He left Felicidad's before dawn, but as he rode across her spread toward Manzanita, he noticed a couple of her vaqueros topping a rise to his right. They didn't seem to be coming at him, so he waved and rode on. They didn't wave back. They didn't act as though they'd seen him at all.

He thought of a phrase from an old song: "All the boys on the rancho are wild about poor Pancho's widow!" But if he was stepping on any toes, it was their own blamed fault. Felicidad's husband had been dead for some time and they'd left the poor little woman playing with herself all alone in that big house long past what common courtesy dictated.

He cut through a grove of live oaks to put some of his new plan into action. As he'd anticipated, the telephone line to Sacramento followed the ridge beyond the grove, strung on ponderosa poles.

He dismounted, tethered the gelding to an oak, and shinnied up a pole in the gray light to cut the wire before he rode on.

When he got back to the hotel, the room clerk told him the Baxters had started earlier for Sacramento. Their key was in the box and they had said they would be back that afternoon. So Longarm went upstairs, forced their door, and started quietly messing things up, grinning like a polecat in a henhouse.

He pulled the mattresses off both beds and slashed them open with his pocketknife, scattering feathers all over. He took Ralph's extra coat from the closet and tossed it on the floor with its pockets turned inside out.

There was a hatbox under Sylvia's bed. He opened it and dumped the contents on her slashed mattress. He noted with interest that she took care of herself with a fancy French douche bag of India rubber.

He opened all the drawers he could find. He stole all the papers and messages. He opened the chemistry kit, and because he didn't really want to do enough damage to hurt the innocent owners of the hotel, he put the acid bottles in his pocket, hoping they wouldn't leak as he scattered the rest of the glassware on the rug and planted a boot heel on it. Some of the stuff fizzed and the rest stank like hell.

He went to his own room and messed it up also, but a bit more gently. Then he went downstairs and yelled angrily at the startled clerk, "Someone's been in my room! It's been searched and torn up. I thought you said you run a first-class hotel here!"

The clerk followed him upstairs and clucked over the signs of forced entry. He didn't enter the Baxters' suite, of course, but when they complained, Longarm knew the clerk could be counted on to tell them the deputy's room had been burgled too. Longarm accepted the man's apology and confusion in good grace, saying nothing had been stolen, and went to have breakfast while the hotel's staff cleaned up the mess.

Some teamsters were having breakfast in the greasy spoon near the jailhouse, so Longarm struck up a conversation with them and explained that he was about to pack it in. He said, "One man can't do it all by himself. I figure I'll hand that high-grading back to old Lovejoy, at least until I can get a whole posse of federal men up here to search every canyon and abandoned mine shaft all at once."

One of the teamsters nodded and said, "We've been jawing about that high-grading some, Deputy. Us mule skinners know nigh every road and byway in these parts, but none of us have cut sign where strange freight wagons have been."

Longarm said, "That ain't the problem. Anyone could hide his wheel marks just by dragging a branch of canyon oak tied to his rear axle. The problem is that there are so many trails. I've been in all the likely hideouts, but that doesn't mean much. One rider can only be in one place at a time and I think they've been playing a razzle-dazzle, shell-gaming the poor, lone lawman by moving about like spit on a hot stove."

The teamster frowned and said, "All that ore, Deputy? Meaning no disrespect, I haul stuff for a living. This is right rough country to be scooting all over the map with tons and tons of rock!"

"Hell," Longarm swore, "they've likely dumped the ore down any of a hundred canyons. You can scoot tolerably with empty wagons, even big ones."

The two teamsters exchanged glances. Then the one farthest down the counter chimed in, "That don't make sense! Why would anyone want to high-grade the Lost Chinaman only to dump the ore down a fool canyon? Ain't the ore no good?"

Longarm nodded and said, "It tests out as fair ore, but it looks like any other rock. Dumped down a hillside or in a creek, it wouldn't attract notice from anyone passing, who'd just think it was the same old country rock you see all over, here-abouts."

"Well, sure," the third teamster admitted. "But what's the infernal point? You can't spend gold that's just laying in a creek-bed, can you?"

"Not right away. But after the search dies down, say in a year or more, you could just come back, start loading up, and say—if anyone asks—that you just found a new placer. Hell, if they've dumped it all in the same place, they could file a mining claim on it and no one would be the wiser!"

The teamsters gaped at him in dawning understanding and one of them said, "Jesus H. Christ! I suspicion it would *work!*"

His companion added, "Sure it would! That's a right smart answer to how them high-graders have been getting away with the stolen ore. Everybody's been trying to figure how they've hauled it out of the county over the mountains, but if they've been dumping it nearby— Why don't you just form up a posse and start looking for it, Deputy?"

Longarm shook his head and said morosely, "It'd take too long. Like I said, it's just rock to the eye. We'd have to prospect every pile of loose rock with chemicals and such. It'd take for-ever even with a hundred men. Besides that, I might be wrong. Nope, I'm packing it in for now. If the treasury boys want their gold so bad, they can just start looking for it themselves. Justice is handing them back their hot potato."

He finished his ham and eggs and left, knowing the teamsters would gossip. With any luck, he'd just started a gold rush. Every man in Calaveras County who had nothing better to do would be poking around in any brush-filled canyon or abandoned mine shaft he could think of, with no intention of reporting anything he might find, for it was finders, keepers when it came to color lying about in the open.

He moseyed over to the jailhouse and went in. He found Constable Lovejoy tinkering with the telephone on his desk. He said, "'Morning, Lovejoy. I've got a favor to ask."

Lovejoy said, "I can't get this infernal machine to work. What can I do for you?"

"Well, I don't want to play with your talking telegraph. I never thought it was a practical notion anyhow. Kevin MacLeod will be shipping again by this time tomorrow morning. I was wondering if you could lend him a couple of deputies to ride the train with him."

"Reckon I could, but where do *you* aim to be?"

"Halfway back to Denver, Lord willing. I'm as stuck for answers as the rest of you boys."

Lovejoy grinned and said, "So you're giving up too, eh? I thought you was supposed to be such a smart, sassy detective from the big city!"

"Don't rub it in, old son. I'll allow the rascals are slicker than I reckoned on,"

"I thought you had a rep for never giving up on a case," Lovejoy needled him.

"James Butler Hickok had a rep for never getting shot, too. 'There was never a pony that couldn't be rode, and never a rider that couldn't be throwed,' like the song says."

Lovejoy looked unaccountably pleased as he said, "Well, I ain't thanking you for giving this can of worms back to me. But I could have told you it was too big a boo for any one man. Me and the boys will just have to muddle through until they slip up, or until they steal every ounce of gold in the Lost Chinaman and retire for life."

Longarm said, "You just do the best you know how. I'm wiring my boss for permission to crawfish out of here. I'll probably, be around town for a while, so feel free to call on me if you come up with anything before I get clearance."

Lovejoy said, "It's too bad this here telephone is out of order. I could have saved you a trip to the Western Union office at the county seat if the blamed thing was working right."

Longarm said, "I know. But I'll just mosey over to San Andreas. To tell the truth, I figure Marshal Vail's going to ream my ass for failing him, so I ain't in such an all-fired hurry to give him the news."

He departed, leaving Lovejoy grinning from ear to ear, and mounted up to ride out. Before heading for the county seat, he walked the gelding up the trail to the Lost Chinaman, where he found Kevin MacLeod supervising his men as they hauled rock from the mine. Longarm didn't dismount as he smiled sadly down at MacLeod and explained that he was cashing in his chips.

MacLeod said, "You can't be serious! I'm shipping these cars down in less than twenty-four hours!"

Longarm said, "I know. Lovejoy says he'll have some deputies riding shotgun for you."

"Damn it, Longarm," MacLeod protested, "those townies don't have the sense to spit! If they hit me again I'm a goner! My men are asking for higher wages, since Vallejo and those other two got killed. I don't have enough to stay in operation. The ore *has* to get through this time!"

Longarm shrugged and said, "Ralph Baxter's in Sacramento right now, doubtless wiring for permission to up the ante. You and Lottie could live right nicely with over a million by way of consolation."

MacLeod shook his head and said, "I don't want to be just rich. I want to die *stinking* rich. I've lost nearly a million in bullion since they started high-grading me! Do you have any notion what it feels like to be starving on bread and beans on top of your very own gold mine?"

"Pretty frustrating, I imagine. But face it, MacLeod. The rascals are just too much for either of us. I will file a full report and see if I can get some treasury men up here. Meanwhile, having done all one man can do, I have to get back to my office."

As Longarm rode off, MacLeod shouted, "Damn it, come back here! I'll *pay* you to stay just one more day! I'll give you a quarter share of the gold I'll be shipping!"

But Longarm shook his head and rode on without looking back. He headed for the trail to San Andreas, but as soon as he was well clear of the neighborhood he cut upslope and rode into the mountains. He followed a game trail along a ridge until he came to a lookout point dominating the valley below, and there he dismounted.

He gathered dry twigs and used the papers he'd stolen from Ralph Baxter to start a fire. When it was burning properly, he slipped the saddle off his browsing mount and removed the saddle blanket.

He cut some green branches and threw them on the fire, sending up a billowing cloud of white smoke that smelled like medicine. He piled on more green brush and dropped the blanket across the smoldering mass, trying to remember how he'd seen a friendly Sioux do it, over on the other side of the Rockies.

As the smoke puffs rose in a series of balloon-shaped clouds, a voice behind him asked calmly, "Why are you doing that?"

Without turning, Longarm said, "Howdy, Bitter Water. Acorns any good this year?"

The Indian came out of the brush and squatted at his side, saying, "I have heard of smoke talk, but my people do not use it."

Longarm said, "I know. But lots of folks are ignorant. They'll be spotting this smoke talk about now from all over the county. I'm likely scaring the shit out of everybody down there, considering the Modoc war wasn't all that far back, or all that far away."

Bitter Water frowned and said, "My people are not on the warpath. There are no other bands in these hills. Who are you supposed to be signaling? What are you saying with that smoke?"

"Signaling nobody and saying nothing. A Sioux would likely laugh himself to death at me. But it's my hope that any white man who spots this smoke talk will get his womenfolk and kids inside and round up all his stock. I doubt if anyone will be out hunting deer today, either. When there's smoke talk against the skyline, men don't ride out much unless they have a damned good reason."

Bitter Water pondered this as Longarm shook the dust and ashes from the blanket and sat down cross-legged next to the Indian, who finally nodded and said, "Heya! You intend to pin down all the innocent, unimportant people around Manzanita, then see who still rides abroad on more serious business. It is a good trick—for you. But what of me and my people? Won't the soldiers come to hunt your wild Indians?"

"No. I'm riding over to the county seat to send some wires.

I'll tell the officers who loaned me that gelding that you folks are working for me, but not to tell anyone else."

Longarm took two cheroots from his coat pocket and offered one to Bitter Water, who accepted it with a nod of thanks. The lawman lit the Miwok's cigar and then his own with a burning twig from the fire. They smoked in silence for a while until Bitter Water shook his head and said, "The soldiers may believe you, but I think it is a crazy story. What are we supposed to be helping you to do?"

"Look for outlaws, of course. I'm deputizing your whole tribe."

Bitter Water laughed. "Now I know you are crazy. We Miwok are not lawmen. We stay as far from you people and your crazy laws as we can!"

"Just the same, I'm saying I've deputized your band. When you've a mind to, you can drop by the Indian agency and pick up the dollar a day I'm paying, oh, say thirty of you. I reckon the taxpayers owe you that much anyway, considering."

Bitter Water said, "You are generous, but crazy. If I were one of those outlaws I would see through your scheme. You grow weary with chasing them around in circles, waiting for them to make the next move. So now you are stirring up trouble to give *them* something to worry about!"

Longarm grinned and nodded, saying, "You'd make a tolerable lawman yourself, old son. I reckon the two of us had best be on our way now. You hear that distant tinkle?"

Bitter Water nodded and said, "Church bells. They ring the bells in the church at Manzanita when there is trouble."

"Right. They've spotted this smoke talk and someone's excited as all hell about it. If your band is anywhere near here, I'd take them over a few ridges pronto. They'll likely get everyone to cover and sit tight for our whooping attack, but in case anyone feels brave enough to ride up here before the army sends help . . ."

Bitter Water rose soberly to his feet and said, "We are going over the mountains where the Saltu have not yet cut the pinyons for mine props. It is well I found you. What if we had been caught unawares by your foolishness?"

"Hell, I spotted you watching me from that next ridge before I even lit the fire. In my time I've fought Apache, so I know, better than most, where you folks can be found. I see by the polish on that boulder yonder that you've been using this peak as a lookout for a mighty long time."

Bitter Water laughed again and said, "Let us hope the others do not read sign as well as you do. I go with a glad heart. The money you offer will get us through another hungry winter."

Longarm said, "I figured it might. Listen, Bitter Water. Sooner or later you know you'll have to pack it in. You're a smart cuss. Why don't you lead your folks in to the agency and let them eat regular meals? It's late in the game for the old ways in these hills."

Bitter Water shrugged. "We shall last one more winter, thanks to you. Next spring the camus bulbs will be spread upon the table of the Great Spirit, the manzanita apples will ripen as always, and the acorns never fail us. I know what is in your heart, and you are a good person, but we were not put here to be the tolerated pets of your kind. We will live as we have always lived, or we will die, but we will die as real people. I have spoken."

As the Indian trudged away without looking back, Longarm saddled up and headed for San Andreas.

He rode down to the main road through a canyon, then cut to the north. He rode slowly. At the moment he was simply giving his quarry enough rope to hang themselves. As he passed through a road cut, he was thinking of the little librarian. He had no other serious plans for that evening. A bunch of poppies were growing from the rocky bank of the road cut. Longarm reined in and, leaning in his saddle, reached over for a bunch. A distant rifle snapped, and a high-powered bullet whizzed past his left ear like an angry hornet!

He was leaning anyway, so he just kept going, snatching the Winchester from its boot as he dove headfirst off his spooked mount. The gelding ran off as Longarm hit the dirt on his side, rolled over on his gut in the dust behind a fallen boulder, and levered a .44-40 round into the chamber.

He spotted a drifting cloud of smoke amid the branches of an oak grove he'd just ridden past. The bushwhacker hadn't been laying for him there or he'd be dead right now. The jasper had followed him from Manzanita, seen him outlined nicely in the cut, and let fly.

Longarm had a clear field of fire into the oaks. He could

see that there was little cover in the shade of the overhanging branches, except for the tree trunks themselves. The bushwhacker could be behind a trunk, but it hardly seemed likely. When a gent draws a bead on another man's back, and sees that he's missed, he either fires some more or runs away, and there had only been that one shot.

Longarm strained his ears for the sound of hoofbeats. His own gelding had run out the other side of the cut, but it was grazing now, in a patch of lush mountain meadow to the north. Longarm could hear it chomping wet sedge. It sounded like someone chewing celery. He could hear a distant redwing's doorbell cry, too. The cut he lay in was a natural ear horn. He should have been able to hear the bushwhacker's sounds, if the son of a bitch was making any. So he was either long gone or lying low.

Longarm felt like a fool, spread out on his belly like a lizard in the dust, with the bastard who'd shot at him already halfway home. On the other hand, he'd seen many a man catch a rifle ball between the eyebrows by raising his head too soon for a look-see. In his time, he'd put a few impatient jaspers in the ground himself. So he decided he'd just stay put for a spell. It wasn't as though he had anything more important to do that afternoon than just to keep on breathing.

Longarm sniffed uncertainly as a stray current of breeze carried an ominous odor to his nostrils. *Smoke?*

That was a worrisome thought. The son of a bitch bush-whacker might have set fire to the brush to burn him out.

Longarm removed his trigger finger from the Winchester, leaving the gun braced and aimed at the oaks as his left hand grasped it by the forward grip. He wet his finger and held it up. Such breeze as there was came from the soggy meadow behind him. He was upwind of the oak grove, so the bushwhacker wasn't trying to smoke him out. He *couldn't* smoke him out. Even if he'd circled around and crossed the ridge this cut ran through, the meadow was watered by a meandering stream. *Jesus! You're getting old!* he warned himself, as he shot an anxious glance at the skyline to his left and right.

He was down between two rises. They'd told him in the army always to take to the high ground. If the bushwhacker was up on either ridge right now, he could be creeping in Apache-style. If he got to the top of either side of the cut, he could drop anything from piss to bullets on any fool lying spread out below.

Longarm shot one more pensive glance at the oak grove, decided it was the lesser danger, and started to get up.

Something stung him on the right hip. It felt like he had a pocketful of red ants or maybe a lit cigar in his britches!

Certain that he'd rolled on a scorpion in the dust, Longarm glanced down at his side as he started to climb the side of the cut. Blue tendrils of smoke were curling from the side pocket of his frock coat. He swore and started shucking out of the coat. Now he knew what he'd been smelling. It was the acid—the bottle of aqua regia he'd stolen from Baxter's kit. The goddamned bottle had broken when he had dived off the gelding!

Dropping the coat, Longarm kept going up, taking one emergency at a time. Some of the acid had soaked through to his longjohns. Baxter had said the stuff would dissolve pure gold, but a bullet tended to smart where it hit you, too.

There was no sense in sticking one's head over a rim where someone might be expecting company. So Longarm simply leaped over the top of the rise and crabbed to his left, training his Winchester down the length of the ridge. It was covered with cheat grass bleached tawny by the summer sun. The nice thing about cheat was that it only grew a few inches tall before going to seed and dying off. So there was no cover to worry about. The bushwhacker had fired a single shot and lit out, leaving the tall deputy with the ridge to himself and smoke pouring out of his right pants pocket.

Hoping nobody important was coming up or down the road from either direction, Longarm unbuckled his gunbelt and let it fall around his ankles. Holding the rifle in one hand, he started fumbling at his pants as he ran down the slope toward his grazing mount. The gelding shied and loped off a few yards, dragging its reins through the grass. But Longarm wasn't after the canteen hanging from the saddle. Not with a whole running brook right in front of him.

He had the trousers down around his thighs and had unbuttoned the longjohns by the time he ran the last few yards to the brook and plopped down bare-assed, with his hide starting to smell like he'd just been roped, thrown and branded!

As the cooling mountain stream washed over him from the

waist down, Longarm sat there with the Winchester across his knees and began to laugh like a jackass. He was aware of the ludicrous picture he presented—a grown man sitting bare-assed in the middle of a meadow in his shirtsleeves, vest, and Stetson, holding a rifle like a fishing pole. But he kept an eye on the treeline all around, just the same. Explaining what he was doing would be bad enough, if some carriage filled with womenfolk came along. If the bushwhacker was still skulking in the neighborhood, he might laugh too. Then again, he might not. Longarm knew he was a tempting target at the moment.

Gingerly, he rose far enough to survey the damage. The acid had burned through his tweed pants and cotton longjohns. He hoped it had lost some of its strength in digesting less important stuff than human hide. The burn wasn't all that bad. It looked and felt as if he had brushed against a hot stove. He'd been, lucky. The bottle had broken and leaked out into his coat pocket as he lay facedown in the cut, with the coattails spread out to his sides. Most of the acid had simply run into the dirt. What hadn't had ruined his duds and nearly ruined him, but he could buy new clothes and his rump would be all right.

He decided that the running water must have washed the acid away by now, so he pulled on his pants and got to his feet. As he squished back to where he'd left the coat, he explored his pockets. His jackknife was well oiled, so it wouldn't rust. His wallet and paper money were in the coat, on the dry side. He shook out the loose change that had been closest to the acid and whistled. Baxter had been right about the stuff being mean. A couple of silver dimes were stuck together and a penny had been gold-plated. A ten-dollar gold eagle was etched badly and silvered on one side from the dimes. He was glad he hadn't been lying right on top of the stuff.

His coat was still smoldering, so he held it out to one side as he emptied the pockets and carried it over to the brook to rinse it out. By the time he'd gotten it to stop smoking, it was a total loss. A few moth holes were allowable in an old tweed coat, but this was ridiculous. It looked like it had been attacked by wolves.

Longarm picked up his gunbelt and strapped it back on. Holding the rifle and the wet coat, he waltzed across the meadow after the skittish gelding, who seemed to think they were playing matador and bull.

Just as Longarm began seriously to consider shooting the gelding once and for all, it stopped dancing away and began to study a clump of wild onion as Longarm, swearing at it, lashed the wet coat to the saddle skirt, slid the rifle into its boot, and mounted up.

Wet from the waist down and sounding like an Indian squaw pounding her laundry on a rock, Longarm rode on. The thin mountain air was warm and dry, so by the time he got to San Andreas, his only wet clothes were his socks. He knew his boots would curl up like cardboard if he took them off to dry, so he left them on. The leather would mold to his feet and stay supple.

He stopped first at a drugstore. He went in, told the laconic old man behind the counter he'd sat in some aqua regia, and asked what the druggist suggested he do about it.

The old man led him into a back room and ordered him to drop his britches again. As he studied Longarm's rump, he said, "Only a first-degree burn. Lucky for you there was running water handy. I've got some camphorated bear grease we might try."

The deputy grimaced distastefully. "Ain't you got anything that doesn't stink so bad, Doc? I was aiming to buy some new pants, and—"

"We'll just butter your ass a mite with spermaceti, then," the druggist said. "How does that suit you? Sperm whale oil smells sort of sweet."

"Yeah. I'd best spring for some cologne water, too. Every time I inhale, I smell burnt wool. You know, that fool acid smells like metal, even when you wash it away?"

"Metallic ions," said the druggist, as he started to paint Longarm's burn with a cotton swab dipped in the sweet-smelling oil. The old man muttered on about the way acids and alkalies worked, but Longarm was a bit weary of the subject by this time. He was annoyed at himself for ever having taken the stuff, and considered himself more of an expert on aqua regia than he'd ever intended to be.

Leaving the druggist, and smelling much better, Longarm rode the gelding to the livery and bedded it down. He took the ruined coat and walked back the way he'd just ridden, looking for a tailor shop he'd spotted before. He found the shop, and sure enough, the sign in the window said they sold ready-to-wear as well as tailor-made.

He went in to discuss his wardrobe. The tailor clucked over the acid burns and said he had a suit similar to the ruined one. Since Longarm never bought anything but ready-to-wear, this came as no great surprise.

The new coat was almost a perfect match for the tobacco-tweed vest. The pants were a little short, but Longarm said they'd do. A few holes in his longjohns weren't worth getting excited about in summer.

The tailor said, "You could use a new hat, too. I just got in a new line of Stetsons and you've been beating hell out of that one you have on."

Longarm took off his hat and regarded it soberly. Aside from the old bullet hole in the telescoped crown and a little wear and tear, he noticed a dime-sized hole in the brim. He fingered the charred edge. A drop of the acid must have spattered on it, probably when the bottle in his pocket first broke. He was glad it had missed the side of his head, or more importantly, his eyes. The acid had worn itself out eating felt and the hole was dry.

Longarm said he was in a line of work that hardly called for new hats. He paid for the new clothing with a government expense voucher, then he went out, feeling like a sissy and smelling of cologne and moth balls.

He went to the Drover's Rest Hotel and engaged a room, saying he intended to stay in town until he received orders to leave for Denver.

He'd told Lovejoy—and everyone else in Manzanita who'd listen—that he was giving up on the case. The constable had that telephone and would undoubtedly check around the county as soon as the wire was fixed. When he did, he'd find nothing putting Longarm anywhere near the Lost Chinaman or the next ore shipment. Longarm wondered if the Indian trouble would be enough of a distraction. He considered starting a forest fire, but decided it might not be neighborly. A forest fire would certainly distract pure Ned out of just about the whole county, but it was August and the California hills were tinder-dry as they waited for the healing winter rains from the Pacific. A wildfire this time of the year could get out of control and hurt innocent people. He figured at least half the citizens of Manzanita had to be innocent.

He went to the Western Union office. He was aware that the telegraphers were not allowed to divulge the contents of wired messages, but he knew that the pimply-faced kid who ran the office probably drank with Sheriff Marvin and everyone else in town. So, while it meant more time and trouble, he wrote his messages in code.

He sent one to an old friend in the War Department, telling him not to pay too much attention to any rumors he might hear about the bloodthirsty Digger Indians boiling down from the rimrock to rape the livestock and drive off the women.

The young telegrapher stared at the sheet of yellow flimsy and said, "I can't make head or tail of this, mister. This message looks like it was written in Greek, or maybe Chinese!"

Longarm said, "You just send it the way I wrote it, boy. I ain't paying you to understand it."

The youth looked at the address and said, "Oh, War Department stuff, huh? I'll bet you're telling them about the Miwok, right?"

"That's close enough," Longarm said. He'd been told that, to date, the U.S. army had spent over a thousand dollars for each and every Indian, friendly or otherwise, west of the Mississippi. Sooner or later he was going to have to explain his actions to Uncle Sam, and his expense account would hardly cover a fruitless military expedition.

He wet the tip of a pencil stub and composed a longer message to Marshal Billy Vail in the Denver office while the telegrapher sent his coded message to the War Department.

Longarm knew his boss wouldn't go along with half the notions he had in mind, but Vail had warned him not to go crazy anymore without a word of warning or at least some slight explanation. So Longarm brought his superiors up to date. He explained that he was pretending to back off, and then outlined what he intended to do next. He may have skimmed over some details, for he knew Vail was a worrier. That was the trouble with a lawman who worked behind a desk. Out in the field, a man did what he had to. Sitting in an office filled with books of rules and regulations, a man could lose sight of objectives. Longarm wasn't on this side of the High Sierra to enforce pettifogging regulations dreamed up by some idiot in Washington. He was here to find out who was high-grading Uncle Sam's gold, and to make the bastards stop.

It was that one word, *stop*, that caused Vail so much needless worry. The big shots in the Justice Department seemed to think Longarm's job was to build up watertight cases that would hold up in court. But Longarm was not a lawyer. He knew his law well enough, he supposed. He knew how often some son of a bitch got off on a technicality, too. So he tended to settle his cases with more dispatch and permanency than Marshal Vail thought was decent.

He knew it would take his office time to receive and decode his message. So, after paying the confused Western Union clerk, he said he'd be back in the afternoon to see if there was an answer waiting for him. He didn't add that he had no intention of ever letting on he'd received one, if Vail told him not to overstep his authority again.

Longarm looked at his watch and saw that it was nearly noon. So he moseyed over to the library to catch up on his reading—and whatever.

The same librarian was on duty, so he sent her up the ladder after some more chemistry books. He noticed that her ankles were still as pretty as they had been before, so he sent her up again after a tome on ore recovery. The mining book was heavy and she lost her balance on the way down. Longarm caught her and said, "Steady on, ma'am."

The girl flushed as she turned her head away and said, "Oh, I'm so clumsy."

Longarm tended to agree, but it was nice to know she trusted him to catch her.

He said, "My name is Custis Long and, like I said the other day, I work for the Justice Department as a field deputy."

She handed him the book and smiled shyly, saying, "I'm Pru Sawyer, and I wish I worked just about anywhere else."

"Don't you like books, ma'am?"

She brushed a stray tendril of hair away from her face. "There's a limit to what you can get from books, and they start smelling musty, after a time."

She shot him an arch look as she added, "I notice you've put on some cologne since the last time."

"Had to," he said. "I was all stunk up with chemicals and water lilies."

They stood there smiling awkwardly for a few moments. Finally, her hands moved spasmodically, as if she didn't know where to put them, and she went back to her desk.

Longarm sat down too, and began to skim through the books while he felt her eyes burning holes in the back of his neck. Few people seemed to come in here. Her days here were undoubtedly boring for her.

He wondered idly why so many men were put off by educated women. He supposed it was because education gives a person a certain amount of independence, and most men didn't care much for that in women. He smiled at the idea that most men couldn't feel strong and smart except when they could measure themselves against someone weaker and stupider. Longarm was not a man in need of such reassurance. He thought of Nellie Bly, the young lady reporter he had met in the Indian Nation a while back, and remembered with a concealed grin that her intelligence, independence, and strength of will hadn't diminished one whit their enjoyment of each other.

With an effort, he turned his attention to the books before him. There wasn't a thing in them he hadn't already read or been told about. But he had time to kill. None of the professors who wrote about gold recovery had considered high-grading.

Most high-graders tended to be petty thieves who either took a job in a mine or trespassed in the diggings when folks weren't looking. Nine out of ten lumps of ore looked like nothing much before they were crushed and refined. If there was a glitter of color showing, the lump was worth stealing, even a rock at a time. The average high-grader simply filled his pockets with rich ore, carried it off, and did his own refining with a nine-pound sledge and a prospector's pan. A man could wash a few hundred dollars a day from stuff with visible color.

But the Lost Chinaman's missing ore wasn't rich enough to refine by such methods. A thief down in some canyon could work for a month of Sundays with running water and not pan out enough to make it pay much more than if he'd been washing dishes for money instead.

He looked up cyanide. The entry didn't tell him much. Cyanide melted or dissolved the metal from the quartz too, a bit better, although somewhat more slowly, than acid. He knew the high-graders had cyanide; he'd smelled it on the dead men's breath and in the wine they'd been tricked with. But every mine in the county undoubtedly had some cyanide handy, and half the local Mexicans made their own wine. That line of inquiry was too fuzzy to bother following up on.

Pru Sawyer came over from her desk and sat down beside him. They were alone in the place, so he wondered why she whispered as she said, "It's almost siesta time, Marshal. I'm afraid we have to close the library until three this afternoon."

He stretched and said, "I'm about done here, in any case. You folks hereabouts follow Mexican notions?"

"You mean about the siesta hours? I'm afraid we do. Nobody will be stirring in town until later this afternoon, when it starts to cool off." She looked down at her hands, which were tangled together in her lap, and added, "Most of us eat and then go home to take a little nap during the hotter part of the afternoon."

He said, "I know how siestas work. I ain't never been one for snoozing in broad daylight, but I'll find something to do. I have to wait for a telegram before I can ride out, anyway."

"Oh, you're leaving San Andreas? I mean, for good?" she asked with what Longarm was sure was a definite hint of disappointment.

He nodded soberly, and said, "I was starting to like it here, too. I'd, uh, offer to buy you a meal, but I reckon you'll have to go home to your folks, eh? I mean, I notice you ain't wearing a wedding band."

She didn't look up at him as she murmured, "I live alone. I'm not from this part of the country, Marshal."

He grinned and said, "You don't have to keep calling me Marshal; I ain't talking official business with you. Most people I'm friendly with call me Longarm."

She looked a little confused, then brightened and said, "Oh, I see. 'Long arm of the law,' and all that."

"Well," he continued, "seeing as we're both strangers in these parts, with nobody expecting us home for the siesta and all, I'd take it kindly if you'd have a bite with me, uh, before your nap or whatever." Before she could take that the wrong way, he quickly added, "If you know a restaurant that won't poison us too bad, I'm on an expense account and you can eat anything you've a mind to."

She hesitated, her hairline going pink like sunset along a high ridge before she said, "The only café near here serves dreadful food."

He closed the book he'd been reading with a snap of finality and said, "Well, you can't say I never offered, ma'am."

She looked up at him, her eyes moist and thoughtful as she asked, "Will you be by later, Longarm?"

"Doubt it. You're right about books. You can only get so much out of any book. After that, you have to go out in the real world for whatever you're after."

She said, "I know. Uh, we could sort of eat at my house, if you're not in too much of a hurry. I mean, I live just down the street, and—"

Longarm nodded and said, "That's right neighborly of you, ma'am."

Chapter 8

Somewhere a clock chime was tolling two o'clock. Longarm propped himself up on one elbow and muttered, "Got to get on over to the telegraph office." But the girl at his side on the rumpled bedding pleaded, "Don't go yet, darling. We have until three before I have to go back to that dusty old library!"

He smiled at her fondly and said, "I never said I wasn't coming back."

Pru Sawyer was a funny little gal. She'd refused to take her chemise off even after he'd gotten them in bed and down to serious loving after a bit of sparring about across her kitchen table. She made tolerable coffee and awful flapjacks, but he'd eaten four of the damned things. The scattered sunlight through the drawn lace curtains of her bedroom dappled her pale, nude rump and legs with golden spangles as she lay beside him on her belly, one arm across his waist. She said, "You told me about expecting a telegram from Denver, but can't it wait?"

He ran his free hand down her spine and fondled her firm little bottom, explaining, "If I get the authorization I need, I may have to ride into Sacramento. I want to get there before the banks and such close."

"Pooh, the banks close at three. You'd never make it even if you left right now."

"I don't aim to make any deposits or withdrawals, honey. The bankers won't be out of the building before six and I knock plenty loud."

"Are you staying there tonight? I wish you'd take me with you."

He ran his fingers between her buttocks absently and shook his head, saying, "No. I figure on a fast round trip. If you want, you can put a light in your window for me. I'll be back before too late for more of your cooking."

She giggled and said, "You knew from the first I was wild, didn't you?"

He said, "I was hoping so. You must get tired of reading all the time."

"I get tired of the sort of men I usually meet in that, place, too."

Longarm thought it was ironic that mousy little gals who looked like butter wouldn't melt in their mouths were usually wilder than all hell in bed. Probably thinking about it all the time was what made them blush so much.

She arched her back and wriggled her bottom as he explored it, saying, "You're getting me all hot and bothered doing that."

He said, "Just getting to know you better. How come you keep that shimmy shirt on like that? It ain't civilized to make love with half your clothes on."

"I just couldn't let you see me naked in broad daylight," she told him.

"How come? It ain't like we were strangers."

"I know, dearest, but I just feel funny about it." Abruptly she turned over, spreading her legs and pulling him on top of her. She wrapped her naked arms and legs around him as he quickly entered her. The chemise annoyed him and he bent his head down to grab the cotton over one breast between his teeth. She giggled and gyrated as he started pulling it up between their bellies, a mouthful at a time. As their moist, bare bellies rubbed together, she suddenly reached down to grab the hem and pull the shift up over her breasts and beyond, gasping, "Oh, yes, it does feel ever so much nicer naked!"

Still moving inside her, he helped her get it all the way off and she threw it across the room.

By the time they were through, they were halfway on the floor. Her hair was brushing the carpet as she bounced her hips all over the bed. Longarm braced a foot against the wall, and put a palm on the floor to keep from diving out on his head. She was still talking about how good it had been while he pulled on his boots.

As he was buttoning his vest, Pru tried to unbutton his fly. He laughed and shoved her hand away, promising, "I'll be back before you cool off enough to mention, honey. But I've really got to git."

"Are you sure you're not just trifling with my emotions? I've heard about you love-'em-and-leave-'em cowboys!"

Longarm had little doubt that she had. She'd probably worn a few down to a nub, too. But he knew the rules of the game, so he said, "I ain't a cowboy, I'm a public servant. When I ride back this way, I aim to trifle hell put of your emotions and anything else I can get my hands on."

Then he strapped on his six-gun, donned his frock coat, and put his Stetson on, insisting, "Got to get cracking, honey. Leave that light in your window and, like the poet says, 'I'll come to thee at midnight, though hell should bar the way.'"

As he kissed her goodbye and left, she sighed, "Oh, you're so romantic . . . sort of."

Longarm let himself out the side door, but strode boldly out to the plank walk, for skulking out of a lady's home in broad daylight or any other time draws more attention than walking tall, as if he were perhaps a visiting minister, a door-to-door drummer, or whatever.

An older woman in a sun bonnet was coming up the walk as Longarm left Pru's gate. Longarm touched the brim of his Stetson with a friendly smile and said, "Howdy, ma'am. Nice day, ain't it?"

The old biddy sniffed and said, "Well! I never!"

Longarm hadn't asked her if she ever, for she was a bit long in the tooth and as homely as a chicken's ass. He and Pru had probably made her day for her. But it was no concern of his what the backyard gossips said about the new gal at the library. He'd been invited fair and square, and it was up to Pru to consider what her neighbors thought.

At the telegraph office he found Billy Vail's message waiting for him:

HAVE YOU BEEN DRINKING **STOP** US GOVERNMENT
CANNOT BE PARTY TO YOUR LATEST INSANITY **STOP** YOU
ARE OUT THERE TO CATCH CROOKS NOT TO DRIVE
WHOLE STATE OF CALIFORNIA CRAZY **STOP** SUGGEST
YOU STICK TO BOOK AND CONDUCT PROPER

INVESTIGATION **STOP** VAIL US MARSHAL DISTRICT COURT
OF DENVER

Longarm swore softly, balled the telegram up, and threw it
in the tin wastebasket. The adenoidal operator opined, "Whatever that coded message you sent him was, he didn't like it
much, did he?"

Longarm didn't answer. He walked outside, went to the livery, and retrieved his mount. Then he lit out for Sacramento,
riding fast.

The manager at the Crocker bank in Sacramento was an old-
timer who'd panned for color without much luck in the rush of
'49. So he knew about high-grading, claim jumping, and the
other crooked notions gold brought out in people. He was bored
with paperwork, too, so he was more than willing to converse
with a deputy U.S. marshal on almost any subject.

They chewed on the high-grading of the Lost Chinaman
until they had most of the juice out of it and the banker said
he would go along with Longarm as far as the law allowed. He
said some of what the lawman suggested was slightly unethi-
cal, but when Longarm pointed out that high-grading was un-
ethical too, the banker laughed and sent a clerk for the account
records.

Longarm spread the account books out on the banker's desk
and pored over them. As he ran a finger down a line of figures,
the banker said, "I didn't know you rootin', tootin' riders for
Uncle Sam were interested in bookkeeping."

Longarm sighed and answered, "We don't get to root and
toot all the time. Two-thirds of this fool job is just boring routine. Before we get to arrest most folks, we have to ask the same
fool questions over and over, and most of the leads we follow
wind up nowhere much."

"Ain't life a humdrum bitch? What are you looking for there,
Longarm?"

"Lies, mostly. Everyone I've met so far out here has a plau-
sible tale and an innocent reason for being wheresoever and
doing whatsoever. At least one of them has to be a crook."

He found the last entry he was looking for, closed the book,
and sat back, muttering, "Shit."

Then he took out a cheroot and put it between his teeth, neglecting to light it.

The banker asked what was wrong and Longarm explained, "Everyone's told the goddamned truth about their finances. Lucky for me you run the biggest bank in these parts, so everyone who has enough money to mention banks the same place. The Baxters have the credit rating they told me they have. Kevin MacLeod and his wife are almost as broke as they say they are, since their account is running thin. I see the Vallejo family has the wherewithal to lay out the thousand they offered for the land the mine is sitting on, and Constable Lovejoy has no more in his account than modest graft would call for. I notice you didn't show me the records of the mining company at Sheep Ranch."

The banker nodded firmly and said, "I don't intend to show you, either. Folks like the Hearsts, Stanfords, Ralstons, Hopkinses, and such don't take kindly to having their finances bruited about."

"I could likely get a court order."

"From Justice Stephen Field? That's funny as hell. Look, you're a nice young fellow and I like you. But take my advice and back off asking about the big shots who own this state. You'll never in a million years hang a stolen nickel on old George Hearst or his friends."

"Even if I catch them stealing from the U.S. Mint?"

"Shit, Longarm, who do you think *owns* the U.S. Mint?"

"The taxpaying public, according to the U.S. Constitution."

"Son, the Constitution doesn't apply to folks as rich and powerful as those old boys. But aside from the danger to your job if you piss them off, I'd say you were way off base. No big outfit like the Sheep Ranch mine would be interested in stealing ore. They've *got* ore! I'll tell you—off the record—Hearst and Ralston own half of the Big Bonanza over in Virginia City. They've staked claims to the Black Hills ore that Custer got killed over. George Hearst has an interest in that new Anaconda outfit up in Butte, Montana. Hell, all the gold the high-graders have stolen from Kevin MacLeod wouldn't pay the salaries of old George's house niggers!"

Longarm said, "I never suggested that anyone as big as an owner might be high-grading. I don't suspect Huntington or

Stanford of playing games with railroad switches, either. But you're right about lots of folks *working* for those big shots. Many a hardworking cuss has plenty of reasons for wanting a bigger slice of the pie. Don't the branch managers of mining properties work on commission?"

The banker frowned and said, "Now that you mention it, they might. You ain't as dumb as you look. Have you studied the men who run the refinery south of town? They get a bonus on the bullion they extract from ore, too!"

Longarm nodded and said, "I mean to have a talk with them later. I don't think they lied to MacLeod about the ore he's been delivering."

The banker narrowed his eyes and pursed his lips as he muttered, "I know this sounds pretty raw and obvious, but have you considered how easy it would be to give MacLeod a false assay? I mean, we don't know the so-called worthless rock never went through the stamping mill *later*, say around midnight."

Longarm grinned and said, "That was one of the first things I came up with, but it won't wash. I was there when they ran the assay. Later on, I sort of snooped around the rock piles down the track. You see, I took the liberty of marking a few lumps of MacLeod's ore when they told him it was worthless. It's still just lying there. Besides that, they've got too many workers at the refinery to play so rough a game on folks. I've added up such refined-out bullion as there could be in ore twice as rich, and I arrived at a figure for the gang."

"You know how many high-graders there are?" the banker asked.

"Nope. I know how many there might possibly be, though. We're dealing with sophisticated professional thieves, or they'd have been caught by the first lawmen who looked for them. Professionals don't steal pennies. Allowing each possible member of the outfit at least a few hundred dollars each time a shipment's diverted, there can't be more than two dozen or so in on it, counting payoffs to folks who just look the other way. There're just too many folks to pay off down here at the Sacramento end. The ones I want are operating out of Calaveras County."

"That still takes in a mess of folks, son."

Longarm rose from his chair as he said, "I know. And since I don't aim to arrest you, I'd best be on my way. I thank you kindly for cooperating with me as far as your regulations allow."

Leaving the Crocker bank, Longarm walked over to the land office for another visit.

The man who remembered Mark Twain, although not the celebrated Jumping Frog of Calaveras County, was not on duty that afternoon. This did not make the tall deputy at all unhappy, for he wanted to see if they always gave out the same tale to visiting lawmen.

They did. Longarm talked to an almost-pretty girl named Justine. She said she was a miner's widow and that she'd gotten the job on merit. It was amazing how many women were holding down men's jobs, these days. Likely it had something to do with Queen Victoria, Longarm thought. Back when he was a kid, before the War, he never saw women in offices with pencils stuck in their hair. Ever since the English had allowed a woman to be ruler of the British Empire, it was getting harder and harder to say no to a female applicant. Which was the way things should be, he supposed, but he found it difficult to do real business without cussing.

Justine took him back to her cubbyhole and told him she knew all about the Spanish land grants he was interested in. As he sat down across from her, she started by correcting him. "Actually, the so-called old Spanish grants you hear about in California were never granted by the Spanish crown. When Mexico declared its independence in 1821, California was sparsely settled. Aside from the missions, they had a few military garrisons: the San Francisco Presidio, Monterey, and so forth."

Longarm smiled at her, wondering if she wore her hair in that tight little bun to look more down-to-business, or if she really had no notion of fashion. He asked, "Are you saying folks like the Vallejos are full of bull when they brag about all the wild mustard they used to own?"

Justine shook her head and said, "No. Mexico gave away vast tracts of land in hopes of filling up this part of the continent before we got around to claiming it as our manifest destiny. The Russians were moving down the West Coast from Alaska, too, and the Hudson Bay trappers must have worried Mexico City. I know the Vallejo grant. It was one of the big ones. But the family obtained it from Mexico, not Spain."

"Ain't we sort of picking nits, ma'am? I understand the conceit your California Mexicans have about being called Spanish. But I don't see how it matters all that much."

Justine sniffed and said, "It's rather pathetic, but most of the early settlers were Spanish or Mexican *soldados*. Male, of course. The distaff half of the old grandees tended to be Indian squaws. The last Mexican governor of California was a Negro."

"That's what I just said." He frowned. He wondered if she was so precise in bed, and if it would be worth finding out. The girl explained, "The treaty of '48 between our government and Mexico recognized the holdings of former Mexican nationals. A real Spanish-grant would be meaningless unless it had been confirmed by Mexico before the Mexican War and the resultant treaty. Most of the mission lands, for instance, were taken from the Church by Mexico before we got here. So the missions are simply empty shells today."

"What happened to the mission Indians?"

"They, ah, lost out in the shuffle. People like the Vallejos, Irvines, and Castros had sense enough to hire good lawyers."

"I heard about the Irvine Ranch, down past Pueblo Los Angeles. They didn't lose so much as a quarter section, did they?"

"The Irvine holdings are huge, even by land grant standards," she averred. "The Scotsman who married into that family had a good lawyer."

"He was white, too. The way I hear it, how much land you got to keep depended a little on your complexion."

Justine looked pained and said, "That's not fair. Poor Sutter lost his mill and everything else, and he was as white as you or me. The land office is not prejudiced, as some Mexicans seem to think."

Longarm smiled crookedly and said, "Sure it ain't. I've no doubt that all the land that was grabbed was grabbed fair and square. But it's the Vallejo holdings I'm interested in. The Lost Chinaman mine sits smack-dab on land the Vallejos used to own. I'd like to know how come."

Justine said, "I can tell you that without looking it up. Old land grants have priority over homestead claims. Mining claims come before agriculture."

"You mean if I was to find a gold mine on any land at all—even if it was occupied—I could just up and *take* it?"

"Of course. You wouldn't need to strike gold. Copper, silver, or mercury would do as well. Once you'd staked out the limits of your find and registered it with the California Mining Commission, it would be all yours."

Longarm's eyebrows rose. "Back up, ma'am! You mean I could start a mine anywhere at all? Suppose someone had a house already built over it?"

She shrugged and said, "It's happened. It's led to messy gunfights, too. Few old land titles include the mineral rights, as poor old Sutter found out when they panned the soil out from under his mill and general store."

Longarm frowned and said, "That hardly seems fair, ma'am."

"I never said it was. But the men who wrote the California laws were mining men, and the law is the law."

Longarm whistled softly under his breath as he mulled her words over in his head. Then he said, "I can see how the Vallejos lost the land the Lost Chinaman sets on. Is there any legal way they can get it back?"

"Not as long as there's a viable mine site up there. The owner of a mine is the landlord of record. He can transfer the property, hold it for land speculation, or do just about anything he likes. The original owners have no say. The only way they could hope to recover the property would be by buying out the mineral rights. This happens too, occasionally."

Longarm shook his head and said, "Felicidad Vallejo ain't got the wherewithal to buy a going gold mine. But what if the mine was to play out and be abandoned?"

Justine pursed her lips. Longarm noticed that they pursed nicely. She said, "As I recall, the mine you speak of did pinch but a few years ago. But the owners hung on and sold it recently. I could look the new owners up for you, if you like."

"I know Kevin MacLeod and his wife, ma'am. The cud I'm chewing is the final outcome of the mess. Am I right in figuring that the Mexicans who used to own the property could get it back if the Lost Chinaman went out of business for keeps?"

Justine nodded and said, "If the mine shut down and nobody else put in a mineral claim."

He stroked his mustache pensively for a moment, then asked,

"What if the mine went broke, but some other outfit was to buy it?"

"They'd own it, of course. As long as anyone is working a mine, or even sitting tight over a hole in the ground, the original property owners are simply out of luck."

He swore under his breath and said, "I can see I'm chasing my fool self smack down another blind alley, most likely. But I thank you kindly for lighting the way."

She smiled rather warmly, considering the severe way she wore her hair, and asked, "I take it you're working on a process of elimination, sir?"

"You can call me Longarm, ma'am, and I've eliminated myself out onto another durned limb. I've got maybe one more arrow in my fool quiver, and if that doesn't work, I've met up with some cuss who's too durned smart for me."

He started to rise. Then he thought better of it, since he faced a lonely night ride back to the county seat in the first place, and wasn't in all that great a hurry in the second.

He said, "I can see you're anxious to close, ma'am, since it's creeping up on four-thirty. Do you, uh, live around here?"

Justine nodded and said, "Just a few blocks over." Then she added, "With a very possessive gentleman."

He said, "Do tell? I didn't notice a wedding band, ma'am."

Her smile was smug when she nodded and told him, "I never said I was married. I suppose you might call me an emancipated woman."

He shot a wry, wistful grin at her and rose to his feet, saying, "I won't keep you from enjoying your constitutional rights, ma'am."

As he let himself out with a slightly mocking bow, she grinned up at him and said, "Nice try, cowboy."

He left, frowning. He didn't think he looked very much like a cowboy, and his "try" hadn't been much more than common courtesy. He'd seen no need to twist the knife like that.

Then, as he walked out into the sunlight, he began to laugh. It sure beat all how women kept surprising him, but wouldn't life get tedious if a man was right every time? He headed for a café across the street to put away some chili and maybe some apple pie, telling himself, *What the hell, old son, you can't win 'em all!*

* * *

The next twenty-four hours were enjoyable, but had little to do with the case, since he spent as many of them as he could with Pru Sawyer. By the time he said goodbye a second time, she'd gotten over any inhibitions she'd ever had about nudity or anything else. She told him she'd read all the books about such matters that were in the library, but that he'd shown her a few tricks they hadn't mentioned. It was good to know he'd helped a young lady's education; she obviously intended to put it to good use. He almost felt sorry for the next gent she snared with her downcast eyes and shy little smile.

Nobody shot at him as he rode back toward Manzanita. His smoke signals seemed to have left the roads in a deserted condition and nobody was expecting him.

He circled up through the trees behind the Lost Chinaman, tethered his mount in a brushy draw, and eased up to a ridge that offered him a clear view of the diggings.

He'd timed his arrival well. The ore cars had been hauled away.

MacLeod and Lovejoy's deputies were well on their way to the mill with the latest shipment. He watched, chewing an unlit cheroot. He wasn't sure just what he expected to see. But until now, everyone had been watching the ore shipments. That train pulling out was the misdirection the book had been talking about. He was watching the stage instead of the magician's flashing hands.

Nothing much seemed to be going on. Some workmen brought a car of ore up out of the mine. Lottie MacLeod walked over from the cabin and he could see that she was directing them to put it on the lift and load it in the tipple. He could have figured out where the ore should go, but MacLeod had said they were using unskilled help.

The woman went back to the cabin and the men walked slowly back to the mine entrance and disappeared. It was pretty uninteresting. A jay sassed Longarm from an overhead branch for a while. Then, getting no answer, it lost interest too, and flew off to bother someone else.

Lottie came out of the cabin again and began hanging up some wash to dry. Longarm scanned the treeline all around. There wasn't any movement. Nothing worth thinking about was happening down there. But Longarm kept watching. He had no idea what the magician's assistants might be up to as everyone watched where they were supposed to. But if he knew what he was supposed to be looking for, he wouldn't have to look.

He took out his Ingersoll watch and studied it. MacLeod and the others would be on their way back from the refinery by this time. If they came by stage, they'd be back around sundown. If they got the railroad to give them a ride back on the empties, it would be sooner.

The afternoon wore on. Not a damned thing happened. He waited a good two hours, made himself sit there for one more, then grunted, "All right. Either that magic book was wrong, or the pea is under some other shell."

He crawled back to his horse and mounted up. He circled wide of the diggings and rode slowly into Manzanita. He tied the gelding in front of the saloon and went in. He bought a bottle of Maryland rye and took it to a corner table, where he sat with his back wedged in the corner. When a cowhand came in and started to walk over to the music box, Longarm asked him not to play "Garryowen." The cowhand shrugged and settled for a beer at the bar.

After a while Ralph Baxter came in. He sat down across from Longarm and said, "I saw your horse outside. I thought you were leaving."

Longarm said, "I did leave. Now I'm back. My office wants me to look into a few more angles before I'm relieved."

Baxter said, "Our rooms were searched while we were in Sacramento."

Longarm said, "I figured as much. Mine was, too."

"The desk clerk told me. What on earth do you suppose they were looking for?"

"Don't know. What was taken?"

"Nothing. Nothing important. What are you missing?"

"The same. They were likely barking up the wrong tree. You say you went to Sacramento?"

"Yes. I've been authorized to offer two million for the Lost Chinaman, but that's the end of it. If they won't sell at that price, they're welcome to any gold they can get out of there. Frankly, I'd have broken off negotiations at a hundred thousand. That fool hasn't made that much since he reopened the mine."

Longarm poured himself a drink, holding the bottle out to Baxter. The Bostonian sniffed and shook his head. So Longarm sipped at his own drink and said, "So far, nobody seems to want to let him. The bank draft you're offering MacLeod is from the Crocker Trust, right?"

Baxter nodded with a frown and said, "As a matter of fact, it is. How did you know?"

"I rode into Sacramento myself to discuss high finances yesterday afternoon. They tell me your outfit's been known to play rough, but their checks don't bounce. By the way, did you bring your, uh, sister or whatever back to Manzanita this time?"

Baxter flushed and snapped, "Don't be crude, God damn it. We both know what Sylvia is. She tends to gloat about it. The only reason I don't beat the tar out of you is simply that there's a long line ahead of you. I'd have time for little else if I intended to thrash every yokel she's known in the Biblical sense."

Longarm stared down at his glass and said, "Yeah. She is sort of Biblical, but you didn't say where she was at."

"I'm afraid you'll just have to make do with your little Mexican thing tonight. We heard there was Indian trouble up this way, so I left Sylvia in Sacramento. I assume she'll find something to occupy her time while I settle this more important matter."

Longarm didn't ask how the jasper knew about Felicidad. That was the trouble with small towns. He said, "You ain't scared of Indians, huh?"

Baxter grimaced and replied, "I simply want to buy the damned property and get out of this stupid country. I have no intention of riding out into the hills where they can get at my scalp."

Longarm nodded, fished out a smoke, and lit up before he said, "There's one thing I don't understand about your offer or your outfit, Baxter. We both know there's more to worry about out here than a few Indians. That mine's been hit high and low and sideways by high-graders. Three men and a dog have been murdered and nobody has an educated guess as to who's behind it all. Yet you're willing to lay out good money for MacLeod's claim. Do you know something I might not, or were you just born foolish?"

Baxter said in a low voice, "If you haven't guessed, Sylvia and I are working on commission."

"You mean it's not your worry whether your syndicate can make money on the mine or not?"

"I've confirmed that the ore is worth digging. How they dig it out and get it to market is their worry. I assume, once a real mining outfit takes over, these high-graders will find it less easy to do whatever it is they have been doing."

"You have no idea how they've pulled it off?"

"Longarm, I don't even *care*. Every grain of the gold they've stolen so far belongs to Kevin MacLeod. It's none of my business. Once the mine changes ownership, it won't be my business either. I'll have collected my commission and been long gone from here before it can possibly happen again."

Longarm started to observe that he thought Baxter was a cold fish. Then he decided that a man would have to be to stay with Sylvia, so he said, "When I rode down to Sacramento, I dropped by the ore mill to swap some ideas. They tell me you've never been by once. You don't seem to be a very curious cuss, Baxter."

"Why on earth would I want to visit the refinery? I have no ore down there."

"I just sort of wondered if you ever thought to assay MacLeod's ore at that end."

Baxter laughed with characteristic unpleasantness. "Assay it? You must be joking. We all know the high-graders have been switching the shipments for worthless country rock. Are you suggesting that the refinery owners have been tricking MacLeod some way? It never occurred to me to question their assay." He stopped talking and blinked a few times. "But see here," he went on. "If they've been accepting good gold-bearing ore, but reporting it as worthless, that would explain everything!"

Longarm smiled thinly and said, "Well, not everything. We've still got some murders and a few nice tries to study on. The other day, I got shot at near here."

He grimaced, having reminded himself of his sore rump, and added, "By the way, I hope you've still got your assay kit handy."

Baxter said, "As a matter of fact, those scoundrels wrecked my old kit when they tore my room apart. I picked up more supplies in the capital, however."

Longarm nodded. Before he could ask his next question, a gun went off outside and a loud voice cried, "Waaaaahooooo!"

The two of them got up and walked over to the doorway. Out in the street, two men were running around in circles slapping everyone they passed on the back and laughing fit to bust. Constable Lovejoy ran down the walk, calling out to them, and one of them fired his revolver in the air again and yelled, "We made it! Got MacLeod and his gold through slick as a whistle! We was just too much for them pesky high-graders, this time!"

Lovejoy danced a little jig and then, as he spotted Longarm, called out, "You hear that, big federal man? The boys got through, and Manzanita is back on the map as a gold camp!"

Longarm waved them over and said, "In that case, the drinks are on me. I want to hear all about it!"

As Lovejoy, his deputies, and half the town crowded in past him, he asked, "Where's MacLeod?"

One of the deputies said, "Rode fast for his mine, to tell the little missus. He was excited as hell. You know what we think? We think we owe it to them skulking Injuns up in the rimrock. The high-graders must have been camped out there in the woods someplace and likely got kilt or run off by Miwok!"

Longarm followed the crowd inside, tossed a twenty-dollar gold piece on the bar, and told the bartender to keep serving till it was all used up. Lovejoy slapped him on the back and said, "God damn it, I like a good loser! I reckon we've seen the last of them high-graders after all, and my men rate the credit!"

Longarm nodded and said, "Maybe. Ain't you interested in catching them for the killings?"

Lovejoy waved the question away expansively. "Aw, shit, who cares about a few greasers? The important thing is that we got through with the gold this time! MacLeod won't have to sell out and it'll mean jobs and boom times for us all again!"

Longarm noticed that Baxter had slipped out. He shrugged and worked his way to one of the celebrating deputies, saying, "I want to hear the whole tale, pilgrim. Start with leaving the Lost Chinaman."

The deputy swallowed a shot of red-eye, neat, and slammed the glass down for more before he said, "Shucks, there's nothing to tell. We rode the ore cars down uneventful. Kept an eye peeled for Indians as well, but nobody never come near us. We rolled into the mill yards and they took a couple of samples to be tested. Come out to say the ore was medium-high grade, for once. Then they wrote out a check for MacLeod. Oh, the check was what they called an advance. They said they'd have to see exactly how much the stuff runs to the ton before they paid him in full. But he left with a couple thousand, so his troubles is likely over. If he gets another couple of shipments through, and it seems likely, he might be able to get rid of them no-account greasers and hire white men like we told him he should. He said he'd study on it."

Longarm had heard enough. He went outside and mounted up. As he reached the Lost Chinaman, Ralph Baxter was tethering his own bay to the porch rail of the MacLeod cabin. Longarm rode in at a trot.

The door opened as he dismounted. Lottie MacLeod let them both in, but said her husband was up at the mine shaft. Ralph Baxter gave her an officious look and explained, "I have a bank draft for two million dollars here, Mrs. MacLeod. I know your husband got his ore to market this time, but it might have been a fluke. I seriously suggest that you sell before you're robbed again."

Lottie looked excited, but said, "You'll have to talk to Kevin about that, sir. He's in the mine at the moment, but he should be back any minute."

Baxter said, "I have to speak with him at once," and marched for the door. He saw Longarm tagging along behind him and asked, "Where do you think you're going, my good fellow?"

"I ain't your good fellow, but I'm headed the same place. It ought to be interesting to see if he'll sell out now."

They argued about it all the way up the slope and into the mine entrance. Baxter picked up a lantern near the entrance and lit it. As they started down the tracks, Longarm noticed that none of the workmen were on duty. The last shift must have just ended.

With Baxter leading the way, they rounded the turn at the bottom. Longarm noticed that someone had whitewashed the bloodstained standing wall where Tico Vallejo had died. They'd hung up a wreath and the cut-out picture of a saint, too.

Baxter led them to the ore face. But MacLeod wasn't there. The Bostonian looked puzzled as Longarm stared at the wet wall and said, "He must be in the other tunnel. It branches like a T down here."

He stepped aside to let Baxter take the lead with the light. They came to the entrance slope, crossed it, and went down the other tunnel. They found Kevin MacLeod on his hands and knees against another rock face. The air was filled with the smell of chemicals. The mine owner had glass dishes and vials of acid spread out near his knees and he'd been hammering on a lump of ore. He turned to smile up at them.

MacLeod said, "The high-graders missed us this time. We got through with a whole load."

Longarm said, "I figured you might."

Baxter said, "See here, MacLeod. You still need working capital. Even if you *can* get your ore to market, I'm authorized to make you a damned fair offer."

MacLeod shook his head and said, "You must be crazy! Didn't you hear me say I *delivered?*"

"Yes, but what of it? It will take you years to make two million clear profit, even if you have no more trouble with those outlaws." He let that sink in before he added, "And that's not saying you won't! Deputy Long here tells me he still has no idea how they've been robbing you. Isn't that right, Longarm?"

Longarm nodded and said, "I've been shell-gamed pretty good, up till now. How come you're testing that rock, MacLeod? I thought they told you it was good in Sacramento."

MacLeod said, "I have two good reasons. I'd be a fool to accept another man's assay, for one thing. For another, they said it was richer than what we've been digging. I think we may have struck through to another vein of bonanza, but, as you see, it all looks the same."

Before Longarm could answer, the ground tingled under them and the air suddenly got heavier. MacLeod gasped, "Oh, *no!*" as the roar of cascading rock filled the mine!

They froze in place, all three holding their breaths as the roar grew louder still, then faded with a last few crashes of falling stones. MacLeod got up as Baxter raced back along the tunnel with the tall deputy following. Baxter stopped, holding the lantern high, and moaned, "Oh, Jesus Christ!"

Longarm joined him and said, "You can say that again."

The leg of the T was filled with dusty rocks and earth, all the way to the ceiling.

Longarm sniffed the air and said, "Smell those nitro fumes?"

Baxter gasped. "You mean someone dynamited the tunnel, with the three of us down here?"

Longarm said, "Wouldn't have been much point to it if we weren't. You don't have a rear door to this mine, do you, Mac-Leod?"

MacLeod said, "Don't be ridiculous! We're a quarter of a mile under the fucking mountain!"

Baxter put down his lantern and fell to his hands and knees, grasping at a jagged rock. MacLeod said, "Don't do that, you idiot! You'll bring more of it down that way!"

Longarm nodded and said, "Timbers, tracks, and such are likely wedged crossways up the slope, holding back some of the rock. No way we're going to dig our way out from this side!"

Baxter started to argue. Then he brightened and gasped, "MacLeod! Your wife knows we're down here and must have heard the blast!"

Longarm said, "There you go. She's likely running for help right now. We'll just sit tight till they muck out the tunnel." He turned to the ashen-faced MacLeod and asked, "How long do you figure it should take if Lottie doesn't waste time trying to do it herself?"

MacLeod frowned and said, "All night, if she's in town this very minute."

A drop of water ticked the brim of Longarm's hat. He asked if there was a drainage problem and MacLeod shook his head. "It would take a week for enough water to seep in to matter. But the air won't last that long."

Longarm had been afraid he was going to say that.

Chapter 9

Longarm sat in the blackness with his back against the damp wall. He had no idea what time it was. He felt like they'd been trapped since the decline and fall of Rome.

The lanterns were out to save air, but as it was, the air they were breathing was getting sort of gamy. MacLeod was filled with cheerful observations and had explained that it wasn't lack of oxygen that killed men trapped underground. It was the poisonous fumes of their own breathing that did the job long before every bit of oxygen was used up. Longarm sure wished Baxter hadn't put on all that infernal bay rum the last time he washed up. He was stinking up the darkness something fearsome.

The Bostonian asked again who Longarm thought had set off the charge. Longarm hadn't bothered to answer the first few times; it was a stupid question, even for Baxter. To shut him up, Longarm said, "Old son, if I'd had any idea someone was fixing to drop a mountain on my head, I'd have never come down here with you."

MacLeod said, "Listen! Do you hear that?"

Longarm answered, "Been hearing it for a while. It's either the biggest gopher in the world or somebody digging on the other side of that crud."

Baxter started shouting, "Help! *Au secours!* We're down here!"

Longarm snorted and said, "Oh, shut up. They can't hear you for one thing, and if they didn't figure someone was down here, they wouldn't be digging us out!"

MacLeod said, "I just thought of something awful!"

Longarm said, "I figured you would. But go ahead."

"What if that digging we hear isn't a rescue party? What if it's the high-graders?"

"Ain't likely," Longarm answered. "We didn't hear much of a blast down here, with all that rock between us and the dynamite, but I *felt* the bump and it was a big one. The noise would have been louder on the other side, shooting out the side of the mountain like a big cannon shot. They'd have heard it in Manzanita and the town's already on the prod, between high-graders and Indians. Whoever set off that blast aimed to kill the three of us and light out."

He put a cheroot between his teeth and chewed it, dying for a smoke, while Baxter went on about who might have done it and why. He suspected everyone from the other miners over at Sheep Ranch to the Chinese Tongs in San Francisco, but he didn't have anything really sensible to hang his worries from.

MacLeod said, "What I can't figure is why the *entrance* was blasted. Now that I think on it, anyone doing it should have known we were safe enough around a right-angle turn. You're right about the noise carrying, too. Hell, it makes no sense. As a matter of fact, it was a dumb way to try and kill us!"

Longarm nodded and said, "Might have been a spur-of-the-moment thing. Might have been a right slick attempt to scare you into selling this mine quick."

Baxter gasped. "See here! That's a ridiculous suggestion, even from you, Longarm. You may not have noticed it, but I was standing right beside the two of you when the blast went off!"

"I know. And you said Sylvia was in Sacramento, too. Maybe someone else is figuring to top your offer. Or maybe you ain't as upset as you let on. The digging sounds are getting louder. I know *I'd* sit still in the dark for a few hours for the commission on a two-million-dollar deal."

Baxter made a gagging sound and said, "You're insane. Even if I went in for such dramatic methods of persuasion, how could Sylvia and I be sure I'd be safe down here? The blast might well have dropped the whole hanging wall!"

Longarm started to say Sylvia might not care, but he decided it wasn't right to talk about a lady with another man listening. The mention of wives seemed to jog something loose in MacLeod's brain and he suddenly blurted, "Oh, Jesus! I forgot all about Lottie!"

Longarm said, "I doubt if that's her I hear digging. It sounds more like six or eight men with picks and shovels. I can feel the rumble of ore cars with my poor sore behind. This wet, rocky floor leaves a lot to be desired as a place to sit all night."

"You don't understand," MacLeod insisted. "Lottie was up there alone when they hit us! My God, I'm such a selfish brute! I forgot all about her when it looked like we were done for!"

Longarm said, "That ain't as rare a feeling as it's supposed to be, old son. Most of us look out for our own hides when the chips are down."

"Do you think they might have hurt her?" MacLeod asked anxiously.

"Can't say, for sure. Every time I think I've got a line on the rascals, they pull something new on me. Let's eat the apple a bite at a time, though. Does Lottie know anything important enough for whoever's behind all this to want her out of the way?"

MacLeod thought silently as Baxter comforted him: "We left her in the cabin, so it's unlikely she saw anyone. These scoundrels have been almost impossibly clever, up till now. No one has ever so much as had a glimpse of the high-graders. Surely, if they were ready to come out in the open and simply start killing people, they'd have done so before now."

Longarm said, "There you go, MacLeod. Once in a while this gent makes sense. Everything the murderous skunks have done has been done sneaky, I'd be surprised as anything if your pretty little gal isn't right as rain, even though she's likely worried sick right now."

A rock rolled down the pile in the blackness and a hoarse voice called hollowly, "Anybody breathing in there?"

Longarm shouted back, "Is that you, Herc? We're all right."

Romero called out, "We'll have you out in a minute. We rushed over as soon as we heard what'd happened. Found some half-assed Mexicans trying to get down to you with their bare hands, but I brought a crew of real hard-rockers. Somebody's sure as shit *mad* at you, Longarm!"

MacLeod crawled over to the pile and shouted up, "Is my wife all right?"

"I don't know. Who are you and who's your wife?"

"I'm Kevin MacLeod. My wife Lottie was up there in our cabin when the blast went off!"

There was a murmured consultation. Then Romero called down, "There's a Mexican lady up here. No other gals nearby.

The Mex gal's vaqueros were helping your mine crew when we got here. Doing a piss-poor job, but I'll admit they were willing. We put them to work hauling and mucking while we dug."

But MacLeod wasn't listening. He was on his knees hauling rocks from the pile when Longarm thumbnailed the head of a match and relit a lantern. MacLeod was growling and cursing as he dug with his hands. A stream of broken rock and sand cascaded down over his knees and buried him to the waist, but he paid it no mind. Longarm got up, moved over to him, and pulled him back, saying, "This would be a dumb time to bury yourself alive."

"My wife! I have to find my wife!"

"Well, sure you do, MacLeod. But let's get out of here alive first."

Some more boulders and shattered mining timbers slid down the pile. Then Herc Romero grinned down at them through a hole near the overhead and said, "There you go, boys. Just let me widen this a mite and you can crawl up over the shit."

As the burly Italian crowbarred a slab of rock aside he observed, "The way I put it together, someone put a box of dynamite in an ore car, lit the fuse, and sent it down the tracks at you. Lucky for you, MacLeod, you run a shoestring operation here. The car jumped your crooked old tracks a third of the way down, hung up on a pit prop, and went off up the slope. If it had made it to the bottom the way it did when they killed Vallejo, we wouldn't be having this conversation."

MacLeod suddenly scrambled up the slope and shoved past Romero. Baxter turned to Longarm and sniffed, "I'd say you owe me an apology, sir. As you see, it was certainly an attempt to murder all three of us!"

Longarm coughed some rock dust out of his lungs, and said, "No, Baxter, just two of us—me and MacLeod. I don't think they cared about *you*, one way or the other. Let's get out and study on these interesting new developments."

Felicidad was waiting at the top of the tunnel. She sobbed as she threw herself in Longarm's arms. He hung on to her long enough to kiss her and comfort her a bit. But his mind was preoccupied and he untangled himself as soon as it seemed polite to do so.

The whole town seemed to be gathered around. Some fool

was shooting a pistol off in the air as if it were the Fourth of July instead of the middle of August. All the mysterious doings of late had made the whole community skittish, but they'd somehow gotten a load of ore past the high-graders and now, when they saw that the murder attempt had gone sour, they were feeling good. Not a man in the valley had any idea who the high-graders were, or how they'd done their magic, but the spell was broken. The skunks didn't win *every* time, after all.

As Longarm untangled himself from Felicidad, Constable Lovejoy caught his sleeve. "God damn it, Longarm, for a man who thinks he's so all-fired smart, that was a dumb play you just made. Didn't you know the chance you were giving 'em by going down in that fool mine with nobody up here on guard?"

Longarm said, "If I had, I wouldn't have gone down there. Let go of my arm; I've got chores to attend to."

He elbowed his way through the crowd to MacLeod's cabin. He noticed that Felicidad was trotting after him, so he held the door open for her and let her come in with him. Baxter and MacLeod were already inside.

The young mine owner was seated at his kitchen table, signing papers as Baxter stood over him, not bothering not to gloat. MacLeod saw Longarm and the girl and said wearily, "I'm cashing in my chips. I'm whipped. You haven't seen my wife, have you?"

Longarm shook his head and said, "No. She must've gotten scared and run off. Your buckboard was out front when we rode in before. It ain't there now."

MacLeod said, "They must have kidnapped her. Baxter is paying us a lot for the claim. So if they ask for ransom, I'll have two million to pay them."

Longarm whistled and said, "You must want her back a lot."

"She's my *wife*, you idiot!"

Longarm nodded and said, "I doubt she's with the rascal who's been funning us. Kidnapping ain't his style."

Baxter snorted and observed, "Longarm, you don't know who it is or what his style might be! You keep looking smug and acting like you know so much, but he's been making a fool of you from the beginning. How do you know it's a *he*, in fact? I'd say it's more like a *they!*"

Longarm explained, "There can't be more than one or two people involved. I've been shot at and dynamited, and those other boys were poisoned, but that's not the way a gang works. I'd say it's a small operation. As to desperadoes holding a mine owner's wife for ransom, it's a mite late in the game for that, ain't it? If they intended to play that way, why didn't they just start out by kidnapping Lottie and making MacLeod hand over his gold, instead of playing all those foxy grandpa tricks?"

MacLeod said angrily, "Will the two of you shut up and let me sign these infernal deeds? Whatever's happened, my wife is missing and I have to find her!"

Longarm said, "You got a check from the refinery in Sacramento earlier today. Do you have it on you?"

MacLeod looked surprised. He got up from the table and rushed over to a green tin box on the kitchen counter. He opened it and swore.

Longarm said, "There you go. She's likely on her way to the Crocker bank in Sacramento to cash her own chips in. You're supposed to be dead at the bottom of the mine."

As MacLeod gaped at him in horror, Felicidad gasped, "*Querido*, what are you suggesting?"

Longarm finally lit the cheroot he'd been holding in his teeth, and said, "Ain't suggesting—saying. Lottie's a pretty little gal with her best years ahead of her. She's probably found living up here in this shack tedious as hell, but she knew sooner or later they'd sell out and she could be living higher on the hog, with someone else to do the laundry and rustle up the grub."

Baxter looked thunderstruck as he asked, "Do you mean Lottie MacLeod sent that car filled with dynamite down the shaft at us?"

"Hell, it wasn't filled. Romero said it was only a box. Tonight you told her you were willing to give them two million dollars for this claim, but MacLeod here was being stubborn about the sale. I reckon that riled her some."

MacLeod said, "I don't believe you! We've been married four years!"

"Longarm's voice was sympathetic as he answered, "You believe me; you just don't want to *say* you do. I'm as sentimental as the next gent, but if I was a lady, I'd have to like someone an awful lot to go on washing socks for him with two million dollars hanging over me and him acting like he *enjoyed* the rustic life."

MacLeod stared at him in sick horror as Baxter asked, "Have you forgotten I was down there with the two of you? I could hardly sign a bank draft for any amount if I was dead, you know."

Longarm said, "I know. But some other jasper could have. You ain't buying the mine personally, Baxter; you're only working for an Eastern syndicate. Lottie never tried to wipe *those* rascals out—just her husband. The two of them have a joint account at the Crocker Trust, so she has enough to live on from the ore sale till they send your replacement out with the two million for her mine. She figures it's her mine now. Herc Romero wasn't supposed to find us alive."

Felicidad asked, "What are you waiting for, then, *querido*? Why are you not chasing the murderess?"

The deputy arched an eyebrow at her. "Forty miles in the dark, chasing a lady who's good at killing? It was her who killed Tico Vallejo and those other two, you know."

MacLeod sputtered, "You can't prove that!"

Longarm nodded and said, "It might be hard to prove in front of a jury, but she did it. It had to be her. You were in Sacramento. She mixed some of your assay chemicals in wine and gave it to them. Then, with them out of the way, she just rolled that car down at us. It missed Romero and me, but . . ."

Baxter said, "The poor woman must be mad! Are you suggesting that she was behind the high-grading of her own husband's mine?"

Longarm took a long drag on his cheroot, and exhaled a billowing cloud of blue smoke.

"Nope. She just helped out by killing folks who came too close to figuring out the game."

"Then you *are* saying she was in on it?" Baxter pressed.

"There had to be somebody watching this end of the operation. None of the Mexicans working here knew much about mining, but Vallejo was bright and learning, so he had to go."

MacLeod asked, "Have you forgotten they killed Lottie's dog that afternoon?"

The marshal regarded the glowing tip of his cigar as he said patiently, "She did that herself to draw suspicion away from her. She had no alibi to speak of, but who suspects a pretty little gal who's all cut up about her poor dog, Rex?"

MacLeod said incredulously, "I don't believe a word you're saying. If you thought for a minute that Lottie had done half the things you say, then Señorita Vallejo's right. You'd be after her this minute."

"Oh, I'll use Lovejoy's line to Sacramento in a few minutes to call the marshal down that way. They've been peeved at me for sticking my nose into their jurisdiction, anyway. I'll have them pick her up when the bank opens tomorrow morning. It'll make them feel good to be in on the capture."

MacLeod scribbled hastily on the last paper and stood up again, holding it out to Baxter, as he said, "All right. Give me the bank draft. I haven't got time to listen to this maniac! I have to find out where my wife is!"

To his credit, Baxter wasn't a complete fool. He looked quizzically at Longarm, who nodded and said, "Sure, give the man his money. That's what you came all the way out here to do."

Baxter bent over and endorsed the bank draft, muttering, "For a moment I expected you to accuse *him* of murder!"

Longarm smiled crookedly, and said, "Nope. He's got enough on his plate with one murderer in the family."

Baxter handed MacLeod the draft and the miner stuffed it in his shirt pocket, hardly looking at it, then stepped over to his gunbelt hanging from a peg on the wall, strapped the revolver on, and headed for the door.

Felicidad asked Longarm, "Aren't you going with him to help look for her?"

Longarm shook his head, walked over to the stove, and picked up the coffeepot. He got three cups from the china cabinet, came back to the table, and poured coffee for Baxter, Felicidad, and himself, saying, "We might as well set a spell. I want to give him a good lead. He took a shot at me the other day, and he shoots tolerably well."

The other two gaped wide-eyed at him, ignoring the coffee as Longarm pulled up a chair and sat down. He said, "Come on, nobody's going to fuss at us for helping ourselves. Neither of them ever intend to come back here to this cabin."

Baxter sank down into a chair, obviously puzzled, and asked, "Just what in God's name is going on around here?"

Longarm took a sip of his coffee before answering, "He's likely going to kill her when he catches up with her. She wasn't supposed to double-cross him like that. In all modesty, I played a right neat trick on the two of them. They call it misdirection in the magic book I was reading over at the county seat."

Felicidad stared in horror at him as she asked, "You *want* him to kill his wife?"

Longarm said amiably, "Sure. I'd never in a million years get a jury to believe she was guilty. I'd have a hard row to hoe proving it was MacLeod who played all those games with the ore, too. This way I figure to get two birds with one stone. He's too blamed mad at her to think straight, and I'll sure as hell prove he shot his wife. I just have to give the rascal time, is all."

Baxter exploded, "The hell with his damned wife! You just said MacLeod was behind the high-grading, but damn it, it was *his* ore they were stealing!"

"Hell," Longarm said, "there never was any ore to steal. The Lost Chinaman was played out years ago. MacLeod and Lottie bought it for a song, aiming to sell it to some pilgrim like yourself."

"That's impossible! Have you forgotten that I assayed the ore personally? You had me check it out the day you rode down the mountain on it with MacLeod."

"Yep, and when we got to the mill, it was worthless. That was even more impossible. I don't believe in spooks and my fool rump was holding the stuff down all the way to the mill. So somebody had to be a liar. I figured for a while it might be you, but there was just no way to make you fit. A man doesn't salt a mine to *buy* it. He salts a worthless mine to *sell* it."

He saw the stricken look on Baxter's face and said soothingly, "Don't feel so bad. They fooled Herc Romero too, and he's an experienced hard-rock miner. MacLeod was too slick just to blast gold birdshot into the rock. He dissolved maybe a hundred dollars' worth in aqua regia, then let it soak into the rock face and some sample lumps he left about for snoopy folks to pocket. Did you notice, when we were down in the mine before, that they weren't working that face at all? He had his greenhorn Mexican help digging pure quartz in the *other* tunnel!"

Baxter shook his head in confusion. "Never mind the mine itself. Damn it, we took random samples from two whole cars of what you claim was worthless rock. I tested them with my own aqua regia. You saw the gold that settled out."

"Sure I did. That was pretty slick on their part. You see, they switched bottles on you. There are a dozen ways they could have worked it, since all those little brown bottles look the same. Either one of them only needed a moment to open your kit while you weren't looking and . . . hell, you're a bright lad. Explain it yourself to the señorita here."

Baxter's mouth was hanging open as though he were trying to catch flies, so Longarm told Felicidad, "Gold dissolves in aqua regia. It stays dissolved and invisible till you neutralize the acid with alkali. Then the gold settles out, no matter what else you may have put in the test tube. I read that in a book."

Baxter's face brightened as his confusion cleared. "Yes, by God, I can see how that would work! If my acid was contaminated with gold, it would assay almost anything as gold-bearing ore!"

Longarm said, "I know. I got a drop on my hat, and when it dried, I had a medium-high-grade Stetson. That was me who busted up your room, by the way. We call it misdirection, among us magicians. I found out about the gold in your acid when the bottle busted on me."

"Hah! I knew you were behind that mess! But you're missing something. They got through with two whole carloads of real ore, the last time!"

The deputy smiled slyly. "No, they never did. That was misdirection, too. I asked the folks down at the mill to lie for me. They just *told* MacLeod he'd brought real ore this time. It must have surprised hell out of him. Did you notice that he was down there looking for a vein he hadn't known he really had?"

"But they *paid* him for the ore. Damn it, *I* just paid him, too! Oh, my God, if I just paid two million dollars for a salted mine . . ."

"Now don't go blubbering up on us, old son. The bank's agreed not to cash either check. I had a talk with the president of the bank and he thought it was a right good way to trap the two of them."

Felicidad said, "I still can't understand why she tried to murder her husband."

Longarm put down his cup, leaned back expansively, and said, "I figured I'd drive a wedge between them when I fooled MacLeod with the false assay at the mill. You can both see how hard it would be to prove any of this in court if they just stuck together. I was foolish to go down in the mine that way after seeing she was all riled that he was hesitating with their prize in sight. But I figured she'd argue with him some before she turned on him. Lottie was smarter than she let on. She must have figured I'd outfoxed them some way, and that he was playing into my hands. So, seeing she had us in a right convenient place, she just put a box of dynamite aboard a car, lit the fuse, and let her roll. She had no way of knowing we'd come out alive. She probably lit out before folks who might have heard the blast could ask pesky questions. She aims to hear the sad news in Sacramento, where she doubtless went to buy supplies or something. Her plan is to come back up, all sad-eyed, and sit tight until some other fool drops by with another bank draft."

Baxter said, "Ah, *that's* why you're sitting here so unconcerned! You expect her to return to the scene of the crime!"

"Not hardly. When she hears about the cave-in, she'll hear that the boys from Sheep Ranch dug us out, too. We'd best go out and take them down to the saloon, by the way. I'd say we owe those boys a drink."

Baxter looked at Longarm with newfound respect. "This time I'll pay. I'll even buy a drink for *you*, Longarm! But if you don't expect them back, shouldn't you be looking for them?"

Longarm looked at Felicidad and grinned, saying, "Later. I'm in no hurry to ride. At least not before sunrise."

Longarm made sweet love to Felicidad as the dawn light crept in on them through her bedroom window. But the woman was upset, knowing it was probably the last time they'd be together, even though Longarm lied and promised the way a gentleman was supposed to.

He was feeling a mite wistful, too. Felicidad was pretty as a picture, in or out of her dress, and he'd been right about one thing: she was better in bed than the librarian in San Andreas. Pru was wilder, but Felicidad was sweeter and warmer. He knew he was going to miss her, and that some night when he was all alone, he was going to think back to this moment and cuss himself for being such a tumbleweed.

Common sense told him a man was far better off with some sweet little gal waiting at home for him with his pipe and slippers, only Longarm didn't smoke a pipe and he owned no slippers. He was a hard-driving lawman with a job to do, and such pleasures as life handed out to him had to be enjoyed on the fly.

For the fifth or sixth time Felicidad pleaded, "Can't I come back to Denver with you, *querido?* There is nothing to keep me here. I promise not to get in your way."

He fingered her pert brown nipple absently and soothed, "We'll talk on it later. I have to ride down to Sacramento after the MacLeods in a few minutes, honey."

She sobbed, "You are never coming back this way. Your work here is finished!"

"I don't know," he equivocated. "My office might want me to clear up a few loose ends. It doesn't seem likely that anyone around here was in on that confidence game with them, but old Billy Vail might want me to make sure."

"Do you promise, then?"

He shook his head and said, "Don't ask for promises, honey. Many a gal has chased a man out of her corral by trying to brand him with promises just as he was starting to eat out of her hand. I said I'll be back if I can make it. Let's leave it at that."

He made love to her one last time, a bit annoyed that she didn't seem as pleasured this time, then he sat up and pulled on his clothes. As he stood in her doorway, she stood up, naked, and came over to kiss him goodbye. She was well worth remembering as she stood before him in the rosy light. He kissed her deeply and with meaning, then he turned away and walked off quickly, not looking back.

He saddled his gelding in the barn and rode out, cutting across the rolling fields of wild mustard in the mountain sunlight. The air was cool and the gelding was frisky, so he rode northwest at a lope, jumping rail fences and feeling sort of good.

He told himself, *You really are a shameless skunk with women.* But he was grinning like a kid stealing apples just the same.

He rode the forty-odd miles to Sacramento, taking most of the morning and leaving the horse lathered and not so sassy at the army remount station just outside of town.

The remount officer started to give him hell for treating government property that way with an Indian uprising brewing, so Longarm said, "You must not have gotten word from headquarters yet. There ain't any Indian uprising. Old Bitter Water is a friend of mine. We used to bust out of jail together all the time."

"What are you talking about? The boys up in Calaveras County report smoke talk from a hundred hills. Some livestock is missing, and—"

Longarm interrupted him. "Now don't get your balls in an uproar. There was only one fire. I was there. As for missing stock, there's always missing stock. Cows don't have a lick of sense."

The officer blinked and asked, "You were *with* the Miwok when they started sending those smoke signals?"

Longarm didn't know just what the army regulations had to say about white men sending Indian smoke signals, so he hedged a little and said, "I just told you Bitter Water is a friend of mine. He was signaling his band to gather for the acorn harvest or something. They're sort of like squirrels when it comes to gathering nuts for the winter. But like I said, it never meant anything."

"Damn it! They have half the county holed up with loaded rifles! They had no right to scare folks so!"

"I know," Longarm soothed him, adding, "I told them they should put on overalls and start looking for steady jobs. Bitter Water says he won't send up any more smoke signals. Meanwhile, if you'd see about shipping my saddle and possibles back to Denver, and tell me how I'm to get into town without a mount . . ."

"I think the mess officer has a buckboard going into Sacramento for supplies. If you leg it over to the gate in time, you'll be able to hitch a ride. I sure don't want to issue you another horse! You ride like a goddamned Sioux on the warpath!"

Longarm suppressed the desire to observe that this attitude might be the reason the army had so much trouble chasing Indians. He simply waved and started dogtrotting away from the corral, holding his holster in place with his left palm to keep it from slapping.

He reached the gate as the chuckwagon was pulling out. He yelled, ran after it, and jumped aboard.

They rode him in to the crowded streets of the city and he dropped off near the federal building, dodging a clanging streetcar as he crossed the street.

He went upstairs to a frosted glass door and introduced himself to a morose assistant marshal from the Sacramento district. He didn't know if this was the son of a bitch who'd gotten him thrown in Lovejoy's jail by disputing his jurisdiction, but it was water under the bridge now. The older federal man had doubtless gotten the word that Longarm was being backed by Boss Buckley, so he was trying to be friendly.

He said, "We have a flier out on the MacLeods, and the Sacramento P.D. is cooperating. But so far, nobody's seen a trace of them."

Longarm brought his fellow employee up to date and the man sighed, "I don't know why you've been playing chess when the game is checkers, Longarm. I mean, you *had* Kevin MacLeod up there at the Lost Chinaman, but you simply sat there like a big-assed bird and let him get away!"

Longarm took out a cheroot, thumbed a matchhead, and lit up before he explained, "Lottie MacLeod took off after trapping us all in the mine. I figured if I arrested her husband on the spot, we might never see her again."

"Good riddance, I'd say. The husband is the one we want."

Longarm shook his head and said, "Nope. He's pretty slick, as we learned the hard way. But Lottie *kills* folks. She's a bitty little woman who looks helpless and harmless. A gal can change her dress and dye her hair to where a man who's bedded her might miss her in a crowd, too. I figure her husband has a better chance of catching up with her than anyone working on our side."

The older man fumbled with a pencil and growled, "Maybe. She ain't been to the bank to cash that check she stole."

Longarm said, "Hell, the news that we were rescued was in this morning's issue of the *Sacramento Bee*. She'd be a fool to try and cash it now. He'll know better than to try and spend the two million they paid him after all the trouble the two of them went to. He must be mad as hell."

For the first time, the older lawman grinned sincerely as he nodded and said, "I'll allow that you really messed them up by getting the bank and the refinery to play along with you like that. But the two of them have a good twelve hours' start and there's no telling where in God's name either one of them has lit out for. We ran MacLeod through the wanted files; he has no paper on him at all."

Longarm nodded and said, "Meaning they were using a fictitious name. Everybody leaves a trail of paper behind as he passes through this wicked world."

"I know. But there's no army record. Nothing to point to a hometown back East that they might be running for."

"Hell, no slick owlhoot runs for home after the first time. MacLeod may be somebody else, but he's been on the dodge before. If we could find out who he was or where he came from, he knows we'd be looking for him there. After we find Lottie, I'll catch the steamer down to Frisco Bay. He'll figure on hopping a boat out, sure as hell."

"Are you crazy? There must be a dozen clippers putting out through the Golden Gate with every tide!"

Longarm nodded and said, "Yep. But like I said, the jasper is slick as well as ornery. He won't catch just any boat. He'll want one headed for some port that has no extradition treaty with Uncle Sam."

The other lawman looked sheepish as he admitted, "I, uh, have some fellows covering the Mexican and Canadian borders, Longarm."

Longarm shook his head and said, "Queen Victoria's Mounties are nosy as hell about strangers up their way. As for Mexico, they might wink at a cow thief or two. But murder is serious on either side of the border. MacLeod would stand out down in the Baja like a sore thumb, and the rurales would nail him pronto."

The older man studied his pencil before he sighed and said, "You're likely right. I understand the Vallejo family is offering a reward for the murderers of their kinsman."

Longarm nodded, adding, "The Vallejos are sort of important folks, too. I know one who figures they'll be able to get back some of their old lands now, since the mine was a bust. But getting back to the wheresoevers —I don't figure MacLeod will try a run for it over the Sierra, since there ain't too many railroads for us to watch. So we're back to an escape by sea. We ought to be able to whittle the ships leaving for an owlhoot's likely ports of call down to a tolerable list."

"Shouldn't we get cracking, then? What's to stop MacLeod and his woman from being there right now, about to leave?"

Longarm said, "A couple of things. For one, a man traveling alone has a better chance. For another, she tried to kill him. She's a tolerable-looking gal with a nice figure, but he's likely feeling testy. She knows too much, too. If he was to get rid of her and make it out of the country . . ."

"I agree he has the motive to kill her twice over, damn it. But while we're sitting here, jawing about it, the two of them are out there someplace and you still haven't told me where."

Longarm blew a smoke ring and explained, "Hell, if I knew where she was, I'd have arrested her already."

"Agreed, but what if MacLeod can't find her either?"

"We'll be in a hell of a fix, won't we?"

The Sacramento marshal drummed his pencil on the desk blotter and mused, "On the other hand, they've traveled and plotted together all this time. MacLeod should know his wife's habits—the sort of places she'd be apt to stay, the sort of stores she shops in. If she's in the habit of changing her appearance, he'd know that too, and what to look for."

Longarm said, "There you go. My plan ain't as dumb as it looks, once a person takes the time to study on it some."

As he rose to leave, the other lawman asked, "What if *she* nails *him?* We know she's tried once, and what you said about their knowing one another better than we do applies in her case as well, doesn't it?"

Longarm nodded. "Yeah. But I purely hope she doesn't get lucky. I know I can likely catch *him.* But I ain't ever been one for trailing after womenfolks."

The older man, who'd heard a lot about Longarm, grinned slyly and said, "Oh, I don't know. The way I hear tell, you sort of like to go after gals. You figure, after you catch her, she'll be in shape to stand trial?"

Longarm replied morosely, "I ain't ever loved a gal to death yet, and besides, Lottie is a mite more passionate than I care for. I'd be willing to let her *try* and screw me to death, but she doesn't fight fair and I've had all the chemistry lessons I need."

Longarm went to the bank, but his hopes failed to pan out. The bank manager gave him a cigar and explained his plans in case either of the missing MacLeods tried to cash their worthless checks. He sounded like he was enjoying the change from his usually somewhat dull routine. But while the armed guards out front in plain clothes were dramatic, it didn't seem likely that either of the MacLeods would turn up.

The banker mentioned that Herc Romero had been promoted by his boss, the enthusiastic tycoon George Hearst. The Hearst holdings had offered a substantial reward for the capture of the murderers, perhaps to butter up the local Mexicans.

Longarm said, "I got to wondering about the other mines shortly after I got to Calaveras County. Old Hearst is unpopular with the local folks, likely for being so rich. But I looked into it and saw that the Hearst holdings weren't robbed. That sort of struck me as strange, since robbing an unpopular absentee owner with a richer ore body looked a damned sight easier than whatever was going on."

The banker nodded and said, "Now that you've explained it, we should all be ashamed of ourselves for not seeing it right off. I mean, damn it, there wasn't any way to steal ore from a guarded moving train, was there?"

Longarm puffed on the banker's fine Havana tobacco, and said, "Don't fret about it. I thought they'd done it too, the first time it happened. I'll admit I wasted time thinking up all sorts of tricks, and I'll allow I had some thoughts on the late Joaquin Murietta's ghost. But it slowly sank into my thick skull that I didn't believe in spooks and that I'm likely as smart as any other old boy when it comes to stealing. In my line, you get to meet a mess of thieves, and in my time, I've probably heard of every way it can be done."

"In other words, if you simply couldn't see how they were stealing the ore, they simply couldn't be stealing it?"

"That's about the size of it. Modesty doesn't pay off worth mention."

"So now all you have to do is figure their next move?"

"Nope. I know MacLeod's next couple of moves. I just wish the son of a bitch would get cracking and figure it out himself!"

Chapter 10

At Sacramento police headquarters, Longarm introduced himself to the desk sergeant. He was led to a squad room where he sat down to converse with two plainclothesmen. The one who did all the talking was named Flynn. Longarm never caught the name of his small, skinny partner. The man was too busy chewing and spitting to have much to say.

Flynn explained that they'd searched high and low for both MacLeods or the remains of either. Then he added his considered opinion that they were not in Sacramento. He said, "If I were one of them, I'd be on a clipper headed for China about now."

Longarm said, "It's good to see that you agree with me about his wanting to get clear out of our jurisdiction. But he won't want to leave his woman behind for us to pick up. To us, he's just a nondescript cuss in worn pants and miner's boots, but she knows his real name and such. And it ain't like they're *friends* anymore."

"All right," Flynn said. "Let's try it this way. Say he's already found her, killed her, and lit out. There are a thousand places you could hide a body in these parts."

"Maybe," Longarm conceded, "but we know she had a good lead on him. So if and when he caught up with her, it'd be daybreak, or too close to matter. They don't own property here in town. So he has no basement at his disposal to plant her in. Someone would have noticed, had he gunned her down on the streets. That means they have to be someplace private for whatever. And that means a *rented* someplace private."

Flynn nodded. "We have men out checking the shabbier parts of town. There are lots of nasty alleyways down near the tracks, and if he caught up with her in some whorehouse—"

"Back up," Longarm cut in. "Lottie MacLeod is too high-toned to hide out in the tenderloin. Not because she might not screw as well as poison, but because she'd stand out. I'd say she'd aim for a more respectable part of town—a medium-priced hotel or a respectable rooming house."

"I read your drift. She ain't such a needle in a haystack after all."

"Her husband would know that, too. There's no telling how much money they still have between them, but she likely has some left over from their last flimflam. She wouldn't rent a place by the month, but she might pay a week in advance. She'd avoid the kind of hotel frequented by whiskey drummers with an eye for an ankle on a woman alone, too. Most towns I know of have respectable boarding houses catering to women only. That's where I'd start looking for her."

Flynn made a notation on a slip of paper. He rang a bell on his table and a uniformed patrolman came in to take the note. As he read it, the policeman said, "That's funny, Sarge. A couple of the boys just answered a call at an all-female rooming house out on the north side."

Flynn asked, "What kind of a call?" The patrolman replied, "Dead woman. Found by her landlady just a few minutes ago. The woman came in to change the linens and—"

But Flynn was on his feet and moving, with Longarm and Flynn's silent partner right behind.

They ran out a side entrance and piled into a waiting police van. The uniformed driver clucked the team forward and they boiled out of the alley, with the van's bell clanging.

It only took them a few minutes to reach the scene. It was a mustard-yellow frame building with a mansard roof. The whole neighborhood had gathered out front, where a patrolman was comforting an hysterical fat lady on the postage stamp-sized lawn.

Flynn asked the cop where his partner was and was told, "Up-stairs in the back, Sarge. This lady here says she's sure no men have been on the premises since she locked up last night."

The three of them edged past the fat lady as she protested loudly that she didn't run that sort of a rooming house.

They climbed the stairs as women peered out through slitted doors with worried looks.

He knew they were in the right place as soon as they got to the open doorway of Lottie MacLeod's rented room. A patrolman stood near the bed, taking notes and trying not to look as sick as he must have felt.

In life, Lottie had been pretty. Her death had been ugly. Uglier than Longarm had counted on, and he felt a twinge of guilt as he swallowed the bilious taste in his mouth. He stared down at the figure sprawled on the blood-soaked mattress, and said, "I'm purely sorry it had to end this way, ma'am, but you did have some ornery notions about killing folks."

Lottie MacLeod lay stark naked in a thickening, glutinous mass of blood and her own innards. She stared at the ceiling, smiling widely up at the gray, cracked plaster as if it had said something amusing. Her throat had been slit from ear to ear. Then her killer had run the knife down from her neck to her pubic bone, slicing her open like an overripe watermelon. Her still-shapely thighs were spread wide, as if her smile were meant as an invitation to a lusty lover. But while she lay spread-eagled and naked, there was little in the way of obscene exposure. Her blood-smeared breasts were visible, but her torn-out guts covered her private parts like some gory apron of tangled wet coils.

Flynn's partner went to the window, opened it, and spit a stream of tobacco juice out into the sunlight. Flynn said, "They don't grin like that until they've been dead about three hours, right?"

Longarm nodded and said, "Found an old boy the Apache had left on an ant pile once. *He* was grinning like he enjoyed it, too."

Longarm spotted a slip of paper on the rug and bent to pick it up as the detective said, "Of course, we can't prove it was MacLeod without witnesses."

Longarm held out the paper and said, "This was part of the rubber check I had the refinery pay him for his worthless gold. They likely had words, with her taunting him some, before he went sort of crazy."

Flynn frowned and said, "I thought she had a worthless check."

"She did. You ain't listening. If both checks were here in this room when she died so messy, this scrap of paper puts him in here with her. Let's see what else we can find."

As Longarm found a woman's carpetbag and began to go through it, Flynn said, "You're right. I wasn't thinking. But what's this you say about her taunting him? How do you know he didn't just bust in and go for her with that knife?"

Longarm pointed with his chin at a nightgown draped over a chair in one corner of the room. He said, "Not many gals sleep naked when they're alone. The landlady said she didn't hear anything, and the door wasn't forced. She let him in."

Flynn gulped. "Jesus! Knowing he was going to kill her?"

"Not hardly. I'd say that part came as a surprise. Most women feel they have certain powers over a man, spread out naked. If they didn't meet outside, he likely came here and signaled. They were good at signals other folks weren't supposed to know about. I'll let him fill in the blank spaces after I catch him."

Flynn stared down at the grotesquely mutilated body and said, "Yeah. She must have thought he wanted to screw her, and for all we know, she let him. But what was that about her taunting him?"

Longarm took a glass vial from Lottie's bag, sniffed it, and said, "Cyanide. Gals are funny that way. You'd think they'd learn that the last thing a man wants to hear right after some good loving is how dumb he is. But it does seem that they always pick just that time to let us have it."

Flynn smiled wryly and said, "Say no more. I'm a married man myself. I can see how it must have happened. They got back together and started to make up. But she was still sore at him and—"

"She was buying time, hoping for a chance to poison him. Only she said the wrong thing, or maybe he was just smarter than she'd counted on. Anyhow, she's out of the way, so we don't have to worry about some fool jury letting her off just for being so pretty and helpless."

"And now?"

"Now I'd best get cracking after MacLeod. I was worried some about presenting my case to a judge and jury, seeing how complicated it was and how little I could really prove."

He stared thoughtfully down at the mangled cadaver before he suggested, "It might be a good idea to get a photographer up here to take some pictures. He may try to brazen through

his story about his high-grading confidence scheme, but no lawyer born of mortal woman is going to get him off for doing
this!"

Flynn observed, "You sound pretty confident, considering
the lead he has on you, Longarm."

Longarm put a cheroot in his mouth, chewed it, and said,
"Hell, he can't have gone that far, poor bastard."

A foghorn moaned through the morning fog of San Francisco as
Longarm lounged between two stacks of redwood lumber. The
tall three-master moored to the end of the quay had finished
loading and would be leaving with the next tide, bound for Australia. The gangplank was still down and he could hear the
sounds of crewmen as they went about their chores on the ship's
deck. He couldn't see them at this distance in the fog.

Longarm stiffened, gun in hand, as he heard the grating of
shoe leather on wet cobblestones. He peered out between the
stacks of lumber and saw a seaman moving toward the gangplank with a duffle bag on his shoulder. The man didn't look his
way. It was just as well. Longarm didn't want to have to explain
why he was skulking about with a .44 in his fist at this hour.

He took out his watch and consulted it by the dim gray light.
The clipper would be leaving soon. He was probably wrong.
He'd been wrong about the last two ships he'd come down to see
off. Could the idiot be dumb enough to make a run back East
with only three railroads to choose from and U.S. deputies
watching every one?

The trouble with being a tricky knave was that it narrowed a
man's options. Longarm wouldn't have known where to start
looking for a wilder sort who simply cut and run. But MacLeod
was shifty as hell and seven times smarter than he ought to be,
so he could be counted on to do the smartest thing. He'd undoubtedly fooled a lot of people in his day. By now he might
have figured out how he'd been flustered. He was probably
pretty angry about it, too.

The sound of footsteps was coming down the quay again.
Longarm glanced out, saw another dim figure toting a sailor's
duffle, and began to back off. Then he noticed that the man was
wearing miner's boots.

Longarm cocked his .44 and stepped out, calling, "Just freeze right where you are, MacLeod. I won't say it twice!"

The figure stopped and slowly turned. Then he suddenly dropped the bulky bag and fell behind it on the cobbles! A flash of orange winked at Longarm, and the lawman fired. A piece of redwood slapped the side of Longarm's cheek and his own bullet exploded socks and underwear out of the ripped-open duffle. Longarm dropped and crabbed sideways as MacLeod put another round where his head had just been. He knew he was invisible in his space between the lumber, so he fired once for effect, then turned and ran back. He grunted himself through a slit at the rear of the piled lumber, moved down two stacks, then holstered the gun and climbed to the top.

He crawled across the damp boards to the forward edge, drew his gun again, and peered over. From his new vantage point, he had a bird's-eye view of MacLeod behind his improvised cover.

He called out, "Give it up, old son. I've got you cold."

MacLeod rolled wildly and fired up at him. The bullet hit the wood just under Longarm's gun hand, driving a big splinter into the heel of his palm and knocking the Colt from his grasp!

"Aw, shit," he muttered, as the gun clattered to the paving below. Then MacLeod was up and running as Longarm rolled off his gut and fumbled the derringer from his vest pocket. He aimed the little brass pistol in his blood-slicked hand and got off a shot as MacLeod was running up the gangplank. Naturally, the shot missed at that range.

Longarm got down off the lumber and picked up his Colt with his left hand as he put the derringer away and sucked at his injured right hand. He took out a kerchief, bound it around his injury, and shifted the .44 back to his right hand as he walked slowly toward the gangplank.

A crewman up in the rigging called down, "What's going on down there?"

Longarm called back, "I'm a deputy U.S. marshal chasing a murderer. Did you see where he went?"

"Everyone on deck's took cover, Marshal. I don't see *nobody* down there."

There was the sound of a shot and the crew member yelped, swinging himself behind the thick pine mast as he yelled, "He just took a shot at me from the poop deck! He's down behind the skylight, for'd the wheelhouse!"

Longarm ran to the gangplank and moved up it, ducking his head as he reached the well deck. He dropped behind a pair of lifeboats on a hatch cover before risking a cautious peek aft.

There was nothing much to see. The railing of the higher poop deck was silhouetted against the skyline of San Francisco. MacLeod was too slick to have his head in view there.

There was a ladder leading up on either side, near the rails. Longarm figured MacLeod would have them both covered. So he decided not even to consider getting there that way.

He called out, "Damn it, MacLeod, you're just making things complicated for no good reason! This ship ain't about to carry you to Australia or anywhere else!"

A voice called back, "I'll stand pat, you son of a bitch! How'd you know where to find me?"

"I figured you'd want to get someplace out of my jurisdiction. You're too smart to book passage on just any ship. So I had a talk with the harbormaster. This clipper stops at Valparaiso on its way to down under, and we don't have an extradition treaty with Chile, so— Hey, why don't you pack it in, and I'll explain it all as I take you to the federal building."

"You'll never take me alive, you bastard! What did you do to turn Lottie against me?"

"You did that yourself by being too greedy. Did you really think you'd somehow bought a real gold mine?"

"I've figured out how you tricked me with that false assay, God damn your eyes. You want me, come and take me!"

Longarm noticed that a member of the crew was staring out at him through a doorway leading to the quarters under the poop deck. He motioned the man back, even though MacLeod couldn't see him from up on top.

He knew MacLeod had no line of sight on his position either, so he broke cover and ran to the doorway, shoving the crewman inside.

He found that they were in a low-beamed corridor, running toward the stern. He whispered to the crewman, "Show me where the helm is, quick!"

The sailor led him back, muttering, "No way you can get at him without getting your head blown off, friend. There's a couple of hatches leading topside, but he's got everything for'd the wheelhouse under his gun!"

They moved back to a wardroom and Longarm saw the skylight overhead. He moved along the shadows of the port bulkhead as he kept his muzzle trained on the glass. There was nothing staring back at him but gray sky and, way up, a gliding seagull.

The wardroom ended, aft, in two more doorways on either side of what looked like a big wooden chimney. He pointed at it with his chin and asked, "Is that where the chains from your wheel run down to the rudder?"

The crewman nodded, but said, "You can't get inside. Wouldn't do no good if you could. The wheelhouse sits smack-dab on top."

Longarm thumbed the spent shells from his .44 and reached into his coat pocket for spare ammunition. The crewman whispered, "You're bleeding."

Longarm muttered, "I know I'm bleeding. Keep your voice down and get back out of my way."

He reloaded his revolver as, overhead, MacLeod called out, "God damn you, Longarm! Come out and fight like a man!"

Longarm raised the muzzle of his .44 above the level of his own head, aiming at the ceiling.

He waited until MacLeod called out again and he heard an overhead board creak. Then Longarm fired four times in rapid succession.

The sound was deafening in the low-ceilinged wardroom, but he could hear MacLeod yelp like a coyote being run over by a train, so he fired once more, directly up at the sound.

Up on deck, propelled by flying splinters and a .44 slug directly up his rectum, Kevin MacLeod took off for the sky!

He didn't get there. His froglike leap shot him out over the skylight, screaming in agony. Then he belly flopped down on the panes of glass and just kept coming as Longarm and the startled sailor moved back out of the way.

MacLeod landed face down on the wardroom floor in a windfall of shattered glass. He rolled on his side in agony and drew his knees to his chest, his gun hand pinned to the blood-spattered flooring as he glared with hate-filled eyes at the tall figure looming above him in the blue haze of gunsmoke filling the room.

Longarm muttered, "Aw, shit," and stepped forward to kick the gun out of MacLeod's hand. It banged against the far bulkhead, out of reach, so Longarm knelt beside the gutshot killer and said, "I'll bet that smarts. I'll send for a doc, old son."

MacLeod coughed blood, licked his lips, and said, "You've killed me, you son of a bitch! I might have known you'd pull another of your dumb tricks!"

Longarm said, "For a man with a bullet up his ass you sure have a poor opinion of everyone else. I'd say you were right about one thing, though. You're dying, sure as hell."

He started, reloading his .44 as he added, "Before you go, would you mind confessing a few things in front of me and this witness?"

"You can go to hell."

"Thanks just the same, but I had Denver in mind. With you and Lottie both dead, a few loose ends hardly matter, seeing as how neither of you has to stand trial."

Other crewmen were coming out of the woodwork to admire Longarm's handiwork. A man with the four stripes of a captain on his sleeve asked, "What's this all about, Marshal?"

Longarm said, "I ain't a marshal, just a deputy. And my tale is too long to be told before I have to catch the ferry back to Oakland and hop the C.P. back to Denver. Let's just say this poor cuss here was too smart for his own good."

He looked down at the dying man as he said, "You and Lottie should have ridden out your pat hand, MacLeod. You know I never could have proven my notions in any court of law, don't you?"

"The bitch tried to kill me. So I paid her back good. *That* was your doing too, wasn't it?"

"Yep. It's called 'divide and conquer.'"

He looked up at the captain and asked, "Do you mind sending one of your men for a doctor and the local P.D.?"

The captain said, "I already did, as soon as it was safe to move. They'll be here any minute."

Longarm nodded and told MacLeod, "There you go, old son. Just rest easy and we'll see how bad you're hurt."

MacLeod didn't answer. He couldn't. Longarm felt the side of his neck as a crewman said, "Jesus, I think he's dead!"

Longarm said, "You're right. He did say something about me killing him. First time the bastard's told me the truth since I met up with him."

The San Francisco police asked a lot of tedious questions, considering how simple it all was. But in the end they said it was all right for a federal marshal to shoot wanted killers on the waterfront, so Longarm went down Market Street and caught the ferry across the bay to Oakland.

He thought he'd probably missed the train to Cheyenne, and he'd already seen what there was of Oakland. So he hurried to the depot, hoping he was wrong.

As he stepped through the glass doors, he thanked his lucky stars for blessing him with good eyesight.

Felicidad Vallejo was standing by the ticket counter, as if she were expecting to meet someone.

A few feet farther on, standing with her arms crossed and tapping her pretty little foot on the cement, he noticed Pru Sawyer.

Neither woman knew the other, and Longarm surmised that it might be a good idea to keep it that way. So he crawfished backward out the door before either girl could spot him. He didn't consider himself a coward, but there is such a thing as pure common sense, and he'd rather have faced an armed band of Apache than get into a hair-pulling contest between two jealous females!"

He circled the big brick depot and found a board fence separating the yards from the carriage road. He put his hands up and hauled himself over the top.

He landed inside on the gritty cinders and started legging it across the yards. The dusty maroon sides of the eastbound express were just starting to pull away from the platform, so Longarm started running.

A yard bull saw him and yelled out, "Hey, you ain't supposed to be in here, cowboy!"

But Longarm paid the bull no heed as he chased the train. He ran down the tracks after it, slowly gaining on the rear platform as the train moved out through the yards. A girl in a big hat and a pinch-waisted dress was staring at him from the platform as he slowly caught up with her and the express.

Longarm reached forward, grabbed the brass railing, and was

almost dragged before he could get an instep on the rear coupler and haul himself aboard, saying, "Howdy, ma'am."

The girl said, "Well, hello! Do you always board trains that way?"

He climbed over the rail, grinning sheepishly, and answered, "Only when they try to leave without me, ma'am. My name is Custis Long and I work for Uncle Sam."

She laughed a pretty skylark laugh and said, "I'm Melony Evans and I don't. Are you going all the way? To Cheyenne, I mean."

He said, "Cheyenne and then some. I've got to get back to Denver before payday."

"How interesting. I'm on my way to Denver myself. We live on Sherman Avenue."

"We, ma'am? You don't seem to be wearing a ring"

"I'm not married. I live with my aunt and uncle in Denver."

"Oh," he said. "Well, I'd best go in and see if the conductor has a compartment he'll rent me. I purely hate trying to sleep sitting up in a day coach, and I figure at least two nights aboard this fool train."

As he eased past her, Melony said, "Perhaps we'll meet later, in the club car. You can let me know if they have a sleeping compartment for you."

He started to ask if she had one, but considered it a mite early to be so forward, so he just grinned and said, "I'll do that, ma'am. I'm sure I'll find someplace, or other to spend the next couple of nights."

NOVEL 8

———◆———

Longarm
and the
Nesters

Chapter 1

Longarm didn't wait to see where the shot had come from. He knew the sound of a rifle from its whiplash crack, and his reflexes sent him rolling out of his saddle before whoever had triggered it could pump a second cartridge into the chamber. The yellow dust raised by the slug that had plowed into the ground between his horse's hooves was still settling when Longarm landed on his feet and crouched in back of the animal. He stood at the roan's hindquarters, where its hind legs and haunches would give him the greatest protection, and bent forward to keep his head from becoming a target while he waited for a second shot to follow the first.

Enough seconds ticked by to give Longarm time to think about trying to grab for his own rifle, but the .44-40 Winchester was resting snugly in its boot on the wrong side of the horse. There was no way he could reach it without exposing his head, arm, and shoulder.

Seconds dragged into minutes, but the shot he was waiting for still didn't come. Longarm credited the bushwhacker with enough intelligence not to waste ammunition on an invisible target. He wondered how long it would take the shooter to think of the obvious next step. He got ready to drop to the ground in case the bushwhacker brought down his horse and stripped him of his protective cover.

Instead of another shot, though, a man's voice, not too far distant, shouted, "A varning it vas I give you, *nesakonnley*! I see you turn off from the train track and ride this vay! Now, I tell you to go back! You put your hands on my fence, then it don't be the ground I shoot at next time! I kill you dead!"

Frowning, Longarm tried to riddle out the strange accent that colored the man's speech. Billy Vail had explained that there would be a lot of foreigners involved in the assignment that had brought Longarm to southern Kansas, but the chief marshal had been somewhat vague as to the country of their origin. The accent was one Longarm hadn't encountered before, even though he'd run into representatives of most of the European nationalities that were part of the population of the West of the 1880s. It seemed to him sometimes that the whole damned world was moving into the wide-open, unsettled prairies and mountains on the sunset side of the Mississippi. There wasn't much time for him to think about that at the moment, though. From the sound of the bushwhacker's voice, the unknown man was edging up on him a little bit at a time.

He called to the still-unseen rifleman, "You got me mixed up with somebody else, mister! My name ain't Connolly. I'm Custis Long, a deputy U.S. marshal, and I ain't a damned bit interested in your fence, except maybe to look at it!"

"You say to me you don't ride for Clem Hawkins?"

"I never heard that name either, any more'n I know this fellow Connolly."

"Is not somebody, *nesakonnley*," the stranger called back. "Is how you call a bad name. Bastard." There was a brief silence, then the unknown assailant went on, "Maybe I make mistake, mister. I don't shoot no more yet, but you prove to me you are vhat you say."

"I ain't taking your word you won't drop me if I show myself!" Longarm protested. "Anybody'd who'd drygulch a stranger ain't much in my book for telling the truth!"

"I do not make lies. I vill not shoot!" the man insisted.

"Tell you what," Longarm called. "You stand out in the open, where I can see you plain, and put your rifle on the ground. I'll hold up my badge and you can take a look at it. Does that sound fair enough?"

"*Da*. So I vill do."

Peering under the belly of his horse, Longarm got his first look at the stranger. The man stood with his empty hands outstretched, though the green thigh-high wheat sprouting up around him kept Longarm from seeing whether he'd really laid his gun on the ground, or whether he'd leaned it against his leg where he could grab it quickly. That wasn't important to Custis

Long. He knew he could get off two slugs from his own .44 Colt Model T before the bushwhacker could pick up a rifle and shoulder it. Just the same, he studied the other man for a long moment before offering himself as a target again.

Except for his headgear, the stranger might have been any farmer or cowhand. He wore a denim jacket over a butternut shirt, and his jaws were heavily bearded, although his upper lip was shaved clean. His nose came down straight from thick, black brows and flared into a bulbous tip. His eyes were dark, his cheekbones high. It was what the other wore on his head that Longarm found strange. Instead of the usual wide-brimmed, high-crowned felt hat that almost every outdoorsman in the West wore winter and summer, the stranger was wearing a floppy, round cloth cap with a short, shiny bill.

Satisfied that there was no chance he'd be beaten to the first shot if further gunplay ensued, Longarm stepped from the shelter of the roan's rump and walked slowly toward the fence that ran between the two men. The other started equally slowly to meet him. Longarm casually pulled aside the flap of his long Prince Albert coat. The stranger spread his outstretched hands wider apart when he saw the Colt that Longarm wore butt-forward, high on his left hip, but Longarm was careful to keep his hands well away from the gun. He moved deliberately, taking his wallet from his inside breast pocket, and let the coat drape forward over the pistol as soon as he had the wallet out.

Flipping open the wallet, he held it up so the man could see the deputy U.S. marshal's badge pinned inside its fold. He said, "Now then. Unless you've got some reason why you'd be bashful about meeting up with the law, that ought to satisfy you."

"You said it is Long, your name?" the stranger frowned.

"That's right. Just like it says in the engraving on the badge."

"How am I knowing this? If it is not yours, the badge—"

Exasperated, Longarm interrupted, "You're the damnedest, most suspicious fellow I've met up with for a while. You act like you're an owlhoot on the prod—which you could be, for all I know. Well, if you are, I'll find out about it, and if you ain't, then you'll just have to take my word that me and the badge belong together."

Unexpectedly the man smiled, showing two rows of gleaming white teeth. "Now I believe you. If it vas you are not who you say, you vould this minute be trying to proof to me still more. *Dobro*. Me, I am Nicolai Belivev."

"Glad to make your acquaintance." Longarm looked past Belivev for a house of some kind, but saw none. "You live around here close?"

"There." Belivev pointed to what looked like a hump in the ground on the far side of the wheatfield.

"A soddy?"

Nodding, Belivev replied, "Is vhat they are call, here. Next year, *pri Bog shini,* I build a real house on top of the ground, then ve don't live no more like rabbit in hole."

"You been here long?"

"Five years." The man's voice was proud. "This year, I come to be citizen of U.S.A."

"Mind telling me where you come from, Mr. Belivev? You throw out a lot of words I never heard before."

"From Russia ve come," Belivev answered. Then, bitterly and with hatred in his tone, he continued, "Mother Russia! A mother like nobody needs!"

"You said 'we,'" Longarm frowned. "You mean there're a lot of settlers around here from Russia?"

"*Da*. Ve are many." Belivev turned and waved his arm. Beyond the hump of the soddie, Longarm saw the mounds of other sod houses, as well as a few dwellings built from wood.

"How'd it happen that all of you picked out Kansas?"

"It vas from your railroad line, you see? They send men over to tell us they sell land for a few kopecks that ve pay each year, until the land, it belong to us."

"From what you said a minute ago, I got the idea you weren't too sorry to leave Russia," Longarm observed.

"*Da*. Is true. Is not Mother Russia any more, like vhen our grandfathers go there from Germany long ago." Belivev hesitated before adding, "Is not here like vhat the men from your railroad tell us it is being, maybe. Mr. Long, you are—" he hesitated, searching for a word— "law-bringer for the U.S. government, is true?"

"I'm an officer who upholds the federal laws, if that's what you're asking me."

"*Da*. Is vhat. You tell me, then— Is lawful a man puts up a fence to guard his vheat while it grows, and other men cut it down so they can run it over with the feet from their cattle and horses?"

"That ain't exactly covered by federal law," Longarm said. He fished a cheroot out of his vest pocket, flicked a matchhead with his thumbnail, and puffed the cigar into life. Then he went on, speaking slowly and thoughtfully. "Fence-cutting's mostly covered by state laws, Mr. Belivev. Of course, here in Kansas they've got a law that makes trespassing on another man's land illegal, but you've sure got a right to put up a fence to keep people from damaging your crops."

"Then vhy the men who raise cattle cut our fences down? And vhy the sheriff don't make them stop vhen ve ask him to?"

"There might be a lot of reasons." Longarm saw no reason to tell Belivev that one of those reasons was probably responsible for his having been sent to Kansas in the first place.

"Tell me them," Belivev asked. Then, before Longarm could reply, he shook his head. "No. A better thing it vould be if you tell them to Mordka Danilov. He can more clear than me explain to the others vhy. Marshal Long, you vill go vith me to see Mordka, *da*?"

"Well—" Longarm looked at the sun, beating down from the unclouded sky as it started its final slide to the west. The heat made a liar of the calendar, which said it was now autumn. He asked Belivev, "Just who is this Mordka fellow?"

"Mordka Danilov is the elder of the *Bratiya*," the Russian said. He explained, "In your language, *Bratiya*, it means Brethren. This is religion I speak about, our religion that causes us such trouble in Russia that ve move now to your country."

"Uh-huh. Sort of your pastor, you might say?"

"Mordka guides us, he advises us. He does not preach at us."

"Oh. I see," Longarm said, though he wondered at the distinction. He thought for a moment, then nodded. "All right. If you think it'll help, I'll talk to him. Where's his house?"

"If you vill come vith me, I take you there," Belivev offered. "Is not far away."

Longarm indicated the fence with its stretched wire strands studded by barbs. "How am I going to get my horse on the other side?"

Belivev pointed to the hump that marked the sod house in which he lived. "The path to Mordka's house goes that vay. If you ride around my fence, and I go across through the vheat, then ve get to my house at same time. From it, there is just little vay to Mordka's."

Longarm nodded. Nicolai Belivev turned away, stooped to pick up the rifle he'd laid on the ground, and started trudging through the wheatfield without looking back. Longarm watched the Russian for a moment, then mounted and nudged the roan with his toe. Turning the animal, he rode parallel to the fence until it ended in a corner, then reined along it on a rough path toward the soddy. Before he got to the hump, Belivev came out without the rifle, and was waiting when he rode up. Longarm reined in.

"Which way now?" he asked.

Belivev said, "Ahead. Is not far. I valk by your horse and show you the vay."

With Longarm on horseback and Belivev on foot, conversation between them was impossible as the Russian led the way along the fenceline to a rambling crazy quilt of a house, a quarter of a mile distant. When his guide stopped and pointed to the house, Longarm dismounted.

"Come," Belivev said. "You can please explain to Mordka about the fences. Is better he tells us in our own language vhat he hears from you. Some of the *Bratiya* don't know so much *yashlkne Ameriska* as like I do."

A tall, raw-boned woman, her head bound up in a scarf, opened the door to Belivev's knock. She kept her pale blue eyes fixed on Longarm while she and Belivev exchanged a few words in their own tongue. Longarm heard the name "Mordka" repeated several times, but that was all he understood. After their parley ended, the woman stood aside and motioned for them to enter. Belivev almost pushed Longarm into the house.

After the bright sunlight, the interior seemed dim, almost to the point of utter darkness. Like so many homesteaders' dwellings, the house had few windows, and all of them were small because of the scarcity and high cost of glass. When Longarm's eyes had adjusted to the lack of light, what he saw was an almost exact duplicate of the homes he'd seen elsewhere in places where settlements were just springing up.

There was a table and three or four straight-backed chairs. A woodburning range stood in one corner of the room. On the walls, shelves held bags, cans, and wooden boxes. Cooking utensils were hung on nails behind the stove. A low bench held a bucket and a washbasin; a towel drooped from a nail over it. At the table, a man sat with a book open in front of him. For a moment the man did not raise his head, and Longarm followed the example of Belivev and the woman, who stood quietly, waiting.

When the man closed his book and looked up, Longarm found himself the object of the scrutiny of a pair of the most piercing blue eyes he'd ever seen. They seemed to shine under bristling, snowy brows that matched the long, square-cut beard rippling down over the seated man's chest. Though the beard was full, Longarm noticed that, like Belivev's, this man's upper lip was clean-shaven, revealing full, red lips outlined by deep creases that slanted down from a hawklike nose.

"Nicolai," the man said. His voice was deep and resonant.

"*Kum* Mordka," Belivev replied. "*Ero gostya imya Long.*"

"Mr. Long." Mordka Danilov nodded without rising or offering to shake hands. "*Pazhalasta.* I make you welcome to my house." He said to the woman, "Marya. *Sedalische. Sbteen.*"

Quickly she brought chairs for Longarm and Belivev, placing them at the table, with Longarm facing Danilov, and Belivev between them. The woman stepped to the stove and busied herself with the steaming kettle and thick, tall glasses. She carried the glasses to the table, set one in front of her husband, then served Longarm and Belivev.

Mordka raised his glass. "To your good arrival, Mr. Long."

Longarm picked up his glass and, following the example of the other men, sipped the hot liquid. He recognized the flavor of honey, diluted by the hot water, and decided that a good tot of Maryland rye would have improved the brew.

Setting his glass back on the table, Nicolai Belivev told their host, "*Sodar Long ero priditi ohpravleny.*"

"*Na zemstud*?" the older man asked.

"*Nyet,*" Belivev replied. "*Centrovley.*"

Mordka Danilov frowned thoughtfully, looking at Longarm. He asked, "You come, as Nicolai says, from the central government, Mr. Long? From Washington?" His English was much better than Belivev's.

"Not Washington. Denver. That's in Colorado. But I'm a federal officer, so I guess you could say I'm from Washington, in a manner of speaking. I'm a deputy U.S. Marshal, Mr. Danilov."

"Ah." Mordka nodded. "You do not belong then to the ranchers, as the sheriff does?"

"I don't *belong* to anybody but myself," Longarm said emphatically. "I've got a job that I do, seeing that the law's upheld. That's all I'm interested in. It doesn't matter who breaks the law, I arrest him, whether it's you or the sheriff or the richest rancher in the county."

"Why have you come here?" Danilov asked. "Who among us is breaking the law? Surely not the *Bratiya*?"

"As far as I know right now, nobody's broken any laws I'm obliged to enforce. My chief sent me down here to make sure there's not any crookedness in the election that's coming along."

Mordka smiled somewhat bitterly. "I see. You do not interest yourself in trespassers who cut fences and destroy crops, then?"

"Not usually," the deputy answered. "That's the sheriff's job."

"If he refuses to do his job, then can we turn to you for help?"

Longarm wasn't sure exactly how he wanted to answer a question of that kind. He took his time in replying, and chose his words carefully. ".The law's a pretty broad thing, Mr. Danilov. Federal officers are only supposed to handle cases where there's been a federal law broken. There are times when we've got to step in, like when a local officer breaks a law or doesn't do his job right. But it's not real easy to set up rules in cases like that."

Danilov nodded thoughtfully. "You have not been here long, have you?"

"I just got in last night. Right now, all I'm doing is sort of looking around."

"Nicolai has told you of the troubles we of the *Bratiya* are having?"

"About all he's told me so far is that you're having a bad time." Longarm decided it was time for him to take control of the questioning. "You and Mr. Belivev keep talking about this thing you call the *Bratiya*. Do you mind telling me exactly what it is?"

"We have no secrets, if that's what your question means," Danilov replied. "In your language, Mr. Long, *Bratiya* means Brethren. It is our religion. It is each man's personal freedom to choose his religion in this country, is it not?"

"It sure is," Longarm agreed. "Though I can't say I've picked one out yet for myself."

"You will, someday," Danilov said with a smile. "But if you

are not a pious man, I can understand why you would be puzzled by our religion. Tell me, do you know of the Anabaptists? Have you ever heard of the Mennonites? The Amish, I think they are called in America."

"There were some Amish folks up north of where I grew up, I recall. I don't guess I've heard about the others."

"They're much the same, Mr. Long. I'll try not to make my explanation too long and tiresome. The Mennonite beliefs were established three hundred years ago, Mr. Long, by a priest named Menno Simons, who found the rituals of the Roman Church too elaborate, too worldly. He began to preach only what is in the Bible itself—simple worship of God and Christ, without altars or incense or fancy robes. Menno Simons made many converts, who called themselves Mennonites. They renounced worldly trappings not mentioned in the Bible, and vowed to live in peace with all men. They put aside weapons and all acts of violence."

Longarm broke in, "Wait a minute. That doesn't square up with Mr. Belivev taking a shot at me, telling me he'd shoot me if I put a hand on his fence."

"Be patient, please," Danilov said. "I will try to make that clear later. Menno Simons began his preaching in the sixteenth century, by your calendar. Even before he died, though, in many of the countries where he made converts, the Roman and Protestant churches as well as the secular governments had begun to persecute those who had adopted Menno's beliefs. His followers refused to serve in armies, or to take oaths in courts of law. The ancestors of our own people, those of us who now live here, were promised freedom to follow their own beliefs by the Tsarina of Russia, who came to be known as Catherine the Great. They migrated to Russia, most of them from Germany." Mordka paused to sip his cooling honey mixture.

Longarm took the opportunity to insert a question. "That must have been a long time back. Dates ain't my strong suit, or history either, but wasn't she the Russian queen a hundred years ago?"

Danilov nodded. "Yes. A hundred years. For eighty of them, our families lived peacefully in Russia. Then a new Tsar came to the throne, and he decided that Russia must become one land, one people, with one language and one religion. Our fathers learned Russian, and taught us to speak it, but they would not give up our religion for the official Russian Church, and they would not serve in the Tsar's army. So the persecution began once more. For a while our families bowed under, but when the Tsar sent his Cossacks to imprison and kill those who would not worship as he ordered, or join his church, some of us reluctantly decided that we must fight back. It made us very sorrowful, but we learned to shoot and to do the other deeds a man must do to protect his family. Of course we could not do this and still follow all of Menno's teachings, so we kept what we could of our old beliefs and called ourselves the *Bratiya*."

Mordka Danilov paused and looked piercingly at Longarm with his flashing blue eyes. "You understand, Mr. Long, it was not easy for us to do this, and our hearts were heavy. So, when the agents from your railroads came to find people who wanted to come to America and buy the land they were selling so cheaply, we saw that we could be free in America to follow our religion as we wanted to. That is why we emigrated; that is why we are now here in your state of Kansas. But even here, we are finding that we must still fight to protect ourselves. Does this help you understand why we ask you where we can find help?"

His face sober, Longarm nodded slowly. "I guess it does, Mr. Danilov. Only from what I've gathered, your troubles here don't come from what you believe in, but from putting your land into wheat, and fencing it off."

"Only partly, I think," Mordka said. "Perhaps if we had chosen to raise cattle, there would be no trouble. But we are farmers. We must work now and raise crops to pay for our land, and even to earn money for our food and clothing."

"Oh, I understand that part," Longarm told him. "The thing is, I don't see much I can do to help you, except to have a talk with the sheriff. Maybe I can get him to keep things peaceful, if he's not doing it now."

"We would be grateful," Mordka said, rising to his feet. Longarm and Belivev stood up also. Mordka went on, "It is close to the hour I spend in meditation. Nicolai, will you stay and join me? I'm certain Mr. Long can find his way back to town without help."

"Sure," Longarm agreed. He added, "And I'll come back and talk to you some more in a few days, Mr. Danilov. Maybe I'll see some way that I can ease things a bit."

"You will be welcome in my house at any time," Danilov said. "And if you are curious about our religion, you will also be welcome at our small church near the town."

"Thanks. And if anything happens that you want to tell me about, I'm staying at the hotel."

Outside once more, Longarm mounted with a thoughtful face and started the roan back toward the settlement. As he rode, he studied the fences that paralleled the crude road. He hadn't been assigned before to a case that took him into an area where Glidden wire was used. The barbed fencewire had appeared on the market fairly recently, and he'd heard the wire discussed—but mostly cussed—by cattlemen who'd encountered it. As he looked closely at the tautly stretched, saw-toothed wire, he could understand the reason for their displeasure.

Even at close range, under the declining afternoon sun, it was hard to see the fence against the growing wheat. At night, or in a storm, unless a horseman happened to notice the posts that supported the fence, it would actually be invisible. A horse moving at any pace faster than a walk could barrel into the sharp teeth of the Glidden wire and scrape cuts on its chest and legs that might cripple the animal. The top strand of the wire was just high enough to catch the legs of a mounted man, and against its barbs, the soft leather of boot uppers would provide no protection at all.

He could see, too, how cattle being driven across open prairie could pile up on a fence like that until the pressure of the herd on its leaders snapped the posts. That very pressure would shove the leading steers into the sharp, thin strands and cut them to ribbons as they reared in panic from the pain of the metal points stabbing into their flesh. *It'd be easy as hell for a rancher to lose a good handful of steers that way,* Longarm thought as he let his horse set its own pace between the lines of posts.

I guess if I had a ranch around here, I wouldn't cotton to seeing the prairie all cut up this way, Longarm told himself. *I'd be real tempted to carry a pair of nippers in my saddlebag and snip those wires, if it was my animals they were likely to tear up. But it'd be just as tough if I'd put my sweat into raising a crop and had a herd of steers or a bunch of riders cut my fence and trample my land. Damn it,* he thought, *this is one place where a man can have trouble making up his mind who's right and who's wrong, where these Glidden wire fences are concerned.*

His thinking didn't comfort Longarm a great deal. It only aggravated what he'd felt about this assignment from the moment Billy Vail had handed it to him in Denver.

Vail was in a testy mood, and Longarm wasn't happy either. He'd just seen Julia Burnside off on the morning express; she was moving with her father back to Atlanta, and he hated like hell to see her go. Julia had been good company as well as a good bedmate for Longarm during the several months since they'd first met. Tired after a long night of lovemaking, and two hours late because the eastbound express didn't pull out of Denver until ten A.M., Longarm snapped back at Vail when he made his usual remark about his deputy's tardiness. Usually the chief marshal's comment was half-joking, but this time it was completely serious.

"Damn it, Billy, I ain't married to this office the way you are," Longarm retorted. "Seems to me you'd allow for all the times I work day and night on a case, when I show up a few minutes late."

"If you call two hours a few minutes, you need a new watch," Vail shot back, glaring out from under his heavy eyebrows. "I've got a new assignment for you, and now you'll have to hump it to catch the noon Santa Fe train to Fort Dodge."

"I'll be glad to hustle, if it gets me out of this office. What's wrong at Dodge?"

"Nothing, except you'll have to stop there to pick up a horse. Where you're going is about fifty miles east of Dodge, some wide place in the road called Junction. If it'll make you feel better, you can ride the Santa Fe spur that goes right to the town, and save fifty miles on horseback."

"Who am I going after, at this Junction place?" Longarm asked.

"Nobody. You'll be looking *at*, not *for*. There's a big squall blowing up down there. It seems the locals are ready to fight over who they'll elect to run the county. There're rumors of plans to stuff ballot boxes and keep a lot of people from voting."

"Now hold up, Billy. That's for Kansas to worry about, not us. Hell, why are we sticking our noses into a local election fuss?"

"It's not just local," Vail informed him. "You know this is a presidential election year too, and the big men in Washington are afraid it's going to be a close race. The smart money's betting there won't be ten thousand votes nationwide between the winner and the loser. They say even a few hundred votes are important in this one."

"In a place like that, there can't be much over a hundred votes."

"Maybe not. But when I get a wire from Washington telling me to send a good man to keep an eye on things, I know they're really worrying."

"But damn it, Billy, it's not a job for a lawman!" Longarm protested. "What you need there is a nursemaid."

The portly chief marshal pounded his desk with a large hand that showed the scars and calluses of a far less sedentary life than the one he was now leading. "Then, by God, you'll be the nursemaid! Now, I don't want to hear any more arguments. You get that noon train, and you see that the voting's honest. If it's not, you can call for a fresh vote. Is that clear?"

"Clear enough," Longarm grumbled. "But I don't like it."

"Nobody asked you if you did," Vail said curtly. He picked up a fresh sheaf of papers from his littered desk, his signal that the time for talking had ended.

Longarm carried the grudge over his new assignment, together with his unhappiness about Julia's departure, on the train that took him down the eastern slope of the Rockies and across the broken Kansas prairie to Fort Dodge. He had to kill a night and most of a day there, waiting for a cattle train that eventually creaked its way across the flatlands on the spur that ended at Junction. His butt sore from the unpadded seat in the caboose, he reached railend a little before midnight, put his horse in the settlement's livery stable, and himself into a room in the town's one hotel. Then, after sleeping late, he set out to scout the territory he'd be working in, and wound up getting shot at when Nicolai Belivev mistook him for a fence-cutter.

As he rode back toward Junction in the red sunset glow, Longarm was more certain than ever that Billy Vail's assignment was going to be a nasty one to carry out.

Chapter 2

Junction was a bit livelier than it had been when Longarm had ridden out of the town at noon. Evening had brought in some of the hands from the ranches closer to town, their numbers swollen now by extra men hired for the autumn roundup and shipping chores. There were also a number of the *Bratiya* homesteaders on the street. The Brethren were easy to recognize, not only by their full beards and shaven-upper lips, but by their clothing. Some of them clung to the short boots and baggy tucked-in trousers that they'd worn in their homeland; even those who'd become Americanized to the extent of adopting Levi's still wore belted blouses with full sleeves gathered tightly at the wrists, and almost all of them had on the short-billed cloth caps of the type Nicolai Belivev wore.

Longarm left his horse at the livery stable, slid his Winchester out of its boot, and tossed his saddlebags over one shoulder for the short walk to the hotel. He stepped into a saloon and purchased a bottle of Maryland rye. When he emerged a moment later, he noticed that dusk was gathering rapidly, and lights were beginning to show inside the crude, unpainted buildings that stood widely spaced on Junction's only street. From the three stores and two saloons the town boasted, from the hotel and the restaurant across from them, as well as from the doctor's office and the barbershop, lamplight spilled across the rutted street in yellow rectangles.

Longarm kicked the door of his room closed behind him, stood his rifle in a corner, dropped the saddlebags, and took out the bottle of Maryland rye he'd tucked under his arm. A quick swallow washed the dust of the afternoon's ride from his gullet. He poured water from the pitcher on the nightstand into the washbasin, and got rid of the clinging film of Kansas soil that had accumulated on his face and hands. Having dried himself with a huck towel, he fished a cheroot from his vest pocket and flicked his thumbnail across the head of a match to light the cheroot before letting another small sip of whiskey trickle down his throat. Then he put his coat back on and went down to look for supper.

A quick glance at the free lunch counter in the Ace High Saloon—the one nearest the hotel—showed him that nothing had been added to the dessicated bologna, dry, cracked rat cheese, and dusty hard-boiled eggs he'd seen there at noon. At the bar, he nursed another tot of rye while trying to decide whether or not to investigate the possibilities of the other saloon, made up his mind it'd be a waste of effort, and crossed the street to the café. A slab of fried steak with an egg and potatoes fried in the same fat wasn't much tastier than the saloon's offerings, but at least the food was hot, and there were pie and coffee after the meal.

By the time Longarm stepped back out to the street, darkness was complete. The last flurry of business activity had ended for the day. The stores were now closed and the only lighted buildings were the hotel, the restaurant, and the Ace High and Cattleman's saloons. The only traffic was an occasional cowhand returning early to his bunkhouse, or moving from one drinking place to the other. From the Cattleman's Saloon he heard the thin tinkle of a honkytonk piano. He hadn't yet visited the Cattleman's, so Longarm crossed the street to have a close look at the place. Casual talk overheard in bars had given him a lot of valuable leads in the past, and he didn't see any reason why Junction's saloons shouldn't be a similar source of information. He stepped across the board sidewalk and pushed through the batwings.

Two poker tables and the faro layout were getting a good play, but the bar was almost deserted. There were tables along the wall opposite the bar, as well as a few scattered between the bar and the wall. At three of them, men sat talking to the saloon girls.

Like its counterpart up the street, the saloon's interior was a long rectangle with a stairway leading to a half-balcony in the back. The gaming tables sat under the balcony. At the end of the bar a piano stood; the player was a seam-faced, derbied man who might have been forty or sixty. He was holding a stein in one hand while the other wandered idly over the keyboard.

Longarm stopped at the middle of the bar. There were no customers to his right, but two or three men stood fairly close on his left side. When the barkeep came up, Longarm said, "Maryland rye, if your stock's good."

"Labeled bottles," the man told him. "We don't buy barrel rye, anyhow. This is mostly bourbon country." He took a bottle from the backbar and set it with a glass in front of Longarm. "Stranger, ain't you?"

Longarm tossed a dollar on the bar. "Got in late yesterday."

"Going to be around awhile?" The barkeep made no move to pick up the money.

"Long as I need to be, I suppose."

"Cattle buyer? Or wheat broker? You don't have the look of a working cowhand, and you sure as hell ain't a dry-goods drummer." When Longarm didn't reply, the barkeep shrugged. "Well, I don't guess it matters all that much. Whatever your line is, the first drink's on the house. Sort of a welcome to Jayhawk Junction."

"Jayhawk?" Longarm frowned. "I thought this place was just called Junction."

"It is. Temporary, though; there's another Junction up north. Jayhawk's a sort of joke. Mostly the folks who settled here after the War were jayhawkers. That was before the foreigners started coming in."

"What kind of foreigners are they?" Longarm tried to sound as if he were only idly curious, not really very interested. "I sure noticed a lot of 'em around when I rode in."

"Well, hell, what can you expect from a foreigner? I guess they're all right. Mostly farmers, wheat-growing farmers. Keep to themselves, got a church out a ways from town, spend a lot of time praying. I damn sure don't see any of 'em in here. If they do any drinking, they order from someplace else and drink at home."

"Do the jayhawkers give them a bad time?"

"Well, they don't love 'em, if that's what you mean. But there hasn't been any real trouble in the five or six years since the first ones started coming in."

"I heard some talk of fence-cutting," Longarm suggested.

"Oh, sure. But there's bound to be some of that wherever fences go up on what's always been open range. Of course, I've heard—" The barkeep stopped suddenly.

"Heard what?" Longarm asked.

"Nothing that'd interest anybody who don't live here," a new voice at Longarm's elbow said. "What Bob's been telling you is just idle gab."

"That's right," the barkeep agreed as Longarm turned to look at the man who'd spoken. "This is our sheriff, Jim Grover. Maybe he can tell you better than I can about how the foreigners and the rest of us get along."

Longarm nodded in Grover's direction. "Pleased to meet you, Sheriff. I was going to look you up tomorrow, anyhow."

"What about?" Grover asked.

"Suppose we just carry this bottle over to a table where we can talk private?" Longarm suggested. He indicated the rye. "This is what I'm drinking, but if you'd rather have bourbon—"

Wordlessly the barkeep set a second bottle out. Grover picked it up without taking his eyes off Longarm. Longarm took the rye and followed Grover to a table, isolated in the middle of the saloon. They sat down.

"All right, who are you and what kind of private business have you got with me?" the sheriff demanded.

Longarm slid out his wallet and flipped it open to show his deputy marshal's badge. "Name's Custis Long, Sheriff. I work out of the Denver office."

"Who are you looking for down here?"

"Nobody, yet," Longarm replied evenly.

"You damn sure didn't come all this way just for the ride."

"Oh, I've got business here, all right," Longarm said, his voice carefully casual. "That's what I was going to look you up about."

Grover grunted, a surly snarl. "Since I've saved you the trouble of looking for me, and since you're in my jurisdiction, suppose you tell me what your business is, then."

"Sure. But let's get this matter of jurisdiction straight, first," Longarm shot back. He'd encountered hard-nosed local sheriffs and marshals before, who resented the interference of outside officers. "I'm here on federal business—the election that's coming along soon."

"Hell, it's a local election," Grover protested. "Local and state and—" he stopped short. "Guess I forgot. We don't pay all that much mind to picking out a new president around here."

"Maybe not. But the men in Washington do. Just to refresh your memory, you'll be voting for a U.S. senator and congressman, too."

"All right. That makes it federal jurisdiction, I suppose. But why's the government so interested in a little place like this? Hell, there's not five hundred votes in this whole county."

"That's right," Longarm agreed. "But what I've been told is that it's such a close race that just a few thousand votes one way or the other could swing things either way. And the men in Washington want to make sure there's no monkey business. No ballot-box stuffing, no repeaters, no fighting around the voting places, nobody kept away from them."

"You saying there's supposed to be any of that going on here?" Grover demanded truculently.

"My chief in Denver's got word from Washington that there might be some local trouble, yes."

"What kind of trouble? Who'll be making it?"

Longarm shrugged. "Nobody's pointing any fingers, Grover. But from what little I've seen since I got here yesterday, I'd guess that bunch of homesteaders from Russia are mixed up in it some way."

"Nesters!" Grover snorted. "Damn foreigners bring trouble every place they try to push in! The goddamn Santa Fe's to blame! You know they got the idea of sending land agents over to Europe five or six years ago? To sell all them sections the government handed over to 'em for pushing the rails through?"

Longarm nodded. "I know. All the railroads are doing the same thing, though. Union Pacific in Nebraska, Northern Pacific in Dakota Territory, they're sending agents to Europe, just like the Santa Fe is. All of 'em have got more land than they know what to do with, and I guess they need whatever money they can get out of it."

"Oh, you can't blame the railroads for turning a dollar," Grover agreed. "But will you tell me why the hell they can't sell that land to ranchers, instead of a bunch of billy-be-damned dirt scratchers? Every one of them foreigners that comes in here gets himself a plow and starts breaking sod."

"Sure. The railroads pick out farmers because they want crops off that land to haul for freight. That's why they're making it so easy for the homesteaders to buy it."

"Ranchers ship cattle, don't they?"

"Yep. But ranchers look on any land that ain't fenced in as being theirs to use free."

"Now, damn it, Long, anybody with enough sense to pound sand in a gopher hole knows you can't dry-crop in these parts. All in God's name this prairie's good for is cattle range. Them goddamn nesters are just ruining good rangeland, putting up their damn Glidden wire fences and closing it off like they are."

After a moment's thought, Longarm said, "Well now, Grover, it looks to me like you don't need to worry much if they can't make a crop. They sure won't be here long unless they can. But their wheat looked pretty good to me when I rode out and took a look around today."

"It looks good now, maybe. But it won't head out, or a snow's liable to come early and kill it off."

"Did they make a crop last year?" Longarm asked.

"Last year and year before both, but it was fluky weather. You'll see."

"That's as it may be. But we're getting away from the election, it seems like. How many of those homesteaders will be able to vote?"

"Half, maybe three-fourths. Most of 'em have been here long enough to be citizens."

"And the ranchers just might try to stop 'em? Is that where trouble could start?"

Grover took his time, pouring himself a fresh drink and taking a long, slow sip from his glass. Finally he said, "Guess it won't make much difference, Long, since you're going to be nosing around anyhow. You might as well hear it from me as somebody else."

"Maybe I'd sooner hear it from you," Longarm replied. "Don't overlook that we're in the same line of business, in a manner of speaking."

"I guess you've heard the damn nesters are running one of their own people against me?" the sheriff said.

"Matter of fact, I hadn't."

"Ain't that a hell of a note, Long? A good hundred-percent

American having to fight to keep a foreign nester from taking his job away from him?"

"I'd say you've got to look for something like that, as long as we live in a free country," Longarm answered mildly.

"Oh, it's pretty easy for you to talk that way. You federal marshals don't have to go up for election every two years, put your job right out where anybody who takes a notion can grab for it."

"You worried about your chances?"

"Wouldn't you be?" Grover asked. Then, when it struck him that he might have said too much, he added quickly, "But I'm not any more worried than usual, don't get me wrong. It's not the first time I've had to run against somebody to keep my job."

"Let's lay the cards face up," Longarm proposed. "There's got to be something special about this election, or I wouldn't have been sent down here to take a look at things."

"Listen, Long," Grover said, dropping his voice, "I'll tell you the—"

Whatever the sheriff had intended to say was lost in the echoes of a woman's scream that cut through the saloon, drowning the subdued rumble of voices from the gambling tables and the piano's tintinnabulations. The sudden unexpected shrilling brought the drinkers at the tables and the gamblers at their games onto their feet, and the piano player up from his stool, and turned the eyes of the men standing at the bar from their drinks to the back of the saloon as they looked for the source of the scream.

Longarm saw it at once. Halfway down the stairs that led to the balcony, one of the saloon girls was struggling with a young cowhand. The girl stood on a step lower than the man. He had his hands locked around her wrists, and she was pulling vainly in an effort to break free. A trickle of blood came from her mouth. The whiskey-flushed face of the youth—Longarm judged him to be less than twenty years old—was twisted in anger.

"Now, by God, Ruthie!" he yelled, "You ain't going to work here another night, you hear me? Damn it, I want you to marry me!"

"Let go, Fred, please!" the girl begged. "Come on, let's go sit down at a table and talk it over. It won't help a bit for you to get all wrought up this way."

"I've talked all I'm going to!" he retorted. "And I've waited as long as I can!" He freed one of his hands from the girl's wrists, drew the pistol that dangled from his gunbelt, and pressed its muzzle to her head. "Like I told you upstairs, if I can't have you all to myself, nobody else is going to have you!"

Everyone in the saloon was frozen, watching the deadly drama on the staircase. Only Longarm moved. He started in a slow, deliberate walk toward the struggling pair, and had gotten halfway to the staircase before the young cowhand noticed him.

"You there! Stop right where you are!" the youth called. He swiveled the pistol's muzzle away from the girl's head and waved it in Longarm's general direction. "You take another step, and I swear to God, I'll plug you!"

Longarm stopped. He said mildly, "Now, you don't want to pull a fool trick like that, Fred. How do you think Ruthie's going to feel if she has to watch you dangling off the wrong end of a hanging rope because you gunned down somebody you don't even know?"

"I don't give a damn whether I know you or not!" Fred shouted. "I'm taking Ruthie out of here, and nobody's going to stop me!"

"What makes you think I want to stop you?" Longarm asked. He watched the young cowpuncher's face as the drunken youth tried to grasp the meaning of the question. The cowpoke was still shaking his head worriedly when Longarm went on, "I'd say Ruthie's got the right idea, Fred. Maybe she'd be willing to tell you why she didn't want to go with you, if you were to talk things over. Then you might be able to argue her around. Why don't you and her come on down those stairs and set a while, talk about it?" As he spoke, Longarm took another careful step or two toward the stairway.

"Damn you, I told you to stand still!" Fred called.

When Longarm didn't stop his slow forward movement, the youth triggered off a shot. The slug was wide by a yard. It crashed into an unoccupied table, cut a white groove along its top, and set the table to rocking unsteadily.

Fred yelled angrily, "You'll get the next one, unless you stop trying to get to me!"

Still inching steadily forward, Longarm said soothingly, "Now, that wasn't a right smart thing, Fred." He spread his empty hands in front of his body. "Look here. I've got no gun. You wouldn't want to shoot at a man who's not shooting at you, would you?"

Ruthie's mind worked faster than Fred's. She said, "He's right, Fred. If you killed an unarmed stranger, they'd hang you for sure. Then how could we go off together, the way you want to?"

Fred took his eyes off Longarm and gave all his attention to Ruthie. "You told me you didn't want to go away with me!"

Longarm used the opportunity to gain three more careful steps in the direction of the staircase, but he was still too far away to jump the cowboy.

Ruthie said, "Don't you know a girl wants to be persuaded, Fred honey? You never did really ask me, you just *told* me."

"I didn't!" he protested. "I asked you to marry me the best way I knew how!"

Again Longarm gained a step or two. This time his movement caught Fred's eye. He leveled his revolver at Longarm once more.

"Now damn you, mister, I told you to stand still!" the youth said menacingly. "I don't want to have to kill you, but I damn sure will, if you keep snaking up on me!"

Ruthie interrupted again. "Fred. If you really want me to listen to you, you'll have to listen to me first. Let's go down the stairs now, and sit at a table and talk, like I've been begging you to."

With a drunk's unpredictability, Fred suddenly snarled, "Damn it! You're pushing at me, all of you! Quit it now!"

He raised the revolver and fired at the ceiling. Wood splintered as lead tore through the ceiling and roof.

It was the chance Longarm had been waiting for. Before Fred could lower the muzzle of his pistol, Longarm leaped across the short distance that now separated them. He closed the gap with two bounding, catlike strides and grabbed the youth's wrist as the gun started down. The two wrestled for a moment, their arms seesawing, as Fred tried to bring the pistol down and Longarm, at a disadvantage on the step below him, fought to keep the menacing weapon pointed upward.

For a moment they swayed, almost falling, then Longarm got a foot on the next higher step. There, his superior height and strength quickly settled the contest. With both hands on Fred's wrist, Longarm's callused, steel-strand fingers put such a punishing pressure on bones and nerves that the younger man's hand was numbed. The gun fell from his limp grasp. Longarm pressed his advantage. He brought the cowhand's wrist down with a whiplash jerk and twisted his arm, throwing the youth off balance. When Fred turned, trying to stay on his feet, Longarm twisted the wrist back and upward until the hand that had held the gun was between Fred's shoulder blades.

"Damn it, you're killing me!" Fred panted. "Let go!"

Without bothering to answer, Longarm grabbed the young cowpoke's free wrist and twisted it too, behind his back. Then he used the painful pressure to force the youth down the steps to the floor of the saloon. Ruthie stood aside, pressing against the wall, to let them pass.

When they reached the bottom step, Longarm didn't pause. He forced Fred across the floor ahead of him until the two reached the table where Sheriff Grover still stood.

"I'll give him over to you, Grover," Longarm said. "Lucky for him, about all you can lock him up for is being drunk and creating a disturbance."

"I'll tuck him in jail until he sobers up," Grover said. He pulled handcuffs from his hip pocket and snapped them around Fred's wrists. Then he hesitated. Obviously the next words were hard to bring out. "I—I'm glad you jumped him before he hurt somebody."

"No thanks needed, Sheriff." Longarm stressed the title. "You and me have still got our talk to finish, but we'll do that tomorrow. Right now, you've got a prisoner to book, and I'm going to hit the hay. It's been sort of a long day."

Longarm stood watching as Grover hustled Fred out of the saloon. The brief fracas seemed to have created no lasting excitement; from the way those in the saloon reacted, it was nothing out of the ordinary. Longarm had taken a step toward the batwings when he was stopped by a hand on his arm. He turned. Ruthie stood there, tears in her eyes, but a smile on her lips.

"I guess I owe you a lot," she said in a low voice. "I don't know how to thank a man who's just saved my life. I thought I'd been in every kind of mess a girl can get herself into, but this is the first time anybody's ever kept me from getting killed."

"You don't owe me a thing, ma'am," Longarm replied. "I'm just glad you didn't get hurt."

"I think I owe you a lot, mister." She hesitated before adding, "If—if you'd like to come up to my room with me, I'd be real pleased to show you how grateful I am."

"Now, I wouldn't feel right if I did that. I reckon I know how you feel, and it doesn't mean I think any the less of you if I don't take your offer. But what you need to do right now is go back up to your room and clean the blood off your face. Then get a good night's rest. I'll drop in tomorrow or the next day, and maybe we can sit down and have a drink together. We can talk then."

"If you're sure—"

"I'm sure. You do what I tell you, now. Go on to bed. You've had a tough time, and you need some rest without anybody around."

Reluctantly the girl turned away. Longarm went to the bar and said to the barkeep, "I guess I owe you for whatever drinks the sheriff and I had."

"You don't owe me a damn dime. The shoe's on the other foot, I'd say. Wait a minute." The man went over to the backbar and studied the bottles displayed there. He selected one and passed it to Longarm. "You favor Maryland rye. Compliments of the house."

Longarm saw the label and whistled softly. "Now, that's right proud whiskey. Don't see much of it in this part of the country. It'll slip down right smooth." He nodded his thanks to the barkeep, tucked the bottle under his arm, and walked the short distance to the hotel.

In his room, Longarm made quick work of opening the whiskey and found that it was as silky smooth as he'd known it would be. He sipped now and then while he shed his clothes and puffed on a freshly lighted cigar. Finally he hung his holstered Colt on the left side of the bed's headboard and let himself sink to the lumpy mattress with an appreciative sigh. He was just dropping off to sleep when a light tapping sounded at the door.

Instantly alert, Longarm slid his Colt out of its holster and padded barefoot to the door. Standing to one side of its thin panels, his Colt poised, he called, "Who is it?"

"It's me. Ruthie."

Years of experience had made Longarm cautious. He unlocked the door and cracked it open. When he was sure the saloon girl was alone in the corridor, he opened the door wide enough to let her slip through.

"As long as you're here," he told her, trying to keep the sleepiness out of his voice, "I guess you might as well come in."

Chapter 3

"You're not mad at me because I decided to come see you after all, are you?" Ruthie asked. "I still feel like I need to thank you proper, you know."

"I'm not mad," Longarm assured her. He indicated the long balbriggan underwear he had on. "I wouldn't say I'm dressed for company, though."

"That won't bother me. You're not the first man I've seen in a union suit. Or without one, either," she smiled. She stepped inside.

Closing the door, Longarm moved to the bed and fished a match out of the pocket of his vest, which hung on the headboard. As he lighted the lamp and trimmed the wick down low, he said without looking at his uninvited guest, "Except you don't owe me any more thanks than you've already give me, Ruthie."

"No thanks for saving my life? Listen, I can still feel that ice-cold pistol barrel pushing into my ear. Every time I think about it, I get the shivers."

"Chances are that young fellow wouldn't't've had the nerve to shoot you, even as drunk as he was."

"He was wild." Ruthie shook her head. "I thought I'd seen some crazy men, but he's the worst ever."

Longarm motioned to the single chair the room held. "You might as well sit down and be comfortable while we talk. And I can't think of anything better than a sip of good Maryland rye whiskey to settle down a case of the shivers."

Ruthie smiled as she crossed the little room and sat down in the chair. "This is something I'm not used to, now—sitting down in a chair when I'm in a room with a man. Most of the time, they can't wait for me to flop on the bed. But I guess you're right, I can use a drink. All they let us have at the saloon is weak tea, unless we're at a table with a customer and drinking from his bottle. I guess you'd know how that works, though, being a lawman."

"How'd you find that out?" Longarm frowned. "I don't recall saying anything to you about who I am or what I do."

You didn't." Ruthie was settling herself comfortably in the chair. "Sheriff Grover came back after he'd put Fred in jail. He told Bob, and Bob told me."

"Bob? That'd be the barkeep?"

Ruthie nodded. "Bob said the sheriff didn't place you right off. Then he remembered what some folks call you. Longarm, isn't it?"

"Some do, I guess. Others ain't quite so polite."

"Enough to give you quite a reputation as a lawman, the sheriff told Bob."

With his back toward her while he poured whiskey from the bottle of bonded rye into his only glass, Longarm said, "I've found out that the farther a man gets away from home, the bigger his reputation gets, too. So don't put too much stock in what you hear." He handed her the glass, took the bottle, and sat down on the bed.

Ruthie held up the glass. "I guess I ought to say something, a sort of toast, but I can't think of the right words."

"Let's just forget about things like that." Longarm tilted the bottle to his lips and took a swallow of the smooth whiskey. He got a cheroot from one vest pocket and a match from another. As he lit the cheroot, he reflected that as much as he hated being a slave to tobacco, the combination of a pretty woman's company, a glass of rye, and a good cigar was unbeatable for sheer comfort.

Ruthie was sipping the whiskey. Longarm studied her through the veil of smoke that billowed between them from the freshly lit cigar. She'd put on a street dress before leaving the saloon, and he'd been too busy watching Fred to pay much attention to her earlier, but now he recalled the low-cut, sequined knee-length dress she'd been wearing then. He tried to remember, but all that came to his mind was a vague impression of full breasts, a small waist, and flaring hips emphasized by the cut of her working garb. The drab brown full-cut garment she was now wearing could hide almost any kind of shape under it, he thought.

As he looked closely at Ruthie's face, he realized that she was younger than most saloon girls; her heavy makeup didn't hide the smooth, unlined skin of her face. He saw in it the freshness of a girl in her early twenties, and guessed her teens weren't too far behind her. She'd combed her light brown hair straight back, instead of leaving it in the high puff that he remembered from their earlier encounter. Her brown eyes looked wise, despite some puffy traces of the tears he remembered that she'd shed, tears of fright mingled with relief, but they were only slightly reddened. Her nose was small and straight, her upper lip short, but the rouged lips themselves were full, almost pouting. Her chin was round and firm, her neck as smooth and unlined as her face.

Suddenly Longarm became aware that Ruthie was studying him almost as closely as he was studying her. The little bubble of tension that had been forming between them broke as they both smiled.

"I guess you're wondering what sort of a girl I am," she said. "That's what seems to interest most of the men I meet." Somewhat defiantly, she added, "My customers, if you want to put the right name to them."

Longarm took his time replying. He said, "You know, Ruthie, all I care about is what I see in you right now. You're an honest girl with enough backbone and spunk to look at the world the way it is, instead of trying to fool yourself, the way most folks do. If you're trying to find out if I think any the less of you because of the line of work you're in, the answer's no. You're a girl called Ruthie, and that's good enough for me." Longarm reached across the narrow gap that separated the bed from the chair where she sat and patted her arm.

She cocked her head to one side and looked at him curiously. "You don't act like other men do. You look at me like I'm a real woman, not something you've paid to use for a little while. I still feel like I owe you a lot for saving me the way you did."

"Now, we settled that when you first came in," he reminded her. "Thing is, you're all nerved up, after what you went through. Here." He refilled her glass. "Take some more of this. It'll settle your nerves down."

"I don't usually drink anything, you know. The older girls, the ones that've been around a while, they always tell me that if you lay off liquor, the other—you know what I'm trying to say—the other doesn't hurt you."

"Let's just call this a special time," Longarm suggested. He held up the bottle in salute. Ruthie raised her glass in response, and when Longarm drank from the bottle, she gulped down most of the whiskey in one convulsive swallow.

When she'd stopped shuddering, she asked, "Can I tell you something? You won't get mad if I talk to you, will you?"

"'Course not. Tell me anything you want to get off your mind."

"I guess I was mostly to blame for what happened there tonight, in the saloon. You see, Fred wasn't like most of the men I run into. He was—well, sort of like you, treated me like a human being. And I guess I fell for him, a little bit. Led him on."

"Fred's probably a nice enough young fellow, when he ain't a lot drunker than a man ought to get."

"But it was wrong, don't you see? I shouldn't've done it. If I'd just treated him like I do all the rest, he never would've acted the way he did."

"I suppose so. But you've got to remember, Ruthie, it's a woman's nature to act that way when a man's interested in her."

She smiled sadly. "Oh, I've learned that, Longarm. You might say that was my first lesson. How do you think I got started out?"

"Like most young girls, I'd imagine. You let some randy young rooster sweet-talk you into bed with him. Somebody found out about it, and told you that you were ruined for good just because you did what's humanly natural, and you weren't old enough to know different, so you believed it."

"You're a pretty good guesser, but you missed part of it. I was the one who was randy, and it was me who did the sweet-talking. And it didn't seem to me I was ruined at all. I enjoyed every minute of it, after the first time, when it hurt like I suppose it does all girls who never have been with a man before. But even that didn't bother me much. And nobody found out; it was him who got tired of me after a little while, and told me I was ruined for good, then he went and found himself another girl."

"You ain't old enough for that to've happened very long ago," he said.

"Long enough. I've been in the sporting life over three years."

"Hell, that ain't so long. You can always quit, if you don't like it."

"It's a funny thing." Ruthie drained her glass before going on. "I do like it, for a little while, now and then. When I meet some man who's not a pig, and I can let myself go with him, and not just go through the motions without feeling anything."

She stood up, fumbled for a moment at the neck of her dress, then shook her shoulders sharply from side to side. The drab brown dress slid to the floor. Underneath it, Ruthie wore nothing except her shoes and long net stockings held by fancy red garters at mid-thigh. In the soft warmth of the yellow lamplight her body glowed like a symmetrical pillar of alabaster.

For a moment she stood quite still, inviting Longarm to look at her as the slanting rays of the lamp revealed full, high breasts with warm pink rosettes that were beginning to pucker and push pink tips from their centers. Her tiny waist flared into generous, fully rounded hips; between them, a small, flat belly showed its oval center dimple. Below her lustrous, light brown tangle of pubic hair that caught the lamp's glow in mysterious highlights, slim thighs tapered into slimmer legs.

"You're the kind of man I know I can let myself go with," Ruthie said. Her voice was a husky whisper now, not the light voice of the girl who'd been speaking moments earlier. "And not just because I feel like I owe you anything."

Somehow, Ruthie's words relieved Longarm's mind. He no longer felt that she was offering herself to repay a debt. They could now be simply a woman and a man coming together.

With a single long step she crossed the space that separated them. Her hands brushed lightly over Longarm's cheeks, her fingers crept around his neck and pulled his face to nestle in the warm valley between her breasts. He felt her shiver with anticipation as the rough stubble on his square jaw brushed the tips of her nipples, and he felt himself respond as the warm, perfumed woman-scent of the valley into which his head was being urged filled his nostrils.

For a moment, Ruthie held Longarm's head firmly against her soft breasts, then she moved her hands and began working at the buttons of his longjohns. Longarm pressed against her, nibbling at the waiting flesh with hardened lips. Her hands were busy pulling at his only garment, and the night air was cool on his shoulders and back as the rough underwear dropped to his waist, He stood up. Ruthie pushed the balbriggans down below his hips, freeing his erection to rise, then swiftly she slid a hand down to bring the throbbing shaft between her thighs.

They stood clinging together, Longarm's hands smoothing her back and hips with long, caressing strokes while he rubbed his lips and face over her smooth shoulders and throat. Her cheek slid across his chest and over a shoulder; her warm, moist tongue darted into his ear. Her hips were moving slowly against him, pressing downward.

"Take me standing up," she panted into his ear, her breath hot against his cheek. "Now, right now."

Longarm spread his legs to brace himself and grasped her firmly fleshed buttocks with his strong, callused hands. He lifted her, and as he picked her up, Ruthie spread her legs to encircle his waist, as her hand reached down at the same time to guide him into her. She whimpered softly as he penetrated her, and locked her legs around him to pull him in more deeply.

For several minutes, Ruthie seemed content merely to let him fill her. She kept her legs clasped tightly around him, sighing, now and then, but moving very little. Longarm made no attempt to thrust; he was willing to let her set the pace.

"Am I too heavy for you?" she whispered. "Can you hold me this way as long as I need to come?"

"Take your time, Ruthie. I can hold you up all night; you don't weigh all that much."

She fell silent then, and began to devote all her attention to finding the pleasure she was after. She locked her hands behind Longarm's neck and let her legs relax a bit to settle herself more firmly against the rigid male flesh on which she was impaled. Pressure alone soon failed to satisfy her, and she began to shift the weight of her hips from side to side, gently at first, then so rapidly that Longarm had to dig his fingers into the yielding flesh of her buttocks to keep her from slipping out of his hands.

When Ruthie felt the increasing pressure of his fingers, she asked, "Are you getting tired?"

"Not a bit. Like I told you, take your time."

"I'm never fast anymore," she said, beginning to work her body back and forth between periods of sidewise gyration. "I guess it's because I'm always thinking about getting my customers off as fast as I can, before I really start feeling anything. Oh, Longarm, you don't know how wonderful this is for me! I'm starting to feel like a woman ought to feel."

"Go on and enjoy yourself all you want to," he told her. "I'm feeling pretty good right now, myself."

"You're not about to come, are you? Because I'm not ready yet."

"I'm good for a long time yet. You just wiggle along however way makes you feel best. I'll hold out, don't worry."

"Can you hold me under my arms for a while? Sort of let me swing free?"

"Sure. Whatever you like." He shifted his hands to her armpits, and she stretched her arms, letting her body lean away from him, but still keeping her legs around his waist. He said, "Let go with your legs, if you want to. I can hold you as easy that way."

"God, but you're strong!" Ruthie exclaimed as she released her legs from around Longarm's waist and let them dangle. "And long and big, too. Most men couldn't handle me this way," she said between gasps of pleasure. "But you're better than most men."

Longarm didn't answer. Praise always embarrassed him. Ruthie's body was hanging free now. She wriggled and writhed like a snake on a catcher's hook, gyrating in midair, opening and closing her legs scissor-fashion as she swung, now back and forth, now from side to side. Longarm, his elbows braced on his hips, held her easily.

He'd not yet begun to tire when Ruthie's body began to tremble; he felt her ribs heaving in his hands, and her panting breath was warm on his shoulder, where her head rested. He felt rather than heard the throaty cries that she began to utter, and decided the time had come to help her. Still in full control of himself, Longarm began thrusting, timing his lunges to meet her swings toward him. Her cries grew louder and burst from her throat at shorter intervals. Her quivering increased, and her body's gyrations took on a wilder tempo.

Longarm felt himself building to a climax as Ruthie's reactions showed that she was also reaching hers. He kept control, though, until at last she brought her legs up once again and clamped them around his body. As she pulled him to the deepest possible penetration, Longarm responded with short, hard, rapid thrusts while she clung to him and trembled in what seemed to be an unending, quivering release.

With a throaty sigh, Ruthie relaxed completely. "Lay me down on the bed, please, Longarm," she whispered. "I've never been so pleasured that I can remember!"

Gently he put her on the bed. She lay sprawled and limp, her eyes closed. Longarm fumbled a fresh cheroot from his vest pocket and moved to the bureau, where he leaned over the lamp to puff the cigar into life at the mouth of the lamp chimney. Then he picked up the bottle of bonded rye from the floor by the bed, and sat down in the chair. He'd savored one long swallow and was tilting the bottle for another when he saw the girl watching him. He held out the bottle, but she shook her head.

"I don't need a drink now," she told him. "You just gave me what I needed more than anything in the world." She studied him as he sat in the chair, his legs extended in front of him, and sighed, "If all my customers had what you've got there, I might enjoy my work more than I do."

"No, I don't think you would," Longarm said. "There're some girls who like the kind of work you're doing, and there're others who don't."

"It's the only kind of work I'm fit for," she told him bitterly. "I can't expect any decent man to marry me. Not now."

"Why not? Men have married saloon girls before. They'll marry 'em again."

"And have a husband who'd throw up to you the kind of life you used to lead?" she countered. "No thanks, Longarm."

"There's not any law I know about that makes a woman tell a man her whole life history before they're married," the lawman observed.

She shook her head adamantly. "I won't lie to any man I'd want to marry."

"Who said you had to? All you've got to do is not say anything."

"That'd be dishonest," she replied in a shocked tone.

"That'd be *sensible*," he retorted.

"But how would I find a man, way out here on the Kansas prairie?"

"Damn it, Ruthie, you don't have to stay here. Save your money and go someplace else. Get a job, let on you're a widow or something. If you're patient, you'll meet a man after a while, somebody you'd want to marry."

"Oh, I've got enough money put away. And I've thought about doing that, but I just can't seem to bring myself to do it."

"Well you think about it some more. I ain't trying to tell you how to run your own life, but if I didn't like any job I was doing, I'd get out of it."

She stretched luxuriously. "Maybe I will, at that. Right now, I don't really care what's going to happen. I haven't felt so satisfied for a long time."

"Wish I could say that," Longarm said. He realized how Ruthie might take his remark and added hurriedly, "I didn't mean that about you and me, don't get me wrong. I was talking about this case I'm on."

"Can you tell me about it, or is it something secret?"

"Hell, there ain't anything secret about it. I got sent down here from Denver to make sure there's nothing crooked about the election."

Longarm's statement didn't seem to surprise the girl. She nodded and said, "I've heard a lot of talk about how the ranchers are going to gang up on the nesters. But I didn't pay any special mind to it because I couldn't vote even if I wanted to, which I don't."

"You remember anything about what you've heard, besides that?" Longarm was immediately interested.

"Well—" she frowned thoughtfully. "The sheriff's Clem Hawkins's man, in case you haven't found that out yet. And the nesters have put up one of the foreigners to run against Grover. That's what started everything, I guess."

"I've heard Clem Hawkins's name before. Who in hell is he, anyhow?"

"He's about the biggest man in this part of the country," Ruthie replied. "Has the biggest ranch, hires the most men, ships the most cattle. All the other ranchers do pretty much what he says. So does Sheriff Grover."

"Not much reason for me to ask you how Hawkins feels about farms and Glidden wire fences coming in, I'd say.".

"Or nesters, either," Ruthie added. She waited for a moment before she said, "I've heard some of Hawkins's hands talking in the saloon. None of them's ever come right out flat and said so, but I got the idea that Hawkins has told them to carry wire nippers in their saddlebags and snip every fence they run up against out on what he calls *his* range."

"Just how big is Hawkins's spread?" Longarm asked.

She shook her head. "I can't tell you that, and I don't suppose anybody else can. Maybe not even old Clem himself. He just lays claim to every acre of prairie that he's sure doesn't belong to one of the other ranchers."

"What kind of man is he?"

"That's another thing I don't know, Longarm. I don't think he ever comes to town. When he wants to see somebody, he sends one of his men to fetch him, and they go out to his ranch. I've been here two years now, and as far as I know, I've never seen him."

"Tell me about the foreigners, Ruthie. How do they get along with the people in town? I already know there's no love lost between them and the ranchers."

"There's not much to tell. They don't come into the Cattleman's. I guess it's against their religion or something to drink. I've seen them on the street, when they come in for supplies. They don't act like they're out looking for trouble, if that's what you mean."

"But they don't mix much with anybody, do they?"

"No. They just keep to themselves."

Longarm chewed pensively on a corner of his mustache. "Hawkins sounds to me like a man who's used to keeping his plans to himself, and doing what he feels like, come hell or high water. And the Russians ain't real trusting of folks from outside, either. You know, Ruthie, I might just be here for a while. Looks like I'm going to have to do some digging to find out what I'll need to know."

"Can I help? I haven't paid much attention to the talk I hear at work, but an awful lot goes on there."

"Sure, you can help, if you want to. Anything you hear that fits in with what I just told you, sort of keep it in mind and pass it on to me. I'd be right obliged if you'd do that."

"You know I will, Longarm. You didn't even have to ask me to."

"I'll appreciate it, Ruthie. Because if I can't find out what's going on, I might have to open up a crack myself. And I don't want to do that unless I have to."

She shook her head. "I don't understand what you mean, I guess."

"I mean I'd have to stir things up a little bit. Maybe even a lot. And if I do that, somebody's apt to get hurt."

A smile grew slowly on Ruthie's face. She said, "I know somebody you can stir up again right now, if you feel like it. I like the way you stir, Longarm."

He offered the bottle of rye to Ruthie, but she shook her head. He took a swallow himself and set the bottle down, then went over to the bed. Looking down at her face, flushed now with anticipation, he asked, "Do you want to do it standing up again?"

"Not this time. I didn't know how long-winded you were, before. I was afraid you couldn't hold out, but you're long in every way that counts. Besides, from the looks of things, I'm going to have to stir you up a bit before you'll be ready to stir me."

Longarm lay down by her, and Ruthie began to arouse him with her professional skills. Once, while she was massaging his growing erection against the already moist warmth of her crotch, she said, "You know, I didn't think I'd ever be able to get worked up again. But look at me! Here I am, shaking like a virgin. I can't wait any longer to get you inside me, Longarm."

"Go ahead," he told her. "It'll go in now, and when you lean over here a little, it'll finish coming up quick enough."

She straddled him then, shivering delightedly as she slid slowly with wriggling hips to take him into her, then leaned forward to let him rub his beard-rough face over her breasts. Her quivering increased as his erection grew to fill her completely, and she sighed contentedly when he rolled atop her and began to drive. She rolled her hips to meet his thrusts, and Longarm was surprised when almost immediately she started to writhe and whimper. He increased the force and speed of his strokes, but still she came long before he did. Then he could tell she stayed with him only by an effort of will until he felt her begin to pulse beneath him again, and to respond once more as she had earlier.

"Oh, hurry, now, hurry!" she gasped. "I'm almost there again!"

Longarm hurried, pounding hard, racing her to the end. He

reached his own climax only a few seconds after the girl shuddered into hers. They lay spent and silent in a tangle of, arms and legs.

"Now I know you're a miracle," she sighed wearily but happily. "Oh, God, Longarm, you don't know what you've done for me. First you kept me from getting killed, and now you've made me feel like a woman again." She propped herself up on an elbow and looked at him pleadingly. "You won't send me back to the saloon tonight, will you? Can I stay and sleep with you? I won't bother you, honest."

"Sure you can." Longarm rolled out of bed and blew down the lamp chimney to extinguish its flame. He rejoined her, and Ruthie cuddled into his arms. He said, "You sleep now. I need some shut-eye myself. We'll both feel better in the morning."

Chapter 4

Longarm opened his eyes, instantly alert. He'd awakened earlier when Ruthie had gotten up and quietly put on her clothes in the darkness, then slipped silently out of his room. He'd feigned sleep, then, and when she'd gone, he had gotten up only long enough to lock the door and drain his bladder into the slop jar before going back to bed and falling into a solid, relaxing sleep.

As always, when Longarm woke, he got out of bed at once. The night's exertions had washed away in sleep. He stepped barefoot to the dresser and drove the early-morning sourness from his mouth with a quick gulp from the half-empty bottle of rye. His face looking back at him from the mirror reminded him that the day ought to start with a shave; Longarm hoped the local barber had a steady hand. For the moment, he pushed his longhorn mustache into shape with a forefinger; it needed trimming, another job for the barber.

He performed his morning routine with swift efficiency. Clothes on, stovepipe boots stomped firmly on his feet, he adjusted the gunbelt and holster of his Colt to his liking, then dumped the cartridges on the bed, checked the gun for action, and inspected each cartridge before replacing it in the cylinder. He inspected with equal care the little double-barreled derringer that was attached to his watch chain. Dropping the derringer into his left-hand vest pocket and the watch into its right-hand mate, he slid his arms into the sleeves of his long black coat, set his Stetson at the proper angle on his head, and went out into the morning sunshine.

Junction looked bleak in the glare of the pitiless prairie sun, its lone street deserted. Longarm chose the barbershop first, though his stomach was calling for eggs and bacon, and above all, a cup of hot, black coffee. Food somehow seemed to taste better to him after he'd had a shave.

At the livery stable after he'd eaten breakfast, Longarm asked the lone attendant, "How do I find Clem Hawkins's place?"

"Just go out to the end of the railroad spur. There's three or four sidings beyond the corrals. Just go on to the corrals and then ride north. There's a cattle trail there that'll take you right to Clem's ranch. Can't miss the place. That white two-story house of his sticks up like a sore thumb out on the prairie."

He found the cattle trail without any trouble and turned his roan gelding-onto the wide, clodded swath of partly beaten earth that led vaguely north. For the first two or three miles, there were fenced wheatfields on both sides of the trail, and in a corner or at an edge of almost all the fields a sod house or a makeshift shanty built of boards marked the home of an immigrant. With only one or two exceptions, all the fields were fenced with Glidden wire.

When the homesteads grew farther and farther apart and the trail entered open range, Longarm studied the country as he rode. There were subtle differences between the prairies of southern Kansas and those of Texas or the Indian Nation or New Mexico, but the sun was the same. It glared from a nimbus of molten brass that shaded into an inverted bowl of light blue sky that descended on all sides to meet the shallower bowl of the yellow-tan horizon. Yellow-tan right at this time of year, he reminded himself. Come another couple or three months, snow would turn it white, and make the sky look a brighter blue than it really was. Then, in springtime, the land would be green and the sky even more washed-out-looking than it was now.

It's a hell of a country for women and horses, old son, Longarm told himself as he let the roan set its own pace along the clods and hoof dents that marked the cattle trail.

Whatever the season, he knew there'd never be any shade except along the streams. Wherever water flowed, there were cottonwood trees, the old ones bigger around than a steer's brisket, surrounded by small shoots and saplings as thick as grass. On creeks where the flow was too small or too irregular to let the cottonwoods reach any real size, willows clumped in straggly thickets. In hollows and washes where water collected and stood during snowmelt or while the fierce spring rains pelted the usually dry soil, a few bushy bois d'arc trees had rooted.

Isolated growths of yucca thrust up their long, spiny leaves on a few humps and slopes; in the early days of summer their flowers had been creamy white, but now the flowers had browned to a few dry wisps on top of the shoots. Old-timers on the prairie harvested the yucca, and Longarm supposed the reason there were so few plants was that the new immigrants had learned that yucca—what most homesteaders called soapweed—would provide a gentler soap than that made from lye and ashes. He recalled the times when he'd had to wear underwear and shirts washed in homesteader-made soft soap, and how his armpits and crotch had chafed him until he'd take the garments off.

Like all prairie lands Longarm had ever seen, the Kansas prairie looked at first glance to be a solid stretch of unbroken, level earth, thinly carpeted with grama grass and the stunted, stickery stems of dwarf sunflowers that grew no higher than a man's knee. On closer inspection, though, the apparent level uniformity turned out to be illusory. There were creases and gullies that were almost invisible from a distance cutting through the soil. Some were finger-deep and whisker-wide. Some were wide enough and deep enough to be dangerous to riders; small and narrow and invisible until a horse stepped into them, but deep enough to throw animal and rider, and often snap the horse's leg as well. A few, but only a few, could have swallowed a good-sized house; these yawned as wide as hellgates and were, in midsummer, as hot as hellfire at their bottoms. Any gully that big became a landmark, the equivalent to a crossroads sign in more settled countryside.

As the liveryman had told Longarm it would, Clem Hawkins's house stuck up like a sore thumb on the level prairie. He saw the place from a distance, at about the same time that he began to encounter scattered, small groups of white-faced Hereford steers. Few ranchers still bothered with the rangy, cantankerous longhorns on which the cattle industry of the West had been founded. Not just the leanness and ornery character of the longhorn had led to its decline; when the railroads came in and the great long-distance trail drives began to be abandoned, seven

Herefords could be packed into the same space that the horns of five longhorn steers required in a cattle car.

While he was still at a good distance from the big two-story house, he reined the roan to a slow walk and began to take stock of Hawkins's layout. It was a big one. In addition to the tall main house, there was a bunkhouse, a cookshack, and a haybarn as big as the main house, though not built quite so high. There was also a scattering of working buildings; a toolshed, storage rooms, privies, and a blacksmith shop, as well as a couple of corrals. A windmill spun lazily, barely moving, on its tower beyond the house. The entire array was spread over most of a quarter-section, and made Hawkins's ranch, like most big spreads, a virtual community unto itself.

Old son, Longarm mused as the gelding plodded slowly toward the sprawl of structures, *Clem Hawkins sure ain't hurting for much of anything. A man as well-fixed as he looks to be is bound to figure the rest of the world belongs to him too, and that he's got a right to run it any way he sees fit.*

There was little activity around the buildings, Longarm noted as he got closer. Smoke rose from the cookhouse and an occasional puff burst from the low building close to the corral, which he'd decided must be the blacksmith shop. Two men were working close to the corrals, and once the cookshack door opened long enough for an unseen man inside to dash a bucketful of water out onto the ground.

Longarm reined in at the hitch rail in front of the house. He'd dismounted and was looping the roan's reins around the rail when the door opened and a broad, stocky man came out to the veranda. He studied Longarm for a moment before asking, "Looking for a job?"

Nope. Looking for Clem Hawkins."

"Well, you've found him. I'm Hawkins."

Now it was Longarm's turn to study the man he'd heard mentioned so often since his arrival in Junction. Hawkins looked to be in his middle fifties; his bared head was balding, and what remained of his dark hair was well-shot with gray. In the style of range lords of the day, it was trimmed close. A thick, bushy mustache hid his lips, but his cheeks and chin were clean-shaven. Up to the middle of his brow, his face was deeply tanned; the upper half of his forehead was dead white where his hat cut off the sun's rays. He wore a gray flannel shirt with the collar unbuttoned and trousers with narrow-cut legs that squeezed his fancy-stitched, high-heeled boots.

"My name's Custis Long, Mr. Hawkins. Deputy U.S. marshal out of Denver. I'd like to talk to you a few minutes, if you've got the time to spare."

"What's the trouble? You on the trail of an outlaw, and figure he's hiding out on my place? Something like that?"

"Nothing like that. There's not any trouble, if you want to put it that way. What I'm here for is to see that none gets started."

Hawkins frowned, staring at Longarm, trying to read the meaning of his words. Then he shrugged and said, "All right. You don't make much sense, but come on inside and I'll listen to you."

Longarm followed Hawkins into the house. It was dim and cool. The window shades were drawn, and the varnished wood floor of the main room was bare except for a few Indian blankets tossed here and there as rugs. The furniture was massive: big armchairs, a great oak rolltop desk along one wall, a long table behind a leather-upholstered divan. A gun rack on the wall beside the door held rifles and shotguns. A pair of gunbelts, each carrying a holstered revolver, hung from the bottom of the rack.

Hawkins indicated a chair and, without waiting for Longarm to sit down, dropped into a deep, wide-armed chair that showed signs of plentiful use. He said brusquely, "Cut your palaver as short as you can, Long. We're in the middle of the fall gather and I've put on a bunch of extra hands. I was just leaving to go out and keep an eye on them, fill in the gaps that my foreman and segundo can't cover when we got such a big crew to handle."

"How many head you figure to handle in the gather?"

"About eight thousand. Might go as high as nine, by the time the hands finish working out to the edges of my spread."

Longarm said thoughtfully, "You'll be shipping right on three thousand, then, I'd guess?"

Hawkins nodded. "Something like that. Sounds like you know a little bit about ranching."

"Not much. Only what I've picked up while I was handling cases in cattle-raising country. I do know enough to figure but that you'd need a lot of range to carry a herd that size, forty or fifty sections. The way the grass looks to me, you'd need two, maybe three acres a head to winter a six-thousand herd."

"That's close to being right," Hawkins agreed.

"And to handle a gather," Longarm continued, "you'd've had to put on maybe fifteen extra hands, give or take a man. That right, Mr. Hawkins?"

"Not that it's any business of yours or the federal government's, if you're asking an official question, but I took on fourteen to see me through the gather and the shipping. Why?"

"Oh, I'm just curious. Making conversation, you might say. You ship out from Junction, I guess?"

"Now that's a damn fool question, Long. Of course I ship out from Junction. It took me three years to convince the Santa Fe that with me and the other ranchers around here shipping twice a year, a spur up here from Dodge would pay." Hawkins snorted. "Then, as soon as the damn spur was built, the railroad played us a dirty trick by loading up the country with a bunch of foreign nesters."

"You'll be shipping in maybe a month, I'd say?"

"Unless a spell of bad weather hits and slows us up. The rancher was getting impatient. "Look here, Long, what's a U.S. marshal doing here, nosing into my affairs? You say you're not after a fugitive or an outlaw. Just what in hell *are* you after?"

"I'm a mite curious about those extra hands you took on, Mr. Hawkins. How many do you hire regular?"

"Sixteen, give or take a drifter who'll stick around for a month or so and move on. Now listen here, I don't mind answering any legitimate questions you've got, but all this is a waste of time. Get to the point. I've got work waiting for me."

"No need to get a chip on your shoulder, Mr. Hawkins," Longarm said mildly. "I've got a reason for what I'm asking."

"Tell me what it is, then."

"Sure. The Justice Department back in Washington doesn't want to see any funny business going on when election day rolls around. I guess you know what I mean. Stuffed ballot boxes, repeaters, toughs keeping legitimate voters away from the polls."

"Things like that only happen in big cities, Long. Places where there're a lot of votes, where the rings control thousands of voters. You don't expect me to believe that the people in Washington are worried about a little place like this corner of Kansas."

"Just happens they are, though," the tall deputy said.

"Why, in God's name? There's not a thousand votes between Wichita and Fort Dodge. Besides, it's the state's job to look after the polls on election day."

"You're right all down the line, Mr. Hawkins—up to a point."

"Where's the point, if you don't mind telling me?"

"Might say there's two points. First off, this is a federal election year, a big one. President, senators, congressmen. And I'm told it'll be close. Even a thousand votes could make a difference in the way the state electors vote on who's going to be president."

Hawkins rubbed his chin thoughtfully. After a moment he said, "Damned if I thought this little place could be all that important. I'm still not convinced it is, Long. Why'd you get sent here? Seems to me you'd do more good in the big cities, Kansas City, Topeka, Wichita, where the votes run up into the thousands."

"Oh, I'm right sure there'll be men sent there, too. I just happened to draw this one."

"Why? Why here?"

"Because stories got back to the East that there's likely to be real trouble here."

"It's those goddamned foreign nesters!" Hawkins exploded. "They're the ones who went running to Washington for help! They've been trying to take control away from us native Americans ever since they came in!"

Longarm raised a hand in a calming gesture. "Look here, Mr. Hawkins, I wasn't sent here to help or hurt anybody. Just to see that the voting's fair."

"Don't feed me that bullshit, Long! Your bosses are the same people who've controlled every administration since the War ended, and all that time they've been trying to flood the country with foreigners!"

Longarm remained unruffled. "That's your opinion, Mr. Hawkins, and you're sure entitled to think whatever you please. It's not part of my job to pay that much attention to the political side of things. All I'm interested in is enforcing the law."

"Go look at those damned Russian nesters, then. They're the ones who're not satisfied with the way things are run around here. They're the ones who want to change everything."

"You mean because they're running a candidate for sheriff against your man Grover?"

"Who says Grover's my man? He's a public official. Maybe I supported him when he first got elected, but that's my business. You just got through saying that."

"From what I've heard, you're a pretty big man hereabouts, Mr. Hawkins. I'd bet Sheriff Grover'd think twice before he did something you told him not to."

"People come to me for advice, sure. I give it to them, and if they think it's good advice and follow it, that's sure as hell not my fault."

"I couldn't argue against that. Only there's a big stretch of difference between giving advice and giving orders."

"Exactly why did you come here today, Long? To intimidate me? Threaten me?"

"I can't recall doing either one, Mr. Hawkins. No, sir. The only reason I'm out here right now is to let you know I'm on hand to stop any election day trouble before it gets started. I plan to keep an eye on the voting place, and I won't stand for fights or threats, and there won't be any repeaters or double voting."

"You're not hinting that I'm planning to encourage any of those things? Or that I'm trying to engineer a crooked election?" Under his tan, Hawkins's face was flushing a deep red. "If you are, I'll have your hide nailed to my barn door before election day."

"I know you've got a lot of influence, Mr. Hawkins. You put this county together, and you run it without a courthouse or any elected officials except a sheriff. But I'm not hinting anything. All I'm saying is, if you hear about somebody planning to try to steal the election, you let me know."

"Let me tell you a few facts, Marshal—maybe they'll make you look at this thing differently. We cattlemen *made* this part of Kansas. Why, damn it, when I came here in '69, there were thirty or forty abandoned homesteads, where wheat crops had failed and the homesteaders couldn't make it. This is cattle country, Long, not farmland."

"Sure." Longarm nodded. "I've seen range and I've seen farmland, traveling around the country like I do. I know the difference."

"That's the smartest thing you've said yet." Hawkins's voice lost some of its hostility, "I'll finish what I started to say, if you don't mind. My ranch was the first one here. All the others came later, but all of us ranchers got here before those foreigners came flooding in, cutting up our range with their Glidden wire. We made this place, we got the railroad spur, we made a town out of Junction. And as sure as shit stinks, we don't propose to give up what we made."

Longarm took his time replying. Finally he said, "A minute ago you told me how many sections you've got in this place of yours. Mind telling me how many of 'em you picked up, just for filing fees on those thirty or forty homesteads you said were abandoned when you moved in? If a man picks up a hundred and sixty acres for a two-dollar filing fee, I'd say that's damn cheap. Less than a penny an acre is what it figures out to, doesn't it, Mr. Hawkins? And wouldn't you like to pick up what those new homesteaders have filed on at the same price?"

Anger flooded back into Hawkins's voice. "I took idle land and put it to use! It took a lot of work and sweat to do it, don't overlook that. Sure, I've got a valuable spread here now. And I'll fight to keep it!"

"Well, now." Longarm's voice was quietly level. "You've said right out where you stand, so I'll do the same. As long as what you do is legal, you won't find me standing in your way. Nobody's out to deny you any rights. But nobody's going to deny those farmers their rights, either, whether they're foreigners or whatever else, as long as what they do is legal, too. Not while I'm around, at least."

"I've already told you what you'd better do. Spend your time watching those Russian nesters instead of bothering good American citizens."

"Now, I plan to keep an eye on them, too. Don't worry about that. But I'm going to be watching a few other things, like fence-cutting and trampling down wheatfields."

The rancher pointed a cautionary finger at the marshal. "Be careful, Long. You're stepping outside your authority when you mix into something that's a matter for the sheriff."

"Not when the sheriff closes his eyes to lawbreaking."

"All right. If that's all you've got to say, you can go about whatever kind of business you've got. My work's waiting for me, and it's not going to wait all day."

Longarm stood up. "I try not to keep any man from his honest business. Or to let one get away with any unlawful business. Thanks for your time, Mr. Hawkins. We'll probably run into each other again pretty soon."

Without waiting for Hawkins to show him to the door, Longarm turned and walked briskly across the polished floor, let himself out, mounted the roan, and started back toward Junction.

When he saw in the distance the green rectangles of the homesteaders' wheatfields, he turned the horse west. This was the area he'd started out to look at the day before, when he'd been interrupted by Nicolai Belivev's rifle shot. He was riding now at an angle that would take him to the Santa Fe spur track about four miles outside Junction. In the triangle between his course and the track lay the fields he hadn't looked at before.

A few minutes after he'd turned west, Longarm noticed a small natural ridge. Perhaps the little rise marked the shoreline of a centuries-dry lake, or perhaps it was a wrinkle resulting from some earthquake that had buckled the land in times before men lived on it. The rise stretched roughly along the course Longarm wanted to follow, and he turned the roan to climb it. Though it was no more than a yard or so above the rest of the terrain, even this much gave him an elevation from which he could survey the land more easily.

He was surprised at the area covered by the homesteads. It was impossible to count them, for most of the 160-acre claims had been fenced into wheatfields of forty to sixty acres, as much wheat as a man could tend in a day's work. Counting the number of dwellings was equally impossible, he discovered as the roan picked its slow way along the ridge. So many of the dwellings were sod houses that it wasn't always possible to tell whether a hump inside a fenced field was a soddy in which someone still lived, or one that had been abandoned in favor of a frame house close by. There were, Longarm judged after he'd ridden almost to the end of the ridge, between thirty and forty frame houses, with six or eight more under construction, and at least half again as many soddies as houses.

On his way to Hawkins's ranch, he'd guessed that there were

as many as twenty homesteads east of the cattle trail. If his new estimate was correct, and if each dwelling he'd counted housed only two adults, then the number of immigrants living around Junction numbered a bit more than two hundred. He reached the railroad and turned onto the road that ran beside the track, heading for Junction.

No wonder Clem Hawkins is bothered, Longarm told himself as he swayed to the broken rhythm of the roan's walk. *I'd bet a plugged lead dollar there're just about as many settlers as there are ranchers and hands. It's a cinch Hawkins ain't missed counting noses. I bet he knows right down to the last man how many hands his rancher friends hire, and how many folks live in Junction. And not everybody who lives there is going to vote the way Hawkins and his pals want 'em to. Old son, we've got us a close election here. Billy Vail sure handed me a live one, this time!*

Chapter 5

Breakfast was a long time behind him when Longarm returned to Junction. He'd chewed a piece of jerky from the emergency rations in his saddlebag, but while it kept his stomach from growling too angrily, it didn't give him the sensation that he'd eaten a real meal. His first stop was at the Ace High for an appetizer that he didn't need, but to which he felt entitled after a morning and part of an afternoon in the saddle. Then he crossed the street to the café.

"We sold out everything we cooked for dinner, and ain't got the stuff for supper ready yet," the scrawny proprietor informed him.

"Well, you've got a stove in the kitchen, haven't you?"

"Sure. Now, you oughta know that."

"Then cook me something."

"I guess we can do that, all right. It'll cost you a dime extra for my trouble, though."

"Go ahead. I'll pay it."

"Eggs and a fried steak sound about right? Cost you two bits and the extra dime on top of it."

"I didn't ask you how much, friend. I said I'd pay it. Now go on and cook."

Longarm slid a cigar out of his vest to give his jaws something to do while he waited. As time passed and no food appeared, he was tempted to light it, for the shot of rye he'd had across the street was serving its purpose, and his stomach was crying out in earnest now. The steak and eggs finally came out of the kitchen. He made short work of finishing them off, sipped his coffee, and started for the hotel to drop off his rifle and saddlebags. He planned to spend the rest of the afternoon sauntering around town, striking up a few conversations that might give

him an idea as to how the citizens of Junction itself, small as
their numbers were, felt about the growing feud between the
ranchers and homesteaders. After he'd done that, he'd drop in at
the saloon for a drink and visit with Ruthie awhile, then have a
late supper. Just as he was entering the hotel, he heard his name
called.

"Marshal Long! A moment, please!"

Turning, Longarm saw Mordka Danilov hurrying along the
board sidewalk toward him. He waited for the homesteaders'
spiritual leader to cover the distance between them.

"It is good fortune that I find you," Danilov panted as he
stopped beside Longarm. "Already twice I have asked here at
the hotel, but you have always been away."

"Something come up that bothers you, Mr. Danilov?" Longarm asked.

"Only perhaps. Of it, we cannot be sure."

"Well, come on in and we'll go up to my room. You can tell
me about it."

Mordka hesitated. "It is better that we do not talk now. Some
of the Brethren have things they would like to say, too. They
must work the fields until dark, you see."

"Sure. I know how farming is. Well, bring in whoever wants
to talk to me, Mr. Danilov. We can sit down and palaver this
evening, later on."

"Palaver? This word I do not know."

"It just means talk."

"Ah. *Ya panimayiti* I understand," Danilov nodded. He
looked questioningly at Longarm. "Would you talk with us tonight, then? If you would come to my house for supper—not a
feast, you understand, but such as we have to offer—it would be
easier for my friends to assemble there."

"Why, sure. Only you don't have to bother about feeding me.
I just ate a minute ago."

"No, no!" Danilov insisted. "It would honor us if you break
bread with us. Come at dusk, Marshal. You will have no trouble
finding my house again, *da*?"

"No trouble at all. I'll be there."

During his afternoon stroll around Junction, Longarm found
too few residents who'd talk about the election to give him much
of an idea of the townspeople's feelings. Even at the barbershop,

the barber was not as talkative as those of his trade usually are. In the stores, where he dropped in casually and chatted with customers as well as clerks and proprietors, he could find no clearcut current of opinion. He got the feeling that while their minds might be made up, people hesitated to say anything that might get back to Grover and, through him, to Hawkins. When he'd finished his rounds, he was as much in the dark regarding local sentiment as he'd been before he'd started. Late in the day, with the setting sun warm on his back, he got his horse from the livery stable and set out for Mordka Danilov's house.

Light spilled into the dusk through the open door of the Danilov dwelling, and as he drew closer, Longarm could hear a humming of voices raised in spirited discussion. He tethered the roan to the fencepost nearest the gate and went in. Danilov came to greet him.

"*Dobro pojalovativa*, Marshal Long. I make you welcome. Come and meet my brothers."

For the next few minutes, Longarm went through a bewildering series of introductions to men whose names sounded incomprehensibly complicated. He supposed they were the Russian equivalents of Smith, Jones, and Brown, but his head began to reel as, in quick succession, he met Fedor Petrovsky, Antonin Keverchov, Mischa Evrykenov, Pavel Sednov, Tikhon Gapontski, and Basil Lednovotny. All of them spoke passable English, though some were less fluent than others, and all of them found it easier to speak to their companions in their native tongue. Nicolai Belivev he remembered from the day before; he found a partial solution to his conversational dilemma by addressing only Belivev and Danilov by name.

To heighten Longarm's confusion, there was a strong uniformity of appearance among the other men. All wore untrimmed, chest-length beards and all had shaved upper lips. They were also dressed in much the same manner. All of them had on solid-color shirts—blouses, really—with full-cut sleeves and closely fastened cuffs; the only difference was that a few wore the familiar denim Levi's of the prairie, while the rest had on full-cut trousers of a material coarser than denim, and tucked their trouser legs into calf-high boots.

Mordka sensed his guest's confusion with the unfamiliar names, and tried to lessen it by repeating the names of the Brethren who addressed Longarm during the brief pause that followed the introductions. As soon as the first confused minutes had passed, Mordka announced that supper was ready. He went to the door at the rear of the room, and opened it.

"Marya!" he called. "Tatiana! *Dayti uzhin!*"

Marya Danilov came at once from the adjoining room, followed by a much younger woman; Longarm put her age at eighteen or twenty. They went at once to a table that was covered with a plaid cloth, and transferred the cloth to a second table. Both women worked silently, paying no attention to the men. Both wore plain, drably hued dresses that reached their ankles, and had small white capes draped across their shoulders. Longarm remembered Marya from his earlier visit, but he found his eyes drawn at once to Tatiana.

She was a girl of striking beauty. Dark blond hair, the color of deep honey, was drawn in severe sweeps from a center part into a bun at her neck. The blond hair framed a classic face—a straight nose with nostrils that flared slightly, full red lips, a firmly rounded chin. Under golden blond brows, Tatiana's eyes were a light blue gray, large and luminous. Her hands were large, the hands of a working woman, reddened and rough, but the skin of her face and neck was flawless. The plainly cut dress she wore effectively concealed all of her figure except for her breasts, which bulged fully rounded below broad, competent shoulders.

As soon as the cloth had been removed, revealing an array of dishes piled with foods strange to Longarm's eyes, Mordka held up a hand, raised his face, and closed his eyes. The others did the same.

"*Slava Bog! Slava Christos!*" Mordka said, and at once the guests—except for Longarm, who stood watching—repeated the words. The silence that followed was broken by the host, who took Longarm by the arm and led him to the table. "*Kushaitye, Marshal Long! Kushaitye pojalsta!*" Immediately, smiling, he went on, "It is our way to make a guest welcome in our homes, an old custom, you understand? You would say to me, 'Eat, Mordka, eat heartily,' in your own language."

"I see." Longarm blinked at the dishes. "It—it looks real good."

"It is our *zakuskis,*" Mordka explained. He pointed to the

filled dishes in turn. "Here is chicken *piroshki*, mushroom *piroshki*—" pointing to rounds of pastries spread with ground meat—"*ogurtsi*—" indicating tiny cucumbers smaller than a finger, swimming in a clear liquid—"*sirniki*—" more rounds, which were browned like toast—"*selenye gribi*," indicating mushrooms in a liquid similar to that covering the cucumbers. "Eat and enjoy, Marshal. Here. A *piroshki* is a good way to begin." He picked up a plate filled with meat-spread pastry rounds and held it out to Longarm,

Somewhat gingerly, Longarm took one of the rounds. He bit into it, found it delicious, and this gave him the courage to try another. As soon as he started to eat, the remaining guests joined him at the table. Longarm watched them for clues, and ate as they did, picking up one of the *zakuskis* with his fingers and popping it into his mouth whole. He began sampling the *zakuskis*, and found his mouth filled with flavors that were entirely new to him, though he could recognize the beef and chicken, the eggplant, mushrooms, and cottage cheese that formed the basis for the fillings of the *piroshkis* and the spreads for the pastry rounds.

Mordka appeared at Longarm's elbow, watched him bite into a *piroshki*, and smiled. He said, "I am glad to see you enjoy our little *zakuskis*, Marshal."

"They're plumb good, Mr. Danilov. Where'd you get the makings for all this stuff, in a place like Junction?"

"You must have seen our little gardens. The women attend to them, while we men work in the wheat. After a rain, they go to the unplowed ground and gather mushrooms. Many of the seasonings, like dillweed, grow wild out on the prairie."

"Wasn't it a lot of work for Mrs. Danilov to fix up a spread like this?"

"No, no, she did not make them by herself, Tatiana helped, of course, and so did the wives of the other Brethren. We have learned to share with one another, you see." Mordka looked around. "Ah. You must finish with the *zakuskis* soon, Marshal. It is time now for supper."

"Supper?" Longarm couldn't hide his surprise. "I thought all this *was* supper."

"*Zakuskis* are only to start. Now, we sit down and eat soup with *pelmeni*, and *golubtsi*, and *blinis*, and to finish, we will have a bowl of *gourievskaya kashka*. Come. You must sit at my right hand; you are our honored guest."

Mordka led Longarm to the larger table. While the men had been munching on the appetizers, Marya and Tatiana had unobtrusively set out plates, knives, and forks on the cloth transferred from the *zakuskis* spread. Danilov took his place at the head of the rectangular table and motioned Longarm to sit at his right. As soon as they were seated, the women began filling bowls and platters from the pots that, almost unnoticed, had been kept warm on the kitchen range that stood in the far corner of the room. As though this was a signal for the other men to sit down, they began finding places, and the table was soon filled.

Nicolai Belivev was sitting across from Longarm. He smiled when he saw Longarm inspecting the soup, which was a clear broth that had tiny bite-sized dumplings swimming in it. Belivev said, "Do not worry, Marshal. It is only good chicken soup, and the *pelmeni* are filled with the livers from the chickens."

Longarm took a spoonful of soup and chewed down on the dumpling that he'd carried to his mouth in the spoon. It was not flat and doughy-tasting like the dumplings he'd eaten before. The *pelmeni* turned out to be a thin shell of flaky dough, and the spiced ground-liver filling added a tang to the bland broth.

Belivev had been watching. He smiled. "This is the first time for you to eat Russian-style, *da*?"

"Yep. But I sure don't aim to let it be the last." Longarm looked at the heaped platters in the center of the table. "I don't know what's in all those plates, but I'll bet they're just as good as what I've already tasted."

"We do not eat so well each day, you understand," Mordka told him. "But when we have a guest, we want him to enjoy our best."

"Well, it sure does you proud. These are about the finest little dumplings I've ever tasted."

"Tatiana made them. She has a good hand with pastry dough," Mordka said. "But if you are wondering what is in the platters, I will tell you." He pointed to them, one by one. "Here is *golubtsi*, chopped beef rolled up in cabbage leaves. *Blinis*, what you would call pancakes. In this small bowl is *izra iz Bak-*

lajan, eggplant cooked with onion and tomatoes and green peppers and seasonings. And in the covered bowl is the dessert, *gourievskaya kashka,* made with ground wheat from last year's crop and fruits from your airtight tins. We have not yet had time to plant fruit trees; we are too busy getting our houses finished and caring for our wheat."

"*Eta pravlina,*" the man sitting next to Longarm said. "It was no time for us to do such things yet. Next year it will be better."

"Next year is always better, Fedor," Belivev remarked. "Next year I plant fruit trees, and I also build me for my wife a house. A *salash,* maybe, but is better the worst hut than to live in the ground, like mole or rabbit."

Fedor nodded. "*Da.* If from the wheat we get money enough, so do I build a house, too."

By now, the diners had eaten their soup, and all around the table, plates were being loaded from the serving platters. Encouraged by the soup, Longarm sampled the cabbage rolls, *blinis,* and eggplant, and found them as different as the soup from his daily fare, but as tasty as the dishes he'd enjoyed earlier. He refilled his plate, taking food from each of the platters. The others were concentrating on eating with the same degree of interest that he was, and conversation faded except for a word now and then complimenting the flavor of the *golubtsi* stuffing, or a request for a platter to be passed to someone who could not reach it.

Longarm was satisfied long before the other guests had eaten their fill. He tried to protest when Mordka spooned a large serving of the fruit pudding onto his plate, but his host insisted that a meal was not finished without a helping of a sweet. Longarm tasted the odd-looking pudding somewhat gingerly; desserts, except for pie, were not among his favorite foods. He found that the mixture of coarsely cracked steamed wheat and pureed fruits, with just a touch of ginger and other spices, cleared his palate of the lingering taste of onion from the cabbage rolls and eggplant, and so he managed to put away the pudding without any trouble.

At last the pace of the eating slowed down. A voice from the far end of the table broke the silence that had prevailed since the meal began.

"Have you told yet the marshal *Amirikanits*, Mordka?"

"*Nyet*," Danilov answered. "*Padazhditi nimnoga*, Pavel. There is plenty of time for you to ask questions."

"If you gents want to start our talking while we finish eating, it's all right with me," Longarm offered. His ear was by now keenly enough attuned to the speech of the Brethren to let him recognize the reference to him as "the American marshal." He rubbed a hand over his stomach and shook his head. "I'm all out of room to put anything more in me, anyway. I don't recall when I've tucked away so much food in just one sitting."

"We will not talk yet," Mordka said firmly. "First we will finish supper. He turned to Longarm. "I have seen you smoking your cigars, Marshal Long. Tobacco, we of the Brethren do not allow ourselves, but if you wish to smoke, it will not bother us."

"Well, thanks. I guess you men have all done better than I seem to be able to." Longarm produced a cheroot from his vest pocket and lit it. "I try now and again to go without cigars, but I guess I ain't got enough willpower or something." He leaned back in his chair and puffed contentedly while the others finished clearing their plates.

One by one, the diners pushed away from the table. Mordka looked at them and asked, "*Vi gatovi?*"

A chorus of "*Da*" answered him. They stood up, and Danilov led them outside, saying, "We will enjoy the fresh night air, and it makes no difference where we have our discussion."

Though the evening air was balmy, there was a hint of oncoming autumn in the light breeze. In the blue-black sky the stars were diamond-bright, shining more brilliantly in the absence of a moon. There was silence for a few moments while deep breaths were taken and exhaled with sighs of repletion.

Mordka Danilov began, "When I saw you earlier today, Marshal Long, I did not want to say too much on the street. Others might have overheard us, you understand. But you see now for yourself my second reason. It is time that you hear from more than one of us about what we fear might be coming to happen."

"Well, none of us did too much talking while we were eating," Longarm said. "But I guess what you're talking about is the fence-cuttings and crop-trompings. You men figure they're going to get worse because you're coming up to harvest time?"

"We are still not so close as you think to reaping our crop," one of them replied. In the darkness, Longarm couldn't identify the speaker. The man went on, "It will not be until after the election that we will harvest our crop."

"November?" Longarm frowned. "Ain't that awful late? This part of the country, you can pretty much count on a freeze and maybe some snow before then."

"*Eta pravlina*," another voice said. "We have been here long enough to know the weather. Mordka, tell the *Amirikanits* of what you are saying to us before he got here."

"To understand what I will tell you, I must go back to the time before we came here," Mordka began, his voice thoughtful. "You know why we must leave Russia, where our grandfathers and great-grandfathers had emigrated a hundred years before to escape from Germany, where it was happening to them what came to be our fate in Russia. Because we did not swear oaths or fight in the Tsar's armies, the persecution started. Even so, we endured as long as we could. We did not want to do violent acts, to hurt or maim or kill." He sighed. "But after so many years, when the Cossacks began to come in and ravage our homes, rape our women, and kill our young men, some of us agreed that we must defend ourselves. We could not stay in our church, so we became what you know us as the *Bratiya*, the Brethren. We bought guns and knives and learned how to use them."

"Can't say I blame you a bit," Longarm told the group. "A man ought not to have to do a lot of things, but if it's do or die, he swallows his craw and does 'em."

"So," Danilov continued, "we fought back, and we survived. Now, tell me, Marshal, have you ever heard of a man called Carl Schmidt?"

"No. Can't say as I have."

"You vould have no reason to," Nicolai Belivev put in. "Ve came to know him because he is our great friend and benefactor."

"Most of Carl's family came to America many years before we of the Brethren did," Danilov explained. "They did not abandon our religion, or part of it, as we had to do. But some were in Russia yet, and through them Carl Schmidt learned how we were responding to the harshness of the new Tsar. He found a way to let us come here, through the railroad land. By his cleverness, most of us managed to bring with us a bit of gold, so we could get started here. And so it has been Carl who has helped us to sell our crop each year."

"Is in Russia not like here," one of the men broke in. "We did not own land, you know, Marshal. We worked on one of the Tsar's big estates—*mantulit*, we say—we eat the scrapings off his plate."

"What Tikhon means is that we plant and harvest, and for our work, we get to keep enough grain for living until next harvest, and if it is lucky, we get more to sell for other things we need."

"Sharecroppers!" Longarm exclaimed. "All you were doing was working for whatever bits the boss threw your way."

Mordka said, "We did not learn how grain is sold in America, you see. Why should we, when we had Carl to sell it for us? But now it is to say of what is the past." He paused a moment, as though to collect his thoughts, then went on. "You see, the money we brought with us was not enough to last very long. We did not make a good harvest the first year after we settled here; the time was too little. The next years our wheat was good, and Carl sold it at good prices. But not good at all the last year. The rain was not enough and the wheat did not do well."

"It was a dry year all over," Longarm said. "But you ought to've got a good price. Wheat goes up, just like anything does, when there ain't enough to let everybody have all they want."

"We did not understand this then," Mordka said. "So last year, the year of the small crop, a man came to us. Oren Stone, his name is. He looked at our wheat and he visited us, and offered to buy the whole crop, in the field. Carl was not here. He had gone back to Russia to help others emigrate. He had told us to reap our grain and store it until he got back. But we had very little money, Marshal. We took Stone's offer, and he kept his word and paid us what he said he would, even before the harvest. And because we thought he was our friend, when he offered us papers to sign, promising that we would sell him this year's crop, most of us signed them."

"Wait a minute," Longarm broke in. "This fellow Stone. Did he set a price on your wheat before it was cut, or did he pay you the going figure when you made your harvest?"

"Ah." Mordka's voice was sad. "That is what our friend Carl Schmidt asked us, when he got back and we told him of the sale we had made. You see, Marshal, we did not then know that men can make much money by speculating in your grain exchange in the town of Chicago."

"Which is what Stone was doing, I'll bet," Longarm said thoughtfully. "He was likely traveling as much territory as he could cover, buying up crops, and holding what he'd bought off the market. Then he'd catch a broker on the wheat pit in Chicago who'd made a short sale and couldn't cover it, and gouge a top price out of him, because the broker had to deliver the wheat he'd sold."

"So Carl explained to us," Danilov replied. "He said if we had waited until after harvest, we would have made many hundreds of dollars more than Stone gave us."

"And now Stone's got an option—which is what I'd guess you signed—to buy this year's crop," Longarm said.

"Yes. Tell us, Marshal Long, is this something that is lawful for Stone to do?"

"As far as I know, there ain't any law against it. Maybe there ought to be, but if a man wants to gamble on a business deal, he's pretty much free to do it."

"*Kak eta mozhna?*" one of the Brethren asked. In the darkness, Longarm could not see his face.

Danilov answered, "How is it possible, Tikhon? You remember how Carl explained it to us last year, don't you? He told us how foolish we had been to sign away our crop, if you recall."

"*Ya nipanimauy,*" another of the men said, disgust in his tone.

"You must understand, Pavel," Danilov said patiently. "The man Stone goes around finding ignorant ones like us and cheating us of what we should have for our labor, like the *aristokratiya.*"

"And I don't see that there's much you can do about it," Longarm told the group. "There sure ain't any way I know of that I can help you on something like this. It's a legal business deal, as far as the law's concerned."

"Perhaps if you would talk to Stone?" Mordka suggested.

"Well, I wouldn't mind talking to him for you, except I don't know where I'd find him," Longarm replied.

"He is in Junction now," Danilov said. "He has a railroad car of his own, and it was pulled into town today. Anatoly Yanishev came and told me he had seen the car arrive. I was on my way to talk with Stone when I saw you, Marshal Long. After you said you would meet with us tonight, I did not go to see him, though."

"You understand I can't do much except ask him to let you off on those options you signed, Mr. Danilov? I can't go beyond that."

"Perhaps if Stone thinks you are watching him, he will be afraid," Danilov said hopefully.

"Maybe," Longarm replied, "but I doubt it. A man like him will know what he can and can't do, where the law's concerned."

"But you will see him?" Danilov urged.

"Sure. I said I would. Now, then. Let's talk about the reason why I'm here in Junction, which is the election."

"What is there to talk about?" Nicolai Belivev asked. "We of the *Bratiya* will vote for Fedor Petrovsky, here. That is all we can say, *nyet*?"

"No it ain't," Longarm replied. "I went out and paid a little visit on Clem Hawkins today. I told him just what I aim to tell you now. I don't intend to stand for any fighting or keeping people from voting, or letting anybody vote more than once."

"Marshal Long. We would not do any of those things," Danilov protested. Then he added, "But the ranchers who favor Sheriff Grover, they might."

"I didn't say you folks in the Brethren would get out of line, Mr. Danilov. I'm just telling you what I'm going to be watching for while the voting's going on."

"We will be watching with you," Nicolai Belivev said. "We do not trust Hawkins. We know he's the one who encourages the cutting of our fences."

"I'm betting he ain't the only one, Mr. Belivev," Longarm told the Russian. "There ain't a rancher anyplace who likes a fence chopping up range that used to be open."

"Not all the land to the ranchers belongs," one of the other homesteaders said angrily. "Ve have some rights to keep our vheat from being spoiled, *nyet*?"

"Sure you have," Longarm agreed. "Especially if the sheriff doesn't do anything when you complain to him."

"Sheriff Grover only listens to our complaints," Danilov put in. "He does nothing to stop the fence-cutting. He is—"

Whatever else Mordka had intended to say was lost. A rifle shot cracked from the darkness. One of the homesteaders spun around and dropped to the ground with a cry of pain.

Chapter 6

Longarm reacted instantly to the sniper's shot. He'd been standing facing the house, with his back to the fields from which the
shot came, and hadn't seen the rifle's muzzle flash, but before
the echoes of the shot had died away he'd wheeled, drawing as
he turned, and sent a pair of slugs winging in the general direction of the sniper.

Distantly, a horse's hooves drummed on the hard earth, and,
in a matter of seconds, faded away to silence. Night shrouded
the horse and rider. In the blackness there was no way by which
the direction of the galloping horse could be traced. All Longarm could tell was that the sniper had made good his escape and
that pursuit would be useless.

Holstering his Colt, Longarm joined the homesteaders who
had gathered around the fallen man and were bending over him.
As Longarm moved, shadows blotted out the rectangle of yellow
lamplight streaming from the doorway; Marya and Tatiana
Danilov had crowded up to see what had happened.

"Let's get him inside," Longarm said crisply. "Not much way
we can tell how bad he's hurt, out here in the dark."

"Of course you will bring him in!" Marya called from the
doorway, then turned and, in rapid-fire Russian, rattled off a
series of instructions to Tatiana.

On the ground, the homesteader who'd been hit moaned
softly. The men lifted him and carried him into the house. Blood
dripped from the fresh wound and spattered on the scoured floor
as they stood for a moment, looking for a place to lay the
wounded man.

"Here!" Marya Danilov grabbed a pillow from her husband's
armchair and put it on the floor. "Let him down here, where the
light is good."

Tatiana came from the stove, carrying a basin of steaming water. She had a clump of rags in one hand. Marya kneeled by the wounded man's head, scissors in hand, and began snipping at his bloodstained shirt to pull it away from his shoulder.

Longarm needed only a glance to see that the wound was superficial. The rifle slug had ripped through the man's upper arm just below his shoulder. If it didn't hit bone, Longarm thought, he ain't going to be too bad off. He frowned, trying to recall the homesteader's name, and after a moment it came to him. He was Fedor Petrovsky, the candidate the Brethren were putting up against Sheriff Grover. Then Longarm's frown deepened. He'd been standing just in front of Petrovsky, outside. He wondered if the sniper might have been aiming at him instead of the Russian.

Mordka bent over Petrovsky, who was beginning to recover from the shock of the rifle slug's impact. The elder sighed with relief. "It is not bad," he said to the others. "Fedor will have a stiff arm for a while, but by harvest time his shoulder will be completely healed."

"*Da, ita nilza,*" Marya nodded. "A clean wound. Tatiana, give me the antiseptic."

A sharp, acrid odor filled the room as Marya wet a piece of cloth with liquid from a blue bottle that her daughter handed her. She daubed the wound with the cloth, and Petrovsky twitched his shoulder.

"It hurts," he protested.

"Better to hurt now than to swell up later," Marya told him tartly. "Lie still, Fedor. I must be sure this goes into the hole the bullet made."

Mordka stood up and faced Longarm. "This is what I have feared would happen," he said soberly. "Once men begin to think of doing harm to their fellows, it is a short path that leads to violence."

"It's a violent world," Longarm told Mordka. Always has been, ever since Cain tried to cheat Abel. But I ain't so sure that bullet was meant for your man Petrovsky. I was standing right in front of him. Whoever the shooter was, he might've been aiming at me."

"Who in this place would want to shoot you? You have been here only a few days."

Longarm's smile was grim. "Somebody who couldn't care one way or the other about what's going on in Junction, Kansas. I've put a passel of men behind bars at one time or another, Mr. Danilov. They sometimes carry a grudge out of prison with them, and if they run into me, they're apt to try to work it off with a bullet."

Mordka nodded. "I hadn't thought of that. I was about to ask you if you would try to find out who might have shot Fedor. You will be doing that for your own interest, though, will you not?"

"I sure as hell will be," Longarm assured him. "Not much I can do tonight, but first thing in the morning, I'll be back out here nosying around. And if I can find the sheriff and get him interested enough, I just might be able to talk him into coming along with me."

"And the fence-cutting? The damage to our wheat? We did not even begin to talk about them," Mordka reminded Longarm.

"Not much to talk about. I'll have a word with Grover when I catch up with him. Might be that if he knows I'm ready to step in if he doesn't do something about all that, he'll do his job right."

"What of Oren Stone?" Mordka smiled sadly, shaking his head. "It seems we are asking a great deal of you, but there is no one else to whom we can look for help."

"Ain't much I can do about Stone. But I'll have a try at talking to him, as soon as I finish trying to run down that bushwhacker."

"Thank you, Marshal. Now I must see about getting Fedor made comfortable. I think it will be better if he does not try to move from here tonight."

"You'd know best about that, I guess," Longarm said. "That being the case, I'll just say thank you for my supper, and ride on back to town. I'll report the shooting to the sheriff. He'll probably be out to ask about it later on."

Junction's jail was an unpainted building at the end of the town's only street. It had been constructed by spiking together railroad ties left over when the spur line was completed. The little building had two windowless cells across its back, and space enough in the front section for a desk and three or four chairs. The door was padlocked on the outside when Longarm stopped there after leaving his horse at the livery stable; quite obviously, Sheriff Grover couldn't be inside. Longarm shrugged and started toward the hotel.

He stopped in at the Ace High Saloon for a drink, and found the place nearly deserted. At the back, two poker tables were in operation, catering to the needs of a half-dozen dedicated gamblers, but there was no one at the bar drinking. The barkeep and the saloon girls were clustered at the end farthest from the swinging doors, chattering idly.

After the barkeep had detached himself from his conversation with the girls and served the shot of rye Longarm ordered, he started back to his interrupted gossip session. Longarm stopped him with a question.

"Sheriff Grover been in this evening?"

"Come to think of it, he hasn't. Sorta funny, because most nights he'll stop in once or twice while he's patrolling around town, but not tonight."

"Guess he's out on a case at one of the ranches, or something," Longarm said. He drained his glass and set it on the bar. "Well, it ain't all that important. I'll run into him sooner or later."

Up the street at the Cattleman's a few minutes later, he asked Bob the same question and got the same reply. Before Longarm could carry their conversation any further, Ruthie left the table at which she'd been sitting with another of the girls, and came up to stand beside him. Tactfully, Bob moved away.

I was wondering if you'd be dropping in," Ruthie said. "I sort of thought you'd be in here earlier."

"Why? You got some more troubles?"

"No, thank goodness! And I'm not going to get into any, if I'm lucky." She looked around, and saw that Bob was still standing within earshot. "Come on over to one of the tables and sit with me a few minutes, if you don't mind. There's something I want to tell you."

She led the way to a table against the back wall, across the room from the bar. Longarm followed her, carrying his glass.

When they were seated, she said, "After I got back here from your room this morning, I lay awake a long time, thinking about what you said. And I made up my mind, Longarm. I'm going to do it."

"Do what?"

"Shake this place. Get out of the sporting life. For good, I mean. Listen, I went to the boss as soon as he came in and told him he'd better find another girl to take my place. I'm going to take the first train out of town, even if I've got to ride in the engine cab or in a cattle car."

"Got any idea where you'll be heading?"

"California, I guess. Maybe San Francisco. It's a big enough place that I ought to be able to find a job there. A decent job, I mean." She grinned lopsidedly. "Maybe after a while somebody'll come along who'll want to marry me. And I'll swear to make him the best wife a man ever had."

"Sure you will."

"Even if I can't lasso a man of my own, I'll get along, you know." She paused before asking in a strangely shy voice, "You won't mind if I come to see you again tonight, when I get off, will you?"

"Now, Ruthie, you know you're welcome anytime."

"I hoped you'd tell me that. It won't be late. Things are real slow tonight."

Longarm drained his glass and stood up. I'll be looking for you, then, whenever you get there."

Back in his room, he treated himself to a swallow from the almost empty bottle of bonded rye before he went through his regular nighttime routine. Before undressing, he cleaned his Colt and slid fresh cartridges into the cylinder to replace the two he'd fired at the bushwhacker. As he worked, Longarm wondered just who had fired that shot from the darkness, and whether the target had been the farmer who'd been hit, or the big lawman himself.

I guess that's something I'll find out sooner or later, he told himself as he slid the Colt back into its holster and hung the revolver by his gunbelt on the left side of the bed's headboard.

He still couldn't dismiss the question from his mind, though, while he cleaned and checked his watch-chain derringer. Before hanging the vest on the right side of the headboard, Longarm fished a cigar out of its pocket and lighted it. Then, with the rye handy on the floor and his cheroot glowing comfortably, he propped himself up on the bed, stretched out, and waited for Ruthie. Not until her light tap sounded and he got up to let her in did the nagging question of who'd been the gunman's target leave his mind.

Ruthie said, "I told you I wouldn't keep you waiting long. To tell you the truth, I left earlier than I should've, but I got to thinking about last night, and just couldn't wait any longer." As she spoke, she was unfastening her dress. "It's been a slow night, though. They won't need me as much as I've been needing you."

Longarm had taken the whiskey bottle to the bureau and was pouring a glass for her. Ruthie came and snuggled up to him. She pushed aside the drink he offered her and began unbuttoning his balbriggans. Her fingers slid quickly from the neck button of the longjohns down Longarm's chest and stomach, and she dragged the undersuit off, freeing his crotch to her soft, caressing fingertips.

Ruthie slid between him and the dresser and turned Longarm to face her. Over her shoulder, in the flyspecked, tarnished mirror, he saw the sweep of her bare back from shoulders to buttock crease as she locked her arms around his neck and levered herself up to sit perched on the edge of the bureau. Her legs came up, her knees in Longarm's armpits. Her gusting breath fanned his cheek as she reached down with one hand, groped for a moment, found him, and guided him to touch her. A moment later, her hand closed around him in a convulsive squeeze as she felt him harden in response to the delicate dancing of her fingertips along his shaft.

"Don't make me wait any longer!" she begged as Longarm stood motionless. "Drive on in! I want all of you inside me, hard and deep!"

He responded to her demand with a sudden, rapid thrust that set her body quivering. She leaned back, accepting him, welcoming the piston strokes he pounded into her. Still, she wanted more. She pulled her legs free, twisting to get them from under his arms, and stretched them high, her feet above Longarm's head, the backs of her thighs soft and warm against his chest. Longarm let her move as she wanted to, without interrupting the rhythm of his own deep thrusting. His arms were around her now, embracing her raised thighs as well as her body. He felt for a moment as if he were holding two women instead of one.

"Oh, it's the best this way!" Ruthie moaned. "Now I'm really full of you! Keep going, Longarm! Don't ever . . . ever . . ." Her words became an unintelligible half-moan, half-scream, as her body convulsed in a series of jerking quivers.

Longarm waited until her cries trailed off to whimpers and the uncontrollable paroxysms of her body relaxed. In one quick motion, he lifted her limp form and swung her around. Still hard and deep inside her, he lowered her to the bed, following her without breaking the bond of flesh that connected them. Then he began stroking again.

For several minutes she lay supine, at the threshold of awareness, unable to respond. Bit by bit, she came to life again. Longarm felt her muscles tighten around him, felt her legs trying to work free of his arms. He moved to release her thighs. She sighed contentedly and wrapped her legs around him. Her arms went around his neck, she pulled her firm-tipped breasts to his chest, and nestled her face in the warm, soft hollow at the base of his throat.

"I said you were a miracle last night," she whispered into his chest. Longarm felt the words rather than heard them. "I just didn't have any words to say how big a miracle you are. And I still can't find the words. But you can't keep going forever, Longarm. Don't worry about me. Come whenever you want to."

"I can go awhile yet. Maybe long enough for you to make it again."

He fell silent then and gave himself up to the pleasure of being engulfed in pulsing heat, of feeling the girl's soft body glued to his. He didn't want to stop any more than she wanted him to, and he paced himself to slow his rhythm, to stop now and again while he was buried to the deepest penetration inside her, and press with a gentle, sidewise rubbing, stimulating her while delaying himself, letting each minute stretch until it shattered.

When he felt her beginning to respond once more, he asked, "You still want me to go on and not wait for you?"

"You can tell I don't. You're the damnedest man, Longarm. You've just about got me there again. Hold on for a little bit longer, if you can. I'm loving every minute of it!"

"Take your time, Ruthie. I'm not in a hurry. Not yet."

Longarm prolonged the embrace until he felt her beginning to respond. Then he drove them both to a frenzy with short, quick lunges until their flesh could stand no more and melting spasms shook them, drained them. They drew apart, sighing, and almost at once, both of them fell asleep.

* * *

When Longarm woke, the sunlight was beating against the drawn shade of his room's lone window. He rubbed his face with his hands, the woman-scent of Ruthie recalling the night. Turning in bed, he took his watch out of his vest pocket. The hands showed eleven o'clock.

"She took if out of you right good," he told himself, rolling to his feet. He remembered her leaving; when he'd locked the door behind her, the window shade had been translucent with a faint dawn-gray glow.

"First time I've been in bed this late for as long as I can recall," he muttered. He tilted the bottle of bonded rye and swallowed the small amount of whiskey left in it. Moving swiftly without the appearance of speed, he went through his morning dressing routine, anxious to make up for the time he'd lost in getting the day under way.

Eating breakfast at noon wasn't a new experience for him, but it wasn't one Longarm especially enjoyed. With eggs and steak and three cups of coffee under his belt, he walked to the sheriff's office. The door wasn't padlocked this time; the lock lay on Grover's desk, but the sheriff was nowhere to be seen. Both cells of the cramped jail were empty too, so there was no one to ask when Grover might be back. Longarm weighed the possibility of finding the sheriff in one of the saloons or stores, and decided his best bet was to wait. The unlocked door was, he thought, a pretty good sign that Grover would be back sooner rather than later.

Longarm's hunch proved correct. He'd been waiting less than ten minutes when the sheriff sauntered in.

"Well, Marshal. What's on your mind today?"

"Just a little job of bushwhacking somebody tried to do last night. Nobody killed, but a man got nicked pretty good."

"The hell you say! Where'd it happen, and how come I haven't heard about it before now?"

"Because you weren't around anyplace where I could find you last night. If it'd been a killing or something like that, I'd've waited to run you down before I went to bed, but I figured there wasn't much you could do that couldn't wait."

"Who got shot?" Grover asked.

"One of the wheat farmers out from town to the north. Name's Petrovsky, Fedor Petrovsky."

"Now, hold on! He's the foreign son of a bitch the Brethren are running against me in the election!"

"Sure. I know that. Didn't, though, until last night."

"Too bad whoever shot him didn't aim better. It would've saved me wearing myself out campaigning."

"That's one way to look at it, I guess, but a sort of cold-blooded one, it seems to me."

"Shit, who'd miss anybody like him? We'd be better off if the whole kit and caboodle of them Russians moved out."

Longarm had heard enough. He said coldly, "Look here, Grover, I already know how you feel about those farmers, after what you told me the other night. Which is just about what your boss said when I talked to him yesterday."

"I've got no boss except the people who elected me!" Grover said angrily.

"Sure. That's what Clem Hawkins said, too."

"I heard you'd paid him a visit. Let me give you some good advice, Long. Don't tangle with Clem. He's a bigger man than you are. He's good friends with congressmen and senators, and he can pull strings that just might get you yanked outa your job."

"You let me worry about my job. You've got your own to take care of," Longarm shot back.

Grover was silent for a moment. When he spoke, his voice was calmer. He'd evidently decided that Longarm was right about his own position being none too secure. He said, "There's no use in us locking horns on this. You did me a favor when you corralled that drunk cowhand. I guess I owe you one now."

"You don't owe me anything. All I want is for you to play out your hand the way it's dealt, cards faceup, like you said you were going to do the other night."

"We never did finish our talk, did we?" Grover asked.

"Seems to me we were interrupted," Longarm replied.

"Well, now's as good a time as any, if you feel like it."

Longarm shook his head. "I'd just as soon put it off awhile. Until you get through looking into that shooting."

"How bad's Petrovsky hurt?"

"Not bad. Slug went in high on his arm, clean wound. He'll be up and around in a day or so."

"Well, you seem to've gotten pretty friendly with them nesters," Grover said. "Suppose you tell him to come in, next time you see him, and after I've heard his story, I'll start my investigation."

"Damn it, Grover, I'm telling you right now that there's been a murder attempted. You can't just sit there on your butt until you hear about it from the man who's been shot!"

"Who says I can't? You? This's a local shooting, mister federal marshal. Don't tell me you've got any jurisdiction over it."

"Oh, I wouldn't do that. If I figured I had, I'd've begun looking into it before now. But in case you've disremembered, Grover, the fellow who got winged is up for office in an election I was sent here to watch. It wouldn't take too much of a stretch for me to say I'd *take* jurisdiction."

"Don't threaten me, Long. My hands are clean. I've got nothing to be afraid of, where you're concerned." Grover's anger was surfacing again.

"I didn't mean you had. Except it doesn't set too well with me to hear any officer sworn to uphold the law say he's going to drag his feet looking into a case of attempted murder just because the man who got shot's running against him for election."

"I didn't say that!"

"You didn't miss it by much!" Longarm snapped.

"All right!" The sheriff's voice was calmer. "If it'll make you feel better, I'll go out and talk to Petrovsky. I don't guess he's going to die between now and tomorrow morning, is he?"

"I told you, he's not hurt bad."

"I'll get out there first thing in the morning, then," Grover said. "I've got work piled up that'll keep me busy the rest of today."

"Suit yourself. I ain't trying to tell you how to run your business. But if you don't object, I'll check in with you after you get back. I've got a sort of personal interest in this case."

"You mean you're going to take the nesters' side?" Grover said incredulously.

"I don't aim to take anybody's side. That's not my job. All I want is to see that election run fair and square. And that's what I aim to do."

"As long, as you keep it that way, then there's nothing for you and me to quarrel about," Grover said.

Leaving the sheriff's office, Longarm started to the livery stable for his horse, then thought better of it and turned back toward town. He stepped through the batwings at the Ace High. He told himself that he wasn't avoiding Ruthie, he just needed a spell of being by himself, where he could sit down and do some thinking.

At a table in one corner, with a bottle in front of him, he started taking stock.

Might be I made a mistake not telling Grover that slug could've been meant for me, his thoughts ran. *If I'd told him, he'd maybe look closer at that bushwhacking than he will if he figures nobody but the Brethren are concerned.*

It's too damned pat just to've happened by accident. Longarm frowned, sipping his drink. *Wonder if it could be that cowhand, Fred? He'd feel like he owed me one for taming him down, making him look little in front of Ruthie. But hell, he's just a kid, and kids don't hold grudges the way grown men do. Most of the time, anyhow.*

Couldn't be that Clem Hawkins set somebody on me. He's too smart an old he-coon to pull a stunt like that, at least not till he sees that I'm going to plow up his cabbage patch. Wouldn't put it past him to do most anything, though, if I stepped on his toes too hard.

Maybe a fence-cutter just riding past, who couldn't pass up the chance? Hawkins ain't the only rancher who tells his hands to carry wirecutters in their saddlebags, from what I hear.

Could be it was just a drunk cowhand larking around, who'd heard his boss cussing the Brethren day in, day out, and just took a potshot out of plumb damn meanness at anybody belong, to the Brethren, figuring they were fair game. But not likely, considering where the shot came from. Had to be somebody who took time and trouble enough to find a good place to shoot from.

Come to think about it, I never did see just exactly where the shot did come from. Muzzle flash was over, by the time I turned around to look.

Wouldn't do a bit of harm to ride out and nosy around a little bit. Not much I can do just johnnying here in town, or planting my butt in a chair in front of a bottle.

Inaction had always galled Longarm. He stood up, took the bottle back to the bar, and tossed the money for his drink onto the mahogany. Then he pushed through the batwings and turned up the street toward the livery to get his horse.

Chapter 7

You didn't have enough time to study this mess out proper last night, old son, Longarm told himself as he rode toward the Danilovs' house, the afternoon sun warm on his shoulders. *Not that it would've done much good, what with everything happening in the dark the way it did. But it'd sure help to be on a hotter trail than the one you're likely to find out there, if you find any trail at all.*

As the roan jogged along the road that paralleled the railroad spur, Longarm searched his memory, trying to recall the precise sound the rifle shot had made the night before. Unexpected as the gunfire had been, he'd registered it automatically in his mind for range, and was pretty sure the bushwhacker had fired from a distance of between a hundred and fifty and two hundred yards. That still left a lot of ground to be covered in trying to find the exact spot where the unknown gunman had stood.

Old Lady Luck better be riding on your shoulder today, Longarm thought. *If she ain't, you're going to have one hell of a lot of hiking to do.*

As the Danilov house faced north, Longarm rode on past the rutted land between wheatfields that led to its door. As he'd hoped, a similar passageway had been left between the two fields beyond the Danilov dwelling and the homestead beyond it. He turned up this one, and rode east until he was in line with the Danilov house. There, he began looking across the Glidden wire fence to the wheatfield on his right. When he found no sign of a trail, he went back to the road and turned north again to the lane that divided the next two fields.

This time his inspection of the grain south of the fence was more rewarding. From the fence to the center of the field, an irregular line of displaced stalks showed in the thigh-high grain.

The line was faint, marked chiefly by an occasional sagging head and a broken stalk or two, but it was there, visible to anyone with trail-trained eyes.

As soon as he spotted the disturbed line in the wheatfield, Longarm pulled the roan up short. He didn't want to trample the area ahead; the night-shooter must have tethered his horse somewhere close to the spot where the path through the growing wheat began, and he didn't want his own mount to disturb any sign that might have been left. He didn't hope for much—the soil in the lane was stone-hard—but any tracks would be better than none at all.

Dismounting, Longarm looped the reins around the top strand of the fence enclosing the field, and walked to the point where the rifleman had entered the field. As he'd thought, the dirt in the lane was too hard to show a clean print, but a pile of still-moist dung showed that there'd been a horse left there for a while the night before.

"Hitched his horse to the fence here, all right. Too damn bad the ground's so hard I can't tell whether he followed me or that Petrovsky fellow over to Danilov's and got the idea of potshotting us when he seen us come outside," Longarm muttered as he straddled the fence and went into the wheatfield.

Absorbed in searching the baked ground for footprints, kneeling now and then in the wheat when he discovered a trace of one, Longarm did not see or hear the plodding mule until its rider pulled up the animal at the fence. He looked back only when his name was called.

"Marshal Long!"

Looking around, Longarm saw the mule and its rider. He might not have recognized Fedor Petrovsky if the homesteader had not carried his left arm in a sling. "Petrovsky! What're you doing out here? You ought to be laying still, letting that arm heal up."

"Nyet, eta ni nuzhna," Petrovsky replied cheerfully. *"Ya harasho."* He saw Longarm's puzzled frown and said, "Excuse, please. Sometimes I forget to talk *Amirikanski* vords. I say is not needed I keep in bed, is all right my arm. Vas only little hurt."

"I told the sheriff about the shooting," Longarm said. "He'll be out to talk to you tomorrow morning, see if he can find out who did it."

"Sheriff!" Petrovsky spat into the dust of the lane. "Vould make him happy, the sheriff, vas I hurt vorse or killed."

"Now, that ain't quite right. I don't say he likes you, or your people, for that matter. But I got him to promise he'd do his job right, and see if he could turn up that bushwhacker."

"If is so, then vhy do you come looking for yourself?"

"Well, I figure I've done a mite more tracking than the sheriff has, in a lot more places. Besides, I was standing right close to you last night, remember? That slug didn't miss me by very much."

"Is true. So. If tracking it is you do, is maybe I can help," Petrovsky said.

He slid off the mule, ducked nimbly between the top and center strands of the taut wire, and started into the field. Longarm noticed that the homesteader stayed to one side of the path that led into the center of the wheatfield, and wondered whether Petrovsky was avoiding the broken line intentionally or by accident.

As he approached, Petrovsky explained, "I see you vhen you go up path between here and Mordka's house. I think you come look for tracks. Is all right I am look too, *da*?"

By now, Longarm had learned what the monosyllable meant. He answered, "*Da*. But that's about the only word of your lingo I know, Petrovsky. All right, as long as you're here, come along while I take a look."

Petrovsky indicated the broken wheatstalks. "He is go right here, to vhere he stop to shoot." He pointed ahead to a place where the grain heads were leaning in all directions and some of the stalks had broken to form a small, ragged circle.

Longarm took a second look at his companion. "You act like you know how to read sign. I'd say you've done some tracking before."

"Sign?" Petrovsky frowned. "*Ya nipaninayu*. Excuse. I do not understand 'sign'."

"Tracks. Footprints and suchlike."

"*Da*. Tracks, I know. Is my family—how you vould say it?—animal-look-fors?"

"Gamekeepers?" Longarm guessed.

Petrovsky's face widened in a smile. "*Da*. My father, his father, his grandfather, is tell hunters to go vere they find *medved*.

That is bear, and *los*, like you call elks. So from a little boy I am learn from my father to know how they look, all kinds tracks. Man-tracks too, like other kind."

"Well, now. Maybe you'll see something I might miss." Longarm didn't think so, but it didn't hurt to be polite. He went on, "So far, all I found is where that shooter tethered his horse last night."

Petrovsky nodded. "*Da*. I see *navos* vhere horse stand. Now is to find from man, *nyet*?"

Together, they walked on into the wheatfield. Without a word of consultation, Longarm moved along one side of the trail of disturbed wheatstalks, Petrovsky on the other. They moved slowly, eyes on the broken grain, careful not to disturb any tracks that might be present. Longarm watched his companion as well; after a few moments he was satisfied that Petrovsky was indeed a skilled tracker.

It was an easy trail to follow, but a frustrating one. The field had been sown broadcast, the seed scattered by hand on earth tilled uniformly flat, rather than having been planted in rows. The ground under the stalks of still-green wheat was level, and, unlike the roads and lanes where the dirt had been baked hard, the growing grain had shielded the earth's surface from the blazing summer sun. The ground had a thick crust, but was soft underneath. It held footprints well.

Under the broken grain, though, there were no clear prints to be seen. In making his way through the field, the sniper had obviously kept his eyes straight ahead, watching the lighted door of Danilov's house. He had felt for a path with his feet, shuffling them along on the surface of the ground, depending on his toes to warn him of any obstacles that might be in his way. All that Longarm and Petrovsky could see as they followed the rifleman's trail was a series of long scuffmarks where his feet had pushed along the soil.

Petrovsky shook his head. "Is not good, the tracks. He is valk like old man who cannot his feet lift up."

"Feeling along with his feet while he watched for a target," Longarm said. He stretched out an arm, his fingers pointing at the Danilov house, in clear view across the intervening wheatfield. The door of the house was clearly outlined. "I'd say our best bet to find something's right up ahead, where he must've stood while he was waiting for a shot. Maybe there'll be some better prints there."

"Is not big man, him," Petrovsky said. His eyes were riveted on the scuffmarks. Longarm had already deduced as much. He nodded. The homesteader swept a hand to measure the unknown man's stride. "Is not so big as you. More big, a little bit, than me."

"Looks that way," Longarm agreed. "Weighs about the same as you do, though, wouldn't you guess?"

"*Da.* So much, maybe a little more."

They reached the small, ragged circle in the grain. A glint of metal caught Longarm's eye at once. He leaned over, careful not to disturb the soil inside the circle, picked up a brass cartridge case, and looked at its butt end.

"Shoots a .32-20." He held out the shell casing for Petrovsky to see. "Coyote gun. Most of us favor a heavier one. I'll bet he packs a Colt the same caliber. Our man's likely a range hand."

A moment later, Petrovsky said, "A horseman's boots he vears." He pointed to indentations in the circle, deep crescents made by cowboy boot heels. Then he frowned and knelt at one side of the area to inspect one of the prints more closely. "*Sapojnik*, shoemaker, he should go to. Look vhat I see."

Longarm circled the beaten-down area to join his companion. He peered at the footprint to which the homesteader was pointing. A perfect print of the left sole of a cowboy boot showed a crack in the leather that ran from one edge of the sole to the other, across the spot where the ball of the wearer's foot rested.

"I'd say our man got careless, sometime or other a good while back," Longarm commented. "Took his boots off while they were still wet, and didn't walk 'em dry like a sensible man would. Leather got stiff, and the first thing that happened when he put 'em on again, that sole cracked wide open."

"Vas new, the boots, too. See, is no hole vhere crack is."

Petrovsky had shifted his attention to the area where broken stems drooped among the otherwise high-standing stalks. He pointed to a round indentation in the earth. "Here he kneeled, *nyet*?"

"Yep. Getting himself a steady rest for his rifle." Longarm indicated a pointed oval at one side of the dent. "He put his rifle butt there when he knelt down. And here's where the toe of his boot dug in. Pointy toe. Cowboy boots, like you said."

Petrovsky spread his hands to measure the distance between the knee and toe marks. "Is like I say, too, not so tall as you, not so short as me."

Longarm nodded with a satisfied exhalation. "Well, now. We know what he looks like, pretty much, and we know he's at one of the ranches hereabouts. A little bit of nosying around, and we'll have him safe in jail."

"Nosying?" Petrovsky asked. "*Ya nipani*—Excuse again, please. I do not understand."

"Nosying? Means I'll just go around to the ranches, starting out at Clem Hawkins's place, which is the likeliest one for him to be at. If he ain't there, I'll go on to the others till I dig him up."

Petrovsky shook his head. "Is not maybe so easy."

"It'll likely take some time," Longarm admitted. "But whoever made those prints is sure as hell going to wind up in jail."

"My father, he tell me a long time ago, '*Ne obival medved shkornley ne produal*,'" Petrovsky said. "Means in your language, 'You do not sell his skin before you the bear have catched.'"

Longarm chuckled. "Takes a lot more words in our language than it does in yours, doesn't it? What we say is, 'Don't count your chickens before the eggs are hatched.' I guess it means about the same thing."

Petrovsky smiled. "*Da.*"

"Well, I know if I turn this fellow up on the first try, it'll just be dumb luck. But in my business a man needs some patience, and I've got plenty of that. Come on. We've seen all we're likely to, here. I'd best get moving before the day wears out."

"Now you go vhere?" Petrovsky asked.

"Hawkins's place." Longarm started back toward the fence-line. "Not much else I can do here. Be nice if our man had written down his name in the dirt back there, but I've got enough to go by when I start looking for him."

"*Eta nilza*—" Petrovsky began; he stopped and started over. "Is it permitted that I go vith you?"

Longarm looked at him curiously. "Figuring to get in some practice in case you're elected sheriff?"

"*Nyet.* To be elected, I do not expect. Is enough ve show the ranchers and the people in Junction that ve of the Brethren have a part in living here. You understand vhat to say I am trying?"

Longarm nodded. "I think I do. You're citizens of the U.S.—most of you are, anyhow. And you want everybody to know you aim to be good ones. Is that about right?"

"*Eta pravlina*. This is vhat ve think. Is to get respect ve vant, to show that new *Amirikanits* good as one born here."

"Well, I guess I don't blame you for trying. It's funny how folks forget things. There's an awful lot of men out here in this part of the country who emigrated from someplace in Europe. Why, hell, a big part of the Northern army was recruited out of young fellows who didn't speak English as good as you do. Still a lot of 'em in the service, too."

"*Da*. This is vhat Carl Schmidt have tell us vhen he come to Russia to say the railroad land is to sell."

They reached the fence and Longarm pulled the roan's reins free. Petrovsky freed his mule and stood waiting, a question in his eyes.

"Well, hell, I guess it won't hurt if you come along," Longarm told him. "It ain't likely we'll turn our man up at Hawkins's, and if we do, there won't anything get started that I can't handle. If the old man is at the bottom of this, it might do him good to see you with your arm in that sling."

"*Nichivo!*" Petrovsky shrugged. "It does not the arm matter. It is not hurt me. I have before got vounds vorse as this one, vhen ve fight the Cossacks."

"Just the same, it's a long way back to Junction and then on out to Hawkins's place."

"Is to go back to town no need. I show you shorter vay."

Petrovsky's route may have been shorter, but it didn't seem so to Longarm. He led them in a winding route along the narrow lanes between the fenced fields, jogging left and right as the fencelines required. There was little talk exchanged between them; Longarm was preoccupied. He was trying to figure out how he'd explain to Clem Hawkins why he wanted to inspect the boot soles of his ranch hands in a way that wouldn't arouse the crusty cattleman's instant anger. He gave short replies when his companion tried to start a conversation, and after a few efforts, Petrovsky gave up and spoke only to give directions through the checkerboarded wheatfields. They came to the end of the cultivated land and turned onto the cattle trail. Sooner than Longarm had expected, they saw the big ranch house looming ahead, its white walls tinged now by the drooping orange sun.

"Don't take me wrong, now," Longarm cautioned Petrovsky. "But you'd better not say too much when we get to Hawkins's place."

"*Da*. This I tell myself, Marshal, *Chooyat*. I know this. I am to be small man, say nothing."

"That's the right idea. Hawkins don't like you Brethren, I don't have to tell you that. I ain't looking for him to be easy for me to handle, when you come right down to it."

There was no greeting at the door, this trip. Their mounts tethered at the hitch rail, Longarm and Petrovsky waited several moments after knocking. The man who opened the door was a stranger to Longarm; he'd not seen him on his earlier visit.

"Boss is out at the bunkhouse," he said. "Hands are just getting in from the gather. You better—"

"We'll just step around there, then," Longarm said. He turned on his heel, and before the man in the door had a chance to object, both Petrovsky and Longarm were off the porch.

Clem Hawkins had his back to them when they saw him in front of the bunkhouse, talking to one of his hands. He heard their footsteps on the hard-packed dirt and turned quickly. His lips compressed into a narrow line when he recognized Longarm.

"God damn it!" Hawkins exploded. "You federal men never do seem to get tired of poking your noses into a man's business just when he's busiest! Here I am, trying to find out how many steers I'm going to be able to ship, and you come around again. What is it this time?"

"I'm trying to track down a bushwhacker, Mr. Hawkins," Longarm replied, his voice low and even. "Fellow shot into a crowd last night, wounded this man here, came pretty close to winging me."

Hawkins looked closely at Petrovsky. "You're one of them damn nesters. I've seen you around town."

With dignity, Petrovsky replied, "I am citizen of this country, like you. Difference is, maybe I not so rich."

With a grunt, Hawkins turned back to Longarm. "What'd you bring him on my place for? I told you the other day how I feel about them foreigners."

"I brought him because he's a citizen, just like he said. And he's got the same right you'd have if it was you who'd been shot."

"You saying I had something to do with that shooting?" Hawkins demanded.

"No sir. Not even hinting. All I know right now is that whoever pulled the trigger was a ranch hand. That's how the evidence reads. He could work here, he could work someplace else. I'm going from one spread to the next until I find him."

Longarm's calm, quick answers seemed to mollify Hawkins a bit. The rancher looked Petrovsky up and down again, though, before he said, "I guess you'd know the bushwhacker if you saw him?"

"I'll know him."

"You said the shooting was at night. How the hell could you see him, if he was a rifle-shot away from you?"

"I'll know him," Longarm repeated. "All I want to do is take a look at your men. I'll only need a few minutes. Are they all in from the gather?"

"All but one or two. My foreman's still out on the prairie, and the segundo's up at the tally pasture. All the hands have come in, as far as I could tell. Like I said when you were here the other day, I've hired on a lot of new men for the gather."

"If you're the kind of man I sized you up to be, Mr. Hawkins, you've got no more use than I have for a skunk who'd throw down on a bunch of unarmed folks, potshot at 'em from the dark," Longarm said. "Now, do you mind if I go in your bunkhouse for a look? I'd guess most of your hands are in there, waiting for the supper bell."

"They're in there. And you're right; I've got no liking for a backshooter," Hawkins replied. "Go on in. But I'll come with you and keep an eye on what you do."

Longarm and Petrovsky followed Hawkins into the bunkhouse. The long, narrow building, two bunks wide and thirty long, was crowded with men. Some of them lounged on their bunks, while others were stripping off sweat-wet shirts, getting ready to wash before supper. The air was full of loud conversation, laughter, and the sharp fumes of Bull Durham tobacco smoke.

Hawkins stamped his bootheel on the floor to get their attention. When the buzz of voices died away, he said, "This man's a federal marshal. He wants to take a look at you."

"How come?" called a voice from the back of the building.

"Because I told him he could!" Hawkins snapped. "Now you men answer whatever questions he wants to ask you." He nodded at Longarm. "Go ahead, Marshal. I hope you'll make it quick. Cook'll be ringing the supper bell in about three minutes."

Raising his voice, Longarm said to the men, "I'll leave it to Mr. Hawkins to tell you later what this is all about. Right now, it'll help me a lot if all of you who ain't on your bunks sit down or lay down, and I'll just walk down the middle and take a quick look at you. That way, we'll be finished before supper."

There was a certain amount of under-the-breath complaining, but the men who were on their feet shifted around until each of them had settled on a bunk. Most of them followed the cowboy adage "Never stand up when you can sit down, never sit down when you can lie down." Only a half-dozen chose to sit. To avoid giving away his purpose prematurely, Longarm concentrated first on the loungers. He walked down the aisle between the rows, glancing quickly at the soles of each pair of boots exposed to his eyes. At the back of the room, he turned and started moving forward again.

At the first bunk on which a man was sitting instead of lounging, Longarm said, "Lift your feet up so I can see the soles of your boots, cowboy, if you don't mind."

Though the man he spoke to seemed a bit bewildered by the strange request, he lifted his feet to show a pair of unbroken soles on his scuffed boots. Longarm moved on to the next sitter, who, after having heard the request made of the first one, lifted his feet without being asked. By now, everyone in the bunkhouse was aware that something out of the ordinary was going on. All of the occupants were watching closely. Their stares ran the gamut from amusement to bewilderment to hostility.

One of the scowlers was a heavily bearded man who sat on the third bunk at which Longarm stopped. Though shirtless, he still had on his hat. When Longarm requested him to raise his feet, he replied with a surly, "Why the hell should I?"

"No reason except I'm asking you to. And your boss told you to answer whatever I asked you about."

"I don't always do what my damn boss tells me to, either,"

the cowhand snarled. He leaned back, though, as if to comply with the request.

Something in the man's voice had struck a gong in Longarm's memory. His muscles tensed involuntarily when he heard it, and as the leaning man changed his motion to a rolling reach for the holstered revolver that hung from a peg over his bunk, Longarm had his own Colt out and buried in the cowhand's bare ribs.

"I can pull this trigger a hell of a long time before you can reach that gun of yours," Longarm grated. "Now suppose you just sit back down and raise up your feet."

"You'll have to knock me down!"

Longarm was too wise to risk breaking a knuckle on a hard skull. Without shifting his Colt, he swung his left elbow around and jabbed it into the reluctant cowhand's throat. The objector choked, gulped, and dropped to his bunk, gagging. Longarm pulled on the left leg of the man's Levi's and brought the sole of his boot into view. A crack gaped in the center, running completely across the sole from edge to edge.

He dropped the leg and reached for the cowhand's shoulder. The man's hat had fallen off when Longarm's blow landed, and his half-bald head was exposed for the first time. On the left side of his scalp, a long scar ran from the line where his hat kept the skin from tanning, and disappeared in his tangled black hair.

"Hell!" Longarm exclaimed. "I ought to've recognized you right off. Would've, except you've let your whiskers grow since I put you in the federal pen for twenty years. Last time I saw you, your face was shaved. Prud—let's see, now—Prud Simmons."

"Yeah, damn you! And you oughta remember me. It was you give me this scar on my head," Simmons growled.

"You better be glad my eye was off that day," Longarm told him. "Let's see. Dakota Territory, just outside Fort Totten, along Devil's Lake. A half-inch lower, you'd be dead. Was it me, I'd rather be alive in jail than pushing up daisies." He frowned. "Five years ago, and you got twenty. Even with good-behavior time off, you oughtn't to be out yet. I'd say you escaped, Prud."

"You got too good of a memory, Longarm," Prud Simmons said sullenly. "That's what the cons in the big house says, anyhow. So when I saw you out here the other day, I figured you was looking for me. That's why I begged off sick, told the foreman I was going to town and see the doctor. I thought sure I had you, when I followed you out in the country. Bad luck I missed, damn it!"

Clem Hawkins had pushed his way through the men who'd crowded into the bunkhouse aisle when the brief fracas had flared. He looked from Simmons to Longarm.

"You mean this man's a fugitive from justice, Marshal?" Hawkins asked.

"I sent him up five years ago for attempted murder and bank robbery. I'd bet he's busted out of the federal pen, I just ain't got a wanted circular on him yet."

"Betting's one thing, Long. Being sure is something else. I want you to be damned sure before you haul off one of my men."

"If you want to put it that way, then, I'm sure. I'm sure of something else, too." Longarm fished out the cartridge case he'd found where the night-shooter had kneeled to fire. He passed the brass cylinder to Hawkins. "This is the cartridge case the man who did the shooting ejected out of his rifle. If you take down that rifle over Simmons's bunk, you'll see it's a .32-20, same caliber as this. And if that long-barreled pistol hanging there ain't the same caliber too, I'll bite the barrel in half."

Hawkins stared at Longarm for a moment, then took down the rifle from its pegs and inspected the action. He tossed the gun on the bunk and lifted the revolver from its holster, opened the loading gate, and peered at the inscription stamped on the cartridge case visible through the gate.

"You're right both ways," he said. There was a grudging respect in his voice. "Looks like you knew what you were doing. I hope you're satisfied that I didn't have anything to do with that shooting?"

"I never figured you did, Mr. Hawkins. Worst thing I thought was that one of your hands heard you cussing the homesteaders so much that he figured they were fair game."

Hawkins nodded. "You're going to take the son of a bitch away, I hope? I don't want outlaws on my spread, Long."

"Oh, I'll take him to town and turn him over to the sheriff. I'll ask you one favor, though. It's night, and more'n a two-hour ride to Junction. Prud's got a tricky way of slipping handcuffs—that's how he got shot. He'd been taken by a sheriff up in Dakota, slipped the cuffs off, and shot him. Petrovsky's got a fresh wound, and he'll want to drop off at his house, instead of town. I'd sooner take Prud in by daylight."

"You don't have to ask. You can lock Simmons up in the ice-house after supper. There's no way to open it from inside, and it's built solid. The water drain'll give him air, and there's no ice in it now. There's a spare bunk in my segundo's shack. You can sleep there."

"I guess that includes my friend, Mr. Petrovsky, too?"

Longarm gave Hawkins credit. The rancher hesitated for only a few seconds before nodding. "Seeing he's hurt, I'll let him stay too. But—" for the first time, Hawkins spoke to Petrovsky— "Don't you get the idea you're welcome. You and your kind never will be, on my place." He looked at the men around them. "Hetter, Rob, you two take care of the marshal. Long, I'll expect you to have these men off my place after breakfast tomorrow."

With this, Hawkins turned and stalked from the bunkhouse, leaving his hands to take care of providing the grudging hospitality he'd offered.

Chapter 8

To the left of the three riders plodding along the cattle trail toward Junction, the sun had just cleared the horizon. Longarm and Petrovsky rode abreast. Prud Simmons, not only handcuffed, but tied to his horse by a rope looped around his ankles and passed under the animal's belly, was half a lariat's length behind them. The morning air was crisp and clean, tanged with just a breath of autumn's promise.

Longarm said, "Well, Petrovsky, we cleared up more'n one thing. Prud was aiming at me, not you or one of your friends. And it was a personal grudge that hadn't got a thing to do with the fuss between your friends in the Brethren and the ranchers, or with the election, either."

"*Da.* Is good to get settled, these things." Hesitantly, then, he said, "In *Amirika*, is custom for friends to call first names between each other, *nyet*?"

"Mostly. Or nicknames."

"Ve are friends, Marshal? If is so, you please call me Fedor?"

"Why, sure. And—well, a lot of my friends, and a lot of folks who ain't so friendly, call me Longarm, instead of my real first name, which I ain't particularly in love with, only it was the one my Ma and Pa gave me, so I bear it right proudly."

"Longarm? *Eta mozhna*, I call you so?"

"Sure, if you want to."

"*Spasiba*, Longarm. Is good to have friends like you."

"I'd say the same thing about you, Fedor. You sort of surprised me, being such a good tracker. I thought all you Brethren were farmers."

"*Nyet, nyet!* Here, is farming all ve can do, until after the language and the *Amirikanitski* manners ve learn. But in old country, is Mordka schoolteacher, is Nicolai Belivev work in

store, is Anatoly Yanishev *koosnec*, like you say blacksmith.
Rest of us, *da*, look after horses, cow, make crops in fields."

"And your family were gamekeepers, trackers. From what I
saw yesterday, you did a little man-tracking, too."

"*Da*. To help find criminals, you understand. Not to do anything to help *Okhrana* catch political refugees. Or religious."

"*Okhrana*? That some kind of policeman?"

"Is secret police of Tsar. Is bad, Okhrana. Nobody helps
them."

"Is that why you figured you'd run for sheriff against Grover?"

"Is not my idea, Longarm." Petrovsky smiled at his first use
of the familiar form of address. "Is from Mordka, from Brethren." He thought for a moment and added brightly, "But now, I
help you find Tsimmons, *nyet*? And is be good to help me make
votes."

"Now wait a minute, Fedor. If you start out acting like you're
the sheriff this far ahead of the election, you might not be making a hit with a lot of folks who'd vote for you otherwise."

"Making hit?" Fedor asked. "Vhat means this?"

Longarm grinned. "I guess you never heard about baseball.
It's a game they play back East. One man throws a ball at a man
who's got a club they call a bat, and the fellow with the bat's
supposed to hit the ball. It ain't much of a game, when you put
it up alongside steer-busting and bronc-riding, but the dudes
back there seem to like it."

"Is good thing a hit to make, bad thing not to, then?"

"That's right. The fellow that makes the hits is the one the
folks like. And if these folks around here don't like you, they
ain't going to vote for you."

Petrovsky sighed. "*Amirikanits* talk. Is hard to learn. But I
remember vhat you tell me, I do like you say."

"You understand, I can't take sides between you and Grover.
I've got to stand right in the middle and see you both get a fair
shake."

"*Da*. This I know. Is good thing, I think, *Amirikanits* vay to
give everybody same chance."

"Sure it is. And I wish you luck, come the election."

Ahead of them, a buggy appeared around a curve in the cattle
trail. Longarm pointed to it.

"Well. Looks like old Clem Hawkins is getting an early visitor."

Fedor shaded his eyes with his hand and gazed at the buggy as it drew nearer. "You can see who is him in buggy?"

Longarm looked more closely. The vehicle was now near enough for him to make out the face of the man who was the buggy's lone occupant, but it meant nothing to him. "I see him all right, but I don't know who he is. Somebody from Junction?"

"*Nyet*. Is man Mordka tell you about, man who cheat us on our vheat crop last year."

"Oren Stone? The fellow from Chicago?"

"*Da*. Is him. Still pretty far avay, but him I know, I don't make mistake."

Picking up speed as it left the curved spot in the cattle trail, the buggy was bouncing along at a good clip by the time it reached the riders. Longarm led them off the trail to give the carriage the center of the path. It passed them going fast. Longarm looked closely at the man holding the reins, but got little more than an impression of a stern face and a gray suit and hat.

Watching the dust trail the buggy raised, he said thoughtfully, "Of course, there's other ranches besides Hawkins's along this trail, I'd guess. But it's my bet that Stone's going to see old Clem."

"You think is vork together, Hawkins and Stone?" Fedor asked.

"Right this minute, I ain't sure what to think. It was day before yesterday that Stone got to Junction. If he was real anxious to see Hawkins, why didn't he go yesterday?"

"Is maybe look at vheatfields yesterday," Fedor suggested.

"Yep. That might be the way it is. Well, there's a lot more I've got to find out before I can make up my mind about a lot of things."

Petrovsky frowned, puzzled. "Explain, please, Longarm. *Ya nipanauy*. Is something you think about you don't tell me yet?"

Longarm took his eyes off the buggy. "I'm wondering just how Stone fits into this. Did he ever give you men any idea why he just happened to show up here last year?"

"*Nyet*. Is just come in big railroad car as belongs to him, and start to buy our vheat crop."

"He ever spend any time you know about with Hawkins or the other cattlemen?"

Again Petrovsky shook his head. "If he does this, ve do not know about it."

"Paid you off in cash, I guess? He'd almost have to, seeing as there's not any bank in Junction."

"Gold he gives us for vheat, and more gold to sign paper saying ve sell him crop again this year."

"Well, we'll find out soon enough whether him and Hawkins are in cahoots, but I'm betting he ain't going out there this morning just to shake hands. That's for me to look into later, though. Right now, I've got to get Prud into the sheriff's office and see that he's locked up. No need for you to go all the way into town with me, Fedor. When we get to whatever turnoff takes you home, you'd better go explain to your wife where you spent the night. She's probably getting a mite anxious."

"*Nyet*. Is know, Mariska, I look after myself good. But is better I don't go to sheriff's office vith you, *da*?"

"*Da*, and *da* again. If I was you, I'd steer clear of Grover just as much as possible between now and election day."

Grover's door was open and he was sitting at his desk. He looked up when Longarm pushed Prud Simmons through the door, and when he saw the handcuffs on Simmons's wrists, his eyes widened.

"What the hell have you been up to now, Long?" the sheriff said testily.

"I ran across this yahoo just sort of by accident. He's the man who did the night-shooting."

"Where was he hiding?" Grover asked.

"Best place a man can hide. In a crowd. He's one of the extra hands Clem Hawkins hired on for his gather."

"Damn it! You've butted into my jurisdiction! Now, we agreed—"

"Hold up, Grover," Longarm snapped. "No need to get feisty. Prud here also happens to be a fugitive, escaped from a federal pen. That's right, ain't it, Prud?" Simmons said nothing, but maintained the silence he'd held ever since Longarm had arrested him.

"All right, tell me the story," Grover said, when Prud refused to speak.

"Sure," Longarm replied. "I took Prud in for attempted murder and bank robbery up in Dakota Territory about five years ago. He drew a twenty-year sentence, so the only way he could be outside now is by breaking out."

"Or being pardoned," Grover pointed out.

"Not likely! But it won't take long to make sure."

"What evidence have you got that he's the night-shooter?"

"Enough. Got a shell case from the place he was hiding when he fired off the shot, and a rifle to match it. It's a .32-20, and there ain't many of them down this far south. They favor it for the mountain country up north, where there's a lot of long-range shooting. You might find three or four rifles of this caliber around here, maybe."

"Is that what you're counting on for evidence?"

"It's not everything. Me and a witness found a bootprint out where Prud waited in a wheatfield. Sole's cracked all the way across. You can look at the boots he's got on. The left one matches that print, where I picked up the cartridge case."

"Pretty thin evidence," Grover grunted. "Who's your witness?"

"You'd know him. Fedor Petrovsky."

"What?" Disbelief dripped from the sheriff's voice. "What kind of game are you trying to play with me, Long? You took that nester bastard out with you on a case he's involved in? What kind of witness is he going to make? Hell, he's an interested party."

"He's more than that. Fedor's a trained tracker. His family have been gamekeepers in Russia for years."

"Gamekeepers? What's that mean?"

"Trackers, the way I understand it. They find tracks that show where a bear or elk is hiding out, then they guide the hunters to where it is."

Grover snorted. "Of all the fool things I ever heard! If these gamekeepers know where the animal's at, why don't they just shoot it themselves, and have it over with?"

"I don't know why, Grover. I guess they just do things different over there. But I watched Fedor. He knows tracking, all right."

"Maybe so, but you know how a jury'd take his testimony? Why, they'd laugh it out of court. You'd never get a conviction."

"That's as it might be. You've still got Prud on that Dakota charge."

"Yeah. I guess I can hold him on that. Or could, if you're sure he's wanted for breaking out of the pen."

"It'll only take a couple of hours to find out. I'll go over to the railroad yard and wire my office in Denver. They'll know."

"All right," Grover said grudgingly. "I'll lock him up. You go send your wire. We'll figure out what to do when we've got the answer to it."

"That's fine with me," Longarm said. He started to unlock the shackles on Prud's wrists. Simmons still said nothing. Longarm pushed the man toward the sheriff. "All right, Grover. He's your prisoner now. I'd better warn you, he's real slick at picking locks. If I was you, I'd keep a close eye on him."

"Don't worry about me. Just go get that wire off."

Longarm wasted no time getting to the Santa Fe train shed. As he passed the livery stable, he saw the buggy that had passed him and Fedor on the cattle trail heading back toward town, and made a note in his mind to call on Stone as soon as possible. At the train shed, he wrote out the wire asking about Simmons, and told the lone station agent who also served as telegrapher, "It'll likely be a couple of hours before you get an answer. If you'd bring it to me, I'd appreciate it. You'll find me at the Ace High or Cattleman's, if I'm not at the restaurant or the sheriff's office."

The agent nodded. "Sure, Marshal. You'll have it just the minute I copy it off the wire."

As Longarm started back to Junction, he noticed Stone's private railroad car sitting on a siding beyond the station.

No time like now to talk to the gent, he told himself. *He'll be right fresh from visiting Clem Hawkins, or whoever he went to see this morning. Maybe he'll let something drop if it's fresh in his mind.*

He walked to the railroad siding and knocked at the frosted glass door in the car's front vestibule. He kept from showing his surprise when the door was opened by an attractive blonde woman in her middle twenties.

"Yes?" she asked. Her voice showed a total lack of interest.

"I'm looking for Oren Stone."

"Mr. Stone is out."

"That's funny. I just saw him drive up in a buggy to the livery stable. That ain't more than a few steps away, Miss Stone."

"I'm not Miss Stone, and I don't know when Mr. Stone will be back. I'll tell him you called, if you'll give me your name. Then, if Mr. Stone wants to see you, he'll send for you."

"Well, now. Suppose if I do that, and Mr. Stone sends for me, I don't feel like being sent for? It'd be sort of hard for us to get together if that happened, wouldn't it?"

Her voice was cold. "Mr. Stone usually decides whether he's interested in—as you put it—getting together with someone who comes asking to see him."

"That's funny. I've got the same habit myself. Only I haven't got a pert young lady to answer my door and tell folks about it."

"As it happens, that's my job," she said.

"Oh, I'm sure you're real good at it too. You look to me like you'd be good in any job you cared to take on."

"I find that a very impertinent remark."

"Do you, now? I was trying to pay you a compliment, but I guess you took it the wrong way." Longarm smiled.

"Really? I can very well do without compliments from strangers, Mr. . . . you never did give me your name."

"So I didn't. Now, you know, that just might be on account of what I told you a minute ago. I've got a habit of not liking to have somebody send for me."

"Perhaps if you'd tell me what you want to see Mr. Stone about—" the girl suggested. She was obviously trying to be patient, but Longarm thought she wasn't trying hard enough.

"I'd rather keep that between Mr. Stone and me," he replied. "If I tell him and he tells you, that'd be his business. If I tell you and he thinks I ought not have, that's something else."

"I'd say that's a fair statement," a man's voice said from behind Longarm.

Turning, Longarm recognized the man who'd been identified on the cattle trail by Fedor Petrovsky. He said, "You'd be Mr. Oren Stone, I take it?"

"I am." The wheat broker looked past Longarm to address the girl. "Who is this man, Mae? And what kind of trouble is he giving you?"

"Well . . . not really trouble," she replied, after a momentary hesitation. "He's been insisting on seeing you, but so far I haven't persuaded him to tell me his name or his business."

"Yes, I gathered that from what I overheard," Stone said. "All right." He faced Longarm again. "Now that I'm here, suppose you tell me who you are and what you want."

"The name's Custis Long, Mr. Stone." Longarm slid his wallet out of his inside coat pocket and flipped it open. "Deputy U.S. marshal out of the Denver office. I'd like to talk with you for a few minutes."

"About what?"

"Mostly about some complaints the wheat farmers hereabouts have made to me. That's good enough for openers."

"I can't imagine what they'd have to complain about. I've done a little business with them, but certainly nothing illegal, nothing that would interest the federal authorities." When Longarm offered no explanation, the wheat speculator went on, "Come inside if you want to tell me what all this is about."

Mae stepped aside to let Stone and Longarm pass from the vestibule to the entryway of the private car. She closed the door and followed a step or two behind them.

Longarm took in the interior of the railroad car with a quick glance. It was a standard-sized coach, but its size was the only thing standard about it. Walnut-paneled walls, lace draperies at the stained glass windows, more stained glass in the gaslights' shades, an overstuffed lounge chair, a divan, a mahogany dining table, and a sideboard laden with cut glass turned the front end of the couch into a luxurious sitting room–dining room. At the rear, a narrow door stood ajar, revealing a corner of a kitchen done in Shining nickel-plated metal; a second door beyond that was also half-open, and through it, Longarm could see part of a lavishly spread bed.

Stone motioned Longarm to a chair and settled down on the divan, facing him. Over his shoulder, he commanded brusquely, "Mae, see what Marshal Long will take, and fix me my usual."

"Certainly, Mr. Stone." In contrast to the tone it had held during her earlier exchange with Longarm, the girl's voice was appealingly pleasant. "Mr. Long? Or should I call you Marshal Long? What will you have to drink?"

"Maryland rye without any fancy trimmings, if you've got

some on hand. And it doesn't make any difference what you call me, Miss—Miss—"

"Bonner," Stone put in. "Mae Bonner." To the girl he said, "Be sure to serve the marshal the Gillincrest rye, Mae. If your taste is for Maryland whiskey, Marshal, I think you'll find this one pleasant."

Stone said nothing more until Mae Bonner had poured the drinks and served them. Both men used the pause to size one another up, exchanging looks of frank appraisal, Longarm meeting the broker's close scrutiny with an equally penetrating one.

He saw in him a man in his late fifties, judging by his white hair and faintly lined ruddy skin. Stone favored a straight, full, British-cut mustache. Under it, his lips were red and full. His nose was aquiline, his eyes brown, his full sideburns carefully trimmed. He wore a faultlessly tailored lounging suit of gray cheviot. Longarm remembered that he'd deposited a pearl gray derby on the hat rack in the car's entryway; it matched the spats that covered his ankles above highly polished black shoes. His full-puffed cravat was dark; an opal stickpin glistened in it, and a pair of opals were set in gold links that held his snowy cuffs.

When Longarm had sipped his whiskey, Stone's appraising look changed to one of questioning. Longarm nodded. "This is as fine a whiskey as I've ever tasted. Just wish I could afford it."

Stone smiled. "I'm afraid it's not a matter of price, Marshal. A few of us contract for delivery of the entire output of this whiskey, and there's a waiting list of men who'll take the places of any of us who don't buy our standing order every year."

"However you come by it, this is still damned fine whiskey, Mr. Stone." Longarm took out a cheroot and lighted it. The tobacco smoke and rye flavor mixed blandly on his tongue.

"I thought you'd enjoy it. Now, then." Stone was suddenly all business. His smile vanished, his eyes grew cold. "What am I accused of doing that's set the federal government after me?"

"I'd better straighten you out on one thing, before I say another word. Nobody's accusing you of anything. I'd just like to ask you a question or two, and I figure the best way to run down rumors is to go right to the man who's involved in them."

"Ask ahead. My conscience is clear."

"Fine. You were here in Junction about this time last year, weren't you?"

"Yes. I told you I had some dealings with the immigrants who are growing wheat here."

"You bought their wheat?"

"Certainly. That's my business, buying and selling commodities."

"Did you pay the going price at the time you bought it, or the price it got when you sold it later on the Grain Exchange?"

"That's got no bearing on anything, Marshal. The Justice Department hasn't any jurisdiction over private commodities sales. God help the country if it ever does. You'd have a bunch of know-nothing drones in Washington telling experienced businessmen how to run their affairs."

"Just for my own satisfaction, Mr. Stone, could you see your way clear to give me an answer?"

Stone thought for a moment. "Very well. As long as it's understood that it's given to you privately and unofficially."

"You've got my word on it."

"I did what any broker would have, bought at the current market price and sold at the price that was current when I wanted to dispose of my holdings. In a private transaction, that doesn't come under any kind of government regulation, I might add."

"Sure. I don't say you did anything that wasn't legal. I'm just trying to run down a complaint or two."

Stone seemed mollified. He said, "I think you're intelligent enough to tell the difference between the value of my word and that of an ignorant immigrant, Long."

"I'd sure try to. Now, tell me about the option agreements these wheat growers signed over to you last year, if you don't mind. Do they set a fixed price?"

"Certainly not. They bind the grower to sell his crop on my call at the current market price per bushel. If they don't live up to their agreements, I can sue them. And will, let me assure you. That's legal too, by the way."

"What you're doing is called hedging short sales, ain't it, Mr. Stone? Seems like I've heard it called that, even if I don't set myself up as an expert on how stock and grain markets work. As I get it, we say wheat's priced at maybe ten cents a bushel, and you sell ten thousand bushels on the market, only you don't deliver the grain right then. Is that what you brokers call selling short?"

"Yes."

"Now, supposing wheat goes down to a nickel. You buy ten thousand bushels for a nickel, but you sold for a dime, so you're covered."

"Right again." An amused smile began forming on Stone's face.

"Now, then," Longarm went on. "If wheat goes up instead of down, you might have to pay fifteen cents a bushel to deliver the ten thousand bushels you sold short. But you know some farmers who need money real bad, so you tell them you'll buy for spot cash, if they'll take four cents a bushel. You make a little bit if wheat goes down, but you make a hell of a lot if it goes up. Is that called hedging?" While Longarm waited for Stone's reply, he drained his glass.

"Mae!" Stone called, his tone peremptory. "Serve the marshal again." Then he looked at Longarm, still smiling. "I make a profit either way, of course, because I was intelligent enough to hedge my position. In a totally legal way, I'll remind you again."

"Seems to me you get the poor farmer going and coming. He's the one who loses on a deal like that. And the man who was betting against the market, of course."

Mae brought the decanter over and refilled Longarm's glass. Stone flicked a hand in her direction, as he'd flick away an annoying insect. She hurried out of the room.

Stone said, "The farmer got paid for his wheat. The speculator lost, but the chances are he could afford to. I don't win every time, you know, when I speculate."

"From the way you're talking, Mr. Stone, I'm getting the idea that you're going to hold these farmers here to the options you got them to sign last year."

"Of course I am. They knew what they were signing. The fact that wheat's a few cents above the price I offered them now, and probably will go higher because crop forecasts are bad, hasn't anything to do with the validity of the options." His eyes narrowed. "That's what this is all about, is it? Those foreigners are stirring up trouble for me because they want to back out of a deal they made?"

"Well, they ain't happy with it, that's the truth. But I told them I'd have a talk with you, which is what I came here for."

"I see. This isn't an official call concerning a case you're investigating, then?"

"No. I'm down here in Kansas to keep an eye on the election that's coming up, and make sure there're no vote frauds."

"Odd that a federal marshal would be sent to such a small place, with so few votes, in a national election year. It seems to me there would be a lot of cities where your efforts would be needed, instead of an obscure village like Junction."

"I don't choose my cases, Mr. Stone. I just go where I'm sent."

"Of course. Well, it's of no importance to me. I'm not involved in it, of course."

Longarm tugged pensively at a corner of his mustache. "That's funny. I figured because you were visiting Clem Hawkins today, and he's into the local election so deep—well, I thought you might be, too."

"What in—" Stone began. He stopped short, started over. "I know Hawkins, of course. It was just a courtesy visit."

"Sure. Well, I won't take any more of your time right now, Mr. Stone. Appreciate you talking to me, and I sure enjoyed your whiskey."

"I'm curious to know what you're going to tell the wheat farmers about the options."

The tall deputy rose from his chair and stretched laconically. "Not much I can tell 'em, beyond what you've told me. As far as the option agreements are concerned, they're legal, all right."

"I'm glad to find out you're a reasonable man, Marshal Long. Drop in for a drink whenever you're passing by."

"Thanks. I might just do that." Longarm picked up his hat and started for the door. "One thing I better say before I go, though. If I was to find out you and Mr. Hawkins were aiming to use those options to influence the wheat farmers to vote your way in the election, it'd be vote fraud, and I'd have to do something about it. Now I'll bid you good day, Mr. Stone."

Stone was still gaping at Longarm when the door closed behind him.

Smiling to himself, Longarm walked the short distance to the train shed and stepped inside. The agent recognized him at once.

"Did you get the answer to your wire, Marshal?" he asked.

"Not yet. You mean it came in?"

"About an hour ago. I looked for you where you said to, and when I didn't find you around town, I delivered it to the sheriff to give to you."

"Well, thanks. I'll stop in there, it's on my way."

At the sheriffs office, the door was unlocked and Longarm went in without knocking. Grover was not at his desk. Longarm looked at the cells, intending to ask Prud Simmons where the sheriff had gone. The cells were both as empty as the office.

Chapter 9

For a moment, Longarm simply stared at the empty cells, unable to believe what he was seeing. He looked around the small, square office then, but there was no other door, no window, no closet, no place in which Prud Simmons could possibly be hiding.

Worry crept into Longarm's mind. He knew Prud's way with locks, and had warned Grover about the fugitive's skill at picking them. There was, he thought, a chance that while Grover had had his attention focused elsewhere, Prud had somehow managed to open his cell and jump the sheriff. It would have been easy enough for the convict to have overpowered an unsuspecting man, and Prud was wily enough to choose his time carefully.

After that, with Grover's guns as well as Prud's own weapons, which Longarm had handed to Grover as evidence, the convict would be in full command. If he'd forced Grover to leave with him, nobody would have noticed; the office was too far from the few stores and houses on Junction's street for anyone to have paid attention to a pair of riders leaving the place.

No damned way in the world to track 'em, either, Longarm thought. *Prud's been out on that Hawkins gather, and he's learned every draw and gully inside of ten miles. . . .*

"Where the hell have you been, Long?" The voice came from behind him.

Longarm drew as he turned. Sheriff Grover's eyes popped when he saw the Colt's muzzle menacing him. Longarm lowered the gun.

"Sorry, Grover. When I hear a strange voice at my back, I don't feel comfortable about it."

"Well, you pick a hell of a way to show how you feel."

Longarm holstered the revolver. "Nothing to worry about. I always look before I pull the trigger."

"Where have you been, Long?" Grover repeated. "I've been going all over town, trying to locate you."

"I could ask you the same question, Grover, only I've got a better one. Where the hell is Prud Simmons?"

"I can't say. I let him go when I got that wire your Denver office sent you."

"Let him go!" Longarm exploded.

"I didn't have much choice. Here, read it yourself." The sheriff handed a Santa Fe telegram flimsy to Longarm.

NO ESCAPE FLYER ON PRUD SIMMONS **STOP**
NOT WANTED AS FAR AS KNOWN **STOP**
VAIL PER GLC

"How'd you get hold of this?" Longarm asked. "It's addressed to me."

"I supposed if it'd been something real private, it would've been sealed up in an envelope," Grover replied. "And you oughta know how I got it. The station agent brought it, after he'd looked everywhere else you told him you'd be."

"Oh, come on Grover. You know I don't give a shit if you read the message. But you letting Prud go, that's something else. Damn it, he was my prisoner!"

"Like hell. The minute you passed him over to me, he was *my* prisoner. Remember, you took him on a local charge in my jurisdiction."

"Take your goddamned jurisdiction and shove it up your ass!" Longarm retorted angrily. "Here I bring you in a night-shooter who damn near killed a man, and give you enough to put him away, and you let him go the minute I turn my back!"

"What you call evidence wouldn't hold up in court!" Grover retorted.

"That's your opinion. I've seen men sent up for prison terms on a lot less!"

"Maybe. But not in Junction, Kansas, when a jury's going to be made up of Clem Hawkins's friends, and the prisoner works for Clem!"

Longarm shook his head pityingly. "Is that why you let Prud out?" His anger was still strong, but common sense was holding it submerged. "You figured you'd make Hawkins happy? Think

again, Grover. Hawkins was right there when I took Prud prisoner. He told me to get him off his ranch, said he didn't want
trash like Prud smelling up his place."

"Clem Hawkins said that? Ah, he was just putting on a show
for you, Long. Clem never has cared much who he hires, as long
as the man does his work."

"You know him better than I do, I guess. It'll be interesting
to see if he takes Prud Simmons back on, though I doubt that
Prud's fool enough to stay around here very long. If I know him,
he's cutting a shuck right now to get someplace else."

A new voice at the door interrupted them. The Santa Fe station agent stood there, another telegraph flimsy in his hand. He
said, "This just came over the wire for you, Marshal Long. It's
marked 'urgent,' so I hurried out to find you."

"Thanks." Longarm took the message and read it. When he
looked up at Grover, his eyes were cold. "It appears you're not
the only damned fool in this mess. Listen to what my office just
sent. 'Earlier message re Simmons in error. Simmons escaped
prison Pembina, DT, five weeks ago. Notifying DT authorities
subject held in Junction. They will send deputy to transfer.'"

"That—that's impossible, Long! You federal people don't
make mistakes like that!"

"The hell we don't. Not many, but we make 'em."

"How'd they come to send the wrong information?" Grover
sounded both beaten and bewildered.

"Too damn many people have got their fingers in things."
Longarm took the first message from the pocket where he'd
thrust it, and looked at the signature. "I'll tell you how this happened. Billy Vail, my chief, has got a prissy little secretary
named George Linden Carver. Those are his initials, right on the
bottom of this wire. Little Georgie took it on himself to send that
wire while Billy was out, and he didn't wire the Dakota people
first, just looked through the wanted fliers in the files. Billy got
back, and made him wire up to Dakota Territory."

"But it's not my fault!" Grover protested. "I thought that first
wire was right!"

"Like hell it ain't your fault! You turned my prisoner loose and
didn't wait to tell me you was going to. If you'd kept your prick
in your pants, and not been so damn anxious to do Clem Hawkins
a favor by letting his man go, you'd've been in the clear."

"What are you going to do about it?" Grover asked.

"I don't aim to do a thing. You made the mess; you clean it up. When the prison guards get here from Pembina, you can tell 'em why they don't have a prisoner to take back. And any questions my chief asks me, I'll tell him to look to you for answers."

"Now, listen, Long—"

"No. You listen to me. That rifle slug Prud triggered the other night wasn't meant for the man who took it. That bullet was aimed at me. I'm betting Prud ain't run far. He might be hiding out close by, waiting for another chance to backshoot me. If he does, it won't matter how bad I'm hurt, I'm coming after you and I'll put a slug in you just where Prud got me. Now, chew on that with your supper!"

Pushing past Grover and the bewildered station agent, who'd stood riveted in frozen fascination while the argument went on, Longarm walked away.

Longarm didn't enjoy his supper of steak and potatoes. The food tasted as sour as had the Maryland rye he'd sipped at the Ace High before going to the restaurant. Even his after-supper cheroot had a rank flavor. The night was still in its early half when he went to his room, and to bed. His last thought before dropping off to sleep was a hope that Ruthie wouldn't knock on his door and rouse him.

It wasn't Ruthie who knocked, however. Longarm didn't know how long he'd been sleeping, but knew it hadn't been long enough, when the insistent rapping of knuckles on the door panel brought him awake and to his feet. His Colt was in his hand before his feet touched the floor.

"Who is it?" he called through the door.

"Is me, Marshal Long. Nicolai Belivev."

Longarm recognized the homesteader's voice. He opened the door and Belivev came in.

"Is trouble, mister Marshal," he panted without wasting time on greetings. "Mordka Danilov sent me to tell you, ask you if vill you help us again once more."

"What kind of trouble are you talking about?"

"Same kind as before. Fence-cuttings and tramplings from vheat." In his agitation, Belivev's carefully learned English was deserting him. "Only now, this night, is vorse as before. Not is

just one field, now. Is already three, and Mordka says maybe
before daytime vill be more yet. Six, seven, riding horses, you
understand? They go one place, cut fence, and ride horses over
field, then fast ride mile or two avay and do again, field from
somebody else."

"You mean there's a gang working your crops over?"

"If is six, seven men a gang, yes, Marshal Long. Shoot guns
up in air to scare our vomen, keep us inside vhile they ruin
vheat."

"Damn fool cowhands from one of the ranches, maybe more
than one," Longarm muttered, more to himself than to Belivev.
He went to the dresser and lifted the bottle of bonded rye, estimated that it held just enough for a wake-up swallow, and
drained it. He went on, "Hands heard their bosses cussing you
farmers, got the notion to chivvy you. Or maybe the bosses sent
'em to do it. Hard to know."

"You vill vith me then come?" Belivev asked.

Longarm was already putting on his clothes. "Sure. Only, did
you go by and rouse up the sheriff too? It's his job to keep law
and order around here."

"Try to find sheriff, Mordka tell me, before I come ask you.
Is no use. All over I go, no sheriff is. So to you I come,"

"All right." Longarm stamped his feet into his stovepipe
boots and belted on his Colt. He took his Winchester from the
corner where it leaned and filled a coat pocket with extra shells
from his saddlebag. He told Belivev, "I'll ride double with you
to the livery stable and get my horse. Then we'll see what we
can do about this damnfool night-riding caper."

In the moonless night, they could see lights gleaming here and
there amid the wheatfields soon after they'd left Junction. Where
houses stood, windows and open doorways threw the glow of
yellow lamplight through the blackness. Where there were soddies, the light rays hugged the ground, visible to a distant viewer
only as a golden sheen. Occasionally the shadow of a man on patrol was silhouetted against one of the lighted areas. When they
got closer and turned into the narrow lane that ran between the
fenced fields, they could hear the faint ring of voices calling
through the night.

Mordka Danilov was waiting in front of his house when they

dismounted. He grasped Longarm's hand in both of his and said, "I thank you greatly, Marshal Long, for coming to help us. Believe me, if it was not a serious matter, I wouldn't have disturbed your sleep. But you seem to be the only one we can turn to right now."

"I didn't figure you'd send for me unless you were being pushed hard," Longarm told him. "Besides, I promised you I'd do whatever I could to get you folks out of a scrape."

"You know we're grateful," Mordka said. "This is something we haven't had happen before."

"These night-riders, they just pop up someplace and snip your Glidden wire, ride over your land, and move on? No rhyme or reason to where they hit?"

"There have been four wheatfields trampled so far. They came soon after dark and cut Basil Lednovotny's fences, rode back and forth over his grain. Then they struck the fields of Sergei Tuscheva, two miles from Basil's place. They had just done their wanton mischief at Anatoly Yanishev's farm when I sent Nicolai to find you, if he couldn't find the sheriff first. Anatoly's land is about a mile from where Sergei lives. Since Nicolai has been gone, they struck at Pavel Sednov's. So you see, they don't seem to have a plan, just ride back and forth at random and stop to do their ugly work wherever they please. They are like the Cossacks of the Tsar!"

"Have your folks been fighting back? You've got a right to defend what's yours, you know."

"We were too stunned at first," Mordka said. "But now we are aroused and ready. We want to live in peace, Marshal. We came here to America to find peace. Now, evil and violence is everywhere we look."

"Belivev told me there's been some shooting."

"A few shots, yes," Danilov replied. "Not aimed at anyone, I think. Just wild shots into the air, to frighten us."

"Any of your people shoot to hit the riders?"

Mordka shook his head. "This I do not know. What I have told you has been passed along from one farm to the next until it reached me here. Everything, I do not know. But I do not think the Brethren have aimed their shots. Not yet."

"High time they did, then. The best way to stop a thing like this is to hit back quick, before your people get hurt too bad."

"Marshal Long, we do not wish to fight." There was sadness in Danilov's voice as he added, "But if you say we must . . ."

"Every man has to look after his own, right now," Longarm reminded Danilov. "I can't be everywhere at the same time. Now, I'll pitch in and help you here, but you'll have to help me too."

"Tell me what you want us to do, and we will do it."

While they'd been talking, Longarm's mind had been busy with a plan. He told Danilov, "We'll try to catch the riders at the next place they stop. Now, you said you'd got word about where they've been, passed along from one of your Brethren to the next. That'd work both ways, wouldn't it? You can pass something along from here?"

"Yes, of course. This is a thing we learned to do in Russia, when the Tsar's Cossacks came. We did not think we would need to do the same thing here, so we are not organized so well as there. But tell me the message you want to send; it will go out."

"I need to know a few things first. How far does Fedor Petrovsky live from here?"

"Not far. Five farms down the lane."

"Fine. I'll want three men to ride with me, and he's one of them. Mr. Belivev can be one. You think about another good man who lives close by, somebody with a horse or mule who can be here in a hurry. You know the Brethren a lot better than I do."

"Anatoly Yanishev," Belivev said promptly.

Danilov nodded. "A good choice, Nicolai. He is near, and the riders, have been once to his farm, so they will not come back."

"All right," Longarm said briskly. "Get those men here as fast as they can move. Tell 'em to bring their rifles and some shells. And pass along the word to the rest of your Brethren not to shoot if those damned cowhands hit their place, not even in the air. It's too dark to aim proper, and I don't want those night-riders spooked before we catch up to 'em."

"We would not shoot at all if we did not feel that we must defend our crops," Danilov sighed. "We had no choice but to fight back."

Longarm nodded soberly. "I reckon you didn't. Seeing as how those cowhands started the shooting, your folks couldn't afford to fool around, and I don't blame 'em. But you get those two men on their way here. I aim to get things settled fast!"

In much less than an hour, Fedor Petrovsky and Anatoly Yanishev arrived. Fedor was on his mule, Anatoly on a swaybacked plow horse that he rode bareback. Both men had rifles. Longarm took them to one side and began explaining his plan, He was still going into the details of his strategy when shouts, growing progressively closer, told of the beginning of another night-rider raid.

Mordka came running up to the three men. "The night-riders are at Mischa Evrykenov's farm now! It is close, and if you want to catch them you can! But you must ride fast, before they go!"

"We're ready to ride," Longarm assured him. "Come on, men. We've got a good chance to end this night-riding once and for all! Let's see how those bastards like it when they get jumped for a change!"

Hurrying to their horses, the four-man commando team mounted and rode off. Following Longarm's instructions, Fedor Petrovsky led the way; knowledge of the layout of the fields that made up each homesteader's 160-acre half-section of land was engraved in his trained tracker's mind. With Petrovsky, Longarm had paired Anatoly Yanishev; the two men, he'd found, were neighbors and close friends. In the narrow lanes that separated the wheatfields, there was just room for two horsemen to ride abreast between the Glidden wire fences.

As Danilov had told them, the distance to Mischa Evrykenov's farm was short. Ten minutes of hard riding brought them within earshot of the intermittent cracking reports of the raiders' pistols. Even from a distance, they could pinpoint the spot where the fence-cutters were at work by the muzzle flashes that now and again cut orange-yellow streaks across the moonless sky. Moments after they could see the flashes they were close enough to hear the wild shouts of the cowhands.

A fence-corner loomed ahead. In the field beyond it, the forms of men mounted on galloping horses showed as shadows; the night-riders were shuttling back and forth, the hooves of their mounts breaking and trampling the grain. With all the noise and confusion, Longarm couldn't tell who was shooting, but he hoped the homesteaders were heeding his instructions not to shoot and thus risk driving the raiders away. A pistol shot cracked from the field. In the instant of its flash, the high-crowned Stetson of a cowhand on a plunging horse shone in brilliant light and vanished as quickly as it had been revealed.

At the fence-corner, Petrovsky reined in long enough to let Longarm and Belivev get close enough to see his arm waving them up the lane on their left. Then he kicked his mule's flanks and the beast moved forward, following Anatoly Yanishev along the lane down which they'd been riding. Longarm and Belivev turned and rode until they reached the fenceposts that marked the corner of the field in which the night-riders were still galloping around. They pulled up, waiting for Petrovsky and Yanishev to ride around the field and come up the lane where they were waiting.

"Let's go!" Longarm called to Belivev, when he was sure they'd waited long enough for the other two *Bratiya* to get into position. "Remember now, keep your shots low. Hit their horses. Those cowhands are going to be in enough trouble—hell, maybe all of us will be in a stew—but we sure don't want murder charges to come out of this."

"*Da. Ya panimayu,*" Belivev replied.

They turned their horses into the lane that intersected the one in which they'd been waiting. The noise in the wheatfield was tapering off now. The yells were diminishing and there'd been no pistol shots since those they'd heard earlier. They rode slowly, not to avoid noise, for the sound of their horses' hoofbeats would go unnoticed in the hullabaloo that was coming from the night-riders, but to give them an opportunity to spot the gap in the Glidden wire where it had been cut. Longarm saw the slack fence first, and reined in. Belivev pulled up his mount. The two brought their rifles up.

"All right!" Longarm cried out. "Let 'em have it!"

After the first shots fired by Longarm and Belivev, Petrovsky and Yanishev joined in the shooting. They followed Longarm's orders and aimed low. It was impossible to sight on a target in the darkness, with the night-riders in constant motion.

"Hell! We're being shot at!" a voice yelled from the wheat-field.

"Shoot back!" another voice responded.

Gunfire from the wheatfield joined the cracking rifle shots

that Longarm and his companions were pouring into the field. A horse in the wheatfield whinnied wildly.

"My bronc's hit!" someone shouted.

"Let's get the hell outa here!" another voice followed the first.

"How? They got us cut off from where we cut the goddamn fence!"

"Cut it someplace else!"

"Cut it yourself, damn it! You're closer to it than I am!"

"Quit bitching and let's get the hell outa here! I just got a slug through my hat!"

In the wheatfield, the shadowy figures, almost invisible, moved to the far side and stopped at the fence. In the lane, Longarm's group maintained a steady patter of rifle fire. Another horse neighed shrilly, its scream of pain dying to a choked bubbling in mid-cry.

They got my goddamn horse!" a night-rider shouted.

"Get up here with me!" one of his companions called.

There was a quick burst of hoofbeats along the lane across from the one where Longarm and his men were attacking. The hooves thudded more crisply on the harder dirt of the lane as the night-riders left the field.

A muzzle flash erupted from the retreating riders. Longarm felt the impact of the rifle slug and saw the flash at the same time. A mighty fist hit him in the ribs and tossed him from his horse. Even as he started to fall, the first numbing shock of the slug's impact faded and a merciless hand rammed a red-hot poker through his side. He was conscious when he hit the ground, and the pain doubled in intensity, spreading up and down his left side in a bursting flood.

Distantly, he heard someone's voice shouting, "Is hit, the marshal!"

Then he knew nothing more.

Chapter 10

There was a soft hand on his forehead, a hand Longarm couldn't identify, and a woman-scent that was also strange to him. The light beating against his closed eyelids hurt his eyes. He thought of opening them, but the thought died quickly with the dread that the brighter light this would expose them to would hurt even more than the dim glow of which he was now aware. There was an aching in his back. To ease it, Longarm tried to move. The effort brought a stabbing pain to his left side. It ebbed and faded to a steady, throbbing ache again, and he realized by degrees that he'd been aware of that ache ever since he'd become conscious of the woman's hand, but had been trying to ignore it.

Close to him, and surprisingly loud, a man's voice spoke in Russian, with a rising inflection—a question—and a softer voice, a woman's voice, answered.

Curiosity conquered Longarm's reluctance to move or look. He opened his eyes, and blinked when a rush of tears filled them as the brighter light struck them. Through the fluid he saw two white, moving blurs, one close, the other some distance away. Another blink and the blurs began to resolve into faces. The distant face he recognized at once. It was Mordka Danilov. After a thoughtful moment of struggling with the puzzle, he gave the second face an identity: Tatiana, Mordka's young daughter.

"Ah, good!" Mordka exclaimed when he saw Longarm's eyes open. "It is about now the doctor told us you should again be conscious."

Memory was re-forming quickly in Longarm's mind. The sensation was not a new one. He'd gone through the same experience before when bullets had hit him: the belated shock of impact and the pain of the slug tearing through his flesh; the moments of semiawareness as consciousness returned; the need to refocus eyes glued shut for a long time; and at last, the quick, flooding return to memory of all that had happened, not just during the moments before being wounded, but the entire lifetime of experiences and sensations recalled.

"How long was I out?" he asked.

Mordka shrugged. "Six, perhaps seven hours. Daylight was close by when Fedor and Nicolai and Anatoly carried you here to my house."

Longarm frowned. "That's something I don't remember."

"Is not strange. You have a bad wound, my friend. And a fall from your horse, too."

Longarm looked around. The room he was in wasn't the Danilov house as he remembered it. Mordka anticipated his question.

"No, no. Is not the room where we ate supper, Marshal. Is my little girl's room. Tatiana, you remember?"

"Oh. Sure. I do. I guess that was her I heard saying something a minute ago."

Tatiana came back into the room, and said something in Russian to her father. He nodded, and was about to reply when Longarm spoke.

"I guess I took over your room, didn't I, Miss Tatiana? Well, I'll try not to put you out too long. Soon as I can get up—"

"This will not be for a while," Tatiana said. "But do not worry, is nothing at all."

Mordka said, "She is right, Marshal. You will hear this from the doctor when he comes back, too."

"You mean I've been doctored and didn't know about it?"

"Of course," Danilov replied. "Fedor and the others put only a rough bandage on your side, after they were sure the night-riders—*proklinat kasaki*—had gone. It was then almost daylight. Now it is just beyond noon."

Longarm tried to move again, but grunted and lay still when he found the pain too great. "How bad did I get hit?"

"He did not seem too worried, Doctor Franklin. He will be here soon, he will tell you better than I could. It is a clean wound, he said, and will soon heal."

"How about the others? They all right?"

"None of them were hurt. And only a killed horse was suffered by the night-riders."

"That was about how I figured it ought to be." He nodded with satisfaction. The quick move of his head reminded him of his wound again, as his side throbbed with a sudden, darting pain. "I want to see that horse, as soon as I can get to my feet." In spite of the warning he'd had when he'd tried to move earlier, Longarm started to get up.

"*Eta nilza!*" Tatiana scolded. She stepped quickly to the bed and pressed her hands against his chest, pushing him back down. "To stay still is what the doctor says."

"You been looking after me too, Miss Tatiana?" Longarm asked.

"*Da*. My mother and I have helped to see that you have comfort."

"Having a pretty girl like you look after him makes a man not want to get well too quick," he told her, grinning.

Tatiana's peaches-and-cream skin reddened in a blush. She said, "*Spasiba*. But it is my mother who do most for you."

"Well, she's a mighty pretty lady too, you know." Longarm saw Mordka's face twitch in a smile at the byplay. To him, Longarm said, "It was real good of your womenfolks to take me in. I bet I've been a lot of trouble."

"Don't talk of being trouble, Marshal. You have done much for us. It is our fault you were shot."

"No, Mordka. I was just in the way when a bullet with no-body's name on it came along. Dark as it was, nobody could take any aim. We were shooting blind, and so were the night-riders." He frowned. "But I still want to see that horse. I'm curious to know whose brand it had on it."

"Fedor thought of that," Danilov said. "It was not Hawkins's brand, but a smaller ranch, not even close to him. The Lazy Y, Fedor said it was."

"Just the same, I'd give a lot to know if all the other horses that bunch was riding had the same brand."

Marya Danilov came in. She saw Longarm and her husband talking, came to the side of the bed, and looked down at Longarm.

She asked, "With you it is better feeling now?"

"It sure is. And I don't aim to impose on you, Mrs. Danilov. I'll be out of your way in a day or so."

"Do not nonsense talk. I know how you come to help us

quick when Mordka is ask you. *Prisnatelniey*, Marshal Long. We are grateful. It is much we owe you," Marya replied. "Now you must eat. Soup I make, *pokhlyobka*, with the good mushrooms and vegetables, to keep clean the blood. Tatiana, you get, help Marshal Long to eat. Mordka, come now, we eat in other room like always."

"If your soup's as good as the supper you fixed the other night, I know I'll like it," Longarm told her as she and Mordka left. Privately, he thought he'd just about as soon have a big piece of beefsteak, but he was beginning to feel so empty that even soup would taste pretty good.

Tatiana brought the soup, steaming in a deep bowl, and a plate holding thin slices of crusty bread, sliced from a round loaf and spread with sweet butter. She pulled a chair up to the side of the bed.

"*Teper kushaitye*, Marshal. You must eat good now, to get well," she said. "So I feed you soup and good bread."

"Now, that ain't necessary, Miss Tatiana. I can do for myself," Longarm protested.

"*Nikovag*, Marshal Long. Is to help you I am here," Tatiana said severely.

Longarm tried to sit up, to prove that he could eat without assistance, but the first movement he made sent pains dancing along his wounded side. He sank back on the bed.

"You see? You will tear open your wound if you do not lie quietly," she told him. "Now, so, I fix pillow to raise head, then you eat while I hold bowl and spoon. *Da?*"

"*Da*" Longarm grinned weakly. "Guess I better let you help me."

Tatiana plumped up the pillow to raise Longarm's head, and began to feed him the soup. She tore off bits of bread and dropped them in the thick, vegetable-rich broth to soften. Longarm found that he was ravenous. Each bite seemed to increase his hunger until the bowl was almost empty, then his stomach suddenly felt full and satisfaction spread through his body in a warm glow.

By that time, he was enjoying being pampered. Tatiana's soft hand was warm on the nape of his neck, as she helped him hold his head erect. The woman-scent that he'd been aware of so vaguely when he was just regaining consciousness was closer now, a mingling of the sweetness of field flowers and fresh summer rain that somehow seemed to increase the flavor of the soup and yeasty bread.

"More?" she asked him when the bowl was empty. "Is plenty in pot on stove, if you want."

"No thanks, Miss Tatiana. I had all I can hold."

"Is good. Now I bring cloth and wash face clean."

In spite of Longarm's protests, Tatiana washed his face, the soft cloth of the wet washrag snagging on his stubble. She'd started to wipe his hands with the cloth when a murmur of voices came from the front room. A short, roly-poly man with a Vandyke beard and a full, drooping mustache came in. Longarm looked at the black bag he carried and realized he must be the doctor.

"How do you feel now, Marshal Long?"

"Pretty good, I guess. A mite sore. I guess you know me a little bit better than I know you. I saw your sign there, in Junction, but damned if I can remember your name."

"Franklin. And with commendable patriotism but doubtful judgment, my parents named me Benjamin." Putting his bag on the floor beside the bed, the doctor said to Tatiana, "Why don't you go join your folks at dinner, Miss Tatiana? I'll see to the marshal."

"*Da*. Excuse, please. I do not want to be in way."

After Tatiana left, Dr. Franklin said, "How're your bowels? Can't let your system get clogged up, you know."

"Now, Doc, that's a hell of a question to ask a man who ain't been awake more'n a half-hour."

"You had a movement last night—this morning, rather—before I got here, Mrs. Danilov told me."

"Well, she'd know better than I would. But my guts ain't been rumbling, if that's what you mean. Or griping either."

"Good."

Dr. Franklin pulled back the light blanket covering Longarm and prodded at his abdomen. "That hurt?"

"It don't hurt where you're poking at me, but those pokes sure don't make me feel good where that slug took me."

I'm not surprised." The doctor took a thermometer from his vest pocket, wiped it on his handkerchief, and slid it under Longarm's tongue. "You're a lucky man, Marshal Long. First, because it was a high-velocity rifle bullet instead of a slug from a pistol, or pellets out of a shotgun. They'd have torn you up. As it is, you've got nothing but a nice, clean hole through the fleshy part of your side. Here." Dr. Franklin indicated the spot on his own body.

Longarm wanted to tell him that he knew damn well where the slug had hit, but the thermometer kept him tongue-tied.

"If I'd picked out a place for a body wound, I couldn't have done better," Franklin went on, leaning over the bed to inspect the area around the bandage. "No inflammation, that's a good sign. Yes, you're lucky. An inch higher, the bullet would have hit your ribs and probably been deflected down through your intestines. An inch or so lower, it'd have shattered your hip and more than likely crippled you for life. An inch to the right, and your stomach and kidney would've been ripped up."

Sure, Longarm thought. *An inch to the left, and the damn slug would've missed me entirely.*

"So, as I said, you're not in bad condition at all," the doctor said, taking out the thermometer and peering at it through his gold-rimmed spectacles. "And you don't have any fever, so I'd say you're in excellent condition."

"Damned if you don't make it sound like I got a blessing instead of a bullet hole," Longarm told him tartly. "It ain't the first slug that's hit me, you know."

"Yes," Franklin replied dryly. "I saw your scars when I examined you."

"This one sure doesn't pleasure me much, though," Longarm continued. "How long's it going to keep me all tied down?"

"Three or four weeks, and it'll be healed completely." Franklin raised a hand to stop the protest he saw in Longarm's eyes. "Now just a minute. Right now you're still sore from the shock. The impact of a rifle bullet's greater than a blow from a sledgehammer, damned close to that of a locomotive. You can move around as soon as you stop feeling sore. That should be inside of three or four days. But don't get into any brawls, or gallop a horse, for another week or two after that."

"Now that's more like it." Longarm smiled. The pain was still present in his side, but his mind felt easier.

"Well." Dr. Franklin picked up his bag. "I'll look in on you tomorrow or the next day. If you feel any unusual pain, or if your bowels get locked, you'd better send for me. But I'd say you'll be well a lot quicker than most men. You're a very healthy specimen."

A few minutes after Dr. Franklin had left, Mordka Danilov came in. "The doctor says you are doing well," were his first words. "He told us you must rest, though, and he made us promise to see that you do."

"Now, Mordka, you know I've got no time to rest. There's too many things I still need to find out!"

"They will wait."

"No, damn it, they won't! What you said about that dead horse the night-riders left behind 'em—that's started me thinking. I want to ride out to that Lazy Y ranch and see whose horse it was. Then when I find out who was forking it last night, I'll get him off to one side and won't let up till he tells me who-all was with him."

"Can you be sure that Sheriff Grover would arrest them, even if you gave him their names?" Danilov asked.

"No. Not by any means. But if he won't, I can take 'em in myself. I'll admit I ain't figured out on what grounds, but it wouldn't be the first time I've seen the fetter of the law stretched to cover special cases."

"I do not believe there will be any more night-riders," Danilov said, his voice thoughtful. "And even if there are, we of the Brethren will make plans to take care of our own fields. Our eyes were opened by what happened last night. Before, there has been only one man or two who cut our fences and let his horse trample our wheat. But last night was like the bad days in Russia, and we learned how to protect ourselves then. We can do the same now."

"That's just what I don't want you to have to do," Longarm told him. "It ain't the cowhands who do the fence-cutting that I want to uncover. It's the men behind 'em."

"You mean Hawkins? If he had a hand in what happened last night, we do not know it."

"He might not have been behind it, I grant you. But being the biggest cattleman around here, he'd have to have known it was going to happen."

"Yes. I suppose that is true," Mordka agreed.

"And something else sticks in my craw. I just can't believe it was happenstance, that night raid happening so soon after Oren Stone got here. He's a hard, cold fish."

"You have talked with Stone? About the options he has on our crops?"

"Sure. Like I told you I would. But I ain't got good news. He says the options are legal, and he's going to make you deliver."

"There is no way to stop him?"

"None that I can see right now. Don't give up, though. You've got a while before you have to worry about turning your grain over to Stone."

"Two months, a bit more, perhaps."

Longarm stared at the elder. "Two months! Don't you know the weather turn's going to come along before that? There ain't a year when this part of Kansas doesn't have snow or a hard freeze early in the winter."

"We know, Marshal. It does not bother us."

"It sure better. I don't know about any kind of wheat that'll dry out and get cutting-ripe if it's frozen or snowed on."

"Let us see what the weather brings. As I have said, it will not bother us. You will see."

"If you ain't going to worry about it, I sure won't. I've got other things on my mind."

"Dismiss them, my friend. Apply all the power of your mind to recovering from your wound."

"Oh, I'll take care of that too, Mordka. I'll be out of your way before I wear my welcome out, I hope."

"You know that is not possible to do, after all that you've done for the Brethren. You honor my house, Marshal. Stay forever."

"Thanks, Mordka, but I sure hope it won't be that long."

It seemed to Longarm that it would be forever, though. As Dr. Franklin had predicted, he could stand up and hobble around painfully on weak legs after the fourth day, but only as long as he kept his back bowed. When he tried to stand erect, pain gripped his side and tried to pull him down. He walked better with a hand on someone's arm, and usually the arm was Tatiana's.

During the first days, when Longarm had been confined to bed, she had stood aside, letting Marya and Mordka care for

their guest, though the latter's help had been pretty well confined to helping Longarm on and off the chamber pot, a job that
wasn't considered suitable for a woman. Before it became possible for Longarm to walk, Tatiana had been the one who had sat
in the room while her parents attended to the occasional, field
chores, which diminished each day as the wheat stalks stretched
higher, until they reached a man's waist, and the heads grew
longer and plumper and began to turn from green to gold. Then
Mordka returned to his books, and Marya to her housework, and
it was Tatiana who kept a watchful eye on Longarm, helping him
out of bed and into the sunshine, where he sat on a long bench
in front of the house, trying to flex his sore muscles back to their
usual resiliency.

They were sitting on the bench when a surrey, drawn by a
magnificent sorrel gelding, threaded its way along the narrow
lane and drew up in front of the gate. A derbied man held the
reins. In the center seat, a woman sat alone

"Is this the house of Mordka Danilov?" she called.

"Yes," Tatiana replied. Her eyes widened as she looked at the
elaborate costume the woman wore.

In spite of the warm weather, the surrey's occupant had on a
fur hat and a neckpiece of seal, over a velvet dress of deep blue.
Kid gloves that matched the dress were on her hands. Under the
fur hat, golden hair glistened; it swept in a curve below the woman's ears and was caught up in shoulder-length ringlets at the
back of her neck. Her nose was thin, with a suggestion of an arch
between nostrils and eyebrows; she had full lips on which Longarm recognized the added hue of lip salve, and a full jaw which
swept in a line that would have been totally classic had it not
been for the suggestion of a double chin that was beginning to
bulge beneath it. She could have been any age from thirty to the
mid-forties.

Looking with green eyes from beneath full brows at Tatiana,
she asked, *"Vi panimayu Paruski?"*

"Da," Tatiana replied.

Whatever else was said was lost on Longarm. The two women
spoke briefly in Russian, then the woman began a regal descent
from the surrey while Tatiana went hurriedly into the house. By
the time the new arrival was at the gate, Mordka and Marya were
following Tatiana outside. Even without knowing Russian, Long-

arm could follow what happened then. There were greetings exchanged, and introductions that began with handshakes and bows and ended in embraces. Then the group went inside. Longarm leaned back against the house and inspected the surrey and its driver. His inspection had barely begun when the man knotted the reins around the whip socket, got out of the carriage, and walked over to the bench.

"From the Danilov family you do not belong, yes?" he asked.

"No. They're just putting me up for a few days."

"Ah. Permit me. Is here allowed for servant to speak. I am Gregor Basilovich. I attend on Madame Ilioana Karsovana."

"That's the lady who went inside?"

"*Da.*" Basilovich shook his head. "A sad matter. She looks all over *Amirika* for the brother who for years she has not found."

"Is he supposed to belong to the Brethren?"

Basilovich shrugged. "Once he vas. But to all places yet she has gone, is know him nobody." He took two cigars from his pocket and offered one to Longarm. *"Eta nilza?"*

"If you mean do I smoke, I sure do." Longarm took the cigar and looked at it; it was long, fat, Corona-shaped, wrapped in rich, dark leaf. He bit off the end. Basilovich was ready with a match. Longarm puffed. The smoke was heavy, and sweeter than the cheroots he favored. He nodded. "A real fine stogie. Thanks, Mr. . . ."

"Basilovich, Gregor."

Mordka appeared in the doorway. "Marshal Long, would you join us indoors? Perhaps you can help Madame Karsovana."

"Sure." Longarm made slow business of getting up until the coachman saw his difficulty and offered a hand. "Thanks, Mr. Basilovich. I don't generally need help, but I took a rifle slug a few days back, and I still don't move around so good."

"Ah. I see. To help is my pleasure."

With a hand from Basilovich and another from Mordka at the top of the low step, Longarm got into the house. Chairs had been drawn into a rough circle around the table where Mordka's books still lay open, and steaming tea had been served. Mordka led Longarm to the chair in which the newcomer sat.

"Madame Ilioana Karsovana, permit me I introduce Marshal Long. He is a U.S. government policeman. It may be he can help your search."

"Marshal Long." Madame Karsovana extended a hand, palm down. She had removed her gloves, and diamonds gleamed from rings on her two middle fingers.

Longarm took the extended hand, and found his own grasped in soft but surprisingly strong fingers. "Pleased to meet you, Mrs. Karsovana. Your man outside was just telling me you're looking for your brother, but I don't know as I can be much help to you."

With a sad smile, Madame Karsovana said, "It is a difficult search, you understand, Marshal? Your country is almost as large as ours."

To Longarm's astonishment, she spoke nearly perfect and almost unaccented English. He said, "It's big, all right. But maybe if you've got some idea where your brother was the last time you heard from him—"

"Ah, that's the trouble. But do sit down, please. Mr. Danilov told me you are recovering from a wound."

Mordka helped Longarm to a chair. As he went to his own seat by the table, he said, "Madame is not sure whether her brother was one of the Brethren, or stayed with the main Mennonite community. But I have had to tell her that he is not among us."

"That's too bad," Longarm said. "When was the last time you heard from him, Mrs. Karsovana?"

"This is my problem, Marshal. Since Pimenn left our own country, he has written only one letter. That was from New York, and in it he said only that he was traveling from there west, to join some group that was planning to settle on land the U.S. was offering."

Longarm ran a hand through his hair, and scratched the back of his neck. "West covers a lot of territory, when you're leaving from New York. Now, Mordka'd be more likely than me to know where there's bunches of Russian Mennonites settled."

"Unhappily, I do not," Danilov said. "In Pennsylvania, yes, Ohio, Illinois, these I know. But Madame has already been to these places, she tells me."

"Well, if I can help, you just tell me," Longarm offered. "But like I told you, I'd be about as lost as you are, trying to find just one man in such a big space."

"Yes, of course. It is kind of you to offer to help, Marshal. I may call on you, if I think of any way that you can do so." Madame Karsovana rose, said something to Mordka in Russian.

Out of deference to Longarm, he replied in English. "It was our pleasure, Madame. You will be going, then?"

She shrugged. "Soon. I am very exhausted, and so are my horse and my servant. Perhaps we will stay in the town hotel for a few days before we go on."

There was a flurry of leave-taking in which Longarm did not participate. The Danilovs walked with Madame Karsovana to her carriage, where they stood for a few more moments, then the family came back inside.

"Too bad Mrs. Karsovana's had such bad luck," Longarm remarked. "I'd like to've helped her, seeing she's a friend of yours, but there wasn't much I could've told her but what I did, and been honest."

Mordka Danilov shook his head. A grim smile, one that Longarm had never seen him wear before, was twisting his lips. He said, "Do not waste your time worrying about that one, Marshal."

"Why not? She seemed to be a nice enough lady."

"Seemed to be, yes. But I do not think she is what she pretends to be."

"I guess I don't follow you," the marshal said with a frown.

"That is because you do not understand the Russian government, my friend." Mordka sat down heavily. "The Tsar is a jealous man, a greedy man. To lose even one subject angers and displeases him."

"I don't know much about Russia, like you said, Mordka, but it seems to me the Tsar's got so many of 'em that a few wouldn't be missed."

"So one would think, but you would be wrong. And when hundreds of us leave, as did the Mennonites and the Brethren, the ruler of all the Russias becomes very angry." Mordka chuckled. "I will tell you the truth, we do nothing to quiet his anger. There are, you must understand, a number of secret newspapers in Russia today."

"Excuse me, Mordka. I guess I don't understand. How do you keep a newspaper secret?"

"These are printed in small basement shops, and handed from one reader to another. Many of them have letters from Russians like us, who have settled here or in other countries. These papers the *gaydbeshnik*, the state security officers, will seize. And when a letter from an emigrant, such as we of the Brethren, appears in one, perhaps the writer's name is sent to the *Okhrana*, the secret police. That, I think, is why Madame Karsovana is here now."

"Wait a minute!" Longarm protested. "You mean she's a spy?"

"That is exactly what I mean. I suspect that both she and her coachman are of the *Okhrana*, and are here to make trouble for us!"

Chapter 11

For a moment, all Longarm could do was to stare openmouthed at his host. Finally he said, "I know you well enough by now to know you ain't one to go off half-cocked, Mordka. I guess you've got good reasons for thinking what you do."

"Yes. Marya and I were sure the Karsovana woman is not what she claims to be the minute we heard her talk."

Marya Danilov spoke for the first time. "Her accent. She is not of our part of Russia, Marshal. From St. Petersburg she comes. Even before the Brethren parted from the others of our belief, there was from St. Petersburg nobody among us."

"Her coachman, too, is from the capital," Mordka added. "I knew it as soon as he greeted us." Seeing the doubt in Longarm's face, he shook his head. "Do not question what we know, Marshal. In this country, I understand the people speak differently in different places."

"That's right," Longarm agreed.

"In Russia, it is true as well. Believe me, this Karsovana woman, she is an imposter. She means us no good."

"You've got enough troubles as it is," Longarm said soberly. "Between the cattle ranchers and Stone, you don't need any more."

Danilov nodded. "I am thinking of that. If somehow this woman finds out what problems we have—and the agents of the *Okhrana* are clever, make no mistake about that—then she could join with them to—" he paused and shook his head sorrowfully— "to finish us here."

"I didn't know it was all that bad," Longarm said.

"It is bad, Marshal. We must get a good return from our wheat this year, or we will have no money to see us through the winter and the planting of a crop next year."

"You know," Longarm's voice was thoughtful, "seems to me like you need more help than I've been giving you. I better get back in action right quick, get back to town, so I can start digging where I left off. This ain't any time for me to be pampering myself." He struggled to his feet. "Come on. Let's get my horse saddled up. I'm going back into Junction and go to work!"

In spite of Mordka's objections, Longarm went to the room he'd been occupying, and started to pick up his saddle from the corner where it had been put the night of the raid. He bent down, but when he tried to lift the saddle, a pain of such intensity stabbed his side that he was unable to stand up. If Mordka had not followed him, and been standing close enough to catch him, Longarm would have fallen to the floor.

"No, my friend," Mordka said when he'd helped Longarm to the bed. "You cannot leave here yet. What good would it do you to be in Junction? You can scarcely walk alone, to say nothing of riding a horse."

"I guess you're right. Looks like I've got to put up with being crippled for a few more days. But it's only going to be a few days, I promise you that!"

Longarm's promise proved impossible to keep. A day passed, and another, and though the sharp pain that had caught him when he'd tried to lift the saddle faded away, he still could do no more than hobble about. Mordka sent for Dr. Franklin, who thumped and prodded, and curtly denied Longarm's urgent plea to do something that would let him resume full activity.

"Don't be a damned fool," the doctor said. "It's going to be another week before you're able to get around without hurting."

"Well, if you really want the truth, Doc, I don't feel quite up to forking a horse yet," Longarm confessed. "And even if I could, there's something else that bothers me. I put on my gunbelt this morning, and even if it's my left side that hurts, I can't make a decent draw with my right hand yet. Now why the hell is that?"

"Because that rifle bullet went through two muscles that wrap around from your belly to your backbone. They're called the *mandibula obliquus externus* and the *mandibula obliquus internus*, and they lie on top of one another with the muscle fibers running crossways. There's a membrane between them to let them slide smoothly when you use them. That's three layers of tissue, if you've been following what I've told you so far, and all three of those layers are still raw; they haven't healed fully. The muscles are irritated every time you move. And they're anchored just about where the same set of muscles on your right side are, so when you tighten up the right side, the left side tightens up in sympathy."

"Doc, I just asked why I still can't make a good right-hand draw. I didn't want you to give me a damned anatomy lesson."

"You asked me why; I told you why. I'll tell you something else, Marshal. From now on, I can't give you any medicine that's going to help you. You've got to be your own doctor, starting today. Don't let it worry you, though. The only prescription you'll have to fill calls for a little bit of exercise and a hell of a lot of patience."

"Patience never was my long suit, Doc. But I'll try."

Tatiana came in after the doctor left. She'd joined Mordka in objecting to Longarm's insistence on going back to Junction at once. Longarm had discounted Tatiana's protests. What to him had been a galling period of enforced idleness had become for her a way to see a world about which she was intensely curious, but knew nothing. To the young girl, whose contacts with people had been confined to the Brethren, Longarm was a being from that other world.

As soon as his wound had healed enough for him to sit up, Tatiana had begun peppering him with questions. The more he answered, the more she asked.

"Is so many things *Amirikanits* I do not learn yet," she had said, a small frown puckering her smooth young face. "*Matushka*, she says I do not need to know, only to cook and keep clean the house. But is not enough, I think."

"Well, knowing about some things works two ways, Miss Tatiana. Like in my case, I've learned a lot of things I reckon I'd be better off if I hadn't. Everything ain't nice or pretty, you know."

"*Da*. I know. I am not child still, Marshal. I know is bad in world. But if I do not know bad, how do I tell from good?"

"I guess you just learn to sort 'em out as you go along. If there's another way, I ain't run into it yet."

They spent more and more time together, and when Longarm became able to move around, the restraints that had existed be-

tween them diminished. Even with individuals as different as
Longarm and Tatiana, it would have been impossible for this not
to have happened. From the first day he'd come to the Danilov
house, there had been the physical contact between them of Tatiana sponging his face and arms, of helping him to shift position in the bed. The contact became even more intimate after
Mordka botched his first effort to shave Longarm's sprouting
crop of whiskers, and Tatiana volunteered to take on the job.

After shaving him the first time, her touch light and delicate
with the razor, her hands warm and moist with the soap as she
moved his face to the angles she needed to pass the blade over
his skin, Tatiana asked, "Is all right? I do not hurt you with sharp
edge of razor?"

Longarm felt his cheeks and chin. "Nope. Not a bit. Feels a
lot better than some of the barber shaves I've had."

Blushing, Tatiana confessed, "Is make me nervous, Marshal.
Is first time I feel so much a man's skin."

"I sure wouldn't want to embarrass you, now. Maybe, if it
bothers you, I better let Mordka shave me, till I can lift my hands
up to my face and shave myself."

"No, no. Is all right. I do not mind, so long as I do not hurt
you."

Even after Longarm could raise his arms without pain, Tatiana continued the daily shave. Longarm came to look forward
to the razor, to the feel of her hands on his cheeks. He quickly
got the impression that she was no longer embarrassed by their
contacts, but in the week that followed Dr. Franklin's last visit, it
seemed to him that she let her hand linger a bit longer than was
really necessary when she passed her fingers over his moist face
to explore, for any patches of stubble she might have missed.

Old son, he told himself that night as he lay awake waiting
for sleep to come, *you better start shaving yourself. First thing
you know, that little girl's going to put her hands someplace else,
and you'll be just horny enough so you won't want to stop her.*

When he suggested the next day that he was well enough to
shave himself, Tatiana objected. "*Nyet.* Is not make me feel nervous. Truly. I like." She began blushing as she added in a timid
voice. "Is feel good to fingers, face of a man."

"You're joshing me, Miss Tatiana. A pretty girl like you, why, you ought to have beaux lined up from here to Junction, waiting for you to take notice of them."

She frowned. "Beaux? *Ya nipanimayu*. What means, beaux?"

"Sweethearts. Fellows waiting to court you."

"Ah, *iskateli? Nyet*. Is not possible. Already, you see, *ya pomoluit*. I have betrothed."

"You're engaged to be married? Is that right?"

"*Da*. With Antonin Keverchov, so soon as harvest is finish." Longarm frowned. "Don't guess I've met him."

"He was at supper the first time you are visit. But was so many new faces to you, maybe you do not remember."

"Guess not. Well," Longarm said, "I sure wish you a lot of happiness." Then, jokingly, he added, "If you weren't already spoke for, I'd be tempted to set my cap at you myself—if I was a marrying kind of man, that is."

Again, Tatiana blushed. "Now you make me feel funny some more. Is not for you, plain country girl."

"You might be a country girl, but you sure ain't plain, Miss Tatiana. Come right down to it, you're one of the prettiest girls I've run across in a long time."

"*Spasiba*, Marshal. But girl like me, who knows nothing, is not suited for *boyar* like you."

"What's that mean, *boyar*?"

"*Boyar* is big, important man, is leader for other people."

"You got me wrong, Miss Tatiana. I just work at my trade like your pa does, or like your young man, Antonin whatever-his-name-is."

Tatiana shook her head stubbornly. "You are *boyar*, all right. Is in way you talk, way men do quick what you command them. I know, I see how by you is to lead." She sighed, and to Longarm's surprise, her eyes filled with tears. Her voice was torn between anger and distress as she went on, "You think I don't want to be more as farm girl, marry to farm, work hard all my life? I like better marry man like you, be *boyar*'s wife, lady, live in city, have new clothes, like Ilioana Karsovana. But is not to happen, *nyet*?"

Longarm's hand started involuntarily to reach for Tatiana's face and brush away the tears that were beginning to run down her cheeks. He caught himself in time and pulled his hand back. His impulse was too dangerous to follow, he realized.

Angry for allowing himself to drift into such a situation, he said, "Now, you're just feeling low, Miss Tatiana. You and your young man are going to settle down and be happy. And after you get started, farm life ain't so bad."

"How to be sure this will be the way?"

"I don't guess you can be sure. There's not anybody who knows what tomorrow's going to be like. We just take our chances, go along day after day, and endure whatever we can't cure."

"*Da*. Is what *matushka* tell me all time."

"I guess she knows. And Mordka's a real smart man. Likely he'll tell you the same thing."

"*Da*. He have say this already." Tatiana wiped away the film of moisture on her cheeks and found a smile somewhere. "I am silly girl. *Prisnatelniey*, you don't laugh at me. Now I wash off soap from your face like always." Then, sadly, she said, "But it is not the same again next time, *nyet*?"

"No. I reckon I'd better start shaving myself."

Tatiana finished washing Longarm's face and put the damp cloth back into the washbasin. She placed the palm of her hand on his cheek. "Am to miss shave you, Marshal. I like feel of your face."

"Pretty soon you're going to have a husband, Miss Tatiana. You can shave him."

"*Nyet*. Antonin is *borodach*. Like papa."

"Sure. I forgot. Well, you'll be happy with him, whether he's got a beard or not."

"How to be sure?" she repeated.

"Just make up your mind to be." Longarm stood up. Tatiana had been in the habit of taking his arm when he moved, but this time he caught her hand and gently pushed it aside. "No. I've been leaning on other people long enough. It's time I start to do for myself. The longer a man leans on somebody else, the easier it is for him to keep leaning. Pretty soon he gets to where he can't get along without having somebody carrying part of his weight for him."

For a moment, Longarm thought Tatiana was going to cry again, but she blinked her eyes hard and smiled, nodding. Quietly she followed him into the house.

* * *

As he rode into Junction the next morning after a long series of
goodbyes with the Danilov family, Longarm shook his head and
heaved a relieved sigh.

Old son, he said under his breath, *you just missed that one by
a hair. Next time you need somebody to look after you for a
spell, you get a girl like Ruthie. It's a hell of a lot safer.*

Easily, without even thinking about it, Longarm fell into the
routine that he'd established during the first days of his arrival
in Junction. He'd ridden slowly on the way to town. Each step
the roan took jarred his wounded side. The pain was much less
than it had been even a day earlier, though; it was no longer a
stab, just an irritating reminder to be more careful in the future.

After leaving his horse with the liveryman, Longarm strolled
up the street to the Ace High and stopped there for a drink before
crossing to the restaurant for the steak and potatoes he'd missed
in spite of Marya Danilov's tasty meals. Playing no favorites,
after he'd eaten, he recrossed the street for a second shot of rye,
this time at the Cattleman's.

"Well, howdy," Bob greeted him from behind the bar. "Missed
you while you was gone. First drink's on the house."

Longarm sipped the rye with a sigh of satisfaction. He never
had been able to decide which drink tasted best, the one before
a meal, or the one after. Since he'd long ago given up trying to
make the judgment, he simply enjoyed the whiskey and poured
himself a refill.

Returning from serving, another customer at the far end of
the bar, Bob stopped in front of Longarm and snapped his fingers. "Just about forgot," he said as he opened the till, took out
an envelope, and handed it to Longarm, "Ruthie asked me to
give you this."

Tearing open the envelope, Longarm took out the folded
half-sheet of paper it contained and read:

Dear Longarm,

*One of the Santa Fe brakemen fixed it up for me to ride the
caboose to Dodge tomorrow. There might not be another
chance for me to leave here until the cattle shipments start,
so I guess I'd better grab this one. I went up to your room*

*to tell you goodbye, but you weren't there. When I got back
to the Cattleman's, I heard them talking about how you got
hurt. I hope it wasn't too bad and you'll get over it quick.
I guess maybe it's a good thing you aren't here, because if
you was, I'd feel like staying. Thanks for being so good to
me. I don't expect I'll ever see you again, but you're the
man I'll always remember.*

Ruthie

Longarm's expression didn't change while he was reading the
note. He shredded the paper and dropped it into the spittoon by
his feet at the bar rail. His glass was empty, and he refilled it. His
side was beginning to ache again and he knew it was time for him
to rest awhile; there wasn't much he could do for the next hour
or so, and he could spend the time figuring out where to start
over, and how he'd make up for the time he'd lost. He drained his
glass, put a quarter on the bar for his drinks, and started for the
hotel.

Passing the store, he remembered that his supply of cigars
was running low. He'd finished the box that Fedor Petrovsky had
brought with a change of clothes from the hotel while he was
recovering at the Danilovs', and had only two or three left in
his pocket. Entering the store, he almost bumped into Madame
Ilioana Karsovana. He nodded and touched his hatbrim, and was
going to pass on by when she spoke.

"Marshal Long! How fortunate! I was thinking of going back
to Danilov's house to chat with you again. In the position you
hold, you must know something more that would help me to find
my brother."

He shook his head. "Sorry, ma'am, I told you just about all I
could the other day." Then he frowned and said, "I sort of got the
idea you'd decided your brother couldn't be around here and
you were ready to go on to someplace else."

"I have been traveling many miles, Marshal. I am exhausted.
I need to stop and rest in a quiet place such as this."

"I see." The excuse was a thin one, he thought. He recalled
Mordka Danilov's suspicions of the woman, and wondered if
Mordka might not be right, regardless of how farfetched the idea

was of a Russian secret agent operating in such a remote spot in Kansas.

Madame Karsovana extended a gloved hand. "Will you help me, Marshal Long?"

Longarm had no choice but to accept her hand. She rested it on his wrist, and, lifting the hem of her skirt with her free hand, turned him back toward the door. She kept her hand on Longarm's wrist while they walked the short distance back to the hotel.

"Shall we talk in my rooms?" she asked as they entered the building. "You will find them comfortable, and I can offer you some refreshment."

"Well, even if I don't figure I can tell you much that'll help you find your brother, I sure won't turn down a lady's invitation."

Longarm's surprise at seeing the woman still in Junction was nothing compared to that which stunned him when Madame Karsovana opened the door to her room. At the windows, yards of ivory silk had been hung to temper the harsh sunlight and transform its glare to a soft translucent glow. A large Persian rug covered what Longarm was certain was the same kind of threadbare carpet as the one that was on the floor of his own room. In the softened light, the rug glowed in subtle reds, blues, and purples. The bed was a billowing sea of tumbled furs and satin pillows, the soft, fluffy texture of the rich, creamy furs contrasting with the sheen of the multicolored pillows.

Chairs had been draped with lengths of brocaded velvet, and a large oval table, its legs ornately carved, filled most of the scanty space left in the corner between the bed and the wall. Lace covered the stained top of the battered oak bureau, and a large rectangular pier glass in a chased gold frame had been propped in front of the bureau's own tarnished mirror. It looked, Longarm thought, as if the Karsovana woman was settling in for a lengthy stay.

"I've got to say, you travel in real style," he told her. "Sure beats the way my room looks."

"I cannot be comfortable in unpleasant surroundings," she replied with a small shudder. "I have traveled a great deal, you understand, both here, and abroad, and I find most hotel rooms

dreadfully squalid. So I carry my little comforts with me, and
Boris has learned how to arrange my *milieu* to suit me, when we
stop for more than an overnight stay."

A crystal decanter, flanked by tiny, conical-stemmed glasses,
stood on a mirrored tray on the bureau, amid a scattering of
small boxes of gold, silver, and enamel. Madame Karsovana
took one of the boxes and opened it, offering it to Longarm.

"You will smoke?"

He looked at the cigarettes in the box—overlong, white, thin
tubes—and shook his head "No, thanks. Not one of them, anyhow. I'll have one of my own cigars, if you don't object." He
took out a cheroot.

"No indeed. I enjoy the fragrance of cigar smoke."

She took a cigarette from the box, and Longarm flicked his
thumbnail across the match he'd gotten out to light his cigar and
held it for her, then puffed his cheroot into glowing life.

"Sit down please, Marshal Long."

Longarm settled into one of the chairs. There were pillows
under the brocade that draped it. Madame Karsovana had stayed
beside the bureau, now she came carrying the decanter and two
of the little stemmed glasses. She put the glasses on the table
and filled them, then, sitting in a chair facing him, she handed
him one of the drinks.

Longarm looked suspiciously at the water-clear liquor. "That
ain't gin, is it? Sure don't get any smell from it."

"It is vodka. I must apologize. Boris could find no ice in the
town, and vodka is best when it is as cold as the winds that blow
off the Neva in December."

"This'll suit me just fine, ma'am. I don't cotton much to cold
liquor." He took the glass she handed him, and held it to his
nose. The liquor was as odorless as it was colorless. He missed
the rich aroma of the rye he favored, and thought—but didn't
say—that a stingy little glass like this one sure couldn't hold the
kind of man-sized drink he was used to taking.

Madame Karsovana raised her glass. *"Pei do dna!"* she
smiled, and added, "It is the Russian for what you say here,
'Bottoms up!'"

"That's good enough for me," Longarm said as he tilted the
glass to his lips, prepared to be disappointed in such a pale
drink. The fiery vodka hit his tongue with a smash and left a trail

of liquid fire all the way down his gullet. It took a real effort for him to keep from gulping. When he was sure his throat would work properly, he said, "Now, that's a real-potent liquor!"

"I am glad you enjoy it." She reached for the decanter and refilled their glasses, "*Pei do dna*, Marshal."

Longarm discovered that one swallow of vodka didn't condition a man's throat to a second one right away. He understood now why the glasses were so small. After a puff or two on his cheroot, he recovered the use of his voice and said, "Well, Mrs. Karsovana, you wanted to ask me some more about looking for your brother. Go ahead, ask away."

"Yes, of course. It is good of you to spend your time helping me. Tell me, Marshal Long, is there a way in your country for my brother to have changed his identity?"

"You mean take a new name? One that ain't on his passport?"

"Yes. In Russia we have identity cards which all must carry with us. Even the serfs have them. Is there nothing of that sort in America?"

Longarm shook his head. "We don't feel like a free country ought to have anything like that. If a man wants to take a new name, to help him get a fresh start, that's up to him. Of course, if he's doing it to hide from the law, that's another thing."

"My brother isn't a lawbreaker, I'm sure. He'd have no reason to try to hide. But I'm told that these emigrants who have settled here, these Brethren, as they call themselves, are having a great deal of trouble. Is that true?"

"If you mean are they in trouble with the law, no, they ain't. There's some bad feeling between them and the cattlemen, but far as I know, the Brethren are pretty much on the right side of the law in that mix-up."

"But I heard they fought what was almost a battle, a short time ago, with the older settlers. Surely that's not lawful?"

"They were just standing up for what's theirs, in that fracas. Matter of fact, ma'am, I was on their side, helping them. If you heard the whole story, you should've known that."

"It's hard to tell the difference between truth and rumors, Marshal, as I'm sure you've found out. The stories I've heard don't agree."

"If you'd like the real facts about it, I'll be glad to tell you," Longarm offered.

"I would, very much. I feel a great interest in these poor people, Marshal. I would like to find some way to help them. But before you start your story . . ." Madame Karsovana leaned forward and picked up the decanter to refill their glasses.

For a moment there was complete silence in the room. Longarm was watching his hostess pour vodka into his glass when his ears, always subconsciously attuned to foreign noises, caught the sound of squeaking boards in the corridor outside the door. Then there was a scrape of metal on metal. He glanced over his shoulder, saw the doorknob move a fraction of an inch.

Putting a finger to his lips, Longarm stood up. He moved toward the door, his footsteps silent on the double-carpeted floor. His Colt was in his hand when he reached the door and flung it open.

Gregor Basilovich stood in the hallway holding a revolver.

Chapter 12

Before the Russian could raise his weapon, Longarm jammed his own gun into the man's belly.

"Just don't start to raise your arm, and you'll be all right," he warned.

Madame Karsovana spoke over Longarm's shoulder. "Gregor Basilovich! What is the meaning of this? Put your weapon away at once!"

Basilovich said something in Russian, and the woman answered him in the same language. Longarm neither moved nor spoke, but kept the pressure on his Colt's muzzle that was buried in the coachman's midsection.

Madame Karsovana placed a hand on the deputy's arm. "Please, Marshal, remove your gun from Gregor's body, He meant no harm. There was an unfortunate event in a hotel where we stopped several weeks ago. A burglar broke in and almost escaped before the police arrived. I suggested that Gregor buy a pistol then, to be on guard against another attempt at robbery."

"Ma'am, I learned a long time ago not to take my weapon off a man who's staring me eye-to-eye with his gun in his hand," Longarm said. "Now, you tell this Gregor to hand me his pistol. I'll give it back to him as soon as I unload it."

Again Madame Karsovana spoke to the coachman in their native tongue. Gregor replied in a tone that told Longarm he was objecting to the instructions his employer had given him, but she replied with a second command, and the man handed Longarm the pistol, butt-first. Holstering his own Colt, Longarm looked at the weapon. It was a latch-cylinder Tranter of English make, not a common gun in the land where Colt was king and Remington was crown prince.

Longarm pressed the release latch under the barrel, swung

out the cylinder, and emptied the cartridges into one hand. He locked the cylinder back into position, handed the pistol to Gregor, then returned the cartridges separately. He knew that the gun would accept only the cartridges manufactured by its maker.

"You ain't asked me for any advice, Mr. Basilovich," Longarm said, "but I'm going to give you some. If I'd been a nervous man, you'd be a dead one by now. Keep your gun holstered unless you intend to use it. Oh—if I was you, I'd get rid of that English pistol, too. There's not many places west of St. Louis where you can buy cartridges for it."

"I did not intend to point at you the pistol," Basilovich said apologetically. "It was as Madame told you; I heard voices in the room, and I did not know Madame had returned. My first thought was that thieves were again at work."

"Sure, I understand that," Longarm replied. "I'm just advising you how to act the next time."

Madame Karsovana said, her voice cold, "You may go, Gregor. The marshal and I are having a discussion. I do not need your services."

In a voice almost as cold as hers, he answered, "Of course, Madame. I will wait in my room until you require me."

When the coachman had gone into a room two doors down the hall, Madame Karsovana said, "I am sorry, Marshal Long, but this excitement is bringing on an attack of nerves. Shall we continue our talk later?"

"Sure. Anytime."

"You are staying here in the hotel, I suppose?"

Longarm pointed to his room, on the opposite side of the corridor. "Right over there."

"I am relieved. With you close by, I will no longer be afraid of thieves. Now, if you will excuse me—"

"Of course, Mrs. Karsovana. Like you said, we'll talk later."

In his own room, Longarm went first to the bureau and lifted the rye bottle to his lips. He needed something to wash away the flavorless, scorched feeling left in his throat by the vodka. The rye trickled down with a bite that was satisfying, and left an aroma that told a man he'd had something other than pure, raw alcohol. The flavor was so satisfying that Longarm took another small sip before taking off his coat, vest, and gunbelt and stretching out on the bed.

There's something about that Karsovana woman that don't ring true, he told himself. *Matter of fact, she looks more phony than real to me. . . .*

Mordka might be right, but what in hell would a Russian spy be doing here? Those Brethren ain't big enough or important, enough to get that kind of attention.

Then he recalled what Danilov had said about the underground newspapers circulating in Russia, in which letters from such involuntary exiles as the Brethren were often printed.

That just might be it, he mused. *The way those countries on the other side of the ocean are always having wars and revolutions, they'd be scared of their people learning there's places where they can live better and freer. It ain't just the Brethren busting away from them Cossacks Mordka keeps talking about; it's that what they've done can give the folks still living there the idea of doing the same thing. . . .*

Yep, it'd make sense. If the Brethren went busted here and had to scatter out, or maybe even crawl back to where they came from, why, that'd suit the old Tsar right down to the heels of his boots. And Mordka might just be right, after all. It'd sure explain why that Gregor Basilovich fellow was skulking outside with a gun in his hand. And she was lying to me about that pistol; he never bought that anywhere in this country, he had to've brought it with him from Russia.

Longarm blinked and shook his head to clear it of swarming thoughts, got up, and went to the bureau for another sip of rye. He reached in the pocket of his vest, hanging on the head of the bed, for a cigar. His exploring fingers found only one, and he reminded himself absently that he'd have to remember to get back to the store for a new supply. His mind was still on Gregor Basilovich.

Lucky I drew before I opened the door, or he could've—

Abruptly Longarm's train of thought was interrupted. He didn't remember drawing. His reaction to the hint of danger outside the door had been instinctive. When he'd tried to see if he could whip out his Colt naturally while he was still at the Danilovs', his wounded side had kept bothering him, slowed him down, but when the real cards were being played, he'd had the Colt out with his old easy speed.

"I'll be damned," he muttered. "Looks like I was worrying without any reason to."

Lifting his gunbelt off the bedpost, Longarm strapped it on. He slid the Colt out and shook the shells out of its cylinder. Then he replaced it in the holster and faced the mirror. He drew once, reholstered the gun, and drew again. He breathed a huge sigh of relief. He reloaded the pistol, checking each cartridge as he slid it into the cylinder. Letting the hammer down carefully on the single empty chamber, he returned the gun to its holster and hung the belt back on the bedpost, his mind at ease.

One less thing to worry about, he thought as he lay down again. *I got a pretty full plate of puzzles, sure don't need another one. Hawkins. Stone. The Lazy Y horse that got shot. Now, the Russian woman and her servant.*

Be a damn big mess if those two got together with Hawkins and the ranchers and Stone to put the Indian sign on Mordka's bunch. The way I read it, if them Brethren don't get a good crop, and if they don't get paid a fair price for it, they're just about finished. Wouldn't make much difference then whether they got Fedor elected sheriff or not. Which they just might do, if the voting's fair and square. And which puts me right in the middle of what could be one damn big mess.

Not my mess, either, except that Billy Vail handed it over to me, so I got to keep it in hand. But there's not any reason why I can't pass part of it over to the sheriff. He's the one that it belongs to, by rights.

All his thinking had made Longarm restless, and he'd thought his way to the point where action was the next step. After his long confinement at the Danilovs', the cramped hotel room seemed to be closing in on him. He was still standing beside the bed, and he looked at it distastefully; the time for lolling around like an invalid had ended. Besides, he was out of cigars.

Strapping on his gunbelt again, he slipped his vest and coat on and started for the door. A stop at the store for cigars, then to the sheriff's office to talk to Grover seemed his next move. He wasn't too preoccupied, when he left the room, to take his usual precaution of wedging the stub of a matchstick between the door and the jamb. If nothing more, the presence of the two Russians in the hotel was enough to remind him that he had to keep his guard up.

There was one other customer in the store when Longarm went in: Clem Hawkins. The rancher was standing at the end of the long wooden counter, a sheaf of charge tickets in his hand, leafing through them. The storekeeper stood close to him behind the counter. When Longarm entered, the merchant said, "Be right back, Clem, soon as I wait on this customer."

Without raising his eyes from the papers, Hawkins grunted, "Take your time, Steb. I'll settle with you as soon as I finish looking these over."

Moving to where Longarm stood, the storekeeper asked, "What can I get for you today, Marshal Long?"

"Box of Havana extras. Tell you what, Mr. Stebbins. I'll just tuck a handful of 'em in my pocket now, and you lay the box under the counter for me to pick up on my way back to the hotel."

When he heard Longarm's name, Hawkins looked up. "Heard you stopped a bullet a couple of weeks back, Long. You don't seem to be any the worse for it, though."

"I heal up quick, Mr. Hawkins. And I'll be out to talk to you about what happened that night, as soon as I get caught up with my other business."

Hawkins bristled. "What're you getting at? You hinting that me or my boys had something to do with it?"

"I'm not hinting at a thing. I just want to talk to you again, about that night, and maybe about Mr. Oren Stone."

"Wait a minute, Long. There was a horse shot in that fracas, and it sure didn't have my brand on it. I'm told it was a Lazy Y bronc."

"You were told right. But there were other horses in the bunch and I didn't see any of their brands, in the dark."

"Well, you won't find out that any of my men or animals were mixed up in that set-to. And as for Oren Stone, I know him, sure. But I don't see what that's got to do with anything."

"Maybe it doesn't. But I'm real curious about a lot of things sometimes, things that don't always connect up. Anyhow, I'll get out your way pretty soon."

"Now listen to me, Long. I've got a ranch to run. We'll be starting to ship steers inside of a few days, and I don't have any time to spare in idle chatter with you or anybody else."

"I won't hold back your business, Mr. Hawkins. The way I look at it, you've got a right to tend your ranch without anybody getting in your way or interfering with your work." Longarm began filling his vest pocket with cigars from the box Stebbins had put on the counter. He went on, "Just like those wheat farmers have got a right to raise their crops without anybody cutting their fences or tromping down their fields. You think about that, Mr. Hawkins. And I'll be out to have that talk with you, just like I said."

Longarm closed the lid of the box and shoved it to Stebbins. Then he turned away and walked out of the store.

Sheriff Grover was in his office, for a change, sitting behind his desk. He studied Longarm for a moment without speaking, then waved to the room's other chair and leaned back in his own.

"Hmph. Looks like that slug you caught the other night didn't slow you down too much," he said dourly.

"I didn't enjoy it," Longarm said, firing up one of his fresh cheroots. "And I didn't see you busting a gut to come out and track down the son of a bitch that shot me."

"Maybe you didn't see me, but I did the best I could. Those Brethren friends of yours was closer-mouthed than a clam going into a steam kettle. They sure as hell didn't give me much help. All of them I talked to acted like it was one of them that winged you. Which it might easy have been," Grover added. "At night that way, everybody milling around, shooting blind."

"Maybe they figured you'd think that," Longarm suggested. "If you'd stop to think things out, Grover, the Brethren haven't got much reason to feel you'd give 'em a fair shake at anything."

"Now, you know I don't play sides, Long."

"No. I'll say that much for you. You stick pretty close to one side. Hawkins and his friends."

"I try to stand right in the middle. You can't blame me if I like men I've known a long time better than I do a lot of Johnny-come-lately foreign nesters."

"When does a man stop being a foreigner?" Longarm asked the sheriff. "The way I understand it, most of the Brethren are U.S. citizens now, and the rest of 'em are about to be. But that's neither here nor there. You say you went out and looked into the fracas. Which was right, it's your jurisdiction, and I wasn't in much shape to do it, even if I'd had a mind to. What else did you find out?"

The sheriff sighed loudly and leaned forward, crossing his forearms on his desk. "One thing that might interest you. All the horses those men who cut the fence rode came from the Lazy Y horse pasture. They'd all been stolen. Easy enough to do; the pasture's about a mile from the main house, where the corrals for the working stock are."

"What you're getting at is that those horses could've been rustled out of the horse pasture almost anytime by just about anybody?"

"That's pretty much the size of it. Charlie Bell, the Lazy Y owner, he swears none of his hands was off the place that night."

"You believe him?" Longarm asked.

"Well, Bell's not what I'd rate as a liar, Long. Hell, you know as well as I do that every ranch in this part of the country's in the middle of their gathers. Bell says his men was all in the bunkhouse, tuckered out, that night. They're going to be driving in their market herds to ship out sometime in the next week or two, so if you want to talk to Charlie or his boys, you'll be able to catch 'em here and save yourself a ride to his place."

Longarm shifted his body in the hard, badly-built chair; it was stiffening up his side a bit. "I'll bear that in mind. All the ranches ship pretty much the same time, do they?"

"Just about. The Santa Fe's corrals won't hold the stock that comes in, if they all try to ship at once, so the ranchers get together and start their drives so they get here a few days apart."

"Makes sense. Well, now, all this is real interesting, Grover, but we got off the main track. I'd like to know who potshotted me. How're you aiming to go about finding out?"

"I don't intend to give up, if that's what's bothering you. A man who'll potshoot at night is the kind I don't like to have hanging around. Right now I don't know which way to look, though."

"You thought about looking in Clem Hawkins's direction? Or in Oren Stone's?"

"Stone? That wheat broker with the private car on the back siding? Why'd he be interested in seeing you put under?"

"You're overlooking the main point, Grover. That shot wasn't aimed at me. It was just part of the whole damn raid. And somebody planned it, somebody put them riders up to it, maybe paid 'em to go through with it."

"Oh, that's occurred to me, Long, even if I'm just a little jerkwater sheriff and not a federal marshal."

Longarm ignored the dig. "Stone's first shot out of the barrel when he landed here was to go calling on Hawkins."

"I don't see anything wrong with that. Hell's bells, Stone's been here before, he's met old Clem. Besides, his business is buying and selling wheat. Why'd he be interested in doing anything that'd hurt them nesters?"

"Stone's main business ain't wheat. He's playing the wheat market, which is quite something different from just buying wheat to sell. Sometimes he don't want to see a good wheat crop. He'll make more money if it's a poor one."

Grover nodded thoughtfully. "I've heard about men like him. I didn't put Stone in that class, though. And I still don't see why you keep on bringing Clem Hawkins into it."

"Because he stands to gain the most if this country's kept in open range instead of being fenced into wheatfields. And if you don't see that, Grover, I'd say it's because you don't want to." Longarm stood up. "You let me know if you find out anything, hear? I've got a personal interest in that fence-cutting now."

Outside the sheriff's office, Longarm breathed the cool twilight air. The sun had dropped while he and Grover talked. A red glow was all that remained of it along the straight edge of the western horizon, and the light was beginning to fade. In the middle distance the rails of the half-dozen sidings that straddled the holding corrals showed glints of bright steel amid patches of the rust that had gathered on them since the last cattle bars had rolled out in late spring. On the last siding, as far from the corrals as it could be placed, lights gleamed from the windows of Oren Stone's private railroad car.

Longarm looked at the car for a moment, remembering the special rye whiskey that Stone's bar held. He muttered, "Saloon rye's just not going to taste the same till I forget how good that liquor of his was." He was about to turn away and head into Junction when a shadowy figure darted from a corner of the corrals and hurried in a crouching half-run toward the private car.

Something about the way the man moved was familiar. Longarm strained his eyes through the fading light, trying to place the dimly seen, almost shadowy figure, but at this time of day and at this distance, identification was impossible. There was cause for suspicion, though, in the way the man moved, the route he took. It struck Longarm that someone who didn't want to be seen was going to visit Oren Stone.

He watched while the man ran and hopped across the tracks until he reached Stone's railroad car and disappeared into the vestibule. There was a flash of light as the door opened to admit him. Longarm didn't waste time trying to recall where he'd seen the skulking form before. He started to walk across the siding to the place where the unknown man had vanished.

Placing his steps carefully, and putting his feet down flat to keep the gravel ballast underfoot from grating when he moved, Longarm first circled the railroad car to see if a window might be open a crack to give him a close-up, well-lighted view of the man whose familiar way of walking had led him to investigate. All the windows were closed tight, their shades drawn. No sound of voices was audible. There was only one thing left to do. Returning to the front of the car, he mounted the steps leading to the vestibule and knocked on the frosted glass panel of the entry door.

Through the translucent pane he could see that Mae Bonner was coming to answer the knock. He'd gambled on the chance that Stone would do as he'd done when Longarm visited him, and send Mae on whatever errands had to be done. The girl's silhouetted form blotted out the light from the entry as she opened the door. Before she had a chance to speak, Longarm grabbed her arm, pulled her outside, and clamped his free hand over her mouth.

"Now, I ain't going to hurt you, Miss Bonner," he whispered. "You know who I am, don't you?" When she managed to nod, hampered by Longarm's hand pressed on her face, he went on, "This time I'm here on official business. You make things hard for me, you're liable to go to jail. You understand that?" Another nod. "All right. I'm going to let go of you in about half a minute, if you'll promise me you won't yell or do anything foolish. Can I depend on you if I let you go?" Her response was a third nod. Longarm released the girl.

"What—what do you want this time?" she gasped in a whisper. "You said it was official business. Is Mr. Stone in some kind of trouble?"

"Maybe he is, maybe he's not. I know that whoever's in there talking to him is about to be. You know who the man is with him?"

She shook her head. "No. Oren—Mr. Stone's been very careful not to call his name, and he always sends me out of the parlor when the man comes to see him."

"He's been here before, then?"

"Twice. Once the day after we got here, late at night. I didn't let him in the first time, I was—well, I was busy."

"Then when did he come back?"

"A day or two later." Mae frowned. "I don't really remember. And this time."

"All right. Now I want you to stay out here and keep out of the way. You going to do that?"

"Yes, Marshal Long. I don't want to get into any kind of trouble at all. In fact—" She stopped short and shook her head. "You do what your job is. I won't get in your way."

"What'd you start to say?" Longarm demanded.

"Nothing. Except that when you knocked, Mr. Stone told me to get rid of whoever it was."

"All right. Do what I told you, now. Keep out of the way of whatever happens inside there."

Longarm stepped quietly into the vestibule. The door between the entry and parlor section of die car was closed. He pressed an ear against it, hoping to hear something that would give him a clue as to what was happening inside, but all he could catch was a faint murmur of voices. He turned the knob gently to open the door a crack, but at the midpoint in his turning the lock clicked loudly.

From the parlor, Stone called, "Who was it knocking, Mae?"

"Nobody but me, Stone," Longarm said, stepping quickly into the parlor section of the car.

He took in the scene at a glance. Stone sat facing the door. A small table had been drawn between the broker and his visitor. On the table, gold eagles and double eagles were spread as thickly as sand on a beach. Longarm needed no interpreter to tell him that some kind of payoff was taking place.

Even when Longarm had announced his presence, the man sitting across from Stone hadn't moved, not even to turn his head. All that Longarm could see from where he stood was a broad-brimmed Stetson pushed back on the unknown's head, which hid his neck and upper back from view. The chair in which he was sitting concealed the rest of his body. Longarm stared at a pair of denim-clad shoulders that stuck out on each side beyond the hat brim.

Stone said brusquely, "Get the hell out of here! You're butting in on a private business transaction."

"If that's what's really going on, you got nothing to get upset about," Longarm replied.

"That's all it is," Stone retorted.

Longarm had sat across from too many players in too many poker games to be fooled. He caught the shading of the bluffer in Stone's voice.

"Then you won't object if I ask your friend to turn around so I can see his face," Longarm told Stone.

He shifted his eyes to the seated man, then, and saw the almost imperceptible hitching of the unknown's right shoulder that gave away his intention.

When the man kicked back his chair and swiveled, drawing as he turned, Longarm's Colt was already in his hand. It spat once, and Prud Simmons began to sag, staggering backward.

Stone had leaped up when Prud moved. Longarm paid him no attention; he was watching the fugitive. He didn't see Stone reach for the shotgun that was cradled in a rack above the table until the broker had the gun in his hands and was bringing it down, his thumb spanning both of the weapon's hammers.

Prud was between Stone and Longarm. The outlaw hadn't yet fallen, he stood swaying on his feet. As Stone brought the shotgun barrel down, Prud shifted his legs, trying to keep his balance. His move ended in a lurch that overturned the table just behind him. Gold coins cascaded to the plush-carpeted floor of the car and rolled in all directions.

Prud was beginning to topple. He was still trying to face Longarm, and his movements put his back to Stone just as the broker triggered both barrels of the shotgun. The explosion as the shotgun discharged was deafening in the confined space. Prud's chest bulged forward under his jacket as the compressed mass of pellets fired at point-blank range tore through his body.

Blood and tissue splattered on the polished wood of the car's walls when the shotgun pellets burst out of Prud's chest. He collapsed in a heap on the green plush carpet.

Chapter 13

Stone dropped the empty shotgun and raised his hands. Don't shoot me, Marshal Long! Look, I haven't got a pistol or any other kind of weapon!"

"Oh, put your goddamned hands down, Stone!" Longarm snapped with disgust. He holstered his Colt. "Nobody's going to shoot you."

In addition to being disgusted, Longarm was also angry. He'd shot to wound, not to kill. The wheat broker's shotgun blast might not have been planned that way, but it spoiled the strategy that had flashed fully formed in Longarm's mind in the instant when he'd recognized Prud Simmons from the manner in which the outlaw had moved while he was standing up, before drawing. He'd counted on keeping Prud alive to tell him about Stone's activities. If Prud had spilled the beans, it would have put pressure on Stone to talk, too.

Mae Bonner ran in, her eyes wide, her mouth rounded into an O. She blinked in the brightness of the parlor's gaslights, and a moment or two passed before her eyes adjusted to the change from the darkness of the vestibule. Then she saw Prud Simmons's body, in a crouched position on the floor. A hole that would have swallowed a man's fist gaped in the back of his powder-scorched denim jacket.

"Is—is he dead?" she gasped.

"About as dead as any man can be that took both barrels full of shotgun slugs at close range," Longarm told her. "And don't waste your sympathy on him. If any man deserved to die, it was Prud."

Now it was Stone's turn to blink, but his blinking was to adjust his mind, not his eyes.

"You know him, Marshal?" he asked.

"I know him, all right. I don't know what name he was using in his dealings with you, but he's Prud Simmons. That's the bushwhacker who shot one of the Brethren a little while back. For all I know, that was what you were paying him off for."

"What do you mean?" Stone was regaining, his usual coolness.

"It was easy as hell for me to tell what was going on when I walked in here, Stone. From the looks of that table, all those gold pieces on it, he was collecting from you for the dirty work you'd been putting him up to."

"Now wait a minute!" Stone protested. "You haven't any way to prove that. If you make a statement to that effect in public, I'll have you in court for slander!"

"If I was to repeat what I just said, it'd be in court, all right. Only you'd be in the prisoner's dock, and I'd be giving sworn testimony," Longarm reminded the broker. "I don't claim to be a lawyer, but I know enough law to get me by. Testimony in court ain't slander, Stone, which is something I reckon you know, too, the way you twist the law so you can use it in your business.

Stone did not reply. Mae Bonner, her voice unsteady, said, "I don't see how you men can stand there and talk like nothing's happened, when there's a dead man on the floor in front of you. What in heaven's name are you talking about that's important enough to let you act like nothing's happened?"

"You're better off if you don't know," Stone told her harshly. "Get out of here, Mae! Go to bed! Don't pry into something that's no concern of yours!"

"But I've got a right to know!" the girl insisted.

"Do what I told you!" Stone commanded. "Shut up and get out!"

"You better be the one to shut up, Stone, Longarm said. "The day might come when she'll be testifying in court, too."

"She didn't see anything!" Stone objected.

"Maybe she didn't actually see you kill Prud. But she saw him come in here to talk to you tonight. And she saw him come here other times, too. Times before the night-riding and potshotting started."

"That proves exactly nothing!" Stone retorted. There was fence-cutting and wheat being trampled a long time before I got to Junction, and I can produce witnesses to prove that!"

"Witnesses like Clem Hawkins?" Longarm prodded.

"I'm sure Clem would testify for me, if it comes to that."

"You might find out different, especially since Prud Simmons used to work for Hawkins. I got a pretty good idea why he came to you, too. I'm betting he saw you out at Hawkins's ranch, maybe even heard the two of you talking about breaking up the farms the Brethren are working. You told me yourself that you and Clem saw eye to eye on getting them out of here."

"Why would I want to break up the wheat farms, Long? It's my business to buy and sell wheat, and I can't do that unless somebody grows it."

"That's not what I heard you tell Mr. Hawkins," Mae said. The words were involuntary; she realized too late what she'd said, and brought her hand up to cover her mouth.

Stone's face flushed angrily. "Damn you, Mae, I told you to get out of here! Now do it, before I get really mad!"

She looked pleadingly at Longarm, who nodded. He wanted Stone alone for a while. Mae left the room, reluctance showing in her slow footsteps. The parlor door closed behind her. For a moment the two men faced one another in silence.

Finally Stone asked, "Well, what're you going to do about this, Marshal? You know I shot the man accidentally."

"I know you were about to throw down on me with that scattergun," Longarm replied grimly. "If you hadn't let off both barrels in Prud's back, I'd've had to shoot you to protect myself. If that was an accident, Stone, it's likely the luckiest one you've ever had. It saved you from being stretched out on the floor there next to Prud."

Stone's florid face paled at the picture Longarm had sketched. He asked, "You have any objections to me getting a drink while we talk this thing over?"

"Go ahead." Longarm thought a drink might smooth the edges of the broker's abrasiveness. It was a calculated risk, worth a try.

"You'll have some of that special rye, won't you?"

"No. Pass me by." Keeping the regret out of his voice took an effort as Longarm thought of the fine whiskey he'd savored on his earlier encounter with Stone. "It rubs across my grain to drink with a man who's just tried to kill me."

Stone turned away from the liquor cabinet, glass in hand. He said calculatingly, "You're not going to try to charge me with anything, are you now, Long? You know I'd say I was trying to keep Simmons from shooting you. You'd never make a charge stick."

Longarm started for the door. "I'll let you stew about what I aim to do. We'll talk about it later on. I imagine you're too smart to run, and anyhow, I plan to stop at the station and tell the trainmaster not to couple this car of yours to any train heading out till I tell him he can. I'll report the shooting to the sheriff. He'll likely send somebody over to pick up Prud's body. I'd say your best bet's to lay low a while. I'll stop by tomorrow or the next day and we'll have ourselves a confab."

Outside the car, Longarm found that the weather was beginning to fulfill the promise of the red sunset. A brisk wind had set in, blowing steadily from the north, and when he looked up he could see clouds scudding across the sky, veiling the stars. There were no lights in the Santa Fe station, and the sheriff's office beyond was also dark and locked. As Longarm walked on into town, his stomach reminded him it was past suppertime. Before he reached the restaurant, a few stray snowflakes were already swirling in the rapidly chilling air.

Surprisingly, Clem Hawkins and Sheriff Grover were sitting at a table in the back of the restaurant. Longarm walked over to them.

"Mind if I sit down?" he asked.

"It's a free country," Hawkins said. "Sit wherever you want to."

"I wouldn't bust in on whatever kind of talk you two are having, except that I've got some news to tell you, Grover." Longarm settled into a chair. "You don't have to worry about Prud Simmons any longer. He's dead."

"Why the hell did you shoot him?" Grover demanded. "I know you carried a grudge, Long, but that marshal's badge you carry ain't quite the same thing as a hunting license."

"Never figured it was. Fact is, I winged him after he drew down on me, but I didn't kill him."

"Then who did?" Grover frowned.

"Oren Stone."

"Stone?" Hawkins's jaw dropped. "Shitamighty, Marshal, Stone didn't even know the man!"

"If you'll take the time to listen, you'll find out he did," Longarm told Hawkins. "Stone as good as admitted to me that he set Prud onto the Brethren. He was the one who paid Prud to get a bunch of yahoos together and pull off that night raid where I got shot."

"It's going to take a lot of proof to convince me of that," Hawkins retorted. "Stone's no special friend of mine, but I can't see him pulling off that kind of stunt."

"I didn't say he pulled it off. I'd bet he hired Prud on a sort of blank-check deal, told him to give the Brethren a bad time. Prud didn't expect them to fight back. Things got out of hand, and he went too far."

"Where'd he get the men who rode with him?" Grover asked.

"Oh, hell, Grover, you've been sheriff long enough to know that a man like Prud can find his own kind wherever he goes," Hawkins said. "There's not a spread around here that doesn't hire drifters during the gather. Stands to reason there'd be a bad apple or two among them."

Longarm nodded. "You put your finger on it, Mr. Hawkins. And I'm real relieved to hear you say what you did."

"I don't see why," Hawkins said.

"Because it takes most of the blame off your hands and off the other ranchers. Now, I know and you know that when this fence-cutting got started, it was a hit-or-miss proposition. You let your hands know there wouldn't be any smoke raised if a fence got cut now and then. I'd bet the other cattlemen did the same thing. Then Prud saw a chance to cash in on it."

Hawkins thought this over for a moment. "I guess that's about the way it was," he admitted sheepishly. None of us like Glidden wire. But I don't think any of us realized things would go so far."

"What am I supposed to do?" Grover asked Longarm. I guess it's turned into your case, since Simmons was a federal fugitive. You plan to bring Stone in to stand trial for killing him?"

"Not right now. I've already got plenty on my plate. If you'll have whoever takes care of burying around here go by Stone's railroad car and collect Prud's body, that's all I'll ask you to do right this minute."

Grover nodded. He looked relieved. Longarm turned to Hawkins.

"Now I've got something to tell you, Mr. Hawkins. You and your friends are going to be shipping out your market herds pretty soon. You're going to be driving 'em past the wheatfields on the way to the Santa Fe corrals. Best thing you can do, all of you, is to leave your wirecutters at home. You get the drift of what I'm saying?"

Hawkins nodded. "Long, you've always played your cards face up with me, ever since the first time you came to my place. I like a man who does that, and I'll always do the same with him. I don't want any more trouble with the nesters, no matter how I feel about them. Neither do my friends. All we want is to get our herds shipped out and then go back to our places and get ready for winter."

"That's good. I'm glad you feel that way."

"Besides," Hawkins went on, "we don't have to worry about that bunch of foreigners anymore. They can't get their crop in before the weather ruins it, and they've already optioned what they'll be able to salvage to Stone. Not one of them's going to have enough cash to get through the winter. They'll all be gone before next spring."

"You might be right, Hawkins," Longarm replied. "I don't say you are, I don't say you ain't. I feel sorry for those homesteaders, and I've been helping them when I could, without hurting you ranchers."

"So I've heard. Well, that's your privilege, I guess."

Grover stood up. He was obviously anxious to end the conversation between Hawkins and Longarm. "I'd better go see Stebbins, and tell him to get his burying crew out to fix up a casket."

"I'll walk with you a ways," Hawkins said. He rose and started out, then turned back and said to Longarm, "I guess you'll be leaving pretty soon now. Not much for you to do, with everything peaceful."

The deputy pushed his Stetson back on his forehead. "Oh, you ain't seen the last of me yet. It's still a while before election, but maybe you forgot about that being my real job down here. You won't get rid of me until my business is finished. And that won't be till the last vote's been cast and counted."

Longarm watched Grover and Hawkins walk out of the restaurant. Their heads were together and they were obviously discussing some kind of election strategy inspired by his reminder. He chuckled and signaled to the waiter. The void in his midsection had been getting bigger and bigger while he'd talked, and the steak with fried potatoes he'd come in for was long overdue.

Snow was still falling when Longarm left the restaurant, having eased the grumblings of his belly. It was a typical early-season prairie snow—tiny, soft flakes no bigger than a baby's fingernail, and just about as thick. In most places the snow melted as soon as it touched the warm ground; later, as the earth cooled through longer, chillier nights, the snow would stick. Now it danced erratically in the black sky, and the night wind, which had taken on a real bite while Longarm was at supper, swept the tiny flakes along the street, mixed with the dust that had grown to a thin, irritating layer during the long, dry weeks of the expiring summer.

Feeling the soft, cold touch of snowflakes on his face, Longarm thought about the wheat so laboriously planted and tended by the Brethren. According to everything he'd seen in the past, wheat had always been cut before the first snow. In the fields around Junction, the grain had headed out and was turning to golden yellow, but hadn't yet reached harvest stage. He wondered how the homesteaders were going to make it through the winter if their crop was small, and the options held by Stone kept them from selling it where they could get top market price.

He shrugged off the problem as he stood on the board sidewalk in front of the restaurant, looking across the street at the lights of the Cattleman's and the Ace High, trying to decide whether to cross to one of the saloons. The night was still early, but after a few seconds of deliberation he decided it was time for him to wind up his day. He had a gun to clean, a still-healing wound to rest, and a hell of a lot of thinking to do.

There were few signs of the snowfall the next morning when Longarm rode out to the Danilov house. Except for a tracery of thin white rime along the edges of the wheatfields and a small streak or two in a deep rut of the road, the ground was clear. In the fields, the grain heads nodded as the fitful breeze passed over them. It seemed to Longarm that the wheat had matured to a deeper yellow in the short time that had passed since he'd looked at it when riding back from the Danilovs' to Junction, and that had been only a few days ago.

Mordka kept telling me not to worry about the weather, he thought, *and I guess he knows more about it than I do. The only thing I was ever good at growing is my whiskers.*

Tatiana opened the door. "*Serdechenly privelstvovai!* I make you welcome, Marshal Long. Come, sit down. Is kettle hot on stove, I give you tea."

"Where's Mordka?" Longarm asked as he stepped into the house.

"Is by our neighbors down the lane. Petra Tuscheva is have new baby. *Kum* Mordka and *matushka* go there. But they are to come back soon. Sit, please. I make you tea."

Tatiana acts right glad to see me, Longarm thought, pulling out a chair from Mordka's familiar book-piled table and sitting down. Tatiana was busy at the kitchen range. She moved with graceful speed, putting tea leaves in the pot and filling it with water from the kettle that steamed on the stove. While the tea steeped, she spooned wild strawberry jam into tall, thick glasses, and poured the hot tea over the jam until the glasses were brimful. Carrying the tea to the table, she carefully set a glass at Longarm's elbow, then pulled up a chair for herself and sat facing him.

"Is heal up good, your wound?" she asked.

"Just fine. You did a real good job of nursing me, Tatiana, you and your mother. I'm real grateful to you for tending me."

"Is not require, you thank us. You do for the *Bratiya* very much."

"I'm just glad I could." Longarm sipped the tea, fragrant and sweet with the jam dissolved in it. He smiled at Tatiana. "You look prettier than ever today, Tatiana."

"*Spasiba*, Marshal. Is soon now—"

What Tatiana had been going to say was lost in the banging of the front door as it burst open with such force that it crashed into the wall beside the jamb. Silhouetted in the opening was a man—a big man, his shoulders so broad that they almost spanned the full width of the door, and so tall that his head was within an inch of the top of the frame. A long, curved scimitar dangled from one of his hamlike hands.

Tatiana gasped, "Antonin! What do you here?"

Longarm had leaped to his feet and faced the door when it banged, his hand sweeping his Colt from its holster in reflex action. If he'd seen the intruder before, he didn't recall him, but when he saw that Tatiana recognized the man, he relaxed and lowered the pistol.

"I see the *Amirikanits* ride up," the man said. "I know Mordka and Marya are by Tuscheva house. I come to protect you, Tatiana."

Belatedly, Longarm understood. The man in the doorway was Tatiana's fiancé. He said, "Miss Tatiana doesn't need to be protected from me. I sure didn't come here to harm her."

"Is what you say!"

"Antonin! *Shpapa oobrate!*" Tatiana said angrily, pointing at the sword.

"*Nyet!*" Antonin raised the curved blade and pointed it at Longarm. "*Ero vbibat!*"

Though he did not understand Antonin's words, Longarm got the message of the sword pointed at him. He said, "Now hold on! If you got ideas about us getting into a fracas over Miss Tatiana, you're barking up the wrong tree. I ain't trying to cut you out with her. She's a real nice young lady, and I like her fine, but I know you're the one she's promised to marry."

"*Ubi vesti*, Antonin!" Tatiana snapped. Then, switching to English for Longarm's benefit, "Behave yourself! You are foolish to be so jealous!"

"That's right," Longarm agreed. "We're just sitting here talking, while I wait for Mordka to come back. That's all."

"Is what you say!" Antonin retorted. "Oh, I see you ride up so sly, when you know Tatiana you find by herself!" He swung the sword menacingly and took a step into the room. "Now I stop you from bothering my Tatiana!" He paid no attention to the pistol in Longarm's hand.

"*Bojie moy!*" Tatiana exclaimed. "Marshal Long does not bother! He comes as friend!"

"*Nyet!* He comes to win you from me!" Raising the sword, Antonin started across the room.

Longarm knew he could not use his Colt on the enraged Antonin, but neither did he propose to be sliced up like a side of bacon. He saw at once that his only way out of the situation was to let Antonin back him down, but that had to come later. Picking up the chair in which he'd been sitting, Longarm raised it to ward off the sword.

Tatiana started for Antonin just as he raised the scimitar. He thrust her aside, and she staggered back. Antonin brought the blade down in a sweeping sidewise cut. Longarm turned the chair to catch the glittering edge of the wickedly curved weapon.

With a crash, the scimitar hit the chair, and chips flew. The force of the blow stung Longarm's hands. He reminded himself, while watching Antonin for some hint of his next move, not to underestimate the man's strength.

Antonin yanked the blade out of the wood it had bitten into, and swung it behind him in the beginning of an overhead slash. Longarm raised the chair and took the downward sweep of the scimitar before it had gained enough momentum to strike hard; the blade rang as it bounced off the wood.

His downward swing had pulled Antonin's body forward, and he stepped back to recover his balance. Tatiana grabbed his sword arm, but Antonin was too angry to think. He swung his arm and forced it free.

Longarm took the opportunity to retreat. Keeping the chair between himself and Antonin, he backed across the room toward the doorway leading to the bedroom where he'd spent so many uncomfortable hours recovering from the rifle slug. He reached the door as Antonin stalked toward him, slashing the wicked blade from side to side. It whistled as it cut through the air.

"Troossiha!" the Russian grated. "Stop to fight!"

To slow Antonin down, Longarm tossed the chair at his feet. While Antonin was untangling himself from the chair, Longarm ducked into the bedroom and slammed the door.

Through the wooden panel he could hear Antonin's shouts, and almost at once he heard Tatiana speaking rapidly in Russian. Judging from the fishwife-sharp tone of her usually soft voice, she was berating her fiancé. The argument went on for several moments, until Antonin's voice dropped to a muted murmur of apology. Then there was a long silence.

At last Tatiana called out, her voice proud, "Marshal Long!

Out you can come, now. I have some sense talked into this wild lover of mine!"

Longarm kept up the appearance of fear. Letting himself seem afraid was the only way he could think of to soothe Antonin's pride. He opened the door a crack and looked through the slit. Antonin stood with an arm draped protectively around Tatiana's shoulders. The sword was lying on the floor behind the pair.

"You sure it's all right?" Longarm asked. He opened the door a bit wider.

"Is safe for you, yes," Antonin replied. The rage had gone from his voice. He smiled, his brown beard rippling below his shaved upper lip, and beckoned Longarm to come on through the door.

Longarm stepped into the living room. "You sure put a scare into me with that big toad-stabber. I don't like that kind of fighting worth shucks," he told Antonin.

"Is Cossack sword, I bring from Russia. My father take it from a man who tries to kill him."

Tatiana said, "Antonin is sorry for his mistake. Are you not, *milochka?*"

"*Da.* I to you apologize, Marshal Long. Is that I do not understand, until Tatiana she tell me how bad you get shot."

"Shucks, no harm done, Antonin. You've got a fine young lady here. Tatiana's going to make you a real good wife."

Tatiana smiled. "I do my best to." There was gratitude in her smile, and relief in her voice.

Didn't fool her for a minute, Longarm thought. *But I was right, she'll make that young fellow a good wife, maybe even give him some of her smartness.* He said aloud, "We were just having some tea when you knocked, Antonin. I guess it's cold by now, though."

"You sit, I make fresh," Tatiana said quickly. On the way to the kitchen range, she picked up the battered chair that Longarm had used as a shield and placed it against the wall. She was turning to go back and pick up the sword that had fallen beside it when Mordka Danilov came in the open door.

Danilov's face broke into a smile when he saw Longarm. "Marshal Long, *pazhalasta*. And Antonin. But you have met before, at the supper we shared here."

"Well, I didn't recall him right off," Longarm said. "But now that we've run into each other again, I sure won't forget him next time."

From over by the stove, Tatiana called, "Petra Tuscheva, how is she?"

"She is well. And her child too. A fine big boy," Mordka replied. "Marya will stay there a while yet, to help." He went to the table, frowned when he saw that his chair was missing from its usual place, and noticed the sword on the floor when he looked around to locate his chair. Then he saw the raw wood chips on the floor. "What has been happening here?" he asked bewilderedly.

Longarm spoke quickly. "Antonin mistook me for a stranger. He came running to protect Tatiana, and we scuffled a little bit. I guess we sort of messed things up."

Mordka nodded. "I see. Antonin is nervous, like all of us. We feel we have enemies on all sides, I'm afraid. I was talking of this with the Brethren who came to the Tuschevas' house to wish Petra and Sergei well."

"Maybe you won't need to feel that way much longer, Mordka," Longarm began. Danilov interrupted him.

"Can you blame us, Marshal?" he asked. "Our fences cut, our grain spoiled, our people made the targets of midnight ambushers? Even you, a government officer, have suffered a bullet. Now we have another fear, and though you have done so much for us that I hesitate to ask another favor, I have promised the Brethren that I will."

"You know I'll do anything I can, Mordka."

"Yes. We are lucky to have a friend like you." Danilov hesitated, then said, "Now has come the time when we meet in our church to pray for our harvest. Some of the Brethren fear that the ranchers may cause trouble. It would be so easy for them to do, with all of us assembled in one place. Will you attend the service that night? Our men do not want to bring their weapons into our church, but if we are attacked, we would like to feel sure there will be someone there who is not bound to our vow—someone who can fight back!"

Chapter 14

"Well, I'll come to your prayer meeting if you want me to," Longarm replied readily. "But one of the reasons I came out here today is to tell you you ought not have any more trouble with fence-cutters, or trouble of any kind, from here on out."

"That is the best news you can bring us, except the news that your wound is completely healed," Mordka replied. "I am ashamed that I have waited so long to ask how you feel."

"Oh, I'm doing fine. I've got you and your ladies to thank for that, and I sure won't forget it."

Tatiana came to the table with the freshly brewed tea just as Longarm spoke. She answered before Mordka could do so. "*Matushka* and I are happy that for you we could do this."

"Of course," Mordka agreed. He looked at Tatiana and Antonin and said, "Now, you and your *milochka* take your tea and go outside. You have talk to make to each other while the marshal and I make another kind of talk here."

When the young couple had left, Danilov asked, "Tell me now, why you think our days of trouble are over."

"It seems the ranchers were upset because things went as far as they did. They had some hands who were going way past what their bosses told 'em. Like the shootings. I don't expect you folks will have to worry anymore from now till harvest time," He frowned and added, "If the weather leaves you any wheat to harvest."

Danilov smiled. "You have said before how you worry over the weather, my friend. I tell you again, do not vex yourself about our wheat. Even if the little snow last night had been a big one, even if the sky drops heavy snow tonight, we will have a crop."

"You're so certain-sure, I'm curious to know why. All the wheat I've ever seen anyplace else couldn't live past a snowfall."

For a moment, Danilov sat silently thoughtful. Then he said, "It will do no harm to tell you, I suppose. But I will ask you to tell no one else."

"You've got my word on that," Longarm assured him.

"I would not have expected otherwise." Danilov's brows drew together. "Because you are not a farmer, to understand what I explain might not be easy. In Russia, on the steppes, the summer is short and winter returns early. There, the wheat is planted in late summer."

"Sure. Winter wheat. Even if I ain't a farmer, Mordka, I've been around wheat country enough to know the difference between winter wheat and spring wheat. And I could see right off, the first time I looked at it, that what's in your fields ain't winter wheat, or it would've been cut before I got to Junction."

"You are right, Marshal. Our wheat is spring wheat. But on the steppes in Russia, a kind of spring wheat grows too. The seeds of it came first from Turkey, in the time of our fathers. We call it *Toorciya krasnenkiey*. What you would say, is Turkey Red."

"I never heard of it, but no reason why I should."

"This is the point I make. In America, there is none except—"

Longarm couldn't hold back the exclamation. He broke into Danilov's explanation, "Except what you folks have got planted in your fields. Is that right?"

"Of course. It was our great friend Carl Schmidt who told us that he has experimented here in Kansas, on his own farm, with the Turkey Red. He has learned that the seeds of *Toorciya krasnenkiey* will germinate and mature in a single summer here, and that the early snows which so often sweep over these prairies, as they do over the Russian steppes, encourage it to mature and ripen. Such storms would kill other kinds of wheat."

"How come this Schmidt fellow doesn't go into the seed business, if he's got a start? Why'd he give the secret of this Turkey Red stuff away to you?"

"Carl is still experimenting. He will some day sell the seeds, but he has so little planted that he could not supply us. So he advised us to bring our own seeds when we emigrated."

"And you got here all ready to plant in spring and reap in fall, even if there's a little early snow-blow like we had last night." Longarm grinned. "That's why Hawkins and the other cattlemen didn't bother you when you first came here, Mordka. They saw you putting in a crop, and they figured it was spring wheat, the kind they'd seen homesteaders go bust with before. They waited for you to go bust, too."

Mordka sighed. "I suppose that is how it was. It is a sad thing, Marshal. On these prairies is so much land, surely enough for everyone. We do not try to drive the ranchers away. Why do they try to force us to go?"

"Well, they were here first," Longarm pointed out.

"But we do not take land that belongs to them, only land they have used without owning it."

"Sure. That's happened just about everyplace I've seen where a bunch of farmers have settled in cattle country. Ranchers have had free open range so long they think it's going to go on forever. It's just ornery human nature, I guess, and I don't see any way to change it."

Danilov shrugged. "It is same everywhere. In Russia, the *boyars* and the nobles hold the land, and the serfs, the common people, have none. And over everyone is the Tsar. He owns all, even the land the nobles claim as theirs, even the souls of the people he calls his own."

"I guess that's why he keeps checking up on you," Longarm suggested. "Even when you leave his country, he still claims you." He thought of Ilioana Karsovana, and the questions he'd been leading to earlier in the day, and added, "I had a little visit with those two Russians who were out to see you the other day."

"Karsovana and her servant?" Mordka's heavy eyebrows rose in surprise. "But I thought they were going to travel on without delay, when we told her we knew nothing of her brother."

"I'll tell you something. I don't think that lady's got a brother."

"Nor do I. Why do they still stay in Junction?"

"She says because she's tired. But I'd say they aim to stick around, judging by the way she duded up her room at the hotel."

"You have talked to her, then?"

"Sure. And she was just starting to ask me about the Brethren when we got interrupted." Longarm didn't specify the nature of the interruption, since he saw no need to worry Mordka.

"Inquiring about us?"

"She sure was," the lawman confirmed.

"If she is curious, why should she ask you? Let her bring her questions here, to us. We have no secrets."

"Except your wheat seed," Longarm said, half-jokingly.

"Of course!" Danilov exclaimed. "It had not occurred to me. We brought the seeds from Russia!"

"Is that against the law over there?"

"My friend," Mordka replied sadly, "in Russia the law is what the Tsar and his ministers say it will be."

"Oh, now come on, Mordka! The Tsar's a big, important man. He's got a whole country to run. He's bound to have a lot more on his mind than a handful or two of wheat seeds."

"You do not understand how life is there. In Russia, when we say 'the Tsar,' we mean the whole imperial court, not just the one man who wears the crown. Even a minor official in the Agriculture Ministry, one who has nothing more to worry about than a handful of wheat seed, could be responsible for sending after us the agents of the *Okhrana*."

His voice thoughtful, Longarm said, "You know, Mordka, the other day I didn't pay much mind to what you said about Mrs. Karsovana and her servant being spies sent from Russia. Then, after she snagged onto me and, first thing, started asking questions about the Brethren—instead of that brother she claims to be looking for—I got to thinking your idea's not as farfetched as I'd figured."

"I am right, Marshal. You will see."

"Maybe so. Only I don't see what harm they could do you, here in this country."

"Perhaps they could do no real harm at all, except to find some way to encourage Hawkins and the other cattlemen to keep harassing us. But even that would be a victory for them and defeat for the Brethren."

"Well, I'll keep an eye on them as best I can. Now I better be getting back to town. I've got a little bit of unfinished business I better tend to."

"With Ilioana Karsovana?" Mordka asked.

"No, with another friend of yours. Oren Stone."

* * *

"I'm sorry, Marshal," Mae Bonner said when she opened the vestibule door in response to Longarm's knock. "*Really* sorry this time, not just being nasty-polite, the way I was when you came here at first. But Mr. Stone's not here, and that's the truth."

"You got any idea where he is?" Longarm asked as he adjusted his hatbrim and leaned against the doorjamb.

"No," she answered, seeming a bit puzzled, then went on, "Well, I've got a general idea, but that's all. He's gone out to see the wheat farmers, but I don't know which of the homesteads he planned to stop at."

"I'll make a guess why he went, and maybe you'll tell me if I'm right. He was going to tell them he expects those options to be made good."

"That's right. He—" Mae looked over her shoulder as though she was afraid Stone might somehow overhear her— "he's been like a wild man since the night of the shooting. Drinking more than I've ever seen him do before, shouting, pacing the floor, not able to sleep, not able even—" She stopped short.

On the occasions when Longarm had seen Mae Bonner before, he'd noticed her clear high-colored complexion, her faultless skin. He noticed, now, that she was wearing both rouge and a heavy coat of powder. Looking more closely, he was sure he could see the faint outline of a dark bruise under the makeup on one cheek.

"Not that it's any of my business, but has he been taking his mad out on you?" he asked.

She seemed reluctant to answer. Finally she managed a low-voiced "Yes," and continued in a whisper that wavered between unhappiness and defiance, "But it's not any of your business, as you just said. I'm old enough to look after myself."

"I'm not aiming to butt into anything private between you and Stone, Miss Bonner, but I'm right interested in knowing how he's feeling. I'll be coming back out here to talk to him later on. If he's out in the country, he won't be back until late, I guess, so I'll wait until after supper."

"Shall I tell him you're going to come talk to him?"

"If you feel like it's your duty to tell him, go ahead. If you just happen to forget, it sure wouldn't make me mad."

"I see. Well, I won't make you any promise about that, Marshal. But you'll probably find him here if you come back when you said you're going to."

Walking back across the sidings, Longarm had to move fast. A string of empty cattle cars was arriving from the Santa Fe's mainline yards, and trainmen were spotting the cars on different sets of tracks. Workmen were going over the corral fences and loading chutes, replacing broken boards, testing the drop-gates, and generally getting things in order for the cattle shipments that were due to begin soon. It was a familiar scene to Longarm. He'd seen it repeated everywhere in cattle country, where sleepy towns awoke to sudden life during the two or three times a year when cowhands massed in large numbers rather than small groups during the arrival of gathered or trailed herds at a railhead.

On the last siding, a half-dozen boxcars were unloading the cargoes they'd brought from Wichita and Topeka, and from more distant points such as Kansas City, St. Louis, Chicago, and Denver. Wagons were lined up, waiting for the cars to be unloaded, to carry into town fresh merchandise for Stebbins's store, kegs of beer and cases of liquor for the Cattleman's and the Ace High, crates of eggs and bags of onions and potatoes, hams and slabs of bacon for the restaurant. Junction was getting ready for the fall fling of the ranch hands, most of whom would be anxious to blow off the head of steam built up during their long, dusty days on the prairie.

Longarm waited until a loaded wagon pulled away from one of the boxcars, and hailed the driver. The lift he asked for was given cheerfully, and he leaned back against the hard boards of the jouncing seat while the wagon rumbled into town. The same kind of buzzing activity that marked the railhead was being repeated in Junction, but on a smaller scale. One of the Ace High barkeeps was repainting the sign on the front of the saloon building, incongruous in his apron as he balanced on a ladder to reach the letters above the awning. Windows were being washed at the restaurant and the barbershop. The wizened night clerk of the hotel, who also did the portering chores during daytime hours, was replacing a broken board in the sidewalk in front of the door when Longarm arrived after dropping from the wagon in front of Stebbins's store.

"Hey, Marshal!" the man hailed Longarm, dropping his hammer and reaching into his pocket. "I got a note for you from that foreign lady up in Room Seven. Said I was to give it to you personal, not put it in your box."

Longarm took the slightly smudged and creased envelope the man handed him, and tore it open. The note was brief, inscribed on thick, creamy paper with an embossed, curlicued *K* at the top:

My dear Marshal Long:

I would like to make amends for ending so abruptly our visit which began so amiably. If you have no pressing matters that require your attention, please accept this invitation to call on me for a tête-à-tête this afternoon at any time after the hour of three.

Ilioana Karsovana.

"Well, now," Longarm muttered as he walked up the stairs, "I wonder what she means by a tayte-ah-tayte? Guess I better go find out, seeing as I've got nothing better to do till Stone gets back."

He stopped in his room long enough to run a comb through his wiry hair and make sure his mustache was smoothed down. As an antidote to the vodka that he expected he'd be offered, he took a quick swallow of Maryland rye. Then, with a fresh cheroot clamped between his teeth, he walked across the corridor and tapped on Madame Karsovana's door.

With a flourish that might well have been accompanied by a roll of drums, Madame Karsovana threw the door open. She wore a flowing chiffon tea gown that stopped just short of being a negligee. The gown itself was a light cream, and the sea-green lace with which it was trimmed accented the deep V to which its neckline plunged in front, below, the cleavage of her full breasts. The high collar rose in back and presented a perfect frame to emphasize the golden glints of her hair, which today she wore piled in a loose bun at the back of her head. The lace darkened the ice green of her eyes, which were widened to match the expectant smile on her full, brilliantly red lips.

"It is kind of you to respond to my invitation, after the manner in which I had to end our last chat," she greeted Longarm.

"But come, sit down. We will begin today where we left off when Gregor so foolishly interrupted us."

"Now that ought not to've upset you so, Mrs. Karsovana. Your manservant was only doing what he thought was best."

"Please. Let us put formality aside. You may call me Ilioana, and I will call you— What is your given name, Marshal?" she said, waving him to a chair and taking his hat, which she put on the bureau.

"Well . . . it's Custis, but I don't get called that very much."

"You have a familiar name, then," she guessed. "A *prosvische*, we would say in Russia."

"A lot of folks who know me pretty well call me Longarm."

Madame Karsovana frowned prettily. "Longarm. *Dlinnorroka*, it would be in my native tongue. In yours it sounds better. You will not object if I call you so?"

"Not a bit. Sounds better than my real one to me."

She was still standing at the bureau. "I have a surprise for you. Look." She held up a bottle of bonded Maryland rye, "I instructed Gregor to ask the porter if you did not keep in your room a bottle of your favorite liquor. So now you must drink this, and I will have vodka, which I don't think you enjoyed greatly."

Now that was thoughtful of you, Ilioana. I guess it's because I'm so used to that, your vodka tasted sort of strange to me."

"It is a drink to which one must become accustomed." She brought the filled glasses over, gave Longarm the glass of rye, and took her own drink to a chair across from him. "*Pei do dna*, Longarm."

After taking an appreciative sip of the rye, Longarm said, "Let's see, we were talking about your brother who's missing, the other day. I think I said—"

"No, no," she interrupted. "We had put aside my problem for the moment to talk of my fellow countrymen, who seem to be having such a struggle here."

"I guess we were, at that." Longarm suppressed the smile that tried to struggle to his lips. Ilioana Karsovana had gone a long way toward confirming Mordka Danilov's suspicions with her remark.

Ilioana leaned forward. Longarm's eyes were drawn almost

automatically to the valley between her breasts that the movement displayed, a shadowy, warm-looking crevice between soft, creamy bulges. Even with the distance between their chairs, he could catch the musky fragrance of her perfume.

"Truthfully, my friend, do you think my poor countrymen will be able to sell their crop of wheat for enough ready money to pay for the food they will need during the winter?" she asked.

"I haven't heard any of them complaining that they were about to go bust," he replied. "But I ain't talked to them about things like that. Mostly I've been trying to stop the cattlemen from cutting their fences and tromping down their wheat."

"There is bad blood between them and the ranchers who raise cattle—this I have heard," she said. "Is your federal government worried that fighting will break out between them that might spread into a revolution, like the war between your north and south states?"

Longarm succeeded in keeping himself from laughing. When he was sure no hint of amusement would creep into his voice, he said, "Why, most folks never did call that war a revolution, Ilioana. Anyhow, it was a fuss over a lot more than a few acres of wheat land that used to be used for cattle range. It takes a lot more people than are mixed up in this little argument here to start a revolution."

"But if this dispute here should spread into other places, would not your federal officials act? Is that not why you came here?"

"Not ma'am! I just came down here to keep an eye on the election that'll be coming along pretty soon, make sure everybody gets a fair shake."

A tinge of disappointment crept into her voice when she asked, "Your government would not punish those who began the fight, if it should grow larger? They would not, for example, send those of the *Bratiya* back to Russia?"

"Of course not. Most of the Brethren are U.S. citizens now, and the way our law reads, nobody can send a U.S. citizen back to any country he might've come from."

"Is it permitted for you to tell me what you have said in the reports you make to your government?" she asked.

Longarm was certain now that Mordka Danilov had been

completely correct in identifying Ilioana and her servant as Russian agents. He smiled as he told her, "Why, I don't report anything to anybody until the job I came here for's all finished. Then, when I go back to Denver, I just write down that I closed my case, most of the time."

"What will you write when you go back there from Junction?"

"I don't know yet. The case still ain't closed."

Ilioana got up and took their glasses to the bureau to refill them. When she came back, she set her glass down first, and as she handed his glass to Longarm, she leaned over him. She was standing directly in front of him, and the low, loose neck of her gown gaped open widely. Longarm saw what the plunging neckline of the dress had hinted at: twin globes of translucent cream and the edges of the pink rosettes that crowned their tips. She held her position for several seconds. When Longarm did not move, and kept his face impassive, she slowly brought her shoulders up and stood erect again.

"What will happen then, when you write that your case has been closed?" she asked. Her voice was velvet-soft; it was a tone suited to a seduction, not a question inquiring about a simple fact.

"Just like all the reports I write, it'll be tucked away in a file case in the office."

"Not sent to federal headquarters in Washington?"

Not unless somebody there asks for it." Longarm suspected that Ilioana knew a great deal more about government routines than she was ready to admit. He added, "That doesn't happen more than once in a blue moon. Why are you so interested in the way I do my work, Ilioana?"

"Perhaps because I am beginning to become interested in you, Longarm. Men who wield power have always fascinated me."

"I guess you picked out the wrong man, this time. I ain't got much more power than the left hind leg of a jackrabbit."

"You are modest, but that doesn't deceive me. I know such men when I meet them. One of my lovers—" she paused and looked at him questioningly—"Does it surprise you that I have had lovers?"

The deputy smiled, "Not especially. A good-looking woman

like you are is bound to've had a lot of men running after her. Stands to reason that some of 'em would've caught up with her. Them she wanted to let catch up, that is."

"And you? Do you find me attractive?"

"Why, sure I do. I reckon any man would."

"I am not interested in just any man." She noticed that Longarm still held his drink untouched, and moved away from him a step, to pick up her own glass from the low table that stood between their chairs. "*Pei do dna*, Longarm. We will drink to strong men, and to women who find them fascinating."

They drank, then Ilioana took Longarm's empty glass from his hand and went to refill both glasses from the bottles on the bureau. When she brought his fresh drink, she did not put it down, but handed it to him. Then, instead of going to her chair, she sat on the low serving-table. Her knees were touching his; their faces were on the same level. Longarm did not move.

Ilioana leaned toward him, and her movement sent the musky fragrance of her perfume swirling to his nostrils. She reached a hand up to cup his chin, her fingers stroking first his cheek, then brushing across his mustache, and finally, with a fingertip, she traced the outline of his lips.

"I can give a great deal of pleasure to men who fascinate me," she whispered.

When Longarm neither answered her nor moved, Ilioana's hand brushed down his chest and came to rest on his thigh. Her fingers were moving, exploring. Longarm felt himself responding, growing hard. Ilioana felt his reaction, too. She pressed more firmly with her stroking hand, and as his erection grew, enclosed it as best she could through the leg of his trousers.

Her face was close to his, and her eyes began to close. Her lips parted, her lower lip glistening moistly, curved outward. Her nostrils widened. Longarm forced himself to respond with the cold calculation of a whore. He drained his glass and stood up. Ilioana's eyes followed him, wide with perplexity and a hint of anger.

"What is wrong with you?" she asked.

"Nothing wrong, Ilioana. Not with me or you. But I just remembered, I've got to go see somebody on urgent, government business, and I've got a little bit of paperwork to do first. We'll have to put off whatever you've got in mind until some other time."

He brushed past her as she stood up. Going to the door, he made a long reach and got his hat from the bureau, then turned back to face her.

"Sorry I've got to cut our visit short. I'll knock on your door when there'll be plenty of time for us to visit."

Leaving Ilioana staring after him, Longarm went out of the room. He closed the door carefully behind him.

Chapter 15

Ilioana Karsovana was very much on Longarm's mind while he sat at supper. She'd made her intentions pretty obvious, but he still couldn't find any convincing reason for her to be in Junction. There was still a riddle in the presence of these Russian secret agents that stayed just out of his grasp, and that bothered him. Finally, when he'd drained his second cup of steaming black coffee and smoked half of his after-supper cheroot, he gave up trying to solve the puzzle for the moment and set out for the Santa Fe sidings.

Mae Bonner nodded in response to Longarm's inquiring look when she opened the door of the vestibule. "He's here now, Marshal." She led him through the entry to the parlor section of the coach.

Stone was at the table where he'd been sitting the night Prud Simmons was killed. There was no gold on the table this time. Instead, papers were spread over its surface.

"Who was—" he began, before he saw Longarm. Then he snapped, "Damn it, Mae! I told you I didn't want to be bothered with anything but these—this work, tonight!"

"I'm sorry, Mr. Stone, but Marshal Long insisted," she said, somewhat tartly.

"Don't blame the girl, Stone," Longarm said. He guessed by Stone's remark that Mae hadn't told the broker he'd been there in the early part of the day. He went on, "You saw the other night that if I want to come in, it'll take more than a woman to stop me."

"I suppose." Stone sounded resigned. "All right, Long." He began turning the papers over to hide their faces. "You're here, and I suppose you've got bad news for me. It seems you generally do." He looked at Mae. "I won't need you for awhile. Go rest or something."

"Mind if I sit down?" Longarm asked as Mae left.

"Go ahead." Stone indicated the chair across from him.

Longarm looked at the chair. It was the same one Prud had been using. He glanced at the wall above the table. The paneling had been cleaned and polished, and he wondered whether Mae Bonner had been forced to clear away the unpleasant mess that had splattered the wall when the shotgun pellets tore through the outlaw's chest. He noticed, too, that the shotgun was back in its rack.

"Lucky I ain't superstitious," he said to Stone as he sat down. "Some folks believe it brings bad luck to sit in the last chair a man was sitting in before he died."

Stone's lips tightened, but he made no direct reply. Instead he said impatiently, "If you've got business with me, get down to it. I've got enough work to keep me occupied until midnight."

"My business won't take that long." Longarm lit a fresh cigar. "I told you I'd come to see you after I'd made up my mind what to do about you killing Prud." He spoke through a veil of blue tobacco smoke. "Well, I've done some studying about it. Seeing as Prud was an outlaw and a fugitive, and already had his gun out throwing down on me, I'm halfway of a mind to let you get off light."

"I'd get off light, no matter which way you'd made your mind up to go. I've done a little investigating, Long. There's no jury in these parts that'd find me guilty of anything but helping you subdue a dangerous man who was trying to kill an officer to avoid being arrested."

"Maybe so and maybe not. We both know you had me in mind when you grabbed that shotgun."

"You don't know what I had in mind. Even if you did, you'd never be able to prove it."

"I've proved less likely things," Longarm said levelly. "But that business with Prud was just a sideline to the case I'm here to handle."

"I know that. So is the feud between the cattlemen and the wheat farmers. You came down here to keep an eye on the election. And here you are, mixed up in a lot of local matters over which you have absolutely no jurisdiction."

Longarm smiled. "Sounds to me like you been talking to Sheriff Grover and Clem Hawkins."

"Of course I have. It's just common sense to find out my real position from people who don't have any personal interest."

"I wouldn't exactly say Hawkins and Grover fall into that class."

"I'd take Clem Hawkins's word before I would a lot of men's." Stone's voice was sharpening with impatience again.

Longarm decided it was time to get down to cases. "I'll lay my cards out, Stone."

"Good. It's about time."

Unperturbed, Longarm went on as though he hadn't been interrupted. "I can file a murder charge against you. I can file another charge against you as an accessory to attempted murder."

"Wait a minute," Stone said, holding up a hand, palm forward. "You haven't mentioned that one before."

The marshal crossed his long legs and leaned back. "Because I wasn't ready to. But I've got enough now to make it stand up."

"On what basis? Give me some facts, Long."

"Sure," Longarm agreed amiably. "Fact one: you were paying Prud Simmons for cutting fences and getting up bunches of night-riders to do the same thing for a while. I won't have any trouble proving that." He hoped Stone would be too shaken up by the new charges to question the evidence. "Fact two: there were men wounded by Prud and his bunch, and part of what you paid Prud went to the men riding with him. That's two cases of attempted murder, Stone. And I was the one who was supposed to be killed in one of them, so I've got a real personal interest in it."

Although Stone tried to hide his shock, Longarm could see in his eyes that the wheat broker was shaken. He thought it was time to ease up on the pressure and let Stone dangle a bit more loosely. He leaned back, saying nothing.

"I think I want a drink," Stone said. He went to the liquor cabinet and poured whiskey into a glass, then spurted soda in from a siphon. Turning to Longarm, he said, "I've got plenty of that special rye that caught your fancy. Would you like some?"

"No. I think I'll pass tonight."

Stone brought his own drink, a bottle of the rye, and a glass back to the table. He put the bottle and glass in front of Longarm, saying, "In case you change your mind."

Sitting down, Stone waited until he'd had two big gulps from his glass before looking at Longarm. He asked, "Well?"

"Well, what?" Longarm asked innocently.

"What's my alternative? You say you can bring these charges of murder and attempted murder to court, if you want to. Obviously you're not anxious to do that, or you wouldn't be here talking to me right now."

"I might not be anxious, but don't think I'm holding back, either, Stone. I just ain't made up my mind."

Stone's eyes lit up hopefully. "In other words, you're open to persuasion."

"That's not what I said."

"Long, over the years I've learned a few valuable lessons. One of the most important is not to listen to what a man says, but to find out what he means by what he says."

"If that's the way you read things, what do you think I mean?"

"That you've got your hand out, wanting to dip it into my pocket."

Longarm let the insult pass without comment. He wanted to see how anxious Stone was, or how worried— just how far he was prepared to go.

"Well, now," the broker said briskly. "You don't deny it, I see. But somehow I don't think you're a man who's too interested in money." Stone frowned in concentration for a moment, then pointed to the bottle of rye, which Longarm hadn't touched. "That whiskey seemed to strike your fancy. Now, I know what you're paid as a deputy marshal, and to be blunt as hell, you can't afford to buy it."

"You're right about that; I can't. And I've got sense enough to know it."

"What would you say to a case a month for the rest of your life? Delivered free, of course."

Longarm sat silently for long enough to give Stone the idea that he was thinking about the offer. Then he shook his head.

"You judged me wrong when you figured you could buy me for a few bottles of whiskey, Stone. Even a whiskey as good as that one. You were right about something else, though. I ain't for sale for cash, either."

"Then what the hell kind of bribe do you expect me to offer you?" Stone said. He was obviously losing what little patience he possessed.

"I'm not interested in any kind of bribe. I'm not for sale for money, marbles, or chalk."

"What do you want, then?"

Longarm took a long drag on his cheroot, blew out a long stream of smoke, and smiled benignly. "I think a little bit of a bonfire might satisfy me."

"Meaning what?"

Longarm pointed at the stack of papers on the table between them. "They look like they'd make a real pretty blaze in that little stove you've got over there in the corner. Nights are getting a mite chilly."

"You go to hell, Long! Those options represent a lot of work as well as a lot of money. I'm not going to see either one go up in smoke!"

"Not even if three warrants went up with 'em?"

"What good would it do to burn a warrant that's been made a court record by—" Stone stopped, his eyes narrowed. "You're trying to bluff me, Long. There hasn't been time for you to get a warrant issued by any federal judge."

"You don't know as much as you think you do about federal warrants. Any deputy U.S. marshal can issue a field warrant, just like a judge can issue a bench warrant, without it being recorded until it's served."

"I've never heard of a procedure like that. I still think you're bluffing."

Longarm's eyes grew cold, taking on the dangerous gunmetal dark shine that had been the last color seen on earth by several imprudent gunmen. "Call me, then. If I take you to jail in Junction with any one of these three warrants I've got in my pocket, Sheriff Grover'd have no choice but to hold you until a federal judge validates them." He waited for Stone to reply, and when the broker said nothing, added, "And don't count on bail. Neither Clem Hawkins nor anybody else can post bail while you're being held on a deputy's field warrant. It takes a federal judge to set bail."

Stone said soberly, "If that's true, you could delay sending those warrants in as long as you wanted to. And I'd be in jail until you had them validated."

"You've got it sized up right," the marshal affirmed evenly.

"It sounds illegal to me."

"If you still think I'm bluffing, get your hat. We'll just go to the jail and try it out."

"Now wait a minute, Long. I haven't turned down your trade yet."

"So I noticed. Well, it's up to you, Stone. Just don't put off making up your mind till my patience runs out. But I better say right now, it's wearing pretty thin."

"I could charge you with blackmail, you know," Stone said.

"Yes, I guess you could. It wouldn't be the first time a man getting arrested lodged a charge like that. I misdoubt it'd be the last time, either. But it wouldn't wash in court, and you know it."

"No," Stone agreed reluctantly, "I suppose it wouldn't." Then he added hurriedly, "But I don't think this trumped-up case you've got against me would, either."

"Maybe you'd like to try it out," Longarm offered. "You'd only be in jail maybe a year or two while the case worked through the court hearings."

"Damn you, Long, you've got me coming and going!" Stone exclaimed bitterly. He thought for a moment. There's a time when anybody who plays the market knows he's forced to cut his losses. All right. Take the goddamned options and burn them!"

"I thought you'd come around to seeing it my way." Longarm was careful to keep the triumph out of his voice. "And you can watch the warrants burn along with 'em."

Longarm swept the papers off the table while Stone watched in grim silence. The small, round railroad car stove wouldn't accept them all at the same time. He crammed its cylindrical belly full, and touched a match to the mass of papers, then closed the door. The flames danced up and reddened the isinglass framed in decorative cast-iron curlicues at the top of the door. When the flames died down, Longarm stuffed the remaining options into the stove, and took out of his pocket the three warrants that he'd filled out in his hotel room after he'd left Il-ioana Karsovana. The flames danced a brief encore, and the isinglass went dark. Longarm stood up, and stretched hugely.

"I guess that's all the business you and I have got to deal with," he told Stone. "You don't owe me a thing; I don't owe you. That being the case, I'll take a swallow of that rye now, if it's all the same to you."

"No, by God, it's not all the same to me!" Stone snarled. He picked up the almost-full bottle of special rye and threw it across the car. The bottle shattered on the paneling with a crash, and the scent of rye whiskey spread through the car.

Mae Bonner ran in through the door that led to the staterooms. "What on earth—?" She sniffed. "Somebody spilled whiskey."

"Will you get back to wherever you came from, Mae? And keep your stupid damn comments to yourself!" Stone's voice was bitter.

Longarm saw that it was time for him to go. He said, "I'll let you two quarrel in private. Glad we could finish our business so fast, Stone. Now I'll bid you goodnight."

Later, after two or three drinks of regular bottled rye at the Cattleman's, he tried to convince himself that it was all for the best that Stone had broken the bottle.

A few more drinks of that special stuff, old son, his thoughts ran, *and you'd purely lose your taste for this kind. And this kind is about all you'll ever be able to drink regular.*

Pushing through the batwings when he left the saloon shortly before midnight, Longarm's first thought was that it was Madame Karsovana who called his name from the shadows on the dark side of the saloon. He stopped, trying to think up an apology for having left her so abruptly, and his relief was mingled with surprise when he saw that it was Mae Bonner who'd called to him.

"Marshal Long! Please, I need to talk to you."

"Why, sure." He held out his arm. "We'll just talk while we go up the street. Nobody's around to hear us, or if somebody is, he'll be too drunk to pay any attention to what we say."

"Don't make a joke of it, Marshal, please. I think I'm in terrible trouble."

Longarm saw that the girl was trembling. He became serious at once. "What kind of trouble?"

"I just killed Oren."

"I won't ask you are you joshing; I can see you ain't. Where is he?"

"I left him in the railroad car. I couldn't stay there a minute with his—his body."

"Maybe you better tell me what happened," he suggested.

"Well—" Mae began, then stopped abruptly, unable to say anything more.

"You and him get into a fight of some kind?" Longarm prompted her. "You were beginning to fuss when I left. I guess it got worse."

"A lot worse. Oren kept drinking, and the more he drank, the meaner he got. He—" Mae gulped and went on, speaking more coherently, "I suppose you've guessed that, well, that Oren wasn't just my boss, that I was—"

"You were his lady friend, is that what you're trying to say?"

"Yes. It just seemed to happen, after I'd been working for him for two or three months. That was about a year ago. For a while everything was all right, then he began to snap at me, curse at me sometimes. You heard him tonight. And a few nights ago, he—" Mae stopped short again.

Longarm supplied the words for her. "He beat you up. I saw the bruise on your face, remember?"

"Yes. It wasn't the first time he'd hit me lately, but it was the worst. Then, after you left tonight, he really beat me."

Longarm looked at her closely, but the street was too dark for him to see anything more than a light-hued blur where her face was.

Mae went on hesitantly, "I told him I wasn't going to stay in the parlor with him any longer, and went to my room. He came in after I'd gone to sleep. He wanted to—well, he started to get in bed with me, after I'd refused to go back to his room with him. I got away from him and he chased me. I saw this big skillet when I went through the galley, and picked it up and hit him on the head with it as hard as I could."

"And then what?" Longarm asked, when she stopped talking.

"Then he fell down. I couldn't stay there. I dressed and came to town. You were the only one I could think of who'd help me. I asked at the hotel, but you hadn't come in, so I looked in the saloons. When I saw you, I had to wait until you came out, of course."

"I see. Well now, I'll tell you what. Supposing I take you up to my room, and you lay down and rest while I go out and see what it looks like at the railroad car. We'll talk about what to do when I come back."

"If you're sure it's all right—"

"It's all right. Now come along."

An hour later, when Longarm let himself into his room, Mae
was lying fully clothed on his bed in the deep sleep that follows
physical and emotional exhaustion. The lamp on the bureau was
still burning. Longarm shook her gently by the shoulder.

"What—?" She shuddered as memory flooded back. "Oh,
God! Tell me, however bad it is, Marshal."

"It ain't bad. Stone's as alive as you and me. Not as wide
awake, though. I'd say he's more drunk than hurt, but he's got
a goose egg-sized bump on his head that won't go away for a
while."

"I didn't, kill him, then? Oh, thank God! Did he say anything?"

"He didn't even wake up. I just left everything the way it
was, and came on back. I figured he'll sort things out when he
comes to."

Mae sighed. "Well, I certainly feel better, even if I am out
of a job and don't know what I'll do in a town like Junction,"

"You wouldn't want to stay here. There wouldn't be any of
the kind of work a smart girl like you does."

"I don't know just how smart I am," she said with a twisted
smile. "I don't have a dime, and the only clothes I came away
with are the ones Í have on."

"Didn't Stone pay you?"

"Oh, sure. In a way. When we settled into our—well, our
personal arrangement, he said he'd keep track of my wages. I
just drew money for the expenses of the car—you know, food,
liquor, things like that, out of the cash he kept on hand."

"How much do you figure he owes you in back salary?"

Mae shrugged. "I don't know. It's—well, he stopped paying
me about seven months ago."

"Paid you pretty well, did he?"

"More than most male stenographers make. Fifteen dollars a
week. And of course I didn't have any living expenses as long
as—well, until tonight."

"That'd mount up to a pretty good sum. Let's see . . ."

Before Longarm could multiply in his head, Mae gave him

the answer. "Seven months at fifteen dollars a week would be four hundred and fifty dollars, Marshal."

Longarm reached into the deep side pocket of his coat and produced a handful of paper-wrapped coin rolls. Mae leaped off the bed and came up to him, her mouth agape.

"I figured five hundred," Longarm said. "That's what I've got here, five rolls of gold eagles. Call the extra fifty a bonus, or to pay for the clothes you left behind." He handed Mae the rolled coins. "Now you won't have to go back to Stone for your back pay."

"You took this money out of his safe!" she gasped. "Isn't that stealing?"

"Not as long as it was money he owed you. I wrote him out a receipt and put it in the safe. Anyhow, I didn't have to open the safe. He'd forgotten to close it up."

"Well—" Mae looked at the money. "You don't know what this means to me, Marshal. I just don't know how I can thank you!"

"There's one way I can think of without a bit of trouble."

Mae looked at him for a long moment, her mouth slowly turning down at the corners. Then, with a shrug, she said, "I don't suppose, it matters much whether it's you or Oren Stone." Her hand went to the collar of her dress and she began to undo the buttons.

Longarm took Mae's wrist and pulled her hand away from the button placket. "Sex ain't what I was getting at. Not that I don't enjoy it, but I never did expect a woman to pay me in bed for anything I did to help her."

"Oh," Mae sighed. "After Oren Stone, I guess I've got a pretty low opinion of men. Go on, Marshal. Tell me what I can do for you."

"You've been with Stone about a year. You must've heard a lot of his business talks, and I guess you wrote letters for him too."

"Of course. That's what he hired me for. The personal part didn't start for a while. But I told you that. And even after it did, he didn't let me off any of the work I was supposed to do."

"A man like him wouldn't. Well, what I want you to do, Mae, is to tell me everything you know about why a big important broker like Stone was so interested in this little jerkwater place where there's not enough wheat grown to make a bit of difference to the price-rigging that goes on among the speculators in Chicago."

"You mean you don't know?"

"If I knew, I wouldn't be asking you."

"Of course you wouldn't. Oren and the few wheat pit operators who were in on Stone's deal have kept it a pretty tight secret. And those poor rubes around Junction, the Brethren, or whatever they call themselves, they don't know either, I guess."

"But you do?"

"Certainly," she replied. "Well. Let's sit down, Marshal. It's something of a long story."

Longarm sat in the chair by the bureau, within easy reach of the rye bottle, and lighted a cheroot. Mae looked around for another chair, didn't find one, and sat down on the side of the bed.

"I didn't know any more than any other city girl about wheat, when I started to work for Oren," she began. "Do you know how many kinds of wheat there are, Marshal?"

"Sure, spring wheat and winter wheat."

"That's not what I mean. I mean varieties." When Longarm shook his head, Mae went on, "I'm not sure I remember the names of all of them. Some I do, like Calcutta and Fife and Vilmorin and Lund, but there are others besides those."

"Turkey Red?" Longarm suggested.

"You do know!" she exclaimed. "What kind of game are you playing with me, Marshal?"

"It's not a game, I guarantee you, Mae. It just happens I know about Turkey Red wheat because the Brethren told me. But about all I know is the name, and that it'll grow in the kind of short summers they have in these parts."

"Not only in these parts," Mae said. "It'll mature in Nebraska, Dakota Territory, Montana, Wyoming Territory, and Utah Territory—just about anywhere in the entire West. That's why it's so important to the speculators who operate on the Grain Exchange, and to the cattlemen. Except Turkey Red, there's no other variety of wheat anybody knows about that will make a crop where wheat's never been grown before."

Longarm frowned. "I still don't see what makes it so special."

"Think about it, Marshal. The West's mostly open cattle range, and the cattlemen want to keep it that way. Under the

Homestead Act, any farmer tired of scratching out a living in the East can plant Turkey Red on his quarter-section, and make a living. What's that going to do to the cattle range, when the word spreads that there's a wheat that will do that?"

Slowly, Longarm nodded. "Sure. All those people scratching out a living, from little hard-scrabble farms, twenty or thirty acres, are going to want to get into wheat farming. If enough of them move West, the cattle range is going to be fenced in after awhile, just like it is now around Junction."

"Not only that," Mae said. "The speculators can make a lot of money in the wheat pit now because crops aren't dependable from one year to the next. Bad weather sends wheat prices up. Good weather brings them down. They know that if Turkey Red wheat makes it possible for thousands and thousands more acres of land to be planted in wheat, those price fluctuations are going to even out. Maybe if enough wheat's planted in places where it can't be grown now, there might not be any more wild price changes overnight."

"So Stone found out about the Turkey Red, and set out to— what do they call it when somebody buys up all of everything?"

"Corner the market. Yes. Stone and a few of his cronies set out to corner the market in Turkey Red wheat. And this is the only place it's grown, except for one little farm run by a German fellow named Schmidt, up near Fort Leavenworth. And Schmidt won't sell any of his crop."

Longarm nodded. "It all begins to make sense now. Including why Clem Hawkins and Stone were working together. Neither one of 'em wanted the Turkey Red seed to get out and be spread around."

"That's right. These nesters here don't know what a gold mine they're sitting on. Oren and Hawkins didn't want them to find out."

"Well, I feel better, now that I know." He didn't mention that the Brethren also knew.

"I feel better too," Mae said. "Like I've gotten back at Oren at least a little bit for what he did to me. Of course, I don't have any idea where I'll go, or how I'll get there."

"I'll see that you get out of here without any trouble," Longarm promised. "I can fix it up for you to go out on one of the cattle trains that'll be starting to roll to Dodge in a few days.

From there, you can go on to just about anyplace you want to.
Of course, you'll have to ride the caboose, instead of that fancy
private car you came here in, but I don't reckon you'll mind
that."

"I certainly won't." Mae hesitated. "Can I ask another favor
of you now, Marshal?"

"Ask ahead."

"I'm as nervous right now as a cat with new kittens. I'll get
a room here in the hotel tomorrow, but—do you mind if I stay
with you tonight? Not—well, you know what I mean, just stay
for company? I can sleep on the floor or in the chair. I don't want
to take your bed away from you."

"You're welcome to the bed," Longarm told her. "My bed-
roll's over in the corner there, I'll just spread it for myself.
Wouldn't be the first time I've used it on a floor, it won't bother
me a bit."

"If you're sure . . ."

"I'm sure."

Sometime during the night, Longarm woke up. The room re-
verberated with a noise like a bunch of Comanches on the warpath. He wondered if some of Stone's irritation with Mae might
not have been caused by the girl's snoring. Pulling the blanket
up over his ears, Longarm rolled over and went back to sleep.

Chapter 16

Sitting on the roan in the narrow alleyway between two of the Santa Fe's shipping-out corrals, Longarm watched the Lazy Y hands roust the last dozen or so bawling steers into the loading chute. Across the way, on the other side of the corral, the cattle broker who had bid high on the herd was settling up with Charlie Bell, the Lazy Y's owner. The snow was beginning to fall more thickly now, and the wind from the North Pole whistled in a higher pitch than it had, through the slat fences of the corrals.

Longarm had been there since the first of the Lazy Y's market herd had started trickling in, just before noon. His feet were cold, and his hands, exposed to the freezing air, were colder. Gloves were out of the question in a job like the one he'd assigned himself. There wasn't any way of knowing when—or even whether—he'd see what he was looking for, or recognize it if he saw it.

What he was looking for, of course, were the other three or four men who'd taken part in that night-riding spree Prud Simmons had organized. Since Prud's death, there'd been no more night-riders out harassing the homesteaders, but the ones who had taken part in the fracas in which he'd been shot were probably still among the hands on the ranches dotting the prairie around Junction.

Chances were, Longarm had concluded after studying things out, that those men were all cut from pretty much the same cloth Prud had been.

Some of them might, like Prud, be fugitives with wanted circulars out on them, and Longarm had put in a lot of time at Sheriff Grover's office studying the fliers that had come in from all over the country. Even with the descriptions he'd read, added to those he carried in his memory from fliers he'd looked at in the office in Denver, he wasn't sure he'd recognize any of the wanted men if he saw them. A lot of the descriptions were pretty sketchy. On the other hand, there hadn't been any certainty that he wouldn't spot a bad apple or two among the temporary hands. If he was going to do anything at all, though, he thought he'd better do it while the crews from the ranches were all in Junction for the shipping-out. Once the cattle had been loaded, their jobs with the ranches would be finished, and they'd scatter.

He'd weighed the chances and decided it would be time well-spent. He had little to do now before election day. Oren Stone's private car had been coupled to an engine and was gone. Mae Bonner had left a day before Stone, riding the caboose behind another of the work engines assigned to the tedious job of car-spotting. After his abrupt departure from Ilioana Karsovana's room, she'd showed an icy face to Longarm on the three or four occasions when they'd met on the street or in the restaurant. In fact, he hadn't seen the Russian woman for the last couple of days, or her coachman, either.

Until today, Longarm's hours spent at the corrals hadn't been bad. The weather had been fine, a prairie autumn, never hot enough to raise a sweat, never cold enough to bring up goose bumps. That had changed about midnight, though. He'd felt the cold seeping into his hotel room and had burrowed deeper under the cover. When he looked out of his room's single narrow window a little after dawn, a few snowflakes had begun to drift down, but so far the snow had fallen in fits and starts, not enough to hamper work at the corrals.

Brushing off a few flakes that a vagrant gust of wind tossed under his hat brim, Longarm wondered how it was out on the prairie, whether it had gotten bad enough to delay the market herds still on the way to the railhead. From the saloon gossip he'd picked up last night, the three biggest herds were still due. They were those from Clem Hawkins's C Bar H, from Bill Ta-tum's Double Z, and from the Evans family's Panther Tail. So far, the herds had arrived at pretty well-spaced intervals, on the schedule the ranchers had worked out between themselves. They'd gotten to the shipping corrals from a half-day to a day apart, depending on the number of steers in each herd. The schedule had been planned to avoid the jam-up that would result if a new herd arrived before the last one had been loaded and shipped out, so there would always be empty corrals.

Longarm didn't really mind the days he'd put in around the corrals, watching and occasionally swapping a few words with the hands. His evenings had been divided between the Cattleman's and the Ace High, having a drink or two, sauntering with an idle look around the poker tables. That idle look had concealed his keen inspection of faces and mannerisms as he watched for the telltale signals that men with guilty consciences almost always give off.

At least he hadn't minded the days until the snow had set in. Now about all he could think of was seeing the last of the steers chuted into the waiting cattle cars and getting back to town. The only thing that would warm him up was a long session in one of the big round wood-stave bathtubs in the room back of the barbershop, soaking out the cold in steaming hot water.

What I'd be smart to do, he thought, *is to get out of here right now and make tracks to the barbershop before this Lazy Y bunch finishes and hits town. If I wait, there'll be so many ahead of me that I won't get warm before suppertime.*

Since he couldn't think of a reason to remain at the corrals any longer, he wheeled the roan about and headed toward Junction.

Relaxed and warm once more after his bath, Longarm crossed to the restaurant for an early supper. Ilioana Karsovana was sitting alone at a table against the wall. When she saw Longarm come in, she nodded, and when he acknowledged her greeting with a half-bow, she motioned for him to join her. He hung his hat on the row of pegs by the door and went to her table.

"Would you take pity on my solitude, Longarm, and join me?" Ilioana asked. "Gregor usually serves my meals in my room, but he is away on an errand, and I have to resign myself to eating here." She indicated her half-empty plate. "A dreadful meal."

"Well, it ain't the best cooking in the world," Longarm agreed, "but it keeps you going." He signaled the waiter and nodded when the man looked his way. He'd eaten there so often since his arrival in Junction that he no longer needed to order his unvarying supper of steak and potatoes. He said to her, "It's nice of you to ask me to sit with you. I wasn't sure you'd offer me the time of day again, after I left you in such a rush the other evening."

"It was not a nice thing for you to do," she replied coyly. "At first I was angry, then I thought, you are conducting an important investigation, your duty must come first."

"Glad you understood."

"And since then," Ilioana went on, "I have seen you hardly at all. Always, when we pass on the street, you seem to be in a hurry."

"Well, I have been a little busy," he admitted. Then, to change the subject, he said, "I'm sort of surprised you're still in Junction."

"I have dreaded beginning to travel again. It has been so very relaxing, my stay here. But it may end soon, I'm afraid."

"Something to do with the errand you said your servant was off tending to?"

"Yes. A rumor, nothing more, that may lead to my brother. I had him go to learn if there was any substance in it. If there is, I will leave as soon as he returns." The waiter brought Longarm's food and she waited until he'd put the platter of steak on the table before saying, "But your work is so much more important than mine. I hope it is going well?"

"Oh, I'm reasonably satisfied. Things are beginning to shape up."

To avoid being questioned about details, Longarm quickly took a bite of steak. He supposed Ilioana took the hint, for she sat quietly while he ate. Once or twice she started to say something, but changed her mind. When Longarm had finished eating and was sipping his second cup of coffee, she returned to her questioning.

"Do my countrymen's crops prosper?"

"I guess they do," he answered. "To tell you the truth, Ilioana, I ain't had enough time to go out and visit the Brethren since the last time I saw you."

"A visit which was much too short. I bought a bottle of your favorite whiskey to please you, and you had only one or two small drinks from it. Was it so bad, the whiskey?" she asked, pouting slightly.

"No, no, it was fine Maryland rye," he answered hastily. "And I'm real sorry I didn't have time to stay longer."

She looked around at the small, plainly furnished restaurant and said thoughtfully, "Your country has much to learn from ours, my friend. I would have liked an aperitif before dining, and wine with dinner. Now I think a cordial would be nice. All those we would have in Europe, and perhaps music as well."

"Oh, you'll find cafés like that in big cities. They just ain't up-to-date in little towns like Junction."

"So I've found. But would not you like an after-dinner drink?"

"Sure, but I can step across to one of the saloons for one."

"Which I cannot do. Another barbaric custom, to frown on women entering establishments where liquor is served. But if I cannot join you in a saloon, will you join me in my room for the after-dinner drink you have said you would enjoy?"

"Well . . ." Longarm felt trapped. He hadn't seen the question coming from around the curve. He thought quickly. It was early in the evening for him to take his regular look around the saloon; the time for that would be later, in an hour or two. By seven or eight o'clock, both saloons would be a lot more crowded. And the rye Ilioana had served him the other day was a lot better than any he'd get at the Cattleman's or the Ace High. He said, "Well now, I guess that'd be right pleasant."

Snow was falling more thickly now, and Ilioana held on to his arm as they crossed the street. "Do you like the snow?" she asked.

"Not much. Reckon I've been out in it too many times when there wasn't any shelter."

"Ah, I love snow!" she sighed. "It wraps me up in a little private world, it makes me feel free."

Going up the stairs at the hotel, she kept her hand resting on his arm, and when they reached the top of the stairway, she said, "Please allow me a few moments before you tap at my door. I would like to change into something more comfortable."

Longarm figured her request meant she wanted to use her chamber pot. He said, "Sure. I'll stop off in my room and drop off my hat and pick up some cigars."

Ilioana had really meant what she'd said about changing, he discovered a few minutes later, when she opened her door in response to his knock. She'd put on a negligee of black chiffon, which, as she moved, billowed to conceal or clung to reveal the voluptuous curves of her body.

Tonight, the soft golden light of a single lamp, turned low, gave the room a different look, though the embellishments that had been added to it by the Russian woman hadn't changed. The Oriental rug, the bed strewn with furs and satin pillows, the brocade-draped chairs, had a theatrical look. Longarm was reminded of stage settings he'd seen at Tabor's Grand Opera House in Denver. He looked at Ilioana, her lips touched with rouge, her face carefully powdered, and thought it was a room that just suited her.

She went to the bureau, the filmy black fabric of her negligee pressing against the curves of her breasts and hips as she walked to the bureau and came back carrying the tray that held the vodka decanter, the bottle of rye, and glasses. She put them on the low table between the two chairs, and poured their drinks.

"*Pei do dna!*" she smiled, offering the toast Longarm remembered.

"Sure. Bottoms up!" he replied, tilting his glass. He put the glass on the tray and Ilioana leaned forward to refill it.

"Now you can tell me what you have been doing that has kept you so busy," she said.

"There ain't all that much to tell," he said evasively. "Besides, like I told you in the restaurant, I've been doing other things that've kept me from going out to see how the Brethren are getting along."

"I am concerned about them," Ilioana said with a little worried frown. "If their wheat crop fails, and they have no money, they would be forced to return to Russia, would they not?"

"Now that's something I don't know. I never heard any talk about them wanting to go back there."

"But it would be the best thing for them to do, don't you agree, Longarm?" she pressed. "To go back to their homeland?"

"I guess you'd have to ask them that."

Ilioana went on as though he hadn't spoken. "Should they go home to Russia, they would need money. And friends in the government. I could see that they had both."

"That's a right kind thought, Ilioana, wanting to smooth their way back to Russia for them." He suppressed a chuckle at the blatant transparency of her statement.

"It would be no trouble for me," she said. "I am almost at the end of my search for my brother. Perhaps I would even go back home with them to be sure they reached their native villages."

"Why don't you go see Mordka Danilov, and tell him that?" Longarm suggested. "Seems to me he'd be the one to talk to."

Ilioana shook her head. "No. The Brethren are peasants, and I am of the aristocracy. In Russia, peasants do not trust aristocrats." She looked at him questioningly. "Would you do me a great favor?"

"Sure, if I can."

"Be my messenger to my countrymen. Tell them of my interest in their well-being, convince them that I will help them."

Longarm whistled softly. "That's a pretty big order. What makes you think they'd listen to me?"

"They trust you. And so do I." Ilioana stood up and came to his side. "It would make me very happy if you would do this for me. And I always respond to men who make me happy. I try to make them happy too." She bent over Longarm and lifted his chin with a soft, warm hand. "Men say I have a great talent for pleasing them. You are a man I would enjoy pleasing, Longarm."

Before Longarm could move, her lips were on his. The tip of her tongue traced his mouth from corner to corner before she thrust it insistently between his lips and he opened his mouth to let their tongues meet. Ilioana's arm went across his neck to hold him in an embrace. Her free hand slid across his chest and reached his groin. Through the cloth of his trousers, Longarm felt her fingers exploring him. Her musky perfume filled his nostrils.

Longarm was not aroused at first. Ilioana's headlong approach took him by surprise; he'd expected it to come much later. In a detached way, he lifted his hands to cup her breasts. The film of chiffon lent an unexpected feeling of sensuality to the warm globes that filled his hands. He stroked them with his callused fingers and felt her nipples grow hard under the caress. Her mouth twisted against his, and her tongue darted wildly around his mouth. Her fingers were busy with the buttons of his trousers. Her hand slipped inside the opening and he felt cool air touch him as she freed his erection. Her hand closed around it convulsively and the pressure brought him up full.

Ilioana gasped as her fingers fondled and measured. She twisted her head to break their kiss. "Ah!" she' gasped. I will find it very enjoyable indeed to please you, Longarm. *Chto rogovoey!* Do not wait! Come into me quickly!

She raised the flowing skirt of her negligee, giving Longarm a glimpse of plump, tapering thighs as she straddled him on the chair. Longarm leaned back, stretched his legs straight, and let her lower her hips to engulf him in her hot, wet, quivering depth. He slid the negligee off her soft, smoothly rounded shoulders, and pulled it down to free her breasts. He buried his face between them, pulling their rosettes against his rough cheeks.

Ilioana began to rock. Longarm felt moisture spring out in the valley between her breasts as she writhed and swayed against him. He let go of her breasts and slid his hands down her sides, bunching the fabric of her negligee between their bodies as he grasped her bobbing hips and pulled himself deeper into her. In her excitement, Ilioana reverted to her native tongue.

"Da!" she sobbed. *"Salsychete kobmna! Toroplovsti!"*

Longarm judged that Ilioana was getting near the end of her ride as her head fell back and he felt her sides begin to quiver under his thumbs. He tried to help her by lifting his hips, but her weight pinned him down. Her breasts were heaving now as she struggled to push herself onto him yet farther, and the rocking of her hips speeded up. The muscles of her belly tightened as she writhed in a final effort. Her scarlet lips were drawn tautly over gleaming white teeth, her eyes turned upward. Her blond hair had fallen loose and streamed down her back. She shook convulsively and whimpered in small, sharp cries, torn from deep in her throat. Then she suddenly went limp. Her body lurched forward and she became a dead weight on Longarm's chest, her head lolling on his shoulder.

He held her there until she began to stir. She sighed, lifted her arms, pushed her hands against his chest, and levered her body erect. Only then did she realize that she was still impaled, that he was still hard within her.

Surprise showed in her widened eyes. They were a darker green than he had seen them before. She asked, "You did not go with me?"

Longarm shook his head. "Not yet. Next time I will."

Clumsily, Ilioana lifted herself free. She stood up, her breasts still upthrust, pink now instead of white, her puckered rosettes almost red. Her negligee was draped in folds around her waist; her hips kept it from sliding to the floor. She stared down at him and shook her head wonderingly. "I couldn't wait. I thought only of myself and failed to please you."

"You pleased me enough. Don't worry about it." Longarm stood up beside her. He removed his coat and draped it across the back of the chair. He turned his back to Ilioana as he took off his vest, and while his back was turned, he transferred his watch to the pocket in which his derringer nestled, attached to the watch chain. He wasn't shy about many things, but he hated to expose his ace in the hole. Unbuckling his gunbelt, he went to the bed and hung the belt on the headboard. Turning, he saw Ilioana's puzzled look. "Just in case that servant of yours gets back. He's too nervous with a pistol for me to trust him."

"Gregor is far away. He won't trouble us." Ilioana pulled the negligee up over her shoulders and came to Longarm. She began to unbutton his shirt. "Tonight, I am my own woman!"

He thought the remark odd, but let it pass, as he sat down on the bed and started to work his boots off. Ilioana added her tugging hands to his until both boots were off. He stood up, and Ilioana shook her head sadly. Longarm looked down. His erection had vanished while they'd been distracted by the boots. She looked at him, a question in her eyes.

"I told you not to worry," he reminded her.

Longarm stripped off his longjohns and jeans in one quick, lithe move. Naked, he stepped up to Ilioana. She slid her negligee off her shoulders and let the flimsy chiffon slide to the floor. Almost before it had bared her breasts, she was in his arms again, her body pressing him back toward the bed. He turned her as they moved and fell on top of her. As though drawn by a magnet, her hand sought his crotch.

"So quickly?" she exclaimed, with delight in her voice.

Spreading her legs, she guided him into her. They lay across the bed, Longarm's feet still on the floor. Ilioana's heels dug into his back, locking him to her. He tried to thrust, but the strong grip of her legs held him motionless.

Ilioana felt his effort to move and whispered, "No. Not yet.

Stay in me, so big, so long, so deep. Then I will pleasure you, indeed!"

"Whenever you're ready," he told her. "What pleasures you will do for me."

Bit by bit, her legs relaxed. Longarm stroked, short and hard, and Ilioana laughed deep in her chest. "Oh, you are big," she said. "Never before have I taken a man so big as you. Now let me go, but only for a moment, while I place myself."

Longarm stepped back. He looked down as he withdrew, and his jaw dropped. Instead of the golden pubic hair he'd expected to see, bare skin met his eyes above the pink lips from which his dripping shaft was sliding.

Ilioana gave him no time to think about what he saw. She turned over on the bed, and brought up her legs to kneel in front of him. Longarm stepped up behind her. Before he could position himself to enter her again, Ilioana's hand reached from beneath her body and took firm hold of his erection. He rubbed the shaft's tip between her legs, but when he moved to go into her warm wetness, she held him off.

"No. Not there." A tremble of excited anticipation was in her voice. "Above. As the Turks do."

Belatedly, Longarm understood what she expected. He let her place him, and went into her slowly. She whimpered as she took him in, and pressed him back for a moment. Then her hand relaxed.

"More now," she said hoarsely, her voice muffled. "More."

Once or twice, while he penetrated ever more deeply into the tight orifice, Longarm heard her moan. It could have been a moan of pleasure or of pain, or of the two sensations intermingled. He put his hands on the soft, round cheeks of her buttocks and spread them wide, to plunge still deeper, and her moans increased.

"Nisvergal!" Ilioana groaned throatily. *"Teper!"*

She began to rotate her buttocks as she spoke, and Longarm got the meaning of her demand. He stroked, slowly at first, then, as he felt her tighten around him convulsively, the added friction that followed her squeezing kindled him to an excitement equal to Ilioana's He started to pound furiously. His hands tightened their grip on the soft flesh they were grasping, flesh that was now rippling under his fingers in muscular contractions. He

did not think of holding himself back when he came up to orgasm, but let go to the accompaniment of Ilioana's frenzied
animal cries.

   She lurched forward on the bed. Longarm, gasping for breath,
fell on top of her.

Chapter 17

For several moments the room was silent except for the sound of their harsh breathing. At last Ilioana sighed deeply and raised herself on one elbow to look at him.

"You liked the way I pleasured you?" she asked.

"I told you, what you liked, I'd like too." Longarm hesitated before adding, "But it sounded to me like I was hurting you."

"Ah, but that is the point, Longarm! Without some pain, there is no really great pleasure!"

"I ain't so sure I agree with you, Ilioana. Seems to me the only pleasure I ever got out of being hurt was getting well."

"Reach your hand out to me," Ilioana said. She took the hand he stretched out and put it on her soft breast. "Now, squeeze."

Longarm did as she requested.

"Harder!" she commanded.

He applied extra pressure.

"Harder yet!" she urged him.

Longarm tried, but could not bring himself to use all his strength. He looked at her breast, his fingers sunk so deeply into its softness that mounds of flesh bulged up between them. He shook his head. "It ain't any use. I can't enjoy it when I know I'm hurting somebody."

"But I was enjoying feeling your strength spent on me. Still, it is a feeling common to only a few." She stretched out and sat up. "We should drink again. I would not like to think our evening has ended so soon."

"If I ain't too old-fashioned to suit you, I'm still good for some more. And a drink would go down pretty good right now."

Longarm watched her as she walked naked across the room. She did not go directly to the table where the liquor was, but to the bureau, where she poured perfume from a crystal vial into her cupped hand and rubbed the scent into her body. She stroked herself sensuously, massaging the perfume into her breasts, her armpits, her abdomen.

The aroma of the perfume was heavy in the small room. As he watched her rub the liquid into her pubic mound and between her thighs, Longarm felt himself stirring into another erection. He was still flaccid, though, when she came back to the bed, carrying filled glasses for each of them. This time she did not offer a toast, but merely raised her glass before tilting it to her lips. Longarm followed her example.

His eyes kept wandering to the smooth delta of skin between her thighs. When she put her glass down and reached to take his, he caught her arm and pulled her to him. She dropped the glass to the floor and came to him readily. Leaning with her back on his chest, she guided his hands to her breasts. He cupped them, gently at first then harder, until they were as flat as he could press them. Ilioana inhaled deeply and sighed with a tiny grating sound, like the purring of a cat, deep in her throat. She began rubbing her bare back against his chest.

Longarm could not keep his hands still. He ran them down over her stomach, down to her groin, which he'd found so fascinating. Ilioana spread her legs apart, as though to encourage him. Her hands crept behind her, between their bodies, and found him, still only partly erect. He began to knead the soft, wet lips that she'd opened to his fingers. Ilioana squirmed and brought his hardening erection up between her legs, and now their fingers began to touch and intertwine. He grew hard quickly.

"Look!" she whispered to him.

Longarm had been nibbling at her neck and shoulders. He raised his head, wondering what there was to look at. His eyes traveled the room, and stopped at the bureau. The big rectangular pier glass that had been hung over the bureau's own tarnished mirror had been carefully placed so that it reflected the bed. In the mirror he saw Ilioana sprawled at full length, her legs spread wide, his rigid shaft between them, his fingers buried in the wet pink crevice between her thighs. She moved his fingers aside while he looked, and guided his erection into the spot they had occupied.

She leaned forward slowly, deliberately, to let him slide into her. Longarm watched the mirror. It was his introduction to this refinement, though he'd heard men who patronized whorehouses talk about mirror rooms. He saw Ilioana's breasts in outline as she bent still farther forward, and reached for them. The dangling white globes were just beyond his fingertips, and now Ilioana's body hid their fleshly connection from view. Longarm was aroused enough, though. He lifted Ilioana bodily, lowered her to the bed on her back, and plunged into her once more.

She did not respond to Longarm's first plunges, but as he continued the furious thrusting, her body grew tense. He slowed to a more deliberate tempo, sliding into her gradually, almost gently, and holding his hips pressed hard against her for several seconds at the end of his penetration. Ilioana began to squeeze with her inner muscles to hold him in, and he timed his easy strokes to her contraction and release. She pulled his head down and offered him her lips. He met them and they began a long, deep kiss that soon set her to trembling and brought Longarm close to orgasm.

He sped up, bit by bit, until he was driving into her with full, pistonlike strokes. Her body began to writhe. The writhing became heaving as she brought her hips up to meet his; their bodies collided with soft, fleshy smacks until Ilioana wailed into his ear. Longarm relaxed his control and pounded home a few quick, final thrusts before his relaxing body covered hers and they lay still, bathed in the heady, warm waves of musk that rose from their drained and still-joined bodies.

Below him, Longarm felt Ilioana stir. He moved to relieve her of his weight, and she sat up. The careful outlines of her rouged lips were blurred, and the lips themselves were swollen. Longarm looked from the woman beside him to her image and his, reflected in the pier glass. When she stood up and stretched, the play of the lamplight on her breasts and hips and on the bare vee of skin at the junction of her thighs still fascinated him, but he felt no arousal as he watched her go to the bureau and get fresh glasses. She padded on bare feet to the table and poured them drinks, then came back to the bed and handed him the glass she'd filled with Maryland rye.

"We will talk now?" she suggested, sitting down beside him on the bed.

"Sure, if you want to," Longarm stood up, went to the chair where his vest and coat lay folded across the back, and found a cigar. He took a match from the bundle in his coat pocket and lighted the cheroot. Back at the bed, he asked her, "What's on your mind for us to talk about, Ilioana?"

"What we were talking about before we stopped for pleasure. My poor countrymen, and how I can best help them."

"I ain't so sure they're going to need your help. Now that the trouble between them and the ranchers has been patched up, they'll likely go on and make a pretty good wheat crop."

"How can they? The snows have started; their wheat will be ruined," she said.

"Maybe not. There's always a few short flurries that come in fast and move on, before the real winter sets in," he told her. "They'll have plenty of time to do their reaping and threshing before the weather gets too bad."

"Even if they do, they have no buyer for their grain, now that the wheat broker has gone," Ilioana said thoughtfully, more to herself than to Longarm.

"Oren Stone?" he asked. "How'd you find out about him?"

"Why, Gregor told me that—" she stopped short. "Gregor heard some gossip that he repeated to me."

Longarm's lips tightened. What Ilioana had just let slip was all he'd needed to be sure that she and her servant were the Russian secret agents Mordka Danilov had suspected them to be. Thinking of Mordka reminded him of something else. He tallied the days in his mind and realized that this was the evening he'd promised to attend the service at the Brethren's church, at which the group would offer prayers for a good harvest.

"You sure take a lot of interest in things that don t have anything to do with finding that brother you came here to look for," Longarm observed. "Where was it you said your servant had gone to look for a new lead?"

Ilioana had made a quick recovery. "I do not think I mentioned his destination. It is of no importance."

She looked at Longarm, who caught her eyes and stared her down. Nervously she got up from the bed, filled her glass with vodka, and drained it. Then she picked up her negligee from the floor and busied herself with putting it on. She kept her back to Longarm until the black chiffon was wrapped around her body. When she turned to face him, Ilioana had regained her composure.

"We have pleasured ourselves almost too much, have we not?" She smiled and indicated Longarm's flaccidity. "I know that I am exhausted."

"Maybe I don't look like it now, but I'll be good as new after I rest a little while," Longarm smiled. He wanted Ilioana to dismiss him, instead of having to walk away from her as he had before.

"Later, then. Much later, after I have slept. You do not mind?"

"No. Not a bit. I've still got some work that I need to do." He lifted his gunbelt off the headboard of the bed and went to the chair where his balbriggans and jeans lay in a crumpled heap. He separated them and began pulling his underwear on.

"You'll come back later, then? Or perhaps . . . tomorrow night?"

"One or the other." Longarm stepped into his boots and stamped them snugly on his feet. "There's still a lot of things for us to talk about."

Ilioana did not answer, but lay looking at him. Longarm's back was toward her, but watching her reflection in the pier glass, he saw a small frown form on her face. He finished dressing quickly and went to the door. "I'll see you later then, Ilioana."

"Of course." She forced a smile. "Later."

Walking through the falling snow to the livery stable, Longarm checked his watch to see if he had time to look in at the Ace High and Cattleman's before going to the church. He was surprised to see the hands indicating just a few minutes past eight; it seemed to him that he'd been with Ilioana half the night. He decided he'd better not check the saloons now; chances were the church ceremony would be over in an hour at most. There would still be time for the saloons on his way back,

Keeping the roan at a walk, and his hat brim pulled low to shield his face from the swirling snow, Longarm wondered just what he'd let himself in for by keeping his promise to Mordka Danilov.

You never were much of a churchgoing man, old son. Seems like preachers have a habit of mixing up something they think's

*right with what's set down in Holy Writ. But I guess it's all in
the way you look at it. Maybe the words in the Bible don't say
the same thing to me that they do to somebody like a preacher,
who's studied 'em a lot more careful than I ever did.*

Longarm had never been inside the little church the Brethren
had built, though he'd seen it several times. The church stood
just to one side of the broad cattle trail that ran north from the
Santa Fe's loading corrals; the trail divided the eastern group of
homesteads from those on the west side of Junction. Glidden
wire fences lined the trail for some distance north of the church,
as far as the homesteads extended. The narrow lanes that provided access to the homesteads and their wheatfields ran off the
broad cattle trail at right angles.

No steeple rose above the church to set it apart from the
dwellings, though it was larger than most of the homesteaders'
houses. Longarm had taken it for a house, until Fedor Petrovsky
had pointed the church out to him when they had ridden past it
on their way back from the Hawkins ranch. He'd had no chance
to ask Fedor whether steeples were forbidden by the creed of the
Brethren, or whether they just hadn't taken time to erect a steeple, or lacked the spare cash.

Lighted lanterns could still be seen bobbing along the narrow
lanes leading to the trail, when Longarm reined in at the church.
He was glad he wasn't going to be the last one to arrive. He tethered his horse to the hitch rail; only a few other animals were tied
up, and he realized that most of the Brethren had only a single
work animal on their farms, so when a family went anywhere
together, they went on foot. As he started for the church, Longarm heard the blatting of a few distant cattle, but thought nothing
of it. There were cows on most of the farms, he'd noticed.

Mordka Danilov was standing just inside the door, talking to
Nicolai Belivev. He smiled when he saw Longarm, and said, "I
was sure you would be here, my friend, so I waited to welcome
you myself."

"That's nice of you, Mordka. I'll admit I don't get inside a
church more than once in a blue moon. Of course, with all that
snow coming down outside tonight, a man can't tell what color
the moon might be, hid by the clouds. I hope the snow ain't hurting your wheat."

"It will do the grain no harm," Mordka assured him. "We will have a fine harvest. I have asked Nicolai to sit beside you. If there is anything that puzzles you about our service, he can explain."

"Why, you didn't need to go to all that trouble," Longarm said. "I don't aim to get in the way or be any trouble to you."

Belivev said, "It will be pleasure, not trouble, for us to have you as guest, Marshal. Vhat Mordka means, I think, is to say our service is in our native tongue. He is vorking to make translation in English, so in year or two, ve have no more Russian talking among us."

Longarm nodded. "I see."

He looked around the church for the first time. The interior was simple to the point of being bare. There were sconces on the walls, some holding lanterns or kerosene lamps, others holding candles. In one corner, a big burner gave off waves of heat. Across the front of the building, a low platform, only a foot or so high, had been erected. There was no altar, just a lectern with a wooden cross on its front. The pews were backless wooden benches, set in tiers, with a narrow center aisle. The walls were unpainted, unornamented, and the boards of the floor were rugless.

Longarm noticed that the women and children sat on one side of the building, the men on the other. Some of the women carried babies in their arms. All of them wore the plainest of clothing. The men, for the most part, had on butternut or black suits, and the women's dresses were as devoid of bright colors as were the men's suits. Although the men had removed their hats, the women all wore scarves on their heads. The children's clothing reflected the somber hues of that worn by the adults.

Nicolai Belivev saw Longarm inspecting the church and congregation. He said, "Is not for show, our church, like in Russia big cathedrals, gold vessels for Communion, robes on priests, incense. People say because bright colors and ornaments ve do not have, our lives, too, have no good cheer. Is not true, Marshal."

"No, I've never seen you folks when you weren't smiling and happy," Longarm agreed.

"Is not our vay to show off in front of God," Belivev explained. "Ve go to Him plain, like ve are born."

"I guess it doesn't take a lot of fancy folderol, at that, to catch God's eye," Longarm said cautiously.

"*Da.* You are say what *Bratiya* show each day by vay ve live," Belivev agreed. "But is by Mordka to start vorship."

Danilov had stepped up on the platform and now stood in front of the lectern. Without raising his voice, he spoke briefly in Russian. When he stopped, one of the men in front of Longarm stood and spoke in the same language. He was followed by several others. None of them raised their voices.

Longarm didn't know whether they were praying or preaching, but he noticed that the congregation gave full attention to each speaker. Not a sound interrupted any of those who spoke; even the children gave them silent attention. Once or twice, in the hush that followed each speaker's words, Longarm again heard cattle blatting outside the church. He frowned. The noises still came from a distance, but it seemed to him the sounds were louder than they had been when he'd heard them outside the church.

A stillness settled over the congregation. Apparently, all those who had felt called upon to speak had delivered themselves of whatever was on their minds. Nicolai Belivev whispered, "Is no one man our preacher, you understand? Mordka our leader is, but anybody is vant to praise God is to do it."

Mordka Danilov cleared his throat and said a very few words. A stir ran along the benches. Men, women, and children were getting up. Belivev whispered, "Is now ve kneel down to pray each one." He kneeled. After a look of startled surprise, Longarm did so too. The church was totally still for several minutes. Once again, the cattle could be heard, and this time, Longarm was sure they were much louder and more insistent.

Must be a trail herd pushing on to get to the corrals, he thought. Snowstorm probably slowed 'em down, and they've got to be there tomorrow to dicker with the buyers and load out.

He looked around covertly, but saw nothing except bowed heads and eyes tightly closed. There was no way that he could carry out his half-formed idea of stepping outside to investigate without disturbing the worshippers. He stayed on his knees.

For several minutes, the silence was maintained. Then, one by one, the sounds of scattered voices rose, saying "*Amin.*" The word in Russian was close enough to its English counterpart so that Longarm needed no one to translate. He raised his head and looked around. People were beginning to stand; he rose to his feet with them.

Belivev said, "Is now come near to end of worship. Only is one *obryad* ve do, to vash feet."

"To do what?" Longarm wasn't sure he'd heard Nicolai correctly. The silence that had lasted so long had ended with the prayers, and now neighbors were talking with neighbors; laughter and the sound of children's voices filled the small church.

"Vash feet," Belivev repeated. "Of person next to us, ve vash feet. Like did *Christos* vith disciples. You do not know?"

Dimly, Longarm recalled a Bible reading from his childhood, and, from later, an Easter sermon by an army chaplain in which Christ's washing of his disciples' feet had been mentioned. He hadn't been paying much attention at either time, he remembered. However, he said, "I've heard about it, Nicolai. You folks in the Brethren use it as a sort of guide, I guess?"

"An example, *da*. To show all men are from same clay made, is no one above other one, to show ve are vith *Christos* brothers."

Longarm had been watching the congregation while they talked. From a bucket of water that stood on the base burner, men and women were filling basins. Those still seated were taking off their shoes.

Belivev saw a crease begin to grow between Longarm's brows. He said, "Is not required you vash feet, Marshal. Or have feet to be vashed, if you do not vish. You are our guest, not one of *Bratiya*. But if you vish, I vash for you the feet."

"Now, I appreciate you offering to do that, but I'll pass, if you don't mind. Seemed to me I kept hearing cattle bawling outside while the prayers were being said. Think I'll—"

He stopped short. A rumbling had begun to become audible above the noise of talk and laughter that filled the room. It was not loud enough, apparently, to register on the members of the church, who were absorbed in their conversations, or in preparing for the foot-washing ceremony. Standing, as they were, at the back of the room, Longarm and Belivev could hear it plainly.

Longarm said quickly, "Must be a herd going by on the way to the shipping pens at Junction. I don't guess it's anything to worry about." Then, belatedly, he finished what he'd started to say a moment earlier. "I'll just step outside and take a look."

Grabbing his hat from the peg by the door as he passed,

Longarm opened the door just wide enough to allow him to slip through sidewise, and went outside. The snow was still coming down heavily. The wind had shifted and was now blowing from the south. It carried the sound away from him and made it difficult to judge the distance between the church and the approaching herd. He squinted into the darkness, but his eyes had not yet adapted for night vision, and the dancing snowflakes still further veiled the darkness.

There was a broken rhythm to the hoofbeats that Longarm didn't like. He'd listened too many times to herds moving by night not to know how one sounded when it was ambling peacefully along a trail with the herders riding flank, keeping the cattle from bunching, warding off the sudden panic to which all herd animals are prone. The rumble he was listening to now wasn't just a large cattle herd moving calmly.

It was a herd stampeding, running in wild panic. Within the next few minutes it would be out of control, packed between the Glidden wire fences that lined the trail and stretched on both sides around the church.

Chapter 18

Longarm opened the door a slit and squeezed inside. Mordka Danilov was standing across the room, talking to one of the Brethren. The others of the congregation had resumed their preparations for the foot-washing, or were still carrying on animated conversations.

He went to Mordka and said quietly, "I hate to bust into what you're doing, but we better have a little private talk, real quick."

Mordka said a few more words to the man with whom he'd been chatting and stepped aside to join Longarm. "You look troubled, my friend. Is something wrong?"

"It's too soon to tell. There's a cattle stampede heading this way. You've got no fence in front of the church, remember, and those steers will be packing in between the Glidden wire behind the building and across the trail. Some of them are likely going to bump against the walls. Maybe you better tell your people not to get upset."

"A stampede?" Mordka frowned. "Cattle running wildly?"

"That's about the size of it. And they'll be here in just a few minutes, as near as I can tell."

By now the rumble of hoofbeats had become a deep, steady thunder. The church members were stopping their joyful conversations and straining their ears to determine the source of the noise.

Danilov jumped up to the platform and began speaking loudly in Russian. As he talked, a few small cries of alarm came from the women, and several of the men started for the door. Longarm moved to stop them. He knew the danger that could be caused by a light being flashed suddenly across the path of the stampeding steers.

"Don't open that door!" he called. "Don't go outside!"

His voice was lost in the din that now seemed to come from just beyond the walls of the church. It was a medley of pounding and blatting and the clashing of horns.

One of the men reached the door and flung it open. Light from the interior speared out into the darkness. It showed the brick-red backs and shoulders of steers glistening as they milled around in the area outside the church. The light that appeared so suddenly spooked the steers that could see it. Their resonant lowing became high-pitched squeals. The cattle directly in front of the church turned to run away from the light that had startled them. They collided with others heading in the opposite direction.

Suddenly the panic that spreads so mysteriously among herd animals struck the steers, the equivalent of human mass hysteria. The cattle nearest the church were pressing against those beyond them. The herd began to mill, to turn in a circle with the unfenced grounds of the church at its center. Steers that had been heading down the trail toward town were drawn into the mill. The barbed Glidden wire fences that bordered the cattle trail scraped the hides of the steers and created still more panic.

A fencepost at the corner of the church lot gave way. Wire strands, stretched taut, snapped through the air with whiplash ferocity and stabbed into the backs of the steers nearest the break. Other strands coiled along the ground and snared hooves. Cattle fell. The other cattle sensed the injuries and death and their panic intensified.

As more and still more steers joined the mill, their flanks struck the walls of the church. The building was completely surrounded by cattle now, and its wooden walls started to creak. A board snapped like a pistol shot, then another. The lights on the walls began to sway. Under the tremendous pressure of the panicked cattle, the building creaked more loudly. Women and children began screaming.

Longarm shouted at them to stay calm, but the tumult drowned his voice.

A kerosene lamp on one of the walls crashed to the floor. It broke, and flames danced along the floor and up the wall. Another lamp fell. The walls of the church were being pushed relentlessly inward now under the weight of the steers packed against them on the outside. A roof girder cracked, and another.

"Get under the benches!" Longarm shouted, but only those nearest him heard.

Those who did hear started to crawl under the pews, and others followed their example. Flames burst through broken windows and flared across the backs of the nearest steers. The animals screamed and tried to run, but they were unable to move.

Now the roof was creaking, about to collapse. Longarm looked around. Most of the people were under the benches. Only he, Mordka, and Fedor Petrovsky were still on their feet. Longarm signaled to them to join the others under the dubious shelter of the pews.

With a final keening groan the roof began to fall. From outside came the sounds of gunshots and shouting men. The roof gave way. It fell in, and scattered burning brands across the pews. The gunfire outside increased. The lowing of the cattle diminished in volume, but the ominous crackling of the flames increased to fill the air.

High-pitched cries of children rose and cut through the snapping of burning wood. Women screamed. Boards scraped against one another, broke, and punctuated the pandemonium with loud reports. The tempo of the shots outside the church increased.

"Obotve nobonic obovate!" a woman cried. *"Moy mladenec! Moy mladenec!"*

Longarm was only a short distance from the wailing woman. He wriggled across the floor to her side. She was tugging at the leg of an infant who had been pinned to the floor when a beam had fallen across its chest. Others were crawling to help, though Longarm could tell at a glance that the child was dead. He shook his head at the woman nearest the mother; the woman took the mother in her arms and tried to soothe her. Longarm crouched over the child and wrapped his arms around the beam. The heavy timber lifted to his straining, just enough to allow another woman who crawled up at that moment to slide the small body free. Longarm pointed to the weeping mother and shook his head. The woman cradled the small corpse in her arms.

By now the flames were growing in intensity and spreading rapidly. In a few minutes, Longarm knew, the air trapped under the collapsed roof would superheat to the point where it would shrivel the lungs if inhaled. He looked for a way out.

There was only one hope that he could see—the section of

the roof not yet reached by the flames. He belly-crawled over to the center of the unburned span and looked around. When he rose to his knees it was like plunging his head into a hot bath. He dropped back quickly and looked around as best he could while prone.

A few feet away, one of the roof girders had snapped, and the broken end of the heavy eight-by-eight timber lay wedged between the fallen roof and the floor. Longarm scrambled over to it and tried to pull it free. It was beyond even his strength to do so. A hand touched his shoulder. He looked around to find Fedor Petrovsky at his side.

"Ve both pull," Petrovsky said.

Wrapping their arms around the timber, seesawing it back and forth, lifting it with their combined strength, they worked the timber free. Both men were panting as they inhaled the rapidly heating air at a level of only a foot or so above the floor. Longarm motioned with his fist, driving it toward the roof, which was made of roughcut boards covered with shingles. Petrovsky nodded. Inhaling deeply with their faces close to the floor, they knelt and began swinging the girder horizontally, like a battering-ram.

Again and again they dashed the girder against the roofboards. Shingles flew off, and the boards began to splinter. Their lungs were straining, and they dropped to the floor to inhale again before going back to the attack. At last the board cracked and broke. From the outside, gloved hands appeared, three or four pairs of them, and began tearing at the split boards, pulling them away from the trusses to which they were nailed.

"Yell to them folks to come this way!" Longarm told Petrovsky. "If we move fast, we might get 'em all out safe!"

Petrovsky began shouting in Russian. His calls brought an immediate response. A steady stream of the Brethren began crawling toward the opening, racing the flames that were being drawn by the draft it had created. Longarm and Petrovsky helped those who needed a hand to get through the gap they'd made. Outside, the same hands that had helped break open the roof took the escaping Brethren and aided them in reaching the ground without falling.

Faces became blurred by his smoke-filled eyes as Longarm worked. He recognized those with whom he'd become best acquainted: Mordka, Tatiana, Marya, Antonin Keverchov, Anatoly

Yanishev, Nicolai Belivev. There were others whose faces were familiar, but to whom he couldn't put names. One by one they struggled through the gap until at last there were no more. Longarm gestured to Fedor Petrovsky to leave, and followed him out. The flames had crept more than halfway across the floor by the time he went through the opening.

Outside, angry people plodded around aimlessly on the snow-covered ground. There were shouts everywhere, and arms raised in gestures silhouetted by the flames that now engulfed the entire mass of boards that once had been a church. The fire cast a circle of flickering orange light around the cleared area and across the cattle trail. Longarm could see the carcasses of steers littering the ground. Some of the Brethren seemed too stunned to do anything more than stand away from the flames and stare into them. A few were moving around. Mordka Danilov was going from one cluster of people to the next, and at the edge of the circle of light, Longarm recognized Fedor Petrovsky talking with a group of men.

Cattle were still moving along the trail, but the panic that had gripped the herd had ended as quickly as it had begun. Ranch hands were riding with the steers, and a few saddled horses stood riderless between the stream of plodding animals and the group of people from the church. Longarm recognized the burly figure of Clem Hawkins, and picked his way around the cattle carcasses and clumps of people until he reached the rancher.

"You satisfied now, Hawkins?" Longarm demanded angrily.

"Long? What the hell are you doing out here?"

"Tending to my job. Seems like the Brethren were right when they came and told me they were afraid your bunch was going to pull off one of your dirty stunts tonight."

Hawkins stared. "You think this thing was something we planned? You're crazy, Long. You've been listening to these nesters too much."

"Maybe. All I can believe is what I'm looking at."

"You'll do better to believe me when I say all this was an accident," Hawkins snapped.

"If it was, it was a mighty convenient one. Fits right in with what you and your crowd have been doing all along."

"Now wait a minute—" Hawkins began.

"You shut up and listen to me, Hawkins," Longarm broke in. His anger was controlled now, his steely dark eyes glittered coldly. "There was a little baby killed in that fire your steers caused. I'm going to hold you accountable for that."

"Are you saying I'm a murderer?"

"You're responsible, ain't you?"

"No, by God, I'm not!" Hawkins looked around, and hailed one of the men who stood a short distance away. "Bill Tatum! Come here a minute! Bring Dell and Hetter, if you can find them!" He turned back to Longarm and said, "Now, if you'll just stand still for a minute and listen, you'll see how this all happened."

"All right, Hawkins. I'll listen to your side. But I want somebody else to hear it too." Longarm peered through the snow, trying to locate Mordka Danilov. He saw him at last, talking to a group of the Brethren, and called, "Mordka! Step over here with me, will you?"

Hawkins glared at Longarm while they waited for the others to join them. When the three men he'd called and Mordka Danilov finally got there, the rancher said, "Long, this is Bill Tatum, owns the Double Z. Dell's his drive honcho, Hetter's mine. Long's a deputy U.S. marshal."

Tatum nodded. "I heard you was nosying around," he told Longarm. "But I still ain't quite sure what you're looking for."

"I was sent here to keep an eye on the election," Longarm replied levelly. "Everything else has just sort of happened. I didn't know I was going to get caught in the middle of a fuss between you men and these homesteaders." He indicated Mordka Danilov, "I guess you know who Mr. Danilov is. He's kind of headman for the farmers."

The ranchers and the homesteader exchanged stiff-lipped nods. Mordka was obviously seething, but held himself silent.

Longarm went on, "Now, Hawkins might be right about me having a hard head, Tatum. But I've been lied to and shot at and I've had a bellyful. Now this killing here's come along, and I'm holding you and Hawkins and your men responsible."

"You see what I told you?" Hawkins exclaimed. "He's on the nesters' side!"

"I ain't on their side or your side, either. I'm on the law's side, and that's the straight of it."

"I thought Sheriff Grover was the law here," Tatum said. "That's what he was elected for."

"Grover's not the law," Longarm snapped. "Nobody's the law. Law's what's put down in the books, not what you or Grover or Hawkins or me says it is, or would like to see it be."

"All right, we know that, Long," Hawkins said brusquely. "Bill, this marshal's not going to listen to anything I tell him. You go ahead, explain how this mess tonight began."

Tatum scratched his unshaven chin. "Damned if I know where to start, Clem."

"Go right on back to the first," Hawkins said. "Back to where you and me got our ropes crossed."

"All right." Tatum looked at Longarm and Mordka. "I guess you know that when it comes time to drive our market herds to railhead, all of us raisers get together and draw straws to see who's coming in to the pens, first to last?"

Longarm nodded, "I heard that's how you work it, but I don't see that it's got any bearing on what happened to the church here."

"Damn it, that's why the whole thing happened!" Tatum retorted. "Clem was supposed to be outa my way by the time my herd got this far."

"My drive started on time, Bill," Hawkins put in. "It was this early snow that slowed us down. I couldn't help it, nobody could."

"Oh, sure, I know that, Clem," Tatum replied. "It wasn't your fault, any more'n it was my fault that Dell pushed the Double Z herd faster than we'd figured on, trying to get to railhead before it started snowing too heavy."

Longarm said, "I still don't know what happened. Suppose you do what Hawkins told you to, Tatum. Start from the first."

"What happened first was that Clem's hands got slowed down when this damn snow come along," Tatum explained. "Then Dell, here, pushed my herd faster than we'd figured on moving. Clem's boys had made a dry camp just north of where those goddamn Glidden wire fences these nesters have put up narrows down the trail we've been using ever since there was ranches here."

Hetter interrupted. "I was leery about trying to push the herd on to the shipping pens because it was getting dark and we couldn't see shit for the snow. I didn't want to see our steers tangle with fences in the dark, in bad weather. I sent a man back to tell Mr. Hawkins what I'd done."

"You didn't know the Double Z herd was pushing so close behind you, either, did you, Hetter?" Hawkins asked.

"Of course not. How could I?" Hetter asked.

"All right. I'm beginning to get an idea of what happened," Longarm said. "But you men go on, set it all straight."

Tatum said resignedly, "Clem's men had made dry camp, like I just said. No fires, and with the dark and the snow, Dell didn't know he was about to run into the C Bar H herd."

"It was about that time the wind got to willywawing," Hetter put in. "Our critters was blatting and restless, and we just plain didn't hear Dell's bunch coming."

"So the upshot was that the herds come together," Tatum went on. "Hell, we didn't know. I was riding drag, way back at the tail of my herd. Our flankers tried to turn my critters, but they couldn't see to work."

"Neither could my night herders," Hetter said. "There was a dozen mills begun in no time at all. We tried to break 'em up, but we couldn't."

"Then something spooked 'em," Tatum said. "Long, you know how easy a herd can get spooked?"

Longarm nodded. "I know, Tatum. Before I took this job I'm on now, I worked awhile as a hand. I've made a trail drive or two. It sure doesn't take much."

"Hell, I've seen herds stampede in bright sunshine just because one of the hands in front of 'em flipped out his bandanna to wipe off some sweat," Hawkins volunteered.

"We all have," Tatum agreed. He brushed snow off his face before continuing, "Well, by the time the steers up at the front of Clem's herd caught the panic from my bunch at the back, about all anybody could do was let 'em run. Clem's flankers went wrong, I guess, when they tried to keep his herd headed the way they was supposed to go. The critters got jammed into the trail between them goddamn Glidden wire fences."

"There wasn't any way to go but straight ahead," Hetter said indignantly. "Those damn fences kept my flankers from going

alongside the critters to turn 'em. By the time we'd worked
through the herd as best we could, the steers had spilled out all
around the church."

They fell silent, remembering how it had been. They needed
no reminders other than the dying flames' orange light that flickered off the glistening backs of the cattle still passing along the
trail toward Junction, the thudding of their hooves, the occasional shout of one of the flank-riders who now held the animals
under control. At one side of the trail, where the corner fencepost of the wheatfields adjoining the church had been, the Brethren huddled compactly. There were a few men in the group, but
most of them were women and children, helplessly watching the
flames and occasionally turning their eyes to the group that
stood talking.

All six men in that group were chilled and uncomfortable as
well as still angry. The wind had died and the snow, falling
straight down, mantled their hatbrims and spilled down to their
shoulders. After Hetter's remark, no one seemed anxious to speak.
It was Mordka Danilov who finally broke the silence.

"What you have said is that our fences were to blame."
His lips set in a firm line for a moment before he went on. "No.
This is not true. Mr. Hawkins, you have cursed us and our fences
since we first settled here. You have too, Mr. Tatum. But we will
not take upon ourselves a responsibility that is yours. They were
your cattle, and your men who failed to control them."

"Damn it, our boys did the best they could!" Hawkins as-
serted. He waved a hand at the carcasses of the steers that lay
around the still-burning church. "When I got here, most of the
harm had been done. I saw the critters were about to push your
building over, and I told my hands to start shooting the ones
closest to it."

"More than animals have died," Mordka reminded them. His
voice was soberly accusing. "A woman over there is holding the
body of her murdered child, and weeping for its death. How can
you compare that with the loss of a few of your steers?"

Tatum said quickly, "Clem wasn't trying to do that. And my
brand's on some of them dead steers, but I'm not trying to do
what you said, either. We're all sorry the baby's dead, but I
don't see—"

"She was to blame?" Mordka asked. "The mother whose

child died because she was praying in our church when your animals destroyed it, set it afire?" His voice lashed them with scorn. "Is that what you ask us to accept?"

Hawkins opened his mouth to reply, but could find no words. Before any of the others could speak, a rider loomed through the snow. Until he came closer to them, they could not see that it was the sheriff. Grover reined in and dismounted. He went directly to Hawkins's side.

"What the hell's going on out here, Clem?" Grover asked. "One of your boys said you was having trouble. Them damn nesters acting up again?"

"Shut up, Grover!" Hawkins snapped. "And where the devil were you an hour ago, when you should've been out here?

"I was doing my work in town. Then, when your man found me and I got outside the saloon, I could see the fire. Thought at first it was just one of them nester houses, so I didn't pay it much mind. And I got here as fast as I could. Now, will you tell me what's happened?" He saw Longarm and added, "And why are you stepping into my jurisdiction again, Long?"

Disgusted, Longarm grunted, "You tell him, Hawkins. He's your man."

Hawkins told Grover, "Long was here when the trouble started. He's not trampling on your toes, so don't get riled."

"I still don't know what's been going on out here," Grover complained.

"Keep your prick in your pants and I'll tell you," Hawkins replied curtly. "Bill Tatum's market herd ran over mine in the dark. The damn steers stampeded and knocked the nesters' church building down. It caught fire. That's about it."

"Not quite," Longarm said sharply. "Finish the story, Hawkins. You haven't said a word about the baby being killed."

Danilov spoke up. "I will tell the sheriff what happened, if Mr. Hawkins is ashamed to speak. Aleksandra Toletof's small child was killed when the cattle pressing against our church broke down the walls and the roof dropped in. Mr. Hawkins's and Mr. Tatum's cattle they were, Sheriff. We hold them responsible."

Grover looked at Hawkins for a clue. When Hawkins said nothing, the sheriff asked, "Is that the way it was, Clem?"

"Pretty much, I guess. But hell, none of us knew what was going on inside that place. It was already on fire."

Tatum spoke up quickly. "It was all a damn accident, Grover. You know a man can't be held to answer for something a bunch of dumb animals did."

"A man should be held to answer if his animals were not properly guarded by the men whose job it was to control them," Mordka observed sternly.

"Wait a minute, now," Grover said as he turned to Mordka. "Is that right? You people was all inside the church building when it caught fire?"

"Yes, Sheriff," Mordka said patiently. "That is the way it was. We had been praying when the cattle surrounded the church."

"If you was all right handy there, why didn't you put out the fire?" the sheriff asked.

"We had no water," Danilov answered. "The walls all around us were being pushed in. Already, before the fire, the roof was threatening to fall. We were trying to save our lives."

"I can vouch for that," Longarm said. "I was inside the church when it all started."

"If I want anything from you, I'll ask you, Long," Grover said, without bothering to hide his irritation.

Longarm swallowed his anger and kept quiet.

Danilov told Grover, "Marshal Long was there at our invitation. We were afraid Mr. Hawkins's men might continue the trouble they have been giving us since we settled here."

"Now, that's a lie!" Hawkins flared. "It ain't my men's fault they don't like you nesters! Damn it, you people just don't belong in cattle country, with your wheat patches and your Glidden wire fences!"

"They've got as much right to be here as anybody, Hawkins," Longarm said. "At least they paid for the land they're planting, which is more than you and your bunch are doing for half of the land you run your herds on."

"All we want is our rights as citizens," Mordka Danilov said quietly. "We do not wish any favors." He looked around at the others. "We have let our feelings make us forget what we were talking about. I will remind you again, Sheriff, a child was killed in the church because of the cattle belonging to these men."

"That was an accident, like Bill Tatum just said," Grover replied impatiently. "I don't see that it's got anything to do with the matter."

"We *Bratiya* would not expect you to see anything that might harm the interest of your masters," Mordka replied. "But we will—"

He broke off suddenly and looked to the north. The others turned to look also. A score or more of lighted lanterns were bobbing, moving down the lane on the north side of the church, the lane that led into the cattle trail. The lanterns illuminated the figures of the men carrying them, men of the *Bratiya,* and light danced off the blue steel of the guns they carried.

Chapter 19

Grover asked of no one in particular, "Now just what the hell is that?"

No one answered him. They were all too interested in watching the progress of the lanterns. Suddenly, from the *Bratiya* who still stood at the opposite corner of the churchyard, a chorus of shouts rang out.

Longarm asked Mordka in a whisper, "Do you know anything about this?"

The Russian shook his head, a look of concern on his face. "No. But I have a thought of what can be happening."

"Maybe you better tell me," Longarm suggested.

Danilov took Longarm by the elbow and led him a few feet from the others. Absorbed in watching the progress of the lanterns, the ranchers and Grover did not miss them when they stepped away.

His voice a loud whisper, Danilov said, "Since you and Fedor Petrovsky were shot, the men of the *Bratiya* have been very angry. They have tried not to show this, but I know of it. Yesterday and the day before, I heard whispers that they might come to the services tonight carrying weapons."

"Afraid the ranchers might start something while you were all packed inside the church?"

Mordka nodded. "Yes. When I heard what they might do, I told them they should not bring weapons to a service of worship. Now I think they have gone quietly to their homes and fetched their guns."

"Would they do that without telling you?"

"My friend, I do not rule over the *Bratiya*. No one of us does. Most of them look to me for advice, perhaps guidance, but I cannot order them to do or not to do anything. I can only suggest."

"If they're really coming back loaded for trouble, what are you going to do about it?" Longarm asked.

"I do not want shooting and killing." Mordka's voice was somber. "Still, we must protect what we have built with our hands, with our sweat. And there is both deep sorrow and great anger in their hearts because Aleksandra Toletof's child was killed."

"That ain't what I asked you, Mordka," Longarm said gently.

Mordka looked sad. "I cannot give you an answer, my friend. I can only wait until the men get here and see if they will listen to me."

The tall deputy regarded him silently for a moment, then sighed and said, "I guess you'll do your best."

"You know that I will. I still live for the day when the *Bratiya* can renounce violence and return to the beliefs our fathers held."

Longarm looked at Mordka for a moment. When he spoke, his voice was dangerously calm. "Just remember, those hands working for Hawkins and Tatum have all got guns. If any shooting gets started, this could turn into a fight worse than Bull Run!"

Although the flames of the burning mass of wreckage that was once a church were almost gone by now, the mass of coals still threw out a bright glow. The glow provided enough light for the men who carried the lanterns to be seen clearly while they were still twenty yards from the point where the lane joined the cattle trail.

Longarm recognized Fedor Petrovsky in the front rank of the marchers, and in spite of the seriousness of the situation, he couldn't repress the beginning of a grin. He liked the feisty little Russian, who never admitted to being whipped. Behind Petrovsky were others whose faces he remembered but whose tongue-twisting names he couldn't recall. All of the men carried rifles or shotguns, and a few of them wore pistols. From the belts of a few others dangled the same kind of long, curved Cossack swords that Tatiana's fiancé had wielded when he attacked Longarm.

"That's a goddamn nester army!" Hawkins gasped. He turned to Hetter. "Get our boys rounded up, fast! If the nesters want a fight, we'll damned well give them one!"

"Dell!" Tatum commanded. "Get our hands here, too. We'll back up whatever play Clem makes."

"Just a minute!" Longarm's voice crackled out. "There's not going to be any war started. Not if I have any say-so."

"You haven't!" Grover told him. The sheriff was almost frothing with anger. "I'm in charge here!"

"You sure as hell weren't a while ago, when you ought to've been!" Longarm shot back. "We can argue about who's in charge later. If you've got a nickel's worth of brains in that skull of yours, you'll tell your friends here to hold back."

"This is as good a time for a showdown as any!" Hawkins grated. "It's got to come, sooner or later!"

None of the others were quite sure how it happened, but Longarm's Colt was suddenly in his hand. "If you want to argue it out, I'll help you," he told them. "If you figure on shooting it out, I'm ready for that too. Hetter, you and Dell stand where you are!"

Hawkins said quickly, "Do what he says, boys. You too, Grover." A broad smile crept over his face. "You boys don't have to call anybody. Our men are already here. Long, just look behind you."

Longarm looked around. He knew before turning his head what he'd see, from the ring of triumph in Hawkins's voice. The C Bar H and Double Z hands had seen the *Bratiya* approaching, and had ridden up to investigate. Behind him, Longarm saw at least a dozen ranch hands sitting their horses. A number of them had already pulled rifles out of their saddle scabbards and were holding the weapons ready to shoulder them.

Knowing before he spoke that neither Hawkins nor Tatum would listen, Longarm said, "Tell your men to put their guns away, Hawkins. You do the same, Tatum. One shot fired by your men, or by that bunch coming up, even accidental, this whole thing's going to explode."

"Let it bust, then!" Hawkins retorted. "Those nesters have got their guns out, and if they shoot first, we'll sure as hell give it right back to them!

"I'm standing with Clem," Tatum put in.

Longarm turned to Danilov. "Mordka! Can you talk some sense into your folks, to keep this thing from blowing up into a war?"

Danilov shook his head. "I am not sure, but I will try."

"Hawkins? Tatum?" Longarm looked at the ranchers. "Is that agreeable with you?"

After a quick exchange of glances, both ranchers nodded.

Hawkins said, "Go talk to your men, Danilov. I'll hold my boys back."

"I wish Marshal Long to go with me," Mordka said. "We of the *Bratiya* have trust in him."

"No, by God!" Grover rapped out. "I'm sick of having him push in every place where it's my job to be! If anybody goes with you, it'll be me!"

"I am sorry, Sheriff," Mordka said, shaking his head. "If you go, I will be able to do nothing. All of our people know that you are on the side of Mr. Hawkins and the cattlemen."

"We ain't so damned sure the marshal's not on your side," Tatum said. "I feel about like the sheriff does. It's his place to keep the peace, not some damned outsider wearing a federal badge."

Longarm didn't bother to raise the Colt he still held in his hand. He said quietly, "I don't want to use this argument-settler I'm holding, but I will if I have to."

Over Longarm's shoulder, Hawkins called out, "Ed! Put your rifle sights on the marshal's back!"

"I had him covered for five minutes, Mr. Hawkins," one of the riders called back. "Figured you might be in trouble when I seen him pull that pistol out."

"Take his gun, Grover," Hawkins ordered the sheriff.

Longarm stood motionless and said nothing. He'd heard no trace of bluff in the voice of the cowhand behind him. When Grover reached down and plucked the Colt from his hand, Longarm released it. Grover stuck the pistol in his belt and looked at Hawkins. "What you want me to do now, Clem?" he asked.

"Go with Danilov, you damn fool! Try to help him talk some sense into the nesters. You'd better shake your ass, though, because if you don't, it's going to be too late for talking."

Hawkins jerked a thumb at the marching *Bratiya*. They had now reached the end of the lane and turned onto the cattle trail. They were spread out across the trail, advancing at a slow walk toward the group that included Longarm, Mordka Danilov, and the ranch owners.

Longarm asked Mordka, "Can't you stop them from getting up too close? Some of those cowhands are going to get skittish if your folks come too near their bosses."

Danilov called, "Fedor! Fedor Petrovsky! *Tam ostanova, pojalosta!*"

"Ya nipanimauy!" Petrovsky called in reply. *"Pachimu?"*

"Damn it, cut off your foreign lingo!" Hawkins told Mordka. "Talk so we can understand what you're saying!"

Longarm hadn't understood Petrovsky's words any better than Hawkins had, but he gathered from the tone used that Petrovsky was asking Mordka to give him a reason for halting the *Bratiya*. He called, "Fedor! Those cowboys up ahead have got rifles on your men. Stop 'em where they are! If you don't, a lot of folks are going to get hurt!"

"Ve vill hurt them vorse as they hurt us!" Petrovsky threatened.

"No need for anybody to get hurt!" Longarm replied. "Stop where you are a minute, Fedor! Mordka's coming to talk to you!"

Grover swept his arm around, and shoved Longarm to one side. "Keep your damn big mouth outa this! I got a bellyful of you butting into my business!"

"Just be sure that bellyful don't give you a case of gripe-gut," Longarm told the sheriff. His voice was dangerously quiet. He pointed to the *Bratiya*. They had stopped and were looking expectantly at Danilov.

Hawkins told Grover, "Settle your fuss with Long later. Get on out there and do the job we're paying you for!"

The marshal flicked a cold blue glance at Hawkins, but said nothing.

Mordka tapped Grover's shoulder. "Come, Sheriff. Let us go and speak with them."

Danilov and Grover crossed the trail and stopped in front of Fedor Petrovsky. A number of the *Bratiya* clustered around them at once; the others kept their eyes fixed on the ranch hands, who had not advanced their horses from their position on the south side of the burning debris. Longarm and the ranchers were between the two groups, too far from both of them to hear what was being said by either.

They could catch an occasional word from the men around Mordka and Grover. One word in particular was repeated: *"Boey! Boey!"*

Hawkins turned to Longarm. "You've been around the nesters more than I have, Long. What's that word mean?"

Longarm shook his head. "I wouldn't know. I ain't been around 'em all that much, no matter what you think."

If the ranch hands were talking, it was in whispers, for only an occasional nicker from one of the horses came from that direction.

Those members of the *Bratiya* near the riders were silent too, watching their fellows for some sign of action. The flames of the fire were almost completely gone; only a tiny, pale tongue shot up here and there from a board that still had not been consumed. The glowing heap of dying coals gave little light to supplement that provided by the lanterns of the Brethren. The snow had tapered off; only an occasional stray flake floated down. The wind had changed direction, and was blowing from the east, bringing warmth. Underfoot, an ankle-deep white blanket crunched when anyone took a step.

To those who waited, it seemed that the discussion among Mordka, the sheriff, and the Brethren lasted a long while. At last the men who were crowded around them stepped away. As they backed off, the faces of Mordka and Grover were pink blurs silhouetted against the yellow of the lantern light, but there was no need to see their expressions. Dejection was in the slumping of their shoulders, their slow, deliberate walk. Behind them, the Brethren were re-forming their ranks.

"Well?" Hawkins asked when Grover and Danilov reached the group. "What'd they say?"

"You could hear them," Mordka answered. "Though you may not have understood. Their cry was *'boey'*. It means 'fight'."

Grover said, "That's the stubbornest bunch of bastards I've ever run into! They don't seem to know more'n only two words, *boey* and *nyet*. I heard them words so many times I don't guess I'll ever forget 'em."

"What're they saying no about?" Hawkins asked.

"They say they ain't going to let another steer pass along this trail till they've been paid for their church and that woman whose baby got killed is made some kind of payment too."

"That won't hurt us," Tatum said. "Our herds are already in the shipping pens at Junction."

"They don't just mean now," Grover explained. "They mean from now on. Next year, the year after that, till hell freezes over, from the way they talked."

"Hell, they can't close this trail!" Hawkins sputtered. "It's public, which means us! We've been using it as long as there've been ranches here. It's not their land, anyhow. It's Santa Fe land."

"You think I didn't tell 'em that?" Grover asked. "They said to bring on the Santa Fe, they'll fight them and us both."

"Wait a minute, Clem," Tatum broke in. "Don't they know we can just drive our herds around east of their homesteads and get to the railhead that way?"

Grover answered before Hawkins could speak. "They know that. But they figure it'll cost you money to do it."

Hawkins nodded. "It will, too." He looked at Tatum. "Figure it out, Bill. We'd add better than twenty miles to our drives, twice a year, spring and fall. That's two or three more days' wages for the extra hands we always hire. Comes to a week a year for every extra man. And covering that much more distance will take a lot of weight off our steers. We'll get less for them at the shipping pens."

"I hadn't looked at it that way," Tatum said. "But you're sure right." He asked Grover, "What's the law say about blocking up a public trail like this one?"

"How the hell should I know? I'm not a lawyer."

"Not much of a sheriff, either, for my money." Tatum sounded disgusted. "You could've stopped these nesters from acting up, kept 'em in their place, if you'd been on the job."

"You got no right to say that!" Grover pointed at Mordka. "*He* couldn't do nothing with 'em, and he's supposed to be their boss."

Mordka spoke up. "I cannot command the *Bratiya* to do what I wish; that is not our way. I have told you this before. But it is true, we do not trust Sheriff Grover, any more than we trust you or Mr. Hawkins. And there is still something the sheriff has not told you yet. The fence-cutting must stop, too."

"How come you didn't mention that?" Hawkins asked the sheriff. "Remember what we talked about when it first started? I—"

"I guess I just forgot, Clem," Grover interrupted hurriedly.

Mordka broke the angry silence that followed the exchange between Hawkins and Grover. "I have only one suggestion. If you will pay to rebuild our church, and agree that there will be no more cutting of our fences, I will see that we ourselves satisfy Aleksandra Toletof's need for help."

"Damned if I'll put up a penny to pay for a nester's foreign church!" Hawkins spat out. He asked Tatum, "Bill, how do you feel about it?"

"Same way you do. If we start paying out like that, why, every time one of these nesters has a broke-down fence, or a stray steer gets into his wheatfield, he'll be at our doors with his hand out. That stampede was a pure accident. We didn't make it happen any more than they did."

"They were still your cattle, and your men were not attending to their jobs properly," Danilov said.

"It's blackmail, and I won't pay it!" Hawkins shot back. "We'll fight first! Hetter, go tell the boys to get ready. Looks like there's going to be trouble after all."

"If there is, it will be of your own making," Mordka said soberly.

Longarm had held himself back during the argument. He knew that even his presence there irritated the ranchers and Grover, and he had hoped that if he stood aside, they would be able to settle their differences with the Brethren. Now he gave up hope.

"I think you better do what those people want," he told Hawkins. "It'll be a sight cheaper than fighting. If you begin feuding now, it could drag on for years."

His remark provided an instant trigger for Grover's angry frustration. Secure in the awareness that he was holding Longarm's Colt, the sheriff let go a backhand blow that caught Longarm across the cheek.

"Stay out of this, Long!" Grover snapped. "You've always took up for them son-of-a-bitch nesters! If I hadn't took away your gun, you'd have forced us to settle this their way before now."

Exercising all his self-control, Longarm didn't strike back. The blow gave him the opportunity he'd been needing. He staggered with the slap and purposely lurched into Hawkins. The rancher put out his hands instinctively to catch him. Longarm slid his hand along his watch chain, and when he straightened up, the derringer on the end of the chain was pressed against Hawkins's ear.

"All right, Hawkins. You like to call the shots around here. I'm going to let you go on calling 'em, but from here on, you'll call 'em my way," Longarm said. "Start out by telling your friends to give us a lot of room."

"You heard him!" Hawkins gasped. "Back away, Bill, you and Grover. And for God's sake, don't go for your guns, either one of you! This damn popgun Long's got on me don't look like much, but it'll sure play hell with a man's skull at close range!"

"And don't forget, I've got more than one shot," Longarm warned the others. "The first one might be for Hawkins, but if either one of you starts to throw down, I'll take you first and save him for later!"

"You won't get away with anything, Long," Tatum said. "Clem's man's already started our hands to moving."

Glancing down the trail, Longarm saw that the rancher was telling the truth. The hands from the C Bar H and the Double Z were beginning to walk their horses forward.

"Maybe you forgot I'd already sent Hetter to get my boys ready," Hawkins gloated. "I guess that spoils your little play, Marshal."

"Let's eat the apple a bite at a time," Longarm told his prisoner. "Get on out there with me. We're going to go stand right in the middle of that trail, in front of them farmers."

"Wait a minute! That's going to put us in the line of fire when my hands open up!" Hawkins gasped.

"It sure as hell is," Longarm replied. He pressed the muzzle of the derringer harder into Hawkins's ear. "But I don't see that you've got much choice. When a man's going to get shot, it purely don't matter who pulls the trigger. Now march!"

As he walked out into the trail, into the light of the lanterns carried by the *Bratiya*, Hawkins called back to Tatum, "Tell your men to hold their fire, Bill! And tell mine I said to hold back, too!"

Tatum's warning call stopped the ranch hands' advance; they reined in. Opposite them, the coals still glowed redly and cast a lurid half-light across the trail. They didn't lower their rifles.

Hawkins tried to look over his shoulder to see what response the *Bratiya* were making to the advances of the cowhands, but the cold muzzle of the derringer at his temple kept him immobile. His voice a hoarse rasp, he asked Longarm, "The men behind us won't shoot, will they? If they do, my boys will sure as hell shoot back, and you and me'll be ripped wide open."

Longarm glanced over his shoulder, and saw the Brethren lined up in two rows. Those in the front row were kneeling so the men behind could fire over their heads.

"Fedor!" Longarm called.

"*Da*, Marshal." Petrovsky's voice responded behind him, "I see vhat you are doing. Don't vorry, vhen ve shoot, ve vill aim above your heads. Hawkins is make as good breastvork as line of stones!"

"Oh, my God!" Hawkins gasped. "Marshal, you've got to do something, or we'll both get killed!"

"You were ready enough to have your men start killing, a few minutes ago," Longarm replied coldly. "Makes a difference when you're in the line of fire, doesn't it?"

"Tell me what you want me to do, Long! I won't try anything, I swear! I'll do exactly what you say!"

"Tell your men to toss their rifles on the ground," Longarm ordered. "I'll see if I can't get the Brethren to do the same thing. Maybe if they see your crew's not going to turn loose on 'em, they'll be reasonable."

"Hetter!" Hawkins shouted. "You and the other boys toss your guns down! Do it right now and the nesters won't open up on you!"

Hetter's voice came back, "How do we know that, boss? That'd open us up to getting killed if them nesters decide to take advantage of us!"

"Do it, damn you!" Hawkins replied. "Or I'm likely to be a dead man!"

"Long's trying to trick you," Grover called from the side of the trail where he stood with Tatum. "Don't listen to him, Clem! He's in with the nesters! I've said so all along!" Raising his voice, he called, "Hetter! This is Sheriff Grover talking. I'm swearing you and all the rest of you boys in as my posse. Now, you got the law on your side, and you're under my orders. And my orders are to keep your guns and stand pat!"

From behind Longarm and Hawkins, Fedor Petrovsky called, "Ve are hear vhat says the sheriff, Marshal. Ve must defend ourselves! If one shot from the cowboys comes, ve shoot back!"

In Longarm's ear, Hawkins said harshly, "Well, Long? You've sure outsmarted yourself this tune! Only comfort I've got is that we'll both die together!"

Chapter 20

Longarm did not bother to answer Hawkins. He was trying to think of a way to break the deadlock. He knew that within minutes, perhaps seconds, the tension that had gripped the Brethren and the ranch hands alike must snap. Somebody would pull a trigger.

He got the answer to his puzzle from a totally unexpected source. From the corner of the churchyard, into the shrinking circle of light cast by the orange-red glow of the fire's dying coals, the people of the Brethren who had been watching the confrontation suddenly became participants.

Led by Mordka Danilov, they walked in double file across the trail a few yards in front of the mounted cowhands. Even in the diminished light, it was plain to see that most of them were women and children. Longarm guessed that the men in the group were those who had kept to the creed of nonviolence that had been a founding principle of the sect.

The sight of the slow, steady parade set off a buzz of voices from Fedor Petrovsky's men. The chatter was cut short when Mordka began to speak.

"Bratiya!" he called. "Listen to me! The Marshal has made sure that the men of the ranches cannot shoot at you without the risk of killing their leader! Now I have made sure that you cannot shoot the ranch men without risking harm to your own wives and children!"

"By God!" Longarm muttered under his breath, "I don't guess Mordka's ever heard of one, but he's sure set up a Mexican standoff!"

"Damned if he hasn't," Hawkins agreed. For the first time that night, the rancher's voice sounded cheerful.

"Does it satisfy you, Hawkins? Because you're the man those hands of yours and Tatum's will listen to. If you tell 'em to drop their rifles again, I'm betting they'll do it this time."

Tatum and Grover came running from the side of the trail to join Longarm and Hawkins. Before they got within reaching distance, Longarm called to them, "Stop right there! This ain't settled quite yet, and I've still got this little gun of mine pushed into Hawkins's ear. You get too close and I might get nervous."

His threat stopped the two men in their tracks. Grover said, "It's some kind of damn nester trick, Clem! Don't fall for it!"

"Shut up, Grover!" Tatum commanded. "Clem can handle this without any advice from you."

"Damn right, I can!" Hawkins said. "Bill, whether you agree or not, I'm going to finish up this mess right now, and tell our boys to toss their guns on the ground. I'm gambling that Danilov or Long or both of 'em will tell the nesters behind us to do the same thing."

"You can depend on me," Longarm said. "And I'd guess Mordka will go along, seeing as how setting those folks down there where they are was his idea."

"That's good enough for me," Tatum agreed. "You won't have any trouble from my men, I'll guarantee that, Clem."

Hawkins raised his voice. "Hetter! Tell the boys to toss their guns down to the ground! There's not going to be any shooting, anybody can see that!"

"You Double Z hands do the same thing!" Tatum shouted.

"Mordka!" Longarm called out. "Soon as the ranch hands have got rid of their guns, I'm going to see if Fedor won't tell his men to put theirs down too!"

"And I will join you in urging him," Danilov replied. "Do you hear me, Fedor?"

"Da." Petrovsky's voice came from the ranks of the *Bratiya*. "Ve vill lay our veapons aside. Ve do not vant a fight, but ve vere ready to have one if ve could get justice no other vay."

Hetter's voice came to them within a few moments. "All right, boss. We've done like you said. But yell if them nesters act up. It won't take but a minute for us to get our guns back!"

Muffled thuds began sounding from the area where the Brethren stood, as rifles, shotguns and other weapons hit the snow-covered ground.

Fedor Petrovsky called, "Ve have thrown down our guns, too! Now let us meet together and settle our differences peacefully."

"I guess I've come around to feeling like he does," Hawkins said to Longarm. "Or I will, as soon as you take that derringer away from my head."

"There's one little thing left to take care of before I can do that," Longarm replied.

"Oh? What's that?"

"Tell your man Grover to hand me back my Colt. It was you who had him take it off me, so I figure it's up to you to tell him to give it back. He seems to do just about what you order him to, like any other hired hand would."

Without hesitating, Hawkins told Grover, "You heard the marshal. Give him back his pistol."

"By rights, I oughta be putting a pair of handcuffs on him," Grover said. "If he was anybody but a federal marshal, he'd've been in jail already."

"Sorry you feel that way," Longarm said. He held out his hand. "But I guess you're smart enough to do what your boss tells you."

Reluctantly, Grover slid Longarm's Colt out of his waistband. He held it out butt-first. The light was dimmer than ever, but Longarm's eyes were sharp. He saw that Grover had kept his forefinger in the trigger guard of the weapon instead of holding the gun by its muzzle. He lifted his left hand to take the Colt.

Grover started to spin the weapon on the pivot of his forefinger, but before his hand could close around the gun's butt, Longarm brought the derringer down from Hawkins's head. The wicked little pistol's flat *splat* broke the silence. Longarm caught his Colt in midair as it dropped from the dying sheriff's suddenly flaccid fingers.

Hawkins and Tatum were caught off guard by the shot. Neither of them reached for his gun when Grover crumpled and folded to the ground. Longarm spun the Colt by its trigger guard, as Grover had planned to do, but his spin was completed and the Colt's butt was nestled in his palm, the muzzle casually covering the ranchers, by the time Grover's collapse was complete.

"Your man was a damned fool, Hawkins," Longarm remarked in a chilled-steel voice. "He ought to've known I've had that trigger-spin stunt tried on me before, that I'd be watching for it."

"You didn't have to kill him," Hawkins protested. There was no conviction in the rancher's tone.

"Like hell I didn't. As long as he was holding my Colt, I couldn't risk just winging him. Besides," Longarm added thoughtfully, "There's two things in my book that'll draw a bullet for a bad law officer. One's hitting an unarmed man he's holding a gun on, like Grover did me a while ago."

Hawkins waited for Longarm to go on, and, when he didn't, asked curiously, "What's the other?"

"Selling his badge, the way Grover sold his to you. By rights, you should've got the second slug in this derringer."

For a moment the three men stood silently, looking down at the body by their feet. Then the Brethren and the cowhands reached them, running to find out what the shot had meant.

Over the excited babble of talk, Hawkins shouted, "You C Bar H and Double Z men have got jobs to do at the shipping pens, don't forget! Hoist your butts onto your horses and go back to work!"

Longarm holstered his Colt. He saw Mordka Danilov walking toward them, and asked Hawkins, "You think you and Tatum can settle things peaceful now, with Mordka Danilov and his people?"

"We haven't got much choice, with you looking over our shoulders," the rancher replied.

"Oh, I don't intend to do that," Longarm assured him, "You're all sensible, grown-up men. All you've got to do is act like you are."

He turned and walked away from them, then. Once, before he reached the spot where the hitch rail had been, he looked back over his shoulder. The ranchers and Danilov were still standing where he'd left them, in sober discussion. The hitch rail was gone and so was the roan, but Grover's horse was stamping its hooves at the edge of the patch of gray ash that marked the place where the church had stood. Longarm swung into the saddle and started toward town.

Halfway to Junction, the clouds scudded away and the new moon brought the prairie to life. The Glidden wire fences stood out as black lines around the field where the wheat heads waved in the light breeze. Longarm looked back, but the weaving of the fencelines hid his backtrail.

As he rode on, he thought, *There's nothing that'll tame a man who thinks he's tough quicker than showing him you can be a damn sight meaner than he is. Mordka and the Brethren ought to get along all right with the cattlemen for a while, now. And Fedor Petrovsky'll help when he's elected sheriff. Which he's bound to be, because nobody's going to vote for a dead man, and the ranchers won't have time before election to pick out somebody else to run.*

He left the horse at the livery stable, walked into town, and pushed through the batwings at the Cattleman's. He was working down his second shot of Maryland rye when the Santa Fe station agent found him.

"Thought I might run into you if I looked in here on the way to the hotel, Marshal," the man said. "This wire just came in from your office at Denver. It's tagged 'urgent, deliver at once,' so I closed up to bring it to you."

"Thanks." Longarm indicated the bottle on the table. "Help yourself to one while I read it. I might need to send an answer."

Unfolding the message, Longarm read:

HIGGINS ENROUTE TO COVER ELECTION ASSIGNMENT
STOP NEED YOU HERE FOR MORE IMPORTANT CASE **STOP**
REPORT DENVER AT ONCE **STOP** VAIL

"There's no answer," Longarm told the waiting agent. "But you can tell me if you've got a cattle shipment rolling to Dodge tomorrow sometime."

"There'll be one out about four tomorrow evening. You wouldn't want to leave earlier anyhow, Marshal. It'll get you there in time to connect with the westbound limited. The train crew'll find you a seat in the caboose. I guessed you'd be leaving, as soon as I copied the wire."

"That's fine. I'll have time to tie up a few loose ends, so Higgins won't be bothered with them."

Longarm had taken his seat in the coach and the whistle had signaled that the limited was about to roll when the veiled woman hurried along the aisle and disappeared into the Pullman car ahead. He hadn't seen her face behind the veil that swathed it, but the figure was familiar enough, and there wasn't any mistaking that heavy, musky perfume.

It's a long ride to Denver, Longarm thought, *and a day coach seat's going to get right hard.*

He stood up and followed the woman into the Pullman as the train started moving. He got there just in time to see the woman disappear into the forward stateroom. He walked up the aisle and tapped at the stateroom door.

"Come," the woman called through the closed door. Longarm entered.

Ilioana Karsovana was standing with her back to the door, her arms raised, taking off her veil. Without turning around, she said, "Put my bags—" then she stopped short when she looked over her shoulder and saw that it wasn't the porter.

"Longarm!" she gasped. Dismay spread over her face. "How did you track me? I was so careful to leave no traces—"

"Hell, Ilioana, I'm not tracking you. I just happened to see you go up the aisle in the coach where I was sitting, and thought it'd be neighborly of me to come in and say hello."

"You—you have not come to arrest me, then?"

"Why'd I want to do that? Far as I know, you ain't broken any laws."

"But . . . I was so sure you had deduced that I am—" She stopped and covered her mouth with her gloved hand.

"That you're a Russian government agent?" Longarm smiled and tilted his Stetson back. "I figured that all along. I guess I'd've tumbled to it, even if Mordka Danilov hadn't told me that he suspected you and that servant of yours were there in Junction to check up on the Brethren. That yarn about your brother just didn't square with the way you two behaved."

"Your government does not care that we are here? In Russia, agents are imprisoned without trials as soon as they are detected."

"It's different here, I guess."

There was a tapping at the door. Longarm looked at Ilioana. She shrugged and called, "Come!"

It was the porter with the bags. As the man started to leave, Longarm stopped him. "Has the barkeep in the parlor car got any vodka?"

"Vodka, sah?" The immaculately clad black man scratched his head. "Is that some kind of whiskey?"

"I guess you could call it that."

"Then he ain't got none, sah. Bourbon and English whiskey and Maryland rye's about all he runs to, 'less you fancies brandy."

"Maryland rye's good enough." Longarm flipped the man a half-eagle. "Bring us two bottles, and keep the change." When the porter had gone, he said to Ilioana, "I guess you'll just have to get along with sipping whiskey for a while."

"It will not be the first time I have learned to like something new." She smiled. She'd taken off her hat and veil, and now she slipped out of her traveling coat. "I will wait until the porter has brought our refreshments before I put on something more comfortable."

Longarm looked around the compartment. "I must say, you travel in pretty good style. I guess your coachman's riding a day coach?"

"Gregor? No. Gregor is not with me."

"Are you meeting him in Denver, then?"

"I hope not." Ilioana hesitated. "If you are not going to arrest me, it will do no harm to tell you the truth. Gregor was my superior, in charge of our mission. When I was sure you had discovered what we were really doing, I decided I must run. But not only from you, Longarm. I have tired of an agent's life. So . . ."

She went to the luggage the porter had lined up against the stateroom wall and picked up one of the bags. Putting it on the divan, she opened it. Banded packets of U.S. currency and rolls of gold filled the bag.

"This was the money Gregor was given by the *Okhrana* to finance our mission. It occurred to me that I needed it more than he did."

"Looks to me like that'll do you for a while. But won't Gregor be chasing after you, to get it back?"

"No, no. When we send no new reports, the *Okhrana* will send men to look for both of us. Where Gregor will hide, I do not know or care. As for me, your West is big, and there are many places where I can disappear." She smiled. "Denver is big enough, no?"

"Wouldn't be too hard for you to keep hid there, I imagine."

Ilioana came closer to Longarm. "This is what I think, too. You understand, Longarm, what I have done before was in the

service of my motherland, to please the Tsar. Now, what I do
will be what pleases me only."

When Longarm walked into his chief's office early the next afternoon, Billy Vail looked up from the papers heaped on his desk.
His face wore its usual disapproving frown as he looked at the
clock.

"Godamighty!" he grunted. "Can't you ever get here on
time?"

"Now, Billy, the limited just pulled in from Dodge. I got here
as fast as I could."

"Like hell." Vail sniffed the heavy scent of musky perfume
Longarm had brought with him into the office. "You took time to
stop at a barbershop. Well, tell that barber of yours to change his
brand of macassar oil. You smell like you just left Mattie Silks's
place."

"Now, you know I don't play the sporting ladies, Billy. All a
man's got to do is be patient, and a filly comes along who
doesn't set a price on what she's got. And that kind knows how
to pleasure a man better, too." Longarm smiled, then suddenly
grew serious. "Now then. I sure hope this new case you wired
me about ain't watching an election. Like I said, that's a job for
a nursemaid, not a lawman."

GIANT-SIZED ADVENTURE FROM
AVENGING ANGEL LONGARM.

BY TABOR EVANS

penguin.com/actionwesterns